Russ L. Howard Library for House of Howard Publishing

**The King of Three Bloods:**

Book One: The Sire Sheaf
Book Two: The Frightful Dance
Book Three: Witan Jewell
Book Four: The Isle of Ilkchild
Book Five: The Bok of Syr Folk
Book Six: The King-Queen
Book Seven: The Scynscatha
Book Eight: Brekka
Book Nine: El Yid
Book Ten: The Evil Ennead
Book Eleven: Rebirth of the Elven-Gods

**TheKingofThreeBloods.com**

Visit the author on Facebook:

**TheKingofThreeBloods.com/fb**

BOOK ELEVEN:

# THE REBIRTH OF THE ELVEN GODS

THE KING OF THREE BLOODS

RUSS L. HOWARD

Cover Art: Deranged Doctor Design
Formatting: Deranged Doctor Design
Publishing: House of Howard Publishing

ISBN: 978-1-945130-25-0



**TheKingofThreeBloods.com**

# ACKNOWLEDGMENTS

I EXTEND MY GRATITUDE TO PAULA Riggs whose tireless editing spanned seven years, much of which required her to endure my corny jokes, and to her husband Carl who had to endure the many blood drenched battle scenes in the book. Much appreciated help came from Jeff Day in preserving my sanity through dealing with my hated computer and for computer and technical assistance above and beyond waking hours. Particular thanks to Susie Stokes for her exquisite artistic talents and formatting despite her own busy schedule, and she, too, gave endless hours of technical direction. I give praise to my beloved wife whose constant feed-back and aide has always inspired me, and to my son, Adam, who gave continuous encouragement and deeply thought out opinions when asked. I thank my many children and my devoted friends who repeatedly asked, "Is it done yet?" Unto them I say, "Here it is."

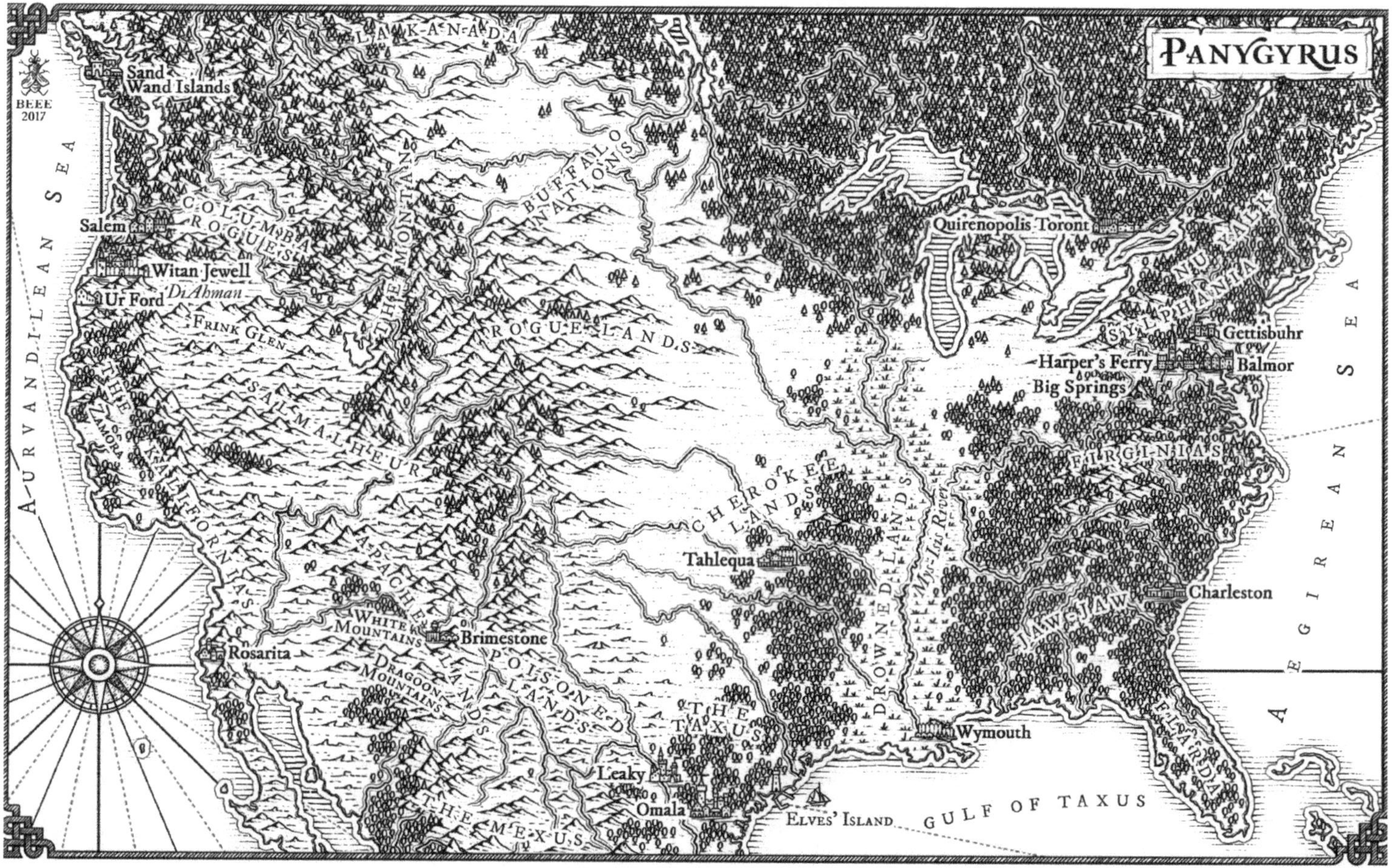
Panygyrus
Lakanada
Sand Wand Islands
BEEE 2017
Aurvandilean Sea
Columbia Rogues
Salem
Witan Jewell
Ur Ford
DiAhman
Frink Glen
The Montan
Buffalo Nations
Rogue Lands
The Zamora
Salmalheur
The Kalifornias
Apache
White Mountains
Brimestone
Dragoon Mountains
Lands
Poisoned Lands
Rosarita
The Mexus
Leaky
Omala
The Taxus
Cherokee Lands
Tahlequa
Drowned Lands
Mys-Isis River
Wymouth
Elves' Island
Gulf of Taxus
Quirenopolis Toront
Nu Valk
Sylphania
Gettisbuhr
Harper's Ferry
Balmor
Big Springs
Firginias
Jaw-Jaw
Charleston
Flarda
Aegirean Sea

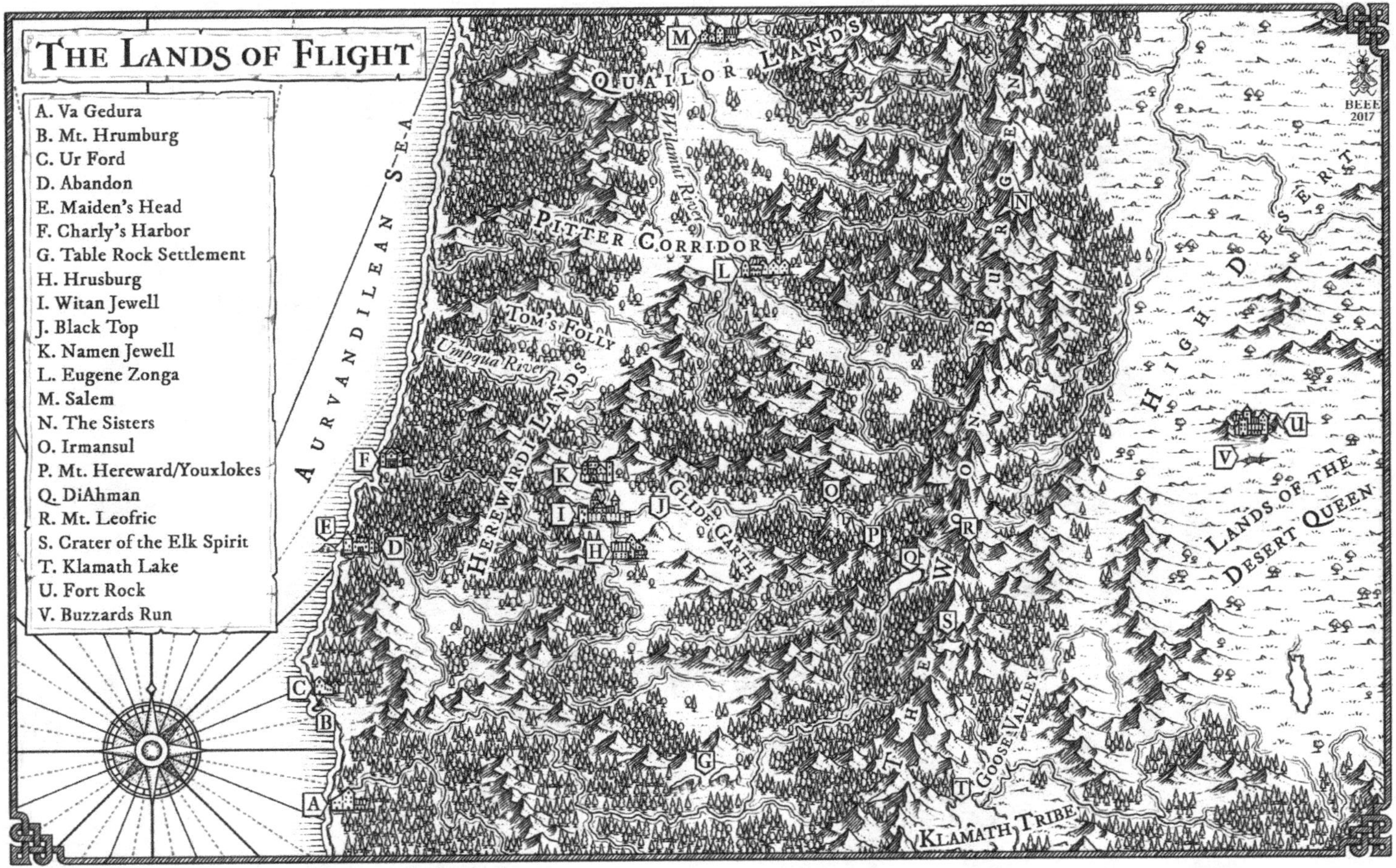

THE LANDS OF FLIGHT
A. Va Gedura
B. Mt. Hrumburg
C. Ur Ford
D. Abandon
E. Maiden's Head
F. Charly's Harbor
G. Table Rock Settlement
H. Hrusburg
I. Witan Jewell
J. Black Top
K. Namen Jewell
L. Eugene Zonga
M. Salem
N. The Sisters
O. Irmansul
P. Mt. Hereward/Youxlokes
Q. DiAhman
R. Mt. Leofric
S. Crater of the Elk Spirit
T. Klamath Lake
U. Fort Rock
V. Buzzards Run
AURVANDILEAN SEA
QUAILOR LANDS
Wilamut River
PITTER CORRIDOR
TOM'S FOLLY
Umpqua River
HEREWARDI LANDS
GLIDE GARTH
HIGH DESERT
LANDS OF THE DESERT QUEEN
GOOSE VALLEY
KLAMATH TRIBE
BEEE 2017

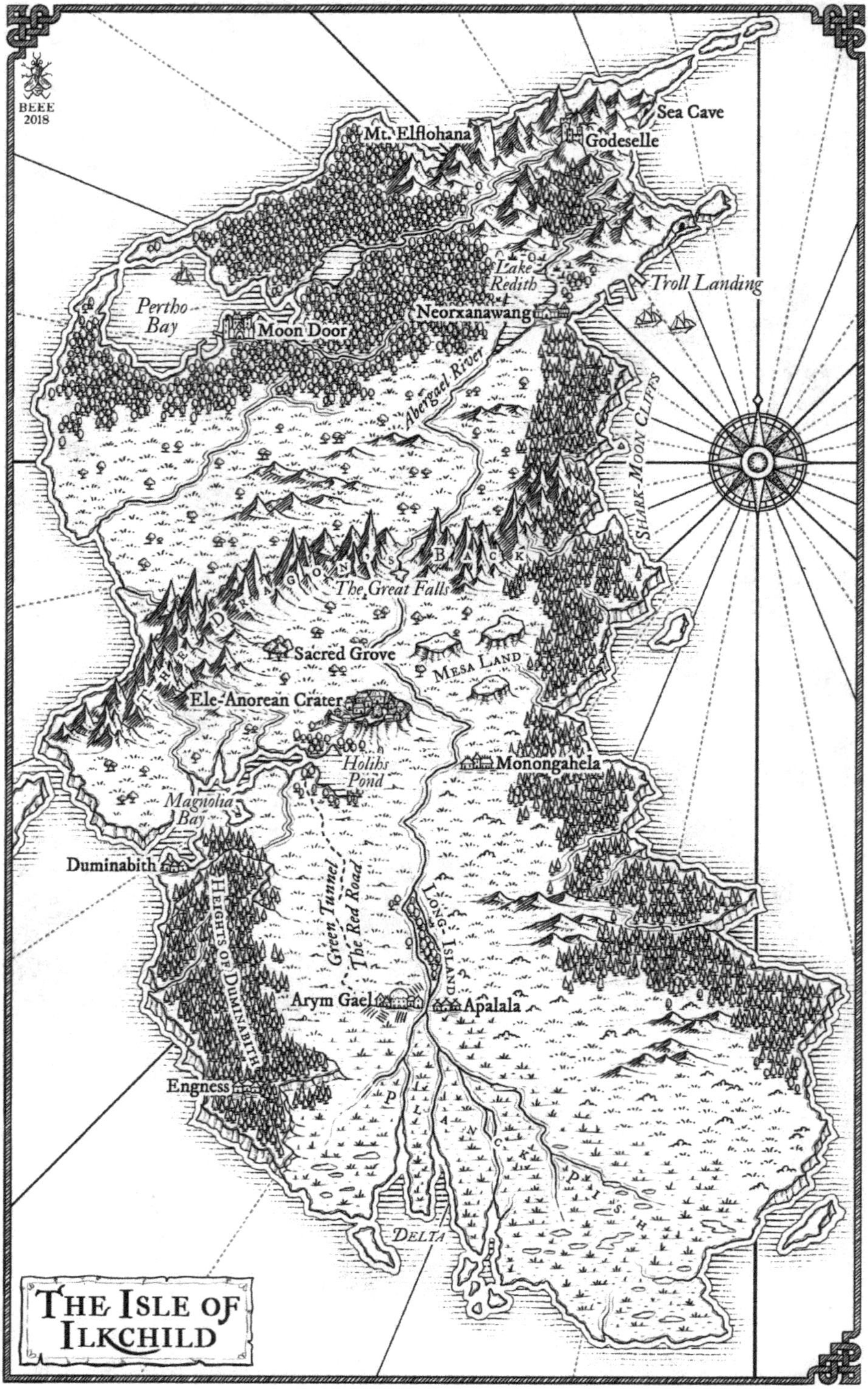
BEEE
2018
Mt. Elflohana
Sea Cave
Godeselle
Lake
Redith
Troll Landing
Pertho
Bay
Moon Door
Neorxanawang
Abergael River
Shark-Moon Cliffs
The Dragon's Back
The Great Falls
Sacred Grove
Mesa Land
Ele-Anorean Crater
Holibs
Pond
Monongahela
Magnolia
Bay
Duminabith
Heights of Duminabith
Green Tunnel
The Red Road
Long-Island
Arym Gael
Apalala
Engness
Planck Pish
Delta
The Isle of
Ilkchild

# TABLE OF CONTENTS


ACKNOWLEDGMENTS……………………………………………9
CHAPTER 1 - The Birth Pangs of the Confederation....................13
CHAPTER 2 - The Dragon's Blood Atonement.............................19
CHAPTER 3 - The Vetting of Brimhilde........................................59
CHAPTER 4 - The Jewel of the South Lands.................................69
CHAPTER 5 - The Norns Bring the Harvest Home.......................79
CHAPTER 6 - The Other Women...............................................109
CHAPTER 7 - The End of the Road is Never the End of the Road...123
CHAPTER 8 - Double Jeopardy..................................................143
CHAPTER 9 - A Miracle Comes on the Tooth of a Serpent .........149
CHAPTER 10 - Rosenkrantz's Ball............................................169
CHAPTER 11 - The Dedication of Mount Heredom...................175
CHAPTER 12 - The Lord of the Forest and the Sprinkling of the May Queen....................................................................191
CHAPTER 13 - The Trials, Tribulations and Passion of the Longfathers.........................................................................199
CHAPTER 14 - The Erection of the Golden Obelisk...................207
CHAPTER 15 - The Well of Urth and the Windows of Heaven......225
CHAPTER 16 - The Wolves Are At the Door.............................263
CHAPTER 17 - Crossing the Rainbow Bridge............................283
CHAPTER 18 - There Was A Queen...........................................299
CHAPTER 19 - There Was A King .............................................321
AUTHOR BIOGRAPHY……………………………………333

# CHAPTER 1 :

## THE BIRTH PANGS OF THE CONFEDERATION

BREKKA SAT ON A LARGE flat rock on the banks of Big Springs. Her heart was troubled and broken for Ruhm. She had lost sleep and ached fiercely for him. It would be hard to choose another man, but thus far he had left her little choice. Only here could she partake of the quiet reflection the matter deserved. In her hand she whiffed the powerful scent of a sprig of faery bush in her hand, hawthorn being one of the four sacred trees. She stared into the crystalline waters percolatirng up from beneath the earth. Peace had become more difficult to obtain than in the many campaigns during the blood drenched Great War against the Pitters. It now befell her to supervise the building of the temple, and as the high priestess, the haligawicca, she had to oversee marriages and all religious services atop Mount Heredom. Adding to her burden was the great responsibility she had taken on of being the nigh-mother for the Young Prince Anghrus. It would be no small matter to educate the future king of the seven nations. She would be in charge of all his tuteledge, training, and upbringing as well as assisting in securing a covey of brides for him. She owed that much to his mother, Wilona, the dearest friend she had ever known.

For the past twenty years, a great moonth's length, all energies had been put into the war. She had fulfilled her obligations which required that she remain a virgin until her commission as the seed of the woman was brought into fruition with the collapse of the Pitter Empire. During those agonizing years of fighting she had drawn very close to her sister knights, several of whom took upon themselves the vows of chastity and formed a sister-bond with her. All those years she knew they were the sisters that would one day make up her bride covey to a worthy man. This meant that whomsoever she married would also be obligated to marry those sisters as well. Freyxus and Verushka had taken these vows, while Wyth and Ysys, though only her personal handmaids, had also sworn the oath. This made the four of them an inseperable pack of sisters forged into a bond whereby they came not as individuals but as a package in any marriage proposal proffered.

All of this presented no problem at all for any Herewardi or even some Sharaka men, but the man she loved was Hickoryan, and further, he was a man of monogamous culture that was dead set against the polygamy as practiced for hundreds of years among the Herewardi people. A practice they would never abandon or deny, for the benefits had proven too many for their survival.

She was only a maid of thirteen winters when she first met Ruhm Lee aboard a ship bound for the Isle of Ilkchild. He was hardly more than sixteen winters himself, a mere young blood. From that moment on she felt a spiritual bond as strong as the pull the moon has for the ea-urth. He had relentlessly pursued her and courted her, but from that first day there was an impassable abyss that separated them. He could not stomach polygamy, and she was bound to her eternal sisterhood and steeped in the teachings of her culture, not to mention she was the Haligawicca, a future queen, and fully invested in the practices of her heathen religion.

Her father, the High King Sur Sceaf had told her that she had made a great offering in having remained a virgin so as to fulfill the prophecy that a virgin's sword would take down the Pitter Empire, but now she was approaching the late summer of age, and she needed to make up for her sacrifices of an empty womb, lost time, and the comforts of a man's bed by wedding as soon as possible, as her high commission had finally been fulfilled. The time frame would be no problem. Her cousin, the young prince Herewose had already proposed they marry several times before, as had her dear friend, Going Snake. She even considered choosing her own man by marrying her uncle, the Wizard Long Swan. What was sure was that she needed to choose one of these three before the next holy moonth unless the handsome Ruhm Lee gave up the exclusive traditions of his fathers and joined her own traditions, not only in their holy practice of polygamy but in her spiritual religion as well, which would place their matrimony at the head of a long line of kings and their queens.

The high king, Sur Sceaf, selected Martinsbuhr, Firginia, as the site of the constitutional convention because it was considered the crossroads of the East, and the hub of the tribes. A very successful dominiker merchant of mysterious origins by the name of Butel Boyd offered the ballroom of his palatial manse to Sur Sceaf to serve as the convention hall. Although the white-columned mansion was a remnant of the early Amerikan days and quite impressive, Sur Sceaf was hesitant to accept an offer from a dominiker, and was about to decline when the man disclosed that he was, in fact, a member of the Sire Sceaf, and proved it by giving the necessary pass words, signs, and tokens. He further revealed that he was Leofric's heir and, even more startling, that as a youth he had once been contacted by Francis Bacon, the Traveler, who told him that the Day of Reckoning would occur within his lifetime.

Seeing the handiwork of the norn sisters in having met with this man in such a serendipitous manner, Sur Sceaf readily accepted the offer of a meeting place as well as his hospitality, which allowed for the representatives to pitch camp on Boyd's extensive lawns.

It was a muggy morning when Sur Sceaf gaveled the assembly to order. Despite some grumbling about the steamy weather, the foul taste of the water in the nearby Tuscarora stream, and the endless annoyance of gnats and harvest bugs, the meeting began with good spirits and high intentions, but soon got bogged down in all the cross intentions and personal interests.

In anticipation of the arrival of the wives and children from the Omala, Prester General A.P. Rockwell in coordination with Beutel Boyd had located suitable accommodations in Martinsbuhr for the various families as well as housing for Amarandel and his team of entered apprentices and skilled craftsmen. To the general's great delight, Merchant Boyd had arranged for Sur Sceaf and his wives and small children to take up accommodations at a large, three story manse situated near Big Springs, once inhabited by the Victor Langsein family, Dominikers who, upon the arrival of the Syr Folk armies at Big Springs, fled to Sylphania, leaving most of their furnishings and supplies behind.

At the urging of Yellow Horse, Sur Sceaf authorized a Grand Fest of High Summer, traditionally held in the Weed Month, which was to begin with the first sliver of the new moon.

Sur Sceaf suspected that Yellow Horse had proposed such an elaborate celebration as part of his anticipation for his wedding to Brimhilde, should Elisheba's vetting result in her full approval. As it was the Herewardi custom for the groom to pay for the wedding festivities, Yellow Horse, ever the frugal, was looking to defray much of the expense by combining the two celebrations into one.

Sur Sceaf had sent a series of harriers down the Pikeside Highway to meet the wagon train due to arrive from the Omala and escort them directly to the Langsein Manse post haste. Full of anticipation, Sur Sceaf found it difficult to concentrate on the myriad details of restoring Mount Heredom.

He and Long Swan were spending the morning touring the sections of Yew Forest at the D'if, purchased for five thousand solidi from the landowners, Roben Brot the Rdokian and Joseph Smith the Hickoryan. In accordance with Herewardi forestry practices, fifty percent of any forest may be harvested for timber, while forty percent must remain standing timber, and fully ten percent of the oldest trees must be dedicated to Odhin as his blot and to forever after remain unmolested, for Odhin had decreed the woods would forever guard his children.

Sur Sceaf had just marked a particularly ancient tree with the honeybee seal, making it untouchable, when Uffa arrived on horseback, blasting his hunter's horn to locate them in the dense forest. Once he honed in on their reply by horn, he rode directly to them. "The wagons have paused for rest and refreshment at Morgan Morgan's Hill on the Opequan, and should arrive at the bastion within four hours, my lord," the youth saluted.

Sur Sceaf exchanged looks with Long Swan. "It will take us at least three hours to return to the bastion by the main trail, but if we take the rough trail from Meadow Branch through Shanghai, we can cut an hour off of that."

"In that case, I vote for the rough trail," Long Swan declared. He untied his mount and vaulted into the saddle. "We can break for a meal at Sleepy Creek and still make it on time."

Sur Sceaf, Long Swan, and Uffa arrived just a few minutes before the long-awaited wagon train just as their families began arriving at the bastion. The word of their arrival had already spread, and the road below the bastion was teaming with family members in eager anticipation of reuniting with their loved ones. It was a most joyous reunion, as families fell on each other's necks with tears and laughter. The little ones were hefted to their fathers' shoulders. Wives were embraced and kissed. Brothers and sisters greeted siblings with jokes and excited inquiries into battles fought and won. The silver harriers carrying dispatches and letters to the Omala had spread word of the bone crushers, vampyrs, gyrlocks, and tyfons and occasionally one had to either be dispatched with spears or arrows or in the case of the monster fyfons with beast stoppers.

Teen boys too young for required military service bombarded their elder brothers in uniform with questions about these monsters, while girls surrounded Freyxus and the lady knights, stumbling over one another with questions about the flying bat-horses. Laughing, Freyxus promised to show some cousins a stable full of them as soon as the activities subsided. A young Rdokian girl, Morgana Logan, serving as a goatherder for Brekka, overheard them and expressed her desire to one day join the lady knights.

Yellow Horse had assigned guides to lead the families to their assigned homes and quarters in Martinsbuhr. However, Sur Sceaf, Long Swan and Arundel accompanied their families to the Langsein Manse, which was commodious enough to accommodate them all with plenty of room to spare.

The wives were thrilled with the beautiful stone-crafted mansion, its two large wings and spacious verandas both top and bottom. Swan Hilde exulted over the beautiful grounds with their vast array of foliage and trees, and was already plotting out her escapes into the garden space where she could also set up a couple of kit-boxes for her high flying pigeons, one of their greatest sources of entertainment on the long journey from the Omala. Faechild immersed herself in the vast displays of bone porcelain and fine cranberry glass lining the cupbords, while Lana fussed over Sur Sceaf and his well-being, sizing him up to make sure he was not nursing any new wounds. "Oh, how I worry for thee, my lord, thou art not in thy youth anymore and it's a lesson thou art too stubborn to learn."

He brushed over her protest with a sweet kiss, and showed the manse off.

While the Lady Paloma was exploring the bedrooms, she decided on where to place each bride-sister according to the numbers of their children. Milkchild and Faechild marveled at the spacious kitchen with its soapstone stove and sinks with running water. Taneshawa, whose proud luck was to have drawn the first stick, put her oldest daughter in charge of her three younger siblings, in order to better focus her attention on Sur Sceaf.

This was the first time since he'd taken Paloma as his faery-queen that Sur Sceaf could enjoy his wives' company without the fear of the Pitter threat that had always lurked in the back of his mind. To enjoy them in the peace of the moment felt deliciously comforting.

After the children had been put to bed with long-awaited kisses and bedtime stories from their father, Sur Sceaf entertained his wives well into the wee hours of morning, at the end of which he and Taneshawa retired to the master suite for a nest of fulfilling love-making, leaving them both sated and joyously reunited.

# CHAPTER 2 :

## THE DRAGON'S BLOOD ATONEMENT

ON THE DAY AFTER THE FESTIVAL of High Summer, Ruhm rose early from his tent at Big Springs, bathed, fed his eagle-owl, Uhu, and then dressed in his best grey and red ceremonial uniform. After making sure he was as resplendent as possible, he picked up his leather pouch containing the white cat skin gloves, fashioned by his mother's hand to be presented to his future wife and headed off in pursuit of his love.

The sun had just sent the first larks to the sky as he walked through a nearby paw paw grove. The light filtering through the leaves was a translucent green before breaking into a brilliant golden field where the camp of the lady knights was located in a circle like a mushroom faery-ring.

The night before, Sur Scetaf had awarded Kanarus and Ruhm the Golden Magnolia wreath signifying stewardship above and beyond the call of duty. During the ceremony the king offered Ruhm accolades that both surprised and pleased him as to their generosity. As his fellow warriors shouted approval, Sur Sceaf drew his famed sword, Snake Fang, tapping each man in turn on their shoulders and heads before dubbing them golden knights for service well rendered.

During those ceremonies the advice of the Ancient One kept going through Ruhm's head. He knew the Harmony-Tongued Herewardi had much secret knowledge hidden in their Wessex Tongue and the Flame Elfabet. He had even been offered the opportunity to learn the

Harmony-Tongue by Kanarus, and now regretted he had not availed himself of that resource. It would have been so helpful. He would now have to figure his approach to Brekka out on his own.

The door to winning Brekka's hand was open but a crack, and he must either act or forever wander the earth in search of snippets of the perfect union that might have been his. Each step brought him closer to the confession that he must soon pour out to Brekka. He clung to the words of his mother when she had given him the gloves. "If you want anything bad enough, you can have it, but only if you desire it with pure intent." Still, he was filled with an inner trepidation he could not peg down. According to Going Snake, Brekka already knew of his lustful swiving escapades in the Shenandoah, and yet, he took comfort that she had in no way shown any displeasure or repugnance toward him.

Bees were humming, birds were singing, and flitting through the nearby leafy canopies. Larks were spilling their songs from the blue skies, and cicadas played their sitar-like songs as he whistled his way into Brekka's camp. He contemplated the warning words of the Ancient White-Haired One that he would have to pass through a crucible designed by the gods. He thought surely his descent into the bowels of the earth to save Brekka must have been that crucible. At least, he hoped it had been.

Upon arriving at Brekka's tent, he heard the ladies inside happily chattering away like a bunch of chickadees in a faery bush. He gave an identifiable yodel to which Wyth opened the tent door, popped her head out through the slit, and was immediately followed by Ynys who said, "Oh! Master Ruhm, Brekka is not here. She went to the stone glade to burn some faggots of hawthorn and bundles of misseltwig to the gods in thanks for the great victory. But it's just past faery-time; if you are lucky, you may find her praying near Wilona's dolman. That's my best guess. Otherwise you will have to wait here with us, and we are not yet finished with our toiletries."

The two girls giggled, and he saw they tracked his every move with blantantly flirtatious smiles. He was flattered and intrigued, but shook his head and said internally, *No more swiving,* before politely taking his leave of these vulnerable game birds.

He had drank a few glasses of Two River's Wine with El Yid the night before, after he had been made a knight. It was after the third glass when Yid had told him of the attack on the Isle of Tangiers and how he had thrown two hundred and fifty plus Pitter heads in the Chesapeake for crab bait from the Pitter merchant ship, The Peggety Sue which he had waylaid. Yid had described how he procured forty chests of rials of plate, five hundred pounds of gold, and seven hundred pounds of silver from the Yengish merchants aboard the ship who had been gleaning hard earned labors of Hickoryans to fatten their purses with.

At first, the merchants were not forthcoming with the treasures, but he told how he offered them murderous words and performed a few false hangings of their captains by placing a noose around their necks and kicking them off ship with just enough rope to fall into the bay and live. The captains were then all too keen to deliver up their treasure troves and hoards without further protests.

Sur Sceaf could barely contain his pleasure as he had commended Yid on his treasure hunts during that banquet. All of which treasure Yid had shipped off to the sea palace. Yid had boasted of it with naked glee, and Ruhm envied the free-spirited pirate, but then Sur Sceaf rose to give Ruhm and Kanarus praise. The Honors Festive Board summarily drank to them. A strong spirit of convivial fellowship prevailed all evening long. He would chalk it up as one of his better festive boards.

After the Occasional Lodge and Banquet, he had retired to his tent. As he had lain upon his bed listening to the swifts twinkling in the sky, intrusive thoughts of Hollyannah, Vicky, Melissa, and even the fiery pounce with Miss Liza that had left him empty of seed stood like silent witnesses in the dark recesses of his mind, haunting him, but in his heart the golden sunlight of his love for Brekka blocked them all out. All the same, his heartstrings twisted for them at some deeper level, and he could not help wondering what would become of them now that he had made his final choice. Despite all the exciting activities and much over-thinking, he still managed to sleep a good sleeping. Today was the choicest day he could remember in a long, long time. Surely that was a good sign in and of its own.

Wyth and Ynys had been in a spunky mood at the tent, and he knew that would likely be reflective of the mood Brekka would be in. At least he hoped it would be so, because today he was resolved to beseech Brekka for forgiveness and ask her hand. He couldn't think of how he could have forgotten such exquisite beauty as she possessed.

His father had often claimed that nothing excited the libido more than exquisite beauty. He found it to be a profound truth. But he also dwelt on the deep spiritual union they had once enjoyed. *Fool! How did our young blossoming love grow into a cage with twisted thorns around my heart after the Taxus Campaign? What set it off course? Maybe it was wisdom that she severed our connection and dismissed me from under her command. But, God, I cannot accept that.*

He had been convinced that she had rejected him and the love he had for her out of some perverse desire to dominate him. Now he saw through the prism of these final days that all his courting gestures and swiving was nothing more than a distraction of his true desire to have her and punish her for her rejection of him. In fact, she had never rejected him at all, only his insubordination in the line of duty.

Before he dared ask her hand in marriage, he knew he first needed to clear the air, confess his sins, bare his back and take the necessary stripes. *The only way I can bare to live with myself is to tell all and hope she does not reject me now for my transgressions.*

Ruhm took to the path that led to the henge of Tor-Ili and made his way up the boxwood lined incline. *Please, Brekka, most beautiful of women, list any penitence. I will traverse parched deserts, climb insurmountable mountains, and endure searing heat and frozen wastelands to regain your love and trust. Just give me but one spark of hope. That's all I require.*

As he passed the Big Springs, he noted a larger than normal green heron on the bank where the Elven Waters began to take their flow eastward. Every feature of the bird's body was focused on its prey as it speared a golden trout, lifting it to a grassy hummock for consumption. *Will I be as successful in convincing Brekka I am a changed man? The Old One said that I have to make a choice, and I have. I've chosen Brekka over the others regardless of what it will take.*

As he crested the hill he saw a faery-like creature of resplendent form and beauty. It was Brekka in her green cotton dress. She sat on a long, moss-covered rock near a curious pile of larger stones. A broken column from some bygone day still stood erect. Her thick red hair had been released from its usual braids, tumbling down her back in shimmering curls and tresses, the ends of which the caressing wind gently tossed.

A moment of fear gripped his heart. His defenses rose like a stone bulwark. *How will I survive if I lose her?* All that was in him bade him not to speak, but his conscience prodded him like a gig. As he drew nearer, he saw she had been weeping over the broken column, and was in the attitude of prayer with her one hand clutching a small branch of Albespiene and the other holding a long white cloth of some sort.

He straightened his shoulders, moved around the hawthorn bush, and patted his leather pouch on his belt for luck. As he approached her, he saw the red, puckered wound to the side of her right eye, then the tears that she attempted to wipe away with the sleeves of her dress. Droplets of tears discolored the bosom of her dress.

"I hope I haven't interrupted your prayers?" he said softly.

She folded a Herewardi Prayer Shawl on her lap, laid the sprig of albespiene atop it, and placed her hands folded upon them.

She looked up with a sad smile. "No, not at all, or at least, I mean, I am finished." She glanced at the stones. "I felt as if Wilona was here communing with me. To me this broken column is a symbol of her unfinished work in the Ea-Urth; a work I am left to put the wings on." She pointed to the broken stele. "This column once bore swan wings and represented the hopes of my people. They called it Irmunsil. It represents the Tree of Life for my ancestor, Widukind. For generations too numerous to count, we Herewardi raise one in every land we sojourn in."

"Why the sprig of hawthorn…I mean albespiene?"

"Oh, I got it from the eildon tree you just passed. Another name we Herewardi use for the hawthorn. You know, when Hrus-Syr-Os was buried, a sprig of hawthorn was placed on his grave to mark his internment. It was prophesied by Lord Elrus that the leaves of this tree shall one day heal the nations. I have contemplated that Hrus-Syr-Os may be the tree of the prophecy of which Elrus speaks, and that we, his children are the leaves. I'm sure you know by now that we Herewardi believe the hawthorn, the magnolia, the oak, and the yew provide us a very special link between Heaven and Ea-Urth, depending on the occasion. I have been scrying where Hrus-Syr-Os was buried, and I also wanted to use the branch to witch out where I should build the shrine of Wilona."

"I do not understand the hexing of witchery, but you two ladies grew very close, didn't you?"

Her expression softened, and the deep green pools of her eyes seemed to radiate both sorrow and love. "Oh, Ruhm, we were sisters of the highest order. Through and through! I learned so much from her.

Wilona put her hands on my eyes and gave me the ability to heal or slay at a great distance. She taught me this knowledge from on high. I never thought we would be separated like this. So many people talk about how when we die we go to the realms above. I just wish there was not such a great chasm between us and the dead. Though I know she has been reunited with the godly hosts in the Summerlands or what we call Elf Home and is probably very happy, it chust doesn't assuage the pain of her absence at all."

"What is that item you hold there? Is it a prayer shawl of some kind?" He eyed the pure white cloth curiously.

"It is the shroud of Wilona," she said with twinkling eyes.

"What do you mean?"

Her face grew somber. "It is what they wrapped Wilona in after they tortured her and before they beheaded her. It bears her perfect image on the shroud. Almost like a painting. Would you care to see it?" She quickly spread it out.

One glance and he saw a mirror image of Wilona unfold before his eyes. "By God, she must have been whipped and bled from every pore of her body to leave such an imprint." He began to worry Brekka had grief sickness of the mind like his mother. She had suffered for seven years from it, after the death of his older brother, Virgil, who died at the hand of a robber band during the days of their wandering. It was as though she had taken herself to a place where neither he nor his father could reach her and he couldn't bare to wade through such sadness again.

"Look here, Ruhm. It even shows that they beheaded her while she was in the shroud, for there is a bloody line right across the neck."

"And that doesn't disturb you to think how much she got tortured and disembowelled? My God, I can't think of anything more horrific. It's too morbid."

She raised her puckered eyebrow. "In truth, she warned me this was coming and that she was in no way afraid, but was eager to rejoin her Heavenly family. She bade me not to grieve too long or too hard for her. But even so, it does bother me that she was tortured. Sure it does. Don't you understand her image is burned on this shroud, not by the blood, but by some sort of light, I'm thinking it was the light of her spirit escaping from her body. Must have scared the hell out of Horquenada." Her face brightened as she reverently folded the shroud and placed it carefully in a red leather basket. Then turned to Ruhm and said, "Why the sad face?"

"I was thinking how tortured I was when I believed you were dead. But that pales in comparison to what Kanarus must be feeling now. He loved Wilona so deeply. Though I know he has other wives, she's practically the only wife he talked about throughout the Shenandoah Campaign. He even called her the perfect faery-wife. The grief he bears has got to be unspeakable. I know he truly loved her as his own soul, and by the gods, I admired his loyalty."

Brekka smiled. "That he did, and she loved him ever as much. It was an eternal love they bore for each other. The fibers of such love can never be disentangled. Death does not take that kind of love away, Ruhm. And you mustn't think he loves his other wives any the less for it; only differently!"

His heart thundering in his chest, Ruhm drew close to Brekka. He cleared his throat and took her hand in his. "Brekka, thrice burned and wounded of eye, and by god, still as beautiful as when I first laid eyes on you," he paused, savoring the touch of her hand and the light of her countenance, "I have two things to say to you. They are the same two things that my soul has agonized over and wrestled over for weeks now." He felt the sickest sense of angst in his stomach as he prepared himself for rejection. "Before you told me it was not the time to talk about such personal matters. Is now the time?"

"The time and place are perfect." Her bright look of anticipation gave him hope. Still he hesitated. She gave him a perky flirtatious look that set his heart to skipping. "Then what are you waiting for, son of Firginia?" She withdrew her hand from his grip and lightly smote him on the cheek. "I am no longer your commander. We are now met here in this holy place stripped of all rank as but man and woman."

He looked down, captured her hand again, swallowing hard. "First off, beloved Brekka, I want to take the Swan Way. I want to become Herewardi."

A cough caught in her throat. "Oh Ruhm, I'm so happy for you. I know you won't regret it." Brekka looked reflective, folded her hands in her lap before soberly answering, "But you should know that becoming one of the Swan Folk should never be entered into lightly and will require every ounce of energy your mind, heart, and body can muster up or spare. I can tell you, being Herewardi is not an easy path. The gods have made it so, for we are lightning rods for prejudice and intolerance. You will find it is a strange mix and balance of being haughty and humble at the same time. You have to tend the needs of your wives and your children just like a shepherd has to take his sheep to good pasture, shelter them, lamb them. There will be times when they lead you to better waters and greener pastures. You must learn when to lead and when to follow. It is an unending labor of love. You would do well to give it further consideration."

"Brekka, I have not done anything else but given it great consideration for the past sixteen years."

"Yes, but is it of your own free will that you have arrived at this conclusion, or think you only to possess my heart without the culture which frames it?"

"For the most part it is. I have prayed to know the truth of your heathen ways." He smiled.

Her face lit up. "So you have experienced the ur fyr burning in your bosom?"

"That was the easy part, I wrestled with my god and your gods and I discovered that my Holy Christ is not only a Virginian, but I came to understand that he is also a Heathen, a Jywd, a Red Man, or a Black Man, but that was the easy part, now for the hard part." He took a deep breath and gave a swift prayer for courage. "I have determined we must have no secrets between us." He marked the tender look in her eyes. "Woe is me! I have transgressed greatly against you."

Brekka was as immovable as the stone upon which they sat. Her worried gaze pierced his eyes. His heart felt like a ship on an angry Sea. Here it was, a wave of condemnation was about to strike. She would either accept him or reject him, but he could no longer stand the suspense of not knowing whether she had heard of his shameful trail of lust that had left a wake of ruin on his march through the Shenandoah, where he practically bedded every woman he met. If she hadn't heard, he decided, she would eventually. Better she should hear it from him.

He took another deep breath and braced himself once again for her rejection. "When you had me removed from your command, I became so angry, Furious! Rageful! I wanted to punish you for rejecting me. I honestly hated you for a while. The logic of it was overridden by the strong emotions I felt for you. Nevertheless, I let my anger and lust lead me into the beds of many strange women. I swived them all! Some of whom I actually came to love." He felt a flush of shame burning his face and could no longer look her directly in the green-fire of her eyes.

She tipped his head up with her hand, forcing him to look directly at her. "Oh, Ruhm, such things are not secret to me. The beetles and harriers, many of whom are my little brothers or cousins, relished the idea of reporting your misbehaviors to me almost on a daily basis."

He was shocked at her response and felt a great sense of relief that her voice held no rebuke or condemnation at all. This remarkable woman could have the hand of any man in the kingdom, and he knew many who had tried to win her. "Going Snake indicated as much," he revealed sheepishly. "I find it difficult to believe you have no eyes of condemnation for me."

"My father told me long ago that the true essence of gold is not marred by falling into the mud. Besides, in the Daleth Tent of Penitence, there is a way prepared to deal with this. There, we will meet the dragon together. A dragon whose blood will cleanse you and me of your sins against yourself, and against me. It sounds to me like you have learned how sweet good fruit is by having sampled it in its bitterest form. Love is always sweetest when it is ripe."

He stared at her in disbelief, his heart pounding. "But I…! But I…! But I betrayed the bond of our love."

"Before you go any further, let me tell you, one night as I slept up here by this broken stone column, I dreamed the future. You and I were laying here in the grass while meadow elves and faeries were dancing in circles around us. I suppose that such knowledge is not given to your people, and therefore you cannot know what it is like to live your life by personal revelation or what it is like to commune with exalted beings. But my people live by the elf-fire of prophecy, and it reveals to us the core of a person's heart, beyond the facade people show to everyone. Truth does not require that you alone change, but that we all change." Brekka placed her hand over Ruhm's heart. "Ruhm, that dream tells me your heart stands pure before me." She hesitated then added solemnly, "Though, there is still much to make right, for no mortal man shall unveil me except Woon shield him."

Her eyes revealed a strong will with no hint of malice or jealousy. His heart leapt beneath the warm touch of her hand. "Does this mean you forgive me of all my swiving?"

"Ruhm, by the Great Birth Mother, Freya, it was everything I possessed to remain chaste in your presence all these years." Her directness and honesty were both genuine and endearing. "I know the power of nature's urges. Believe me. I hope only that you will repent of the shallowness of such swiving with the false promises you surely must have spoken. Women are not toys that you play with and then re-shelve. Once you drill into a lover's heart and plant your seed, it is your responsibility to ever after nurture that seed so that it does not grow into a noxious vine that strangles her soul and the souls of others connected to her."

Ruhm was stunned by the realization that what she said was absolutely true. It was as if one of the heavy henge stones laid upon his heart in place of her hand. "I had never looked upon it that way before," he admitted. "A vine that's torturing the souls of those I've swived. It places a heavy burden of guilt on my heart." He took a bracing breath. "Please tell me, how is it even possible to ever make such things right again, Brekka?"

Brekka smiled. "You may not be able to make it right, but your desire to do all that you can to make it right shows me you are already on the right path. The gods will require that you make amends and atone to each and every one of those women according to your ability to do so. Probably in ways your mind doesn't even entertain at this time. But we Herewardi believe there is always a way to atone. Though I must warn you, it shall not come without struggle, conflict, and great sacrifice. For now, the daleth tent will be the first step in a long and winding journey to wholeness for you. The dragon's blood will invest you with the armoring you and I will require in such an odyssey." She ran her fingers over his cheek and then braced his neck with her hand. "For such atoning will include the both of us. You shall not walk this dangerous path alone."

"But you have done no wrong."

"Try to understand, our souls are so inextricably bound together that your debts must of necessity become mine. It cannot be otherwise in the Swan Way."

"If what you speak is the truth, it burdens me even more to think that I have incurred so many trespasses against you."

She framed his face with her hands and looked directly into his eyes. "Let me reassure you, we look upon spiritual offenses in a natural way. Undergoing the Rite of the Veil in the secret place will be like turning over a field of dead weeds in order to replant it with comely flowers. You may not understand this now, but what is for sure, is that your eyes will be opened to new ways of thinking not given to the understanding of your culture."

As he gazed at her beautiful face, conflicting emotions tumbled through him, coalescing into a bittersweet confusion, yet she smiled warmly at him. It gave him enough hope to blurt out, "Does that mean you would consider marrying me?"

Her eyes radiated deep affection instead of the scorn he had feared would be the case. "If you can truly say that you will abide by the spirit of the forty-four laws as laid down by the Roufytrof in the beginning of times, and if you submit to the rite of the veil in the secret place where you may bathe in the sacred blood of the dragon, then yes, I will happily marry you. After all, it has been my dream since first we met."

His eyes widened in disbelief. He felt his heart race. A great burden fell from his mind. It was all he could do to remain seated and not jump and dance for joy.

Exuberant, he declared, "You may be happy to know that I have studied the forty-four laws diligently of late under Kanarus, read the teachings of the heathen prophets, and I can wholeheartedly declare I will abide by their spirit. His eyes filled with tears. He took both her hands in his and kissed each one gently. "Sweet Brekka Copperlocks, you cannot know how deeply I have longed for those words. They are a balm to my tortured soul. And, yes, so help me god, or gods, I will submit to the rite of the veil in the secret place, face the dragon with you, and pay eternal homage and fealty to the Herewardi forever more."

Wrens spilled their cheerful songs from saffron skies as honeybees kept the silk tree humming above the black Daleth Tent on Tor-Ili. The tent sat in a grove of ancient dark yews atop the Holy Mound, isolated by woods, dolmans, and stone henges. It was a sacred place, a holy place, with roots five hundred years old.

Two weeks had passed since Ruhm and Brekka had pledged their troth at Wilona's dolman. In order to secure complete privacy, Brekka had asked Sur Sceaf to issue an order that the mound would be out of bounds for any exploration. After the three preceding days of rain, the day had dawned sunny and clear with a warm mountain breeze tugging at the ends of Ruhm's long brown hair. As instructed, he had bathed, washed his hair, and dressed in his finest uniform. His Herewardi brothers in arms, on the other hand, were garbed in long black hooded cloaks that flapped in the breeze like ravens' wings as they escorted him along. On their hoods was a golden band of Herewardi knots and runic writing, and from the solemn looks on their faces he knew they took this business very seriously.

Lord Arundel explained, "This is the Daleth Tent and this place upon which it sits was once called Mount Heredom. It was the place of the harrow stone called Ili-Tor, which means 'the Gate of the Gods,' but for some unknown reason came to be called Tor-Ili by the Hickoryans. This sacred place was the Garden of Ea-Urth, the placenta of the Herewardi Nation and is therefore, deeply holy unto us. You are so fortunate to be wed in a place of such powerful ancestral energies. I find it to be curiously remarkable that it is also the place of your origins."

Kanarus placed a hand upon Ruhm's shoulder. "My brother in arms, I have marked a distinct change in your nature over the past moonth. Perhaps it is because the war is over, but you seem much more open to light and things of the spirit. And were it not going too far, I believe I see new light emanating from your being. It pleases me that you have made the decision to undergo the ancient rites of the Herewardi, rites that go all the way back to the Invisible College, yea, even further back into the days of King Alfred and before, and rites that will assist you in becoming Osytru, a Blood Elf, it is the Swan Way." He squeezed Ruhm's shoulder before withdrawing his hand. "It behooves me to reveal to you that three gods favor you. I am impressed to tell you that they are Frey, Ullr, and Heimdall. From henceforth, you will know them as your personal guides in mortality. See to it that you seek them out when you are in need of spiritual counsel. They will never fail you, though they may try you sorely and you may feel all but forsaken."

"Will they be with me now?" Ruhm asked anxiously.

Kanarus nodded. "They have always been with you, but the lust of your flesh blocked them from your view. Fortunately, now you will become receptive to their entreaties. It would behoove you to study their traits so as to not be deceived or tricked by dark elves and other tricksters of Loki's ilk and kind. Apply yourself to one of the skalds or lore masters. Forsetti would be my recommendation."

A bit bewildered, Ruhm simply nodded. He had never considered gods to be more than a great spirit that engulfed all. Dealing with actual beings was going to require a major mind shift. But that would be something he would consider later. At the moment all of his energy was focused on what the Herewardi called facing the dragon and successfully passing through the flames of the rite.

Now that the time had come for Ruhm to enter the tent, the old feelings of trepidation and mystery made his bowels to churn. His face grew hot, then cold. Two large ravens, which Ruhm had learned were the usual companions of the Ancient One, flew into the boughs of the nearest gnarled yew. He looked around for the Old White Hair, he did not see him. He didn't know whether this was a good sign or a bad sign.

As though sensing his uncertainty, Lord Arundel gave him a confidant look and said, "Take fresh courage, for after you're tried and proven, you will step out of this tent a new man and a swan-lord. One cannot unenter this tent without denying the sun at noon day."

With one brother on each side, they led him through the tent door. As Kanarus lifted the flap, Ruhm spied a sizable number of thick golden beeswax candles burning on a small table placed against the right wall of the tent. The air seemed perfumed with the pervasive scent of magnolia and was pleasingly warm. The floor was a bare canvas, black as a collie night. As far as he could see, there were no chairs, only a large concave stone the color of turquoise and the size of a bushel basket, one side of which rose a hand's breadth above the other. In the very center of the tent was a circular mat with a thin outer ring of gold enclosing the golden imprint of a large ewe's hoof. Embroidered in its middle was a golden beehive. This he knew from the Herewardi flags was the Mark of Hrus and represented the Ur Father.

To one side of the stone was a large brazen copper tub filled with hot water with wisps of steam rising from it. On its side was placed a large shallow wicker tray covered with a golden cloth adorned with curious scarlet runes. Lined up precisely on the cloth were a large coil of rope, a shiny sharp golden sickle and a rough wooden flail. There was also a bottle of what looked to be mead, as indicated by the large glass honeybee molded on the bottle, but only one krug made from the deepest blue glass he had ever seen.

Approximately two feet in front of the stone was what at first appeared to be a wall but was actually an aubergine veil with a large shimmering black perthro rune letter embroidered in its center. It was the rune of the womb, and betokened rebirth. The veil, he had been told, covered the secret place, the bridal chamber and the holy bed, but from where he stood, he could not see them.

Arundel indicated they should sit in a semi-circle at the edge of the mat. Kanarus, who was seated nearest to the tray hefted the bottle of mead and, at a nod from Arundel, filled the blue krug. As he handed it to Ruhm, he said, "This is dwale, a combination of mead, barley, wild neep, ergot, and night shade. It will relax you and open the portals of your mind so that the veil of this world may be thinned. The perthro rune represents wyrd, fate, the mysteries of the unknown, and the gate of life and death."

Obediently, Ruhm lifted the krug to his lips and took a tentative sip. It tasted like bubbly, barley bee-ur. To his surprise, it was even more delicious than the usual bee-ur and left a pleasant aftertaste. The more he drank, the more a feeling of warmth and well-being settled over him.

After he drank the last draft of the dwale, Kanarus took the empty krug from him and set it to the side before grabbing the large rope from the tray. "The plant spirit of the barley has entered you. Now, stay seated," He got to his feet and took up his position behind Ruhm. "I place this thirteen-coiled noose over your head to lead you as a collar through the three deaths, that you may enter the path to become an Immortal."

At first, there was a sense of uneasiness as Kanarus slipped the scratchy noose over his head. Brekka warned he must trust the rites in the secret place and follow his conductors' every word or possibly be slain, for the rites were dead serious and the gods suffered none to mock them or to take them lightly. Somehow he forced himself to relax his tense muscles as the noose was cinched tight about his neck. *Arundel and Kanarus have always been my most loyal friends. What's not to trust?*

With little warning, Kanarus tugged on the rope, which tightened even more under his left ear, thus forcing him to rise from his seated position. He sprang to his feet merely to keep from choking. Silently, Kanarus held him in tow and pulled him toward the tub that glistened with reflections of candlelight.

Arundel arose and instructed, "Disrobe completely."

His heart pounded like a hammer as he drew in a breath and kicked off his boots. Piece by piece he shed his clothing until he was completely naked. Silently he prayed this proving wouldn't be as agonizing as that of the Sun Lodge, where he had seen men hung from the flesh of their chest until unconscious. The thought made him queasy; nevertheless, he was prepared to do anything, anything at all to earn Brekka's hand in marriage.

As he stood there trying his best to hide his fear, Arundel stepped in front of him with a calculatingly calm look on his face. As Ruhm stared at his friend, Ary pulled the small golden sickle from beneath his cape. Without a word of warning, Ary held the point of the sickle against his neck under the right ear. Holding his breath and closing his eyes, Ruhm felt the dull drag of the metal as it crossed over the skin of his neck. A sudden bite pierced the left ear lobe with a white-hot sting of pain. Several droplets of blood splashed on his naked shoulder. Lord Arundel clarified, "This represents the cutting of the misseltwig from the bough of the oak, showing that even if you are cut down, you remain green and alive."

Kanarus picked up the flail and motioned for him to lie face down on the mat bearing the Mark of Hrus. Awkwardly, with the noose still uncomfortably tight about his neck, Ruhm laid on his belly with hands outstretched, and braced himself for the thrashing. The first blow lashed diagonally across his back. To his surprise, the pain was little more than a slap. The second was stronger, but easily endured. The third bore the edge of pain. He expected each blow to be progressively more painful. *I can endure this to death if it wins me Brekka.* Seconds passed, but to his relief, there were no more punitive blows.

The two lords lifted him up by his arms, and Lord Arundel explained, "You have been thrashed like the barley, meaning that you have been properly prepared and are now to be laid up for greater works and uses."

Kanarus beckoned him to step into the brazen tub. As he stepped into the tub expecting it to be hot, instead he found it was pleasingly warm. Relieved, he lowered himself until he sat chest high in it. Suddenly, Arundel placed his hand upon Ruhm's head and shoved his head completely beneath the surface and held him there. Water poured over the sides. He resisted the urge to struggle. Instead, he held his breath, telling himself over and over that his friends would not truly let him drown. His lungs ached and starved for air. His blood raced through his head. After what seemed like an eternity, he was released. He sat up and gulped for breath, water dripping over his eyes.

Lord Arundel declared, "Your throat has been cut, you have been strangled, flailed, and drowned as though you were a sheaf of barley. Ever keep in mind that even our death must serve our people, the Herewardi, which you now are born into as a sheath. This rebirth will prepare you for your journey through the remainder of the ritual, and we charge you to ever ponder the meaning of this, the Barley Rite, the Baldurean Death, and the Effusions of Os, which you have just undergone. Thus, having survived the three deaths, you will ever be armored against the dragon. Now you have learned the scary truth, and may forthwith ponder the terrible questions. Suffice it to say for now that you are dead to your old ways and reborn into the Herewardi ways, which will unite you to the holy bloodline of Brekka, who is a true voice, the oracle of the gods in the Middle Garth."

Lord Kanarus charged. "Remember, during your meditations that the ur fyr is like a giant web of shimmering energy, filled with both power and life. Always keep in mind that Brekka is the netter and perceives this net or web better than any of us. This ritual is designed to teach you how to use the net to the best of your ability and will. Do not be fooled by the gentleness of the knowledge you will receive here. This is a place of immense power. All Father Woon is not made powerful by all his silver and gold, nor is he strong by his thunderings and lightnings, but rather by his divine light and intelligence, for he is the master of the ur-fyr and able to cross over the abyss."

Arundel stepped forward to declare, "For you are now born into the House of Swans and are become a son of Odhin, that you may come forth from this tent a true swan-lord."

Both Arundel and Kanarus intoned in unison, "So mote it be!"

As Ruhm rose out of the water, dripping, Kanarus turned a valve that vented the water into a basin outside of the tent. At the same time Arundel retrieved a black towel from beneath the table.

Kanarus grinned, removed the dripping noose and said, "I only hope we didn't give you too bad of a scare. Most Herewardi know what's coming, but this being your first exposure to Herewardi ritual, I can only imagine that it must have been somewhat frightening."

Ruhm choked out a cough and began toweling dry. When he finished, he blotted the blood from his ear lobe which had continued to seep.

"I must admit it helped to know you fellows were my friends, but a noose tightening around one's neck, and a sickle sliding over the throat, gives one great cause for reflection, and briefly, I rode upon a moment of terror. Truth be said, I didn't know how long you all planned on holding me under either. I was starting to think, 'at what point must I begin fighting back?' Kanarus told me no one had died from this ritual, but I began thinking I was going to be the first."

They laughed. "This was the easy part," Kanarus said. "The rest is the real hard work. You must enter the darkness of your heart and ponder the terrible questions of death and the grave and what the true meaning of mortal existence is. Then you must swear by the blood that has flowed under your feet that you will ever avenge the righteous in the Ea-Urth."

"I don't understand. I thought this was the end of the rite."

Kanarus smiled. "Right now you are what the Herewardi consider the newly born, a mere cygnet. As you pass through the ritual, your true self will be fully born and manifested by your full plumage. There is the unself, what you are now, that walks the Ea-Urth, and then you must find the true self which transcends time and place. The second stage of the ritual will call upon your ability to search the depths of your soul for answers as to who you really are, where you came from, and what your obligations as a Herewardi swan-lord will be."

Arundel amplified, "You will be required to remain naked from this point on. For now, you must remain in this tent only. We shall be removing all other objects except for the stone of truth and the mat with the mark of Hrus. If you feel your will fading, go to the stone of truth for strength of purpose. As soon as you hear Brekka approaching, you are to sit on the stone of truth, and not move or pass that veil until Brekka raises you through it."

Lord Arundel and Lord Kanarus assisted him in remembering the ritual words to be spoken when he ultimately encountered Brekka.

Lord Arundel said, "Do you have any questions before we depart?"

"Yes. Why is it I should remain naked?"

Arundel laughed, cupping Ruhm on the shoulder with his large hand. "It is custom if you wish to be married, my man."

Kanarus said with a fox smile, "She will also be naked."

Ruhm's whole body grew hot.

"Come now," Kanarus said, "I will show you where you can anoint your body with the magnolia perfumed oil, the essence of Herewardi presence. With such a becoming blush, I'm sure she will appreciate it."

Lord Arundel nodded. "This is our way. Here is where you enter the door to holy marriage. Finish the contents of the dwale and be prepared for the journey it will take you on. dwale opens the portals of the soul. May Ullr guide you."

Ruhm poured a portion of the contents of the bottle of dwale into the krug and eagerly gulped down its golden effervescence.

After the two lords instructed him further in what ritualized words needed to be spoken where and when in the remaining ritual, Kanarus extinguished the sweet smelling beeswax candles, collected the ritual items and then backed out of the tent door with Arundel, leaving Ruhm naked and alone in the dark.

Lord Arundel said through the tent wall, "Ruhm, this labor is yours, and so is the reward. Yield your heart and soul fully to this holy moment. You must now remain in silence in darkness for four days, until you see the likeness of the sun smite the top of the obelisk. That will be your cue that the trial is over and Brekka has come to raise you to a living perpendicular. By then the dwale will have run its course, and all obstacles will have been removed for you to enter the consummation of sacred marriage."

Kanarus declared, "This tent stands at the intersection of eternity and internity. It is a holy place, the center of the world, unto which you may return many times to restore your soul. It is the place of the days of the future past. Here, the marriage bed is holy. Pleasure is not an obstacle to spiritual life; it's a fountain of it. May you caress what you please and please what you caress." He used a curious Herewardi expression. "We charge you to feed your cat well and take possession of the door to your future kingdom."

They departed, and his soul yearned for their return. Silence gathered around him in the form of insect song. To occupy time he began running the Futhhorc, the Herewardi Elfabet through his mind. He was naked and left to ponder his life alone. Crawling was the safest movement. He felt along the floor until he ran into the tent wall. Gradually, he made his way to the stone of truth and felt its smooth concave surface. Slowly, he started to perceive the initial effects of the dwale. He continued to crawl, felt as if the darkness were a long ribbon that stretched out before him like an endless path into the stars. He felt as if he had been crawling for miles when once again the emptiness was interrupted by the stone of truth.

Against evening, the lady Brekka rode out from Big Springs with Freyxus and Verushka on either side. Donny rode just ahead of them to show the way, and the wyrm-kats kept pace on either side of him, their sleek cat-like bodies strangely reflecting the human seed code in their bi-pedal gait. Just behind Brekka the hounds were being handled by her hound master, Fork Beard, and the rest of the swan maids brought up the rear in no particular order or formation. After all, Brekka determined this was going to be a gleeful coon and marten hunt. Freyxus pointed out the distant landmarks of a hickory and a tulip tree to show Brekka where she planned to build the stables of her flying foxes. She had obtained permission from Sur Sceaf to keep the flying foxes alive, provided she built a stable that would accommodate all one hundred and eight of them. But the tyfons and gyrlocks had been wisely destroyed by gassing them with beast-stoppers, though it was believed several had escaped into the wild during the gassing, and several more had been reported by travelers coming out of the mountains.

Donny turned around on his mule and shouted, "Just there, my Lady Brekka." The portly fellow pointed at a cattail-lined pond. "Up ahead."

Freyxus turned and looked her straight on with a bubbly smile. "You're going to love it, Brekka. Donny and I spied it out yesterday with the wyrm kats."

"How did either of you know it was here?"

Freyxus gave a wide-eyed look. "Why, I simply asked Scratch two days ago to find me a place that was wide open with few to no trees, so I could build a stable for the drogs as well as several barns for the fruities. Yesterday, Scratch led us out to this place. On the map, the local Hickoryans call it Paynesford Pond. It's believed to be a haunted place from which many have reported seeing Herewardi witches, sea-wylfs, and wights flying out of the broad meads in days past."

"Probably why no Hickoryan has claimed it? How did you ever get Scratch to show you?"

Freyxus grinned. "That was the easy part. I promised each of the ketten three chickens if they could find me an open space that ran for at least a mile in breadth. I explained that a mile is the distance between the Big Springs and Chester Duke's chicken farm. They did the rest of the work."

Brekka laughed. "In order for the ketten to have known this place tells me they are hunting far and wide for rabbits and groundhogs."

Scratch ran up to Brekka with an expectant look on his almost human looking face. "Brekka pleased? Brekka give Scratch more chooks."

They laughed and Scratch turned his head side-to-side. "More chooks?"

"Oh, black and blue hell, Scratch! Yes, I'll give you each one more chicken for finding the place, but somebody needs to teach you how to count, and that a deal is a deal."

Scratch sprung nearly as high as the horse's back, twisted in mid air, and then ran up to Mauser and Chloe in a half meow. "More chooks! We gets more chooks to eat!"

One of the reasons Brekka had proposed this hunt was to distract her mind from her anxiety over Ruhm's proving in the Daleth Tent; and the Wyrm-Kats were quite the diversion.

*But can Ruhm endure? Can he truly make the transition to become Herewardi, or will it all be just too terrifying or foreign for him? Oh how I wish we were already married. If he can just make it through this rite we'll be married. Soon, very soon, I shall lie upon your arm Ruhm, and shower you with my deepest affections. How I have waited for this moment. Oh Mother Freya, make the time to lift me upon its swiftest wings and carry me into the arms of my lover.*

Her reverie was broken when Donny drew near on his mule once again, "This is the place, my lady. It is an ideal setting for a farmstead. Is it not?"

She scanned the scene, a broad spanse of flat plain, "That it is, Donny." She looked up briefly to see the first stars appearing in the twilight, before she took a sweeping look across the flat lands and marveled at how few trees there were; a very strange matter for those parts. The well-mowed grass told her the sheep visited there even if the farmers wouldn't. She imagined a sizable barn sitting in the flat lands, and even thought Ruhm would likely love to have a horse stud there. Turning to Freyxus, she asked, "How do you plan on getting this stable built, Frexy?"

“As you see, it’s perfect for my needs, I can grow fruits, and there is water. Donny will be my hostler, and I’ve engaged Wendell, Sur Child’s son, who is almost a master builder. He will build the stables for the drogs. I’ll also hire some of the packers to tend the gardens and plant the orchards.”

Donny said, “They’d work for free just to be in the open air.”

Freyxus declared, “Donny that is not our way. The forty-four laws say clearly, ‘Thou shalt not oppress the hireling in his wages, nor shalt thou muzzle the ox that treads the mill. All my workers will receive a percentage of the profits of this enterprise.”

“It’s an excellent plan.” Brekka said, “I can see you have anticipated every aspect of your stable, but I have to charge you to get it done quickly, Frexy. I have just sent Hirondelle, son of Arundel to D’If in Merry Land, which stretches from Paw Paw to Cumberland and up through Bedford. He is to begin quarrying the marble and granite for the temple I’ll be building atop the Mound of Heredom. Sur Sceaf will oversee the laying of the foundation before he leaves for Godeselle. I warn you, unless the stable is built before all the stone gets here it won’t happen. We will need every man, woman, and child to labor on the Temple until it is done.”

Cisne rode up. “My lady, remember Arundel’s warning that danger still lurks in the night skies. The darkness is swiftly falling. We should give the animals a drink and get into a tight unit before the night hunt.”

Brekka signed for everyone to water their horses. Fork Beard brought the hounds up for a drink. Her favorite faery hound, Puck, lapped up a couple drinks before he sniffed the ground then opened on a coon trail.

Brekka called out, “Let slip the hounds! Let the hunt begin.” She grabbed the hunter’s horn at her side and sounded off. Puck led the pack straight for the wood that ran in the direction of the Holy Mound, just as she had planned. She felt her heart leap at the mere thought of just being in Ruhm’s vicinity. It would be as if their spirits would feel each other’s presence as she passed.

As she and Verushka rode to the rear of the others, Verushka said, “But my lady, this will lead us straight to the Holy Mound, and the Lord Arundel specifically forbade anyone going near unto it until after the rite in the secret place is consummated.”

“Oh Veru you are ever the lawful one. You’ve been with me long enough to know I go where the spirit directs me, with little to no thoughts of the rules of men. Besides, what offense would it possibly give the Lord Arundel if the haeligwaecca toured her mound with her swan maidens?"

Verushka pulled her horse in closer. "My lady, I have been telling myself for the past week to keep my mouth shut, but now it is all boiling up in me, and I feel to explode if I don't say my piece."

"That's never stopped you before, Veru. This must be very serious. Go on, spit out what you are thinking, and let us clear the matter up once and for all. For I am sure, I already know your thoughts."

Veru hesitated.

"Go on! Speak! Be out with it."

"My lady, I did not need to stretch my ears far to hear of Ruhm's disgraceful swiving in the Shenandoah. I thought perhaps you had not heard. Ruhm's a wolf among sheep, and his teeth still drip with the blood of lambs from one end of the valley to the other. Are you prepared to live with that?"

Brekka was shocked at Verushka's boldness, despite the fact she had guessed what her friend was going to say before she said it. But that was why she had chosen Verushka as her second lieutenant. She always confronted the uncomfortable issues that no one else dared address. Now Brekka knew she must make it perfectly clear that she would have no one, not even one of her best friends, question what the gods had so clearly revealed to her.

She thought she would take a more Quailor approach in dealing with her. Turning her sharp gaze on Verushka, Brekka asked, "Would you deny the ghost of God?"

Verushka appeared startled. "Of course not, for to deny the Holy Spirit is the gravest of sins."

Brekka's brow frowned for added emphasis. "Then hear me, my faithful lieutenant. I have scried in the stones regarding Ruhm Lee. And I also know the gods have weighed his heart on the scales of Osgard. Thirdly, the Ur-Fyr bears witness in here." She struck her bosom and spoke out loud enough so that the others could hear. "So I declare to you and all those within sound of my voice, in all plainness; it is woven by the Norns that Ruhm is to be mine under full sanction of the Elf Fire."

Verushka hung her head. "Forgive me for even presuming to counsel you, but it is my sworn duty to protect you from all harm. I only meant to express my concerns to make it right in my heart. I'm sorry you had to make it clear to me that I did not have all the facts. I yield to the will of the ghost of god, my lady."

Brekka thought it was a perfectly logical assumption Verushka had put forth, but Verushka had not been privy to her revelations. "Verushka, I didn't make you my second just so you would say yes to everything I do. I need you to always check me, if you can stand the rebuke of the Elf Fire. Now, if we don't catch up to Fork Beard and those dogs, we'll come late to the tree."

She and Verushka rode hard to catch up to the others who were surrounding an old elm tree where the hounds were hammering out at a coon scurrying through the top branches.

Pata got out her mirrored lantern and flashed the light up at the pair of shining eyes looking down. Scratch said, "Scratch catch coon. Scratch love to eat coon."

Brekka ordered "Chust wait, Scratch. I'll see to it that the three of you get to eat the coon, but let the dogs have fun first."

Scratch skipped away to the tree, encouraging the dogs into a frenzy with his loud cat-screams and clawing at the trunk. He was shortly joined by Mauser and Chloe in a formidable caterwauling that drove the coon to the tip of the branch in despair.

Always eager to be in for the kill, Freyxus moved in close to the tree, leaving Brekka and Verushka to watch from the darkness. Unexpectedly, a strange sound of swooshing came from the tree, startling them. She at first thought it might be Donny making a swishing sound, but in the lamp light she saw his mouth was closed. Before she could draw sword or shout warning, Verushka had been plucked from the saddle and was instantly airborne.

"Yo! Pata, bring the lantern over here! Quickly! Quickly!" With one loud blast from Brekka's hunter's horn, the hounds left the tree and assembled near her. Pata rushed to her side with the lantern. Brekka looked down and commanded, "Puck, find Veru. Go. Sucht, Sucht!"

The hounds rushed off, followed by the ketten. As they pursued the hounds through a hawthorn thicket to the base of a large sprawling oak, Pata held up her lamp and Brekka could see a dark winged creature held Verushka on a sturdy branch like a hawk clasps a squirrel. The hounds bayed ferociously and leapt up the tree. Scratch had just mounted the trunk and made it to the first branches when the dark gyrlock lifted into the air with Verushka dangling from its claws. The dogs pursued it to another large, open oak about fifty yards away.

Brekka, Donny, Pata, and Freyxus rushed through the thicket to the neighboring tree, as the other swan maids pursued with Fork Beard urging on the hounds. As Pata directed the beam of her lamp upward, glowing red eyes looked back down upon them, apparently, most disturbed at all the hounds baying below. There was only a small window of time open to save Veru. The gyrlock was weary of toting her around, and would likely send his worm tongue down Veru's throat any moment.

Brekka reached for her bow, quickly strung it, and nocked an arrow, but before she could draw, loud flapping sounds struck her ears. As the lamp light moved through the branches, she could see Scratch and Mauser were busily shredding the wings of the shrilling were-bat, while Chloe helped Verushka to shimmy down the tree.

Brekka hastily dismounted and ran to her side. "Are you alright, Veru?'

Verushka let out an almost breathless, "I think so. Maybe a little bruised and scratched." She turned to the female wyrm-kat and reached forth a hand to touch Chloe's arm. "Thank you Chloe. I wouldn't have made it out of that tree in one piece without your help. The vampyr was already snaking its tongue toward my mouth."

"Chloe, a lady-knight." Chloe preened, her eyes shining, her cat's teeth bared in a smile.

Brekka smiled, "Yes, Chloe, you are a lady knight." Turning back to Veru, she said, "We've got to finish off the rest of those demons. Not only have they scattered to the four winds, a camp of were-bats has been spotted living in a large cave in the Two Rivers village."

Veru rubbed her elbow. "Count me in on those hunts. Imagine if I had been a child. There would have been no hope of surviving such a beast."

Behind them, branches were snapping. They turned to see the gyrlock on the ground where hounds were tearing the shrieking creature to pieces. Always Brekka's grittiest faery-hound, Puck had the creature by the back of the neck, shaking it furiously as the demon's pink tongue wormed through the air.

Scratch leaped from the lower branches of the oak and came directly over to her, "Dumb dogs! Scratch already kill bat. Bat just make noise."

As Brekka assisted Verushka, Pata shone her lamp toward Donny. He stood transfixed with his eyes as big as tomatoes. "Lordy, was that ever exciting!"

Brekka laughed. "And damned near costly, too."

After the dogs had their play, and Fork Beard had calmed them down, Brekka whistled. Puck ran to her and looked up adoringly, waiting for direction. "Take us home, Puck."

The hound gave his distinct cry and bolted through the wood with Fork Beard, Donny, and the wyrm-kats following. After assisting Verushka to mount, she and the swan maids followed at a more sedate pace. As they passed over the Holy Mound, Brekka spotted the dark outline of the Daleth Tent a plough length away.

*Oh mighty Ullr, be gentle with my love. You proving god, we ask that you judge him mercifully when you weigh his heart against the swan feather. Let it be said in Osgard, the love of Ruhm and Brekka shall endure forever.*

Kanarus had told Ruhm he must start this fast with prayer and reflection. He hugged the stone the way a drowning man hugs a piece of boat, for he found himself thinking he was adrift on a sea of endless darkness. A darkness that left his soul in a morass of aloneness that made him hunger for light and sensual stimulus of any kind.

He prayed, *Oh gods who love me, lead me into the path of the Herewardi and truth. Take away my lonely heart, and send me comfort.*

In that ocean of blackness the baying of Brekka's seven faery-hounds echoed, and it charged his heart with renewed hope. *She's coming for me. She's letting me know that she's coming for me.* Never mind that it would still be three days away. For the first time, he felt a lifeline of hope he could touch with the senses of his soul; for soul and body he felt were fast integrating into one. He was in a space he had never been before.

How many were the hunts he had been on with Brekka and those very hounds! If he was not mistaken, that was the full and melodious cry of the pack leader Puck, which he had heard so many times before. He chuckled knowing that she was such an avid huntress and hounds-woman that she had insisted on bringing those faery hounds with her throughout the numerous campaigns of the war. His mind's eye flew open like a vision. He saw giant faery hounds with red heads and ears leaping over him and running through a dream-like wood. The hounds bayed out as if they were trying to communicate with him personally. He sensed that Brekka was telling him that she would soon be there with him. Radiant warmth filled his body, and his heart eased.

"*Meditation*" the command came from the tent wall. The strange voice resonated with authority. For a brief moment he glimpsed the image of a god that was whiter than the driven snow. From his discussion with Kanarus, he immediately recognized the entity as Heimdall, 'the fairest of the gods.' It was as if the tent was coming alive, and he was in no way prepared for this business of having exalted beings commune with him. The very thought was terrifying; like being visited by a ghost, only worse.

The god spoke with the voice of a trumpet, "Thou art one of the champions I called from the nine worlds. Thy good works shall follow thee and be thine to boast of after thy bad works are set aright."

Fortunately, the apparition disappeared again.

Kanarus had told him to start with the beginning of his life, and to follow the course of his years up to the present day, so as to inventory the landmarks of his journey. As he clung to the stone, the only point of reality left to him, memories bigger than life came to him. Closing his eyes, he smelled his mother's rose-perfume. Time fell away, and he was once more a child being rocked on the porch swing of their old homestead outside the town of Winchester. Gradually, the song of tree crickets and whip-poor-wills filled the tent. Smiling, he reached out to touch his mother with his small infantile hand. Just as he felt the smoothness of her apron beneath his palm, she disappeared into the darkness. "Mama, don't go. Please, don't leave me."

"My sweet Ruhm, go to sleep, my darling, go to sleep." Once again he felt the comfort of her cradling arms, and smelled her scent as he drifted into a cozy slumber.

How long he slept, he knew not. Heart pounding, he opened his eyes to the sight of a Pitter rat pack marching up the red dirt lane. Dust from their black jackboots clogged his throat and assaulted his nostrils. "Go away," he shouted, only to have his father place a strong hand over his mouth. His Papa said, "For the time being, we must submit in order to live. But our day will come, son. There is a rising star in the west, and we shall one day find our way under its protecting rays."

The look on his father's face frightened him as much as the Pitter thieves. So he stood silently while the rat-faced monsters took three-fourths of his family's livestock, including his pet rabbits. Tears were running down his mother's face as the invaders stripped the garden of her carefully tended vegetables. The ones mama had intended to feed the family through the winter.

"Are we going to starve, Father?" he asked as the intruders laughingly hauled off the goods in wagons.

"No, my son, we'll manage. We just have to harvest wild onions, acorns, squirrel, and deer. The good Lord will provide."

"Will they hurt Bun?"

"Would you have me lie to you? Best not to think on such, Boy." As he looked up into his father's face, his father's lips were white, and his brown eyes looked like burning coals against his tanned face.

"Someday, Son," his father said, "we will be free of these bastards forever. In the meantime, my friend, Karl, is due to arrive in two weeks. He will be telling us what we must do, for the likes of us will not be tolerated by the Pitters. Unless we flee, they will drive us into an early grave."

The scene went up in smoke, leaving him in profound darkness once again. Time passed. Minutes? Hours? Again, he knew not. Then, crawling on his hands and knees he found his krug with the bottle of dwale next to it. Kanarus had said this was the only drink or nourishment he was allowed and to ration it accordingly. Taking great care not to spill any, he used his finger as a guide and poured a small measure into his krug.

As he slowly sipped, he felt as though his senses were becoming heightened once again. The sound of a far distant trumpet could be heard as clearly as if it were within sight. He could smell every herb in the drink. A sense of power infused him, and he knew if he only lifted his arms he could fly. It was a curious and wonderful sensation. *Yet* he pondered, *perhaps all I am seeing is no more than the workings of this magical Dwale.*

Just as he was finishing the last drop of his cup, a whisp of light appeared on the tent wall. The wall drew back revealing a familiar scene. In the shadow of Babb Mountain he recognized the little white church in the dale. His father had aged and now sported a mustache. Old Preacher

Tucker appeared. He too, seemed frailer than Ruhm remembered. Yet his voice was strong enough to resonate in his ears.

"It's no use resisting any longer, Jon Lee. These damned Dominiker commissars are hell-bent on us representing Angrar as the only true god, but it's nothing, but lies. I guarantee you, if we don't get out of these parts soon, they'll kill the likes of you and me and send our wives and children to their despicable slave camps faster than an Ala-Bamba tick."

Ruhm strained forward to hear his father's response, but the darkness returned, and all he heard was the sound of air rushing in and out of his lungs. He began to hear the call of gulls, not outside, but *within* the tent. He felt the sting of salt spray against his face. He had to run his hands over the canvas floor of the tent for orientation, but, as he did, the smells of brine and fish filled his nostrils. Before him appeared the image of a powerful god holding a bow. The deity was not only manly and strong, but also possessed the ability to communicate without speaking. He knew this god had protected him throughout their wilderness journey and across the seas. This had to be the god Ullr, his protecting deity. Ruhm's heart was filling from a communication of wisdom in a language he could not understand, but which he knew would someday manifest itself.

Gradually, he was surrounded by the swirling gulls. Out of the darkness came a brilliant vision of a large red-stained boat bobbing up and down against a weathered grey pier. Nearly weighed down by the pack on his back, he followed his parents up the gangplank while he supported his little sister with one hand. Half of the people in the village he had known were already aboard. It had been a long and dangerous trek across wild lands and deserts all the way from Virginia. Often they had to hide in the woods and canyons from Pitter rat packs, who were patrolling the area, as well as the sinister Rogue robber bands that plagued these Western Lands. He could still feel his little sister, Tammy, shivering as he held her close to keep her from crying. He smelled the sweet scent of cherry tobacco wafting from the pipe Karl always seemed to have with him. He was a man of calm in any storm. There he stood, Karl Throckmorton, the pedlar and the man his mama called their savior. He still remembered the night his parents sat around their table and listened to Karl tell them how he could put them beyond the reach of the Pitters. It was the first time he had heard mention of the

Herewardi, and the first time he had seen hope on the faces of his father, Reverend Tucker, and Merriam Wallenwood, his father's closest friend.

Now, as he stepped onto the deck, Karl's jolly voice boomed into his ear. "Ruhm, my boy, you are not going to believe the freedoms and beauty of the isle we sail to today. You're going to think you died and went to heaven."

He felt utterly exhausted. No more quaking at the sound of Pitter jackboots. The large boat raised sail over a bumpy sea. Too exhausted to cheer as some of the others did, he sank down on the plank deck hugging his rucksack. He felt the waves beneath him lulling him to sleep against the ship's railing in the warmth of a briney sun, then he was rocked by a sudden wave. Opening his eyes, he gazed upon the most electrifying sight he had ever seen, a young maiden of exquisite form with red hair and bright green eyes. His breath caught, so astonished was he by her beauty. She smiled an invitation at him with her sparkling eyes. He rose to follow her, but, laughing, she flirtatiously turned away. He shouted for her to wait, but she was spirited away by a frightful large Sharaka Shaman adorned in beaded brain tanned leather. The shaman frowned fiercely at him. Suddenly, Ruhm was alone again on a grey sea that faded into the void, leaving only a vivid memory.

She was more beautiful than any girl he had ever seen; so overly confident, cheerful, and filled with that bubbly energy of those who are truly alive. As the girl walked off, he shouted for her once again and was shocked to realize he had shouted out in the darkness. The memory that had seemed so real a moment ago was now nothing but a deep dark void. He was now left with only his thoughts of how many times he made excuses to travel from Hockney-in-the-Hole to Ele-Anor-Ness just to see the lively redhead once again. He chuckled at the pleasantly intrusive memories.

As the sweet summer breeze rocked the walls of the tent, he contemplated how he had striven throughout the years to win Brekka's love. His mind went to that dark place where his troubles had all begun. *She released me from her command. She rejected me.* The pain of rejection flooded his being.

A massive wound appeared out of the darkness on the black wall. A swirling red tongue swooped around him and swallowed him. He felt engulfed and smothered in burning acid, as if he had fallen into a giant cobra lily. With all the anger and rage he could summon, he slashed and punched until he fought his way out of the wound.

Suddenly, the tent was filled with sunlight once again. He found himself running through a leafy vineyard. Looking down at his naked body, he saw that golden red hair covered his thighs, such as a goat has. Amused, he realized that even his feet were cloven. He felt a strange sensation above his butt cheeks and reached back to feel a short furry tail. *By God, I'm a satyr.* As he looked about, he found he was surrounded by the grapevines of a sunny sloped vineyard.

Through the grape leaves, he could hear the laughter of woodland nymphs. He was propelled by instinct to chase them, swatting vines out of his way as he leapt over tall vines to capture a squirming, giggling nymph and subdue her with his amorous hands and lips. When he had plied his lusts with one, he was back hurling himself though thick ferns and vines at the next beautiful nymph that he was about to ravish when a loud crashing sound came through the idyllic vineyard, like the rolling of a giant boulder or avalanche. The sky went black. The next thing he knew, he was on the rainy earth in Winchester being pummeled and kicked senseless by a gang of ruffians. The darkness was overwhelming, and his eyes burned with searing pain like someone had run red hot arrows into each of them.

As he opened his eyes, the powerful ancient white-haired man had him pinned down with his piercing green eyes. On the ancient's shoulders sat two of the blackest ravens he had ever seen. A thunderous voice addressed him. "You shall drink the bitter dregs of your sins until you are purified sufficiently to join yourself to a Queen of Heaven."

The ravens took flight from the ancient's shoulders. He felt their black wings pounding him from every direction until all he could see were the two piercing green eyes of the All Father, which gradually faded into the blackness, leaving him with an awful sense of foreboding.

He sat motionless, silently counting his thunderous heartbeats, while striving with all his being to find calmness and peace. His hand felt for the krug and the calming bottle of dwale. He poured. As he carefully sipped, a brief image of Brekka sitting gloriously atop her white buffalo rose up before him.

*Clunk!* The sound came from behind him, startling him so much he dropped the krug. Dreading what he might see, he slowly turned to the red eyes of the gyrlocks on the massive iron gates. They were closing on Brekka. *Oh! No! No! Please, not this again.* He found himself falling into a bottomless dark pit, grabbing for a hold, but tumbling into the nothingness of the abyss. Expecting to hit bottom at any moment, he found himself instead curled into a fetal position, screaming bloody murder in agony at not having had the power to rescue Brekka from her fate. He was overwhelmed by his incapacity and weakness to help her. He was filled with the emptiness of her absence. *Dead!* His beloved was dead, and it was surely all his fault.

Brekka's ghost stood before him, clothed in long white robes, flaming white hair, and blazing eyes that shone like amber. She addressed him. "How could you have betrayed me? Why did you besmirch our sacred love?" Another feminine voice cried out in the darkness, from whither he could not discern. It was but one loud word, *Confess*.

His bowels writhed like coiling serpents. Spiritual terror poured into his soul like venom. A vision broke forth in a powerful burst of light. He saw himself on hands and knees, naked before Brekka, who stood in a shaft of golden light, once again in glistening white robes, holding a scale before her in one hand and a sharp flaming ice blade in the other. A voice as the sound of trumpets barreled out: "Who dares to approach the Daughter of King's Blood, the Anointed Virgin of Woon the All-Father?"

"It is I, Ruhm Lee, Son of Virginia."

The voice commanded, "Then look and behold."

Once again, he saw Brekka holding up a scale, and upon one side lay his heart, but on the other side was a list of his sins written on parchment, which turned into a mass of blackest slime squirming and dripping with maggots. He asked, "Is there nothing I can do to save us?"

The brilliant god Ullr stepped forward and placed a swan feather alongside his heart on the scale. "One thing only." He commanded, "Look to the dragon card." The god disappeared, the scale was balanced, and Brekka was gone. Darkness filled the void.

Now, as he looked out into this darkness, it was like a deep pit, and were it not for the stone of truth upon which he clung, all hope of marrying Brekka would have been abandoned in that moment. He felt the cool and smooth stone against his naked skin. Without it, he would have had no center at all. The smooth stone became his compass on a very dark and troubled sea.

Exhausted and weak from his fasting, he drifted in and out of sleep. The passage of time was marked only by fitful dreams of dragons, bloody swords, being burned by dragon-fire, raked by claws. A barely conscious awareness of lark and cricket song marked real time. Through it all, he kept fighting, only to lose time and time again against the many cunning devices of the dragon. He was giving into a despair that drained all hope from the heart. He had lost all that he cared for, all hope of securing Brekka's love, and he was utterly exhausted. He collapsed on the floor and cried out, "Odhin, God of the Herewardi, save me."

A deep and restful slumber followed, during which he dreamed he was riding joyously upon the back of a flying golden-green dragon. He shouted out in such exhilaration in riding on the mount of the gods that it awakened him. He felt rested and suffused with new hope.

*Praise Woon, the All-Father for his all enduring grace. I know now that I must bare my soul to my beloved and accept whatever feat or penitence she sets. I thank you, All Father, that you have revealed that I have the power to subdue and tame the dragon of my passions and turn its power into such a wondrous beast.*

*But, wait, didn't Arundel tell me, it was the dragon that guards the sacred treasures of love? The blood of which imbues the bather with an immortal love. But who sits in the pit? By my sheer confessions, it puts both Brekka and me in the pit, from which we must both be birthed anew. The love born from this rite will truly purify us and make us one. I yearn so to experience that spiritual union I felt long ago in the night vision. By Ullr, I pray it comes to pass.*

What he believed was the fourth day was once again heralded by the morning song of a lark. He was convinced that he had truly come to understand himself at a deep level and that he had safely made the passage over hell and into the favor of the Herewardi gods. He had managed to plumb the depths of his own soul, and to explore the intricate connections he had to everyone important in his life. It finally felt like wholeness was settling into his being, until once again Brekka's words that he would have to atone to all the women he had misused came into his mind. He now understood why that was both necessary and essential, so that the world and hearts might be set aright again.

*But how, my god, how?*

Gradually the image of a well-endowed, robust god in all his naked glory materialized on the veil. "I invest you with *the Fire of Life,* and bequeath unto you the godly powers of fertility. Thou hast earned the crown of life. Now be whole, and fill the mountains and valleys with thy seed, for we the gods are of thy race, and like you, have been created to be greater than those who created us. There is nothing older nor stranger than true royal blood."

Ruhm recognized that it was the God Frey from the amulets that many young bloods sported.

The chirping of tree crickets aroused him from a half-slumber. By his reckoning, he decided it was nearing sunset of the fourth day. Night was approaching. The time must be drawing near. He sat up, looked around, reached out and touched the veil. For a moment he wondered if she were really coming. *Was all this but a vision I have conjured up? Were the visitation of the three gods and their reassuring words simply the final torment of the rite?* Suspense was the ultimate proving. *Is this my judgment, to be kept waiting and longing, but never to be satisfied? If so, I cannot think of a worse or more deserved punishment.*

Inside Brekka's white tent her handmaids had taken great care to prepare her for this momentous occasion, her wedding day. Just before sundown, Brekka had washed her hair and bathed in magnolia-scented soap. As twilight deepened, her mother, Lana, along with her handmaids, Wyth and Ynys, were putting the final touches on Brekka's hair and dress. There was much fuss and playfulness. Merriment filled the atmosphere. Finally, Brekka's mother could be content that her last daughter had married, and in all likelihood the numerous grandchildren she anticipated would soon be following.

Wyth held up a mirror and exclaimed, "Oh, Brekka, I wish I was in your place and getting married to a bronzed man like Ruhm. You are so lucky. They just don't come any handsomer than your Hickoryan."

"Well earned was that luck," Lana gently pointed out. "At thirty-five winters, a woman could count herself lucky enough to even find such a man. Methinketh she waited long enough to marry. Unlike her father, I was surely opposed to her taking up the sword, and I certainly did not like her becoming the woman of blood she's been all these years. All her younger sisters have their men and several weens at their sides, while her womb was as empty as a blown egg. Had she waited any longer, she'd look like me, all memory and a foot in the grave."

"Mother, you should be happy that I am now feathering my nest and shall fill it with grandchildren to overflowing. And you know very well that you are still beautiful and, the gods willing, you shall live to see your fifth generation."

Lana responded. "Yeah, dearling, but thou knowest it's always better to marry in that first flush of youth when the sap runneth strong in your veins. You two maids would do well not to follow her bad example. Marry before ye leave your bearing years. A fallow womb oftimes will not bear. Know ye not that the holy moonth of May is at hand, a most proper time for you all to marry?"

"I'd rather take Brekka's place. Ruhm Lee outshines any man I ever met." Ynys responded. "That is, if you're having second thoughts, Brekka."

Lana smiled. "He is every bit a man of pretty parts. That I can attest to, much like thy father. Although, I hear his rumspringa has certainly gotten him into quite the mess."

Brekka huffed, "Mother, the Hickoryans do not have rumspringa. He was just lust crazed."

"Then whatever thou callest that rakish thing he did."

Brekka gave a sigh, turned to her handmaid and said, "Ynys, I'm having no second thoughts, but rest at ease, you are on my list of sister-brides."

Ynys laughed. "I hope I'm at the top of it. Such hope only makes me envy you all the more this night."

Lana knitted her brow. "I chust hope the groom hath not been exhausted by the ritual preparations. They are rather spooky to an outlander, as thou knowest. There was that man from Hockney. What was his name?"

"Oh, that was Meriweather Madison. He repeated the rite six moonths later and passed. He was unable to deal with the dark side of his mind!"

Ysys sighed, "Don't worry. I am sure he'll be alright the moment Brekka steps inside the marriage chamber."

"Brekka, my dear," Lana said in a subdued tone while reaching into her *beutel,* a small cloth bag Quailor women wore tied to their apron string. "It would please me if thou wouldst wear the swan pendant my mother-in-law, Mahallah gifted me on my wedding day."

Brekka took the golden pendant in her hand and studied the diamond shem on the swan's back, and knew it to be the work of elf-sires from long ago. "Oh, it's so beautiful, Mother. A true elven gem! You can rest assured I'll see to it that my firstborn daughter gets it on her wedding day. Complete with its long chain of history."

Brekka's eyes filled with tears at the thought of the unbroken links of love going back from her grandmother all the way to the days of Turfrida, wife of Elrus the Seer, as first recorded. Its origins were ancient, from the realms before recorded history, even stretching back to the days before the folk memory and into the Drowned Lands.

Lana beamed, pressing a hand to her back. "There shan't be any daughter if we don't leave for the mound right this moment!" It was Lana's way; getting more and more excited before any special event. "Thou knowest thy fa is strategically motivated and is probably waiting outside this tent pacing back and forth right now."

"Fa is always strategically motivated," there came an oaken voice from beyond the tent.

"Chust give us a few more moments," Lana called out as she splashed some fresh magnolia perfume on Brekka's hair and shoulders. "This is a very special day, a holy day, right? If thou rushest us before the bride is in proper spirits and prepared for her holy calling, thou invitest the Muspelli with their tormenting little demons."

Brekka could almost hear her father chomping at the bit to get the marriage underway. At any rate, she was sure the king was cursing the slow women for all their primping and preening, just as he used to do when they were maidens preparing for a dance.

Lana took a step back. "Now, thou lookest exactly like the swan goddess, Yster; bright as a golden May dawn and sweeter than the first cherry of June."

Wyth exclaimed, "She's absolutely right, Brekka! You could take flight any moment and none of us would be the least surprised."

Brekka got to her feet. "My ladies, I thank you for all your fussing and help. I could have never made myself as presentable as you have done. The gods bless you all."

Yyns took her by her hands. "Are you ready for this, my lady?"

Brekka took a deep breath. "I am more than ready. I have done naught but dream of this moment for nigh twenty years!"

As prescribed by protocol, Wyth and Ynys left the tent to alert the lady knights to light their torches for the bridal procession.

Lana was biting back tears as Brekka walked out of the tent into the torchlight. Sur Sceaf stepped back to take a good, long look. Pride lit up his war-weary visage. "You are as beautiful as your mother was on our wedding day." His voice was thick with emotion.

Lana smiled. "I was never this beautiful."

"Oh, but you were and still are, my Freckle-Fox." He leaned down and kissed Lana.

Sur Sceaf took Brekka's arm and squeezed it lovingly, while Lana took the other and staunched her tears with her handkerchief.

Ynys and Wyth lifted Brekka's train and the lady knights led out with torchlight and song:

"Now to the Holy Mound we are ascending. Here comes the bride.

Yonder waits the groom on truth's stone humbly seated. Here comes the bride.

When they join the heavens are waiting. Here comes the bride.

First comes the groom and then the multitude of children. Here comes the bride.

We make this holy declaration. Here comes the bride.

Let the gods rejoice and hear our proclamation.

Bless them ever with luck and higher elven station.

Here comes the bride."

Shortly after washing and preparing the space for Brekka, Ruhm's heart stopped. He heard revelry and the singing of women beyond the walls of the black tent. Muffled whispering voices could be heard outside the tent. Shortly thereafter a bright sliver of light shone through the veil, and now as his heart speeded, the door opened wider and a feminine form was silhouetted in the golden torchlight. She hurriedly closed the door on her company, leaving only the illumination of her brilliant candle to his dark accustomed eyes.

As he sat firmly on the stone of truth, mesmerized, a graceful being approached him through the daleth door. She was clothed in an aubergine robe, carrying a candle in one hand and a golden obelisk, which shone like a spear of sunlight in the other. It was about the length and thickness of her forearm and almost as blinding as staring directly into the sun.

He watched, fascinated by her every move as she set the candle and obelisk to the table. They sat on the opposite side of the veil next to a golden torc and a thick leather pouch which, heretofore, he had not been able to see. She walked gracefully over to the trestle table, surrounded by her golden halo. Near her was an alabaster basin of red wine, the golden torc, and the horn of golden mead, just as Kanarus had described.

Arundel had explained to him in his previous instruction that the obelisk represented not only the lost word of generative powers, but also possessed the power to bestow the knowledge of how to live holy lives. He declared that amongst other things, this jewel included and symbolized the power of multiple marriages which the Herewardi culture centered around.

A chorus of tree crickets accompanied the sacred moment. He sat up straighter on the turquoise stone of truth as he had been instructed, and patiently waited for her to come for him as promised. He was overtaken by a profound yearning so strong and powerful, it was almost painful.

*Come to me my dearest, my darling, my beloved. My heart moves me in deep rivers of longing for you.*

As he wiped the wetness from his eyes, she began disrobing on the other side of the veil. His heart jumped, pounding out a powerful beat in his chest. Her godly form was suddenly unveiled, and she was approached like a graceful faery in the candlelight. Her whole body seemed to radiate a soft golden light that accentuated her sublime figure--full breasts, and shapely hips with a wedge of copper hair accenting her upper thighs.

His mouth went dry. *My god, you are more beautiful than anything I've ever laid eyes on, Brekka. You are like some perfectly shaped marble statue of a goddess, only very warm, pink, gold, pulsating, and vibrating with life.* He wondered for a moment if this might be a dream, for it was entirely too perfect and stimulating.

That thought vanished when Brekka came close to the veil. In the stillness of her movements, he could hear her breathing. All his senses were infused with thoughts of feeling her body pressed lovingly against his.

"I will open to you my beloved, if you will open to me."

The very air grew golden with her voice, as if the sounds made the vibrations of light move in waves.

*Sweet Freya, Mother of Gods.*

As he had been instructed, Ruhm remained seated in the nude and whispered back, "I will open to you, my beloved." He didn't even recognize his own voice.

Smiling, she retrieved the soft vellum pouch and drew out a stave of hawthorn wood, shaped like the Thorn of Life. She whispered in a low breath, "Hawthorn hammer of Thor's protection, shield me and mine."

The father of the Herewardi had received this sacred runic implement from Thor himself, who had appeared to him in the guise of a young man child. It had been fashioned from a stout branch of the holy and most Ancient Eildon Tree.

Brekka left the candle on the trestle table next to the veil. With the Thorn of Life she split the omicron on the veil, then delicately dipped one of the fragments of the veil into the red wine and wetted her lips. With delicate fingers she re-dipped the aubergine cloth in the wine, the very color of blood, and this time wetted Ruhm's lips with it. A sweet taste of full-throated wine coated his tongue. Through the opening she extended the Thorn of Life, which he grasped by the handle. Slowly, smiling into his eyes, she raised him up to a living perpendicular before drawing him through the tear in the omicron veil representing wyrd, fate, and the mysteries of the unknowable in its blood red perthro rune. For an instant he felt like a newborn colt on wobbly legs, and when he had grasped hold of the Hammer Thorn, a power surge entered his body with a perceivable jolt. At the same time coils of energy flowed up and down his spine like electric serpents, causing his skin to tingle and yearn for her caresses. Brekka then loosened his grip with one of her hands and laid the Thorn of Life on the trestle table.

They drew near to one another, face to face. Their bodies pressed tightly. She whispered magical words from the Ur-Tongue that would forever change his life. Words that Kanarus had tried to translate for him, but which he now could barely distinguish. He had, indeed, experienced romantic and emotional love before, but this went beyond, into a new, mystical, and exalted spiritual form he had never quite known. It was a spiritual dimension that magnified all the other forms of love, delicious to the senses and very desirable.

She drew back and looked into his eyes as she sang a whispering song, "I pull you out of your old world into a new world of light, joy, and perfect joining."

In each hand she took up the mead horn and the Golden Omega Torc. She held the torc in one hand, placing the other end of it in his hand. Then she drank deeply from the mead horn and gave him to drink from the same.

She spoke his name as the new word, "Ruhm-Ullr-Lithe."

As instructed, he called her by her new word, "Brekka-Anu-Freyafae." These were the names that they privately would whisper into each other's ears throughout their lives and by which they would be known in the worlds to come.

She looked warmly into his eyes and smiled, then spoke her part, "Oh, Holy Seed Father, warm me with the rays of your love. Cause my mound to rise and give birth to the gods that sleep in the side chambers of my rib."

The language was sensual, and the warmth caused delicate moisture to cling like honey to their skin as their passions stirred in each others' naked presence.

He hesitated, trying to reign in his state of arousal, before saying in a serpentine whisper, "Oh Holy Womb Mother, my beloved wife, spread over me the canopy of your peace. Give my soul rest in your comfort. Lift me up and tear your veil for me. Cover me with the stars of your heavenly love."

Brekka then responded, as he gazed into her inviting face with those emerald stars of her eyes staring back at him so trustingly in complete surrender. "Come with me, my beloved, into the garden of my love, where the hawthorn and magnolia are always in bloom, where the sun always shines, and where the branches of fruit are heavy with the food of love."

She led him back to another veil housing the bridal bed. Ruhm saw that the bed was shaped like a large bed-sled, draped with a gossamer canopy of deep maroon and covered with the softest of furs, mink, and otter.

"The Elf-God, Odhin, taught us that this marriage chamber signifies that all of the world is sealed out, and you and I are sealed in. So shall we two be sealed in the bonds of eternal love, as were the first man and first woman. Many are the marriage beds you shall have, but this bed is thine and mine. Let none other enter here."

They embraced, and the salty taste of her sweet summer sweat wet his lips, as he kissed first her brow, and then moved sensually down her face to her lips. She eased him back on the soft furs with her gentle hands, then arched over him before settling atop him as was custom for this night, the female symbolizing the canopy of the starry heavens.

"As the heavens roll down, and the sun rises up with its penetrating rays, so I take you to be my eternal husband, through night and day, throughout all the revolutions of time, through all internity and eternity. Thou art my swan lord evermore."

# CHAPTER 3 :

## THE VETTING OF BRIMHILDE

AS WAS HER RIGHT, BRIMHILDE HAD asked Freyxus to accompany her to the meeting with Elisheba, who was to vet her as a potential sister-wife for the royal jester, Yellow Horse. While Freyxus was untying the rag curlers she'd done up for Brimhilde the night before, she realized her sister-knight was literally shaking in her boots. In battle Brimhilde was as firm as a rock, always alert for a sneak attack—and, in fact, had saved Pata's life several times. But now, she was fussing over her appearance like an inexperienced maiden on her first promenade with a suitor.

"Relax, sister. I have met Elisheba, and like all Ele-Anoreans, she is filled with grace, intelligence, and the peace of the Tree People. I promise you, there is nothing to fear from her."

Brimhilde turned her head with a look of utter disbelief. "Easy for you to say, you're not the one being vetted. My mother was rejected during her first vetting, and we children felt the effects of that rejection the rest of her life."

"Remember that I will be by your side as your advocate. Yellow Horse has chosen you because of your wit, wisdom, and beauty. Everything commends you. You have nothing to fear."

"But what if she rejects Billy? Perhaps she would be unsettled that I have adopted a Hickoryan orphan, who often throws tantrums and pissy fits in the presence of company."

"Didn't Dr. Shanks assure you that the best thing for him is the stable and nurturing environment you are providing?" Freyxus unwound Brimhilde's thick blonde braids before taking up her brush. "Remember, he said it would take time, but gradually Billy's misbehaviors would dissipate. I can't imagine what the poor little fellow had to endure."

Brimhilde sighed. "The sweet lad still has nightmares about seeing his parents brutalized by the Grand Inquisitor.

I have come to love him so dearly. I will never give him up, even if I have to give up Yellow Horse to keep him."

"Honestly, Sister, I can't imagine either Yellow Horse or Elisheba rejecting you for this act of love and kindness. After all, Billy's story is very much like Yellow Horse's own. He, too, witnessed his parents' getting slaughtered at the hands of the Pitters, and after he was rescued by Sur Sceaf he was taken into a loving family, and took many moonths to come out of the shock."

An hour later they arrived at a charming stone cottage with a reed-thatched roof on the Boyd plantation that Yellow Horse had specifically chosen for Elisheba and their three younger children. As they waited for admittance, Brimhilde nervously chewed on the nails she had so tediously groomed.

Freyxus whispered, "Stop that. You're ruining all my handiwork. Why is it you always picture the worst of anything?"

Elisheba's daughter, Willow Song, opened the door and offered a friendly greeting before leading them to a small sitting room off the kitchen. The interior stonework was parged and whitewashed, though black soot gave the stones of the fireplace a gray cast from backdrafts, testimony of a clogged chimney. The furnishings were of rough-hewn pine, suitable for a temporary residence. Freyxus detected the smell of hickory smoke from the fireplace. The light blue curtains at the windows appeared new, as did the tessellated rug on the oak plank floor. The table was set with teacakes and cheese along with a pot of tea and vase of red daylilies splashed with baby's breath and monkshood. Freyxus felt immediately at home in the cozy cottage.

Elisheba also greeted them with a smile and warm eyes. She was attired in the traditional turquoise Chartreusean gossamer dress, flowing gracefully to her ankles. As Freyxus performed the introductions, she sensed an instant bonding between the two women. "Yellow Horse has done nothing but sing your praises in his letters and has confused to do so since I arrived. He's told me about young Billy in such a way that makes me think he already considers the boy his son. I am eager to meet him and have our children get to know one another."

Brimhilde glanced at the floor for a moment, before blurting out, "Did he tell you that my son suffers from shock sickness?"

"Of course he did, and it breaks my heart to think what he has endured at so young an age. His history reminds me of Yellow Horse's trauma as a child. I must say that your taking him under your wing is an eloquent testament to your character and the heart that you will bring to this family."

Brimhilde glanced at Freyxus, confusion in her eyes. "You mean you approve of me as a sister-wife?"

Elisheba smiled warmly. "Of course, I do. This vetting is simply a formality that must be undertaken under Herewardi law. But I am a seeress, and I have already scryed the blessings you will bring to our family. So I must ask if it is of your own free will and choice that you embrace this holy covenant."

Brimhilde broke into a big smile. "I…it most certainly is. I fell in love with Yellow Horse the moment I met him at a banquet in the stone hall of Godeselle where he entertained us with his wit and wisdom like no other jester I've encountered. And, as I've gotten to know him on a personal basis, I've found that everything he says and does resonates with my spirit."

Elisheba lit up. "I'm so glad to hear you say that you have come to know and appreciate him as I do."

Freyxus interjected, "Though it may not be necessary, I wish to speak to Brimhilde's character and personality. Ever faithful to her oath and fearless in battle, she is true to her sister-knights. You shall find her as true to you as a sister-wife."

"Even though your words are indeed unnecessary, I appreciate your testimony as a confirmation of what I have already scried."

Brimhilde ventured to ask, "Do mine ears fool me? Do you really approve of a marriage between Yellow Horse and me?"

Elisheba took both her hands. "I do indeed approve, and I already love you as a sister. And I know I will love and treat Billy as one of my own nigh children. So do not fret your gizzard anymore on this matter. Let the three of us sit down and make plans for the wedding."

As they took seats, Elisheba offered a dimpled smile. "But I must warn you, Yellow Horse is eager to wed you before the Grand Fest of High Summer in the Weed Moonth. So that gives us no more than three days to pull this together." She paused, her brow wrinkling. "That is, if you so desire."

"Absolutely," Brimhilde enthused. "I would marry today was it not the time of your reunion."

Freyxus noticed a becoming blush warm Elisheba's cheeks and ears. "See, already we know how to put things in balance." She laughed. "How about we have the wedding on the morning of the Grand Fest?"

Brimhilde replied, "It will be the culmination of my two greatest dreams; that of fulfilling my calling as a lady knight, and marrying the man I love."

"In that case, I will order the marriage tent prepared at the foot of the Kings' Mound so that your ancestors may bear witness to this marvelous joining of two noble bloods."

The lady knights all agreed that Brimhilde was a beautiful bride in her gauzy white dress. She couldn't stop smiling as Elisheba, in her capacity as faery-queen and haligawicca, presented her to Yellow Horse at the door to the flower bedecked marriage tent.

Yellow Horse was still breathless from the ceremonial ritual performed by his Sharaka comrades, consisting of heaving him high into the air by means of a buffalo hide bedecked with fertility talismans. He was resplendent in beaded buckskins, hair bone armor, and an eagle, raven, and swan feather headdress. His headdress denoted that he borrowed from the Herewardi culture. He had chosen to hang from his belt the placental talisman given to him by his mother to ever shield him from harm.

While the lady knights sang a wedding hymn, he took the hand of his bride and led her though the flap of the tent. In her capacity as Haeligawaecca, Brekka followed. Once she reemerged and the lady knights finished the last hymn, they hurried to their tent to change into their riding clothes.

Taking up their bows, quivers, and spears, they quickly mounted their steeds which had been saddled by the green beetles, and Brekka took charge of her eager faery hounds. They arrived at the edge of Benders Woods just as Hound Master Fork Beard, son of Elfbeard the former master of the hunt, was lining out his hounds.

In a gravelly voice that carried even to the interior of the wood, he announced, "We dedicate this fox hunt to all the fallen hunters and warriors whose company we enjoyed so much in times past. I am pleased to announce that the great artificer, Amarandel, has crafted a special sword out of star metal and virgin's milk to be awarded to the man or woman who presents the greatest number of trophies."

An enthusiastic cheer lifted up from the hunters.

"Hunters, please take particular note that a horse race is soon to begin from the east side of the woods down the Pikeside Highway and then ending at Kimes Ranch on the far side of Pikeside. So avoid the highway, and should you encounter one of the racers, at all costs, call off your hounds." He suddenly grinned. "The turkeys and the chickens in this region have endured much predation from foxes and varmints that have become way too prolific, so let's even the score and set things back in their proper balance." He then gave the traditional blast of the hunter's horn signifying the hunt was now afoot.

Two hours later Fork Beard once again sounded his horn to recall the hunters in from the hunt. When all returned with their trophies and hounds, it was announced that Lord Arundel on Sun Charger had taken first place in the race. It had been a close contest between the many fine steeds entered. Chise and Arundel had taken turns leading when at the end, Loosestrife on his bay Hanoverian nipped into second place, only a few strides behind Lord Arundel. The prize for the winner was a herd of ten Dzungarian horses, the pride of the Rdokians, donated by Rabenbrot of Paw Paw, one of the far flung guerrilla captains of Hoor's shocktroopers who had the uncanny ability to attack the enemy and then disappear in the ranks of the city his forces had just attacked.

"And now it's time to determine the winner of our hunt. Present your varmints to the beetles doing the count."

When the results were tallied and announced, Freyxus was thrilled to learn she had won the trophy sword with a count of seven kills. Brekka had a count of six, while Going Snake came in third with a count of four foxes and a lone timber wolf, not often seen in those parts. Some even insisted it was no more than a large coy-wolf.

With Freyxus in the lead, holding high the prized star sword, the hunters headed back to Big Springs where crowds were already gathering on the promontory in anticipation of the festivities to come.

Brekka had attended many festive boards, but she had never seen so many tables, rows and rows of them. An army of kitchen helpers, including many of the heretofore captives and packers from the bastion, streamed from the large kitchen tent bearing platters and bowls of fare in anticipation of the official opening of the fest of departure for the king. Many of the benches were already occupied, while other celebrants were spreading blankets all the way to the top of the promontory, nearly as far as Pikeside.

Chartreusean girls in their flowing gauzey gowns were entertaining the crowd with singing and sitars, although their green skins brought the most curiosity. Yellow Horse and his bride-covey of two radiant women, and Going Snake with his covey of seven were busily directing the governors-elect and the newly appointed mayors and administrators of the city-states to their places at the long king's table.

As Brekka threaded her way through the throngs on the way to her tent, she spotted Zschamillah and Arym working their way through a cadre of flirtatious Hickoryan young bloods including the Hickoryan Jokers, who were clearly dazzled and besmitten by the beauties of the Ele-Anorean sisters. They paused to exchange greetings and hugs with Yid and his bride-covey, before steering toward the king's table, presumably to congratulate their sister, Elisheba, and to meet their new sister, Brimhilde.

Many contests had already occurred; archery, wrestling, javelin throwing, foot races and even jousting. Most had been won by young bloods representing all tribes. The awards ceremony with the Lady Paloma presenting the prizes to the winners concluded shortly before midday. Now everyone was looking forward to the official opening of the festive board in honor of King Sur Sceaf.

Before the awards ceremony, Paloma had intended to take a ride in one of the cerulean bal-loons, but the lines of excited children and parents were overwhelmingly long. *Perhaps later*, she told herself as she, along with the throngs, awaited Sur Sceaf's arrival from D'If. As faery-queen she would have the honor of sitting with her husband at the king's table as would the other faery-queens, while the remaining bride-sisters were seated at nearby tables.

A heightened buzz arose, causing her to turn toward the northwest, where Sur Sceaf and Chief Chise, the new President of Panygyrus, led a colorful procession of senior officers and dignitaries, flanked by the king's color guard in their brilliant red uniforms riding their white steeds with their red accoutrement, flags, and banners held high. The Banner of Panygyrus flew, unfurling the marvelous image of the feathered sea-serpent which had come to symbolize the new nation.

Following behind came Arundel in his role as King of Ele-Anor-Ness, Kanarus, King of Taxus, and Mendaka, Chief of Chiefs of the Red Nations, all equally impressive of demeanor and regalia.

Paloma felt a thrill run through her. Though King to others, Sur Sceaf was first and foremost her beloved husband. Now in his late fifties he was even more handsome than on their royal wedding day. For this occasion he was resplendent in the formal attire of the Herewardi gentry and a scarlet gluckspilz cape with its pearly white ermine tails adorning his broad shoulders. Years of struggle and stress had greyed his temples and added a bronzed cast to his skin, but the years had also added the patina of strength and wisdom to his dear face. Her mother's words in the preparatory tent on her wedding day had now come to full fruition. The gods truly had favoured her. For at the time she spoke it, Surrey was the lesser of all his brethren and the least likely to ascend the throne.

The procession ended on the highway between the promontory and the bastion. After all had dismounted, green beetles rushed to lead the white steeds away while Sur Sceaf and the others walked up toward their seats at the king's table. Great cheers arose, and hats were flung skyward in exuberant greetings. A series of lurs heralded his approach, filling the air with an overarching hum like that of a mighty and robust beehive about to swarm.

When Sur Sceaf reached the spot where Paloma stood, he kissed and hugged her, and they looked into one another's eyes. He offered his arm and escorted her to the table. The others did the same with their faery-queens. When all were seated, the crowd settled, waiting eagerly for Sur Sceaf to open the festive board.

He began with the breaking of bread, and the presentation of the ales and bee-urs. The cooks' helpers then brought forth quarters of stags, baked and bronzed turkeys, Paloma's favorite, along with stuffed hens and fatted calves which had previously hung over the fires until tenderly braised. Additionally, they bore forth platters piled high with crabs and crayfish from the Chesapeake, golden geese, fricasseed squirrels, groundhogs, and young rabbits. Leeks, pumpkins and greens were laid at every table along with roasted mutton, catfish and eels. There were enormous pecan, pumpkin, and woven dough apple pies that decorated tables along with pastries in the shape of rabbits, bees, and swans.

Vases of roses, zinnias, pink lilies, day lilies, yarrow, delphiniums and boastful sunflowers adorned each table, along with garlands of evergreen magnolias. Dessert tables held honey cakes, nut breads, fruit cakes and cream puffs. Rounds of cheese were stacked like yellow and white columns, along with a plethora of hors d'oeuves.

It was a feast of laughter and camaraderie and joyous reunions unequaled throughout the whole of Panygyrean Realms. Once everyone had eaten their fill, Sur Sceaf signaled for the music of the sitars to cease. He then rose to introduce each official, beginning with President Chise and progressing through the governors and mayors, freely dispensing accolades to the deserving. A roar of laughter ran through the crowd when Christian Rosenkrantz, the rotund mayor of Winchester, who attempting to rise in acknowledgement, fell over, the result of too many early festive cups, but he was a jolly and beloved chap and true gentleman as ever there was.

Yellow Horse, still in his wedding clothes, shot to his feet and shouted, "I can see that the people of Winchester will soon be drinking ale and bee-ur instead of their famous hard cider." Even Mayor Rosenkrantz laughed as he was hefting himself off the ground trying to resume some modem of dignity.

After all had been introduced and spoken a few words, Sur Sceaf signaled for quiet. “As King, I find myself humbled and grateful for the outstanding service and sacrifice of these men and women now appointed to shape this new world; particularly of our deserving president, Chise. Please join me in wishing them well as they depart for their various stewardships and embark upon this grand government called the Confederation of Panygyrus.”

Long Swan shouted, “So mote it be written. So mote it be done!”

# CHAPTER 4 :

## THE JEWEL OF THE SOUTH LANDS

RUHM LEE HAD SPENT MOST of his time in one delicious honeymoon after another. After taking Brekka to wife, the most thrilling moment of his life, he was still quite in a euphoric state. All his adult life he had striven to be with her. The honeymoon was even more exhilarating and delightsome than he could have ever imagined. Since then, she was like a brilliant dawn that kept renewing itself. Because it had been so fulfilling to be with Brekka, he felt a jolt when she began urging him to marry others. He knew that was an expectation in the Herewardi culture to select a suitable bride-covey, and in fact he had been considering several of Brekka's friends, but he had not expected it to come so soon. When she began urging him to consider the women closest to her, harmony being the backbone of Herewardi marriage, he found she was partial to those he always found most pleasing. In fact, he and Freyxus had already formed a bond of attraction during the exploration of the caverns. Though Verushka had shown him no particular favor, he had always admired her for her steadfast integrity and grit. Both Wyth and Ynys had shown interest in him from the beginning, and Brekka eagerly encouraged them in her own words, 'So that my best friends may be my bride-sisters forever.'

Brekka, as his faery-queen, could suggest bride-sisters of her own liking, while he was free to agree or reject. At the same time, he was free to suggest brides of his own choosing who would then be vetted by the bride-covey. Even though he had observed this process for several decades, he had always been an outsider to its mechanations. Now that he was considering this up close from a Herewardi point-of-view, it was most intimidating. Finding no objection to Brekka's choices, and seeing that he could love them all, he willingly embarked upon a proper courtship of each in turn, taking great care to tailor his wooing to the needs and personalities of each.

These were beautiful and intelligent women, but it was difficult for him to believe he would ever care for them as much as Brekka, yet Going Snake and some of his other polygynist friends assured him that with the passing of time you acquire a great love for all of your wives. He would have to learn how it was the Herewardi men came to love all their wives equally. He would give it time, because this was the package Brekka came with. Each wife in her own way brought out some other hidden aspect of him and enriched their lives together at a deeper level than he could have previously even imagined possible. Each was as pleasing, lovely, and as full of surprises as if they were multiple, beautiful gardens.

As he wed each one in turn, and they became part of Brekka's bride-covey, they seemed to be more filled with joy and exuberance, more especially when they were all together. Even in the kitchen they were like a nest full of singing canaries, joyously adding to one another in an overriding chorus of sisterly love he had seldom observed among other peoples. At first he worried that he might feel left out, the only man in a family of six, but discovered that everything seemed to revolve around their love for him as well as each other, making him feel more strong and content and eager to reciprocate in kind.

At the same time Ruhm found himself astonished at all of the details involved in setting up the virginia viceroyalty. As one of his first orders as governor, he commissioned Flammalf to create an official map of his viceroyalty, which stretched from Merry Land's northern boundary in the north to the Cherokee lands near the dismal swamp in the south to the Oheo River in the west.

During his honeymoon with Brekka, the city hall in Martinsbuhr had been converted to his personal seat of government. Seamisch, in his capacity as one of Ruhm's chancellors, not only oversaw the refitting of the large stone building in the center of the city, but he also hired a number of the former employees of the city government, many of whom had served under Dominiker control and now professed great delight at being a part of the new regime.

Loosestrife, his former lieutenant, was put in charge of the Hickoryan Cavalry. In this role, he tasked the new commander to visit every city-state or major township in the viceroyalty of Virginia in order to promulgate the protocols of the new government. He thought how strange it was that Loosestrife, a confirmed philanderer had no interest in the Herewardi custom of multiple marriage. The matter had perturbed him so much that he asked Loosestrife why he preferred philandering over honest marriage, and his old friend said, "I am not interested in getting to know the women I swive any deeper than a toss in bed. I don't even invest that much energy in my own wife." Despite the man's many moral faults, he was still a superb military officer.

Feeling a bit overwhelmed at his change from cavalry commander to governor, Ruhm leaned heavily on his new father-in-law, Sur Sceaf, for advice and counsel. For his part, Sur Sceaf appeared to be pleased at the acquisition of his new son-in-law, and Ruhm was overjoyed to be treated with as much respect and affection as if he had been one of the king's own sons, but then he had heard beetles and some of the Red Nations leaders praise Sur Sceaf's unabashed friendliness.

Shortly after his wedding to Brekka, a silver harrier brought him letters from Hockney-in-the-Hole on the isle, including one from his mother, one from his father, and to his delight, one from Reverend Tucker. All three expressed congratulations and approval, a fourth letter he received was from Gordon Swinerd who chose to upbraid him for becoming Herewardi. He never really cared for Gordon, a self-righteous prig who took advantage of Herewardi hospitality, but never reciprocated, and chose to place himself above the laws of the isle by cutting down entire woodlands for nothing but a profit motive. Loosestrife had told him that Gordon had even supplied the subversive news paper, Hoth's Kat Sheet with railing accusations against the Herewardi which were later proven to be wholly without truth, but which rumors took years to dispel. Indeed, he had come to hate Gordon, as had his father.

The letter from his mother was especially touching, expressing her admiration for Brekka, and she gave no expression to disapproval of his having chosen other wives as well, although, she did jest that she would have a difficult time remembering the names of all her grandchildren when they came. She also insisted on being the first to be told that she had a grandchild on the way. He suspected he might be writing that letter very soon, but, so far, Brekka had kept it secret, presumably unwilling to offer false hope.

Shortly after his marriage to Wyth, he received word from Sur Sceaf that the Pitter host in the south lands had been routed and all their survivors put to the sword. Great celebration heralded the end of the war and the total victory of the Syr Folk forces. Thereafter, he received a message from Il-Alim requesting his assistance in setting up a proper city-state in Charleston, a city-state that was unquestionably the jewel of all Panygyrus. Ruhm had replied he would be glad to render assistance.

Brekka had further encouraged him. She had said, "Of course, you must go, my darling. It is your duty as governor. I know Fa would appreciate your helping my brother. He is, after all, a warrior and is not schooled in the same diplomacy you've developed. Charleston, having once been the home of a large enclave of Herewardi, is very dear to the king."

"You bring up a good point. Since your father has appointed Rip the Prestor as governor of Ala-Bamba, I need to strategize with Rip and Khem about rooting out the robber bands infecting the surrounding lands. In fact, since Sur Sceaf has ordered Fork Beard's Fyrd to Moby to ensure the shipment of the ginger and turmeric from the plantations, Seamisch and I can travel with them."

She offered a flirtatious smile. "Don't even think about leaving me behind. Since Wyth and Ynys have not had as much time with you for a honeymoon, this would be a lovely opportunity for them to enjoy your company in the jeweled city."

Ruhm laughed. "Aha, now it begins. My faery-queen is managing my life for me. Yellow Horse warned me."

"But, my darling, this is what a marriage partnership is all about. Before your bride-covey, all of your rainbows were in shades of grey. Now, you are surrounded by a spectrum of brilliant colors, each with their own particular radiance. I'm sorry if it's too much for you to handle."

"It's not too much for me to handle." He had to protect his pride. "Besides, if you are to accompany me, it would be helpful to have your handmaids with you."

"Oh no, you don't! You must remember that Wyth and Ynys are no longer my handmaids, but my fellow bride-sisters, equal in status to all the wives."

“I stand corrected, dearling. You must be patient with me while I absorb the intricacies and hierarchies of Herewardi culture.”

“Haven’t I been patient with you for twenty years?” Her eyes twinkled at him, sending a thrill through him. He thanked his newly discovered protector gods every day that she was his wife. Leaning forward, he kissed her and sent a silent prayer of thanksgiving up to the god, Ullr. “Believe me, it wasn’t easy to accept that ‘Stay away from me, I love you’ behavior of yours. But every step of the way is now worth it. And I do agree it will be far more enjoyable traveling with my bride-troupe. They keep things so lively.”

“Not the whole troupe. Freyxus is focused on completing the stables for the drogs, fruities, and your horses before the workmen are needed for the temple. And Verushka will substitute for me over details of the mound excavations.”

He grinned. “So mote it be, my faery-queen.” He felt like Lord Arundel when he first described Zschamillah. ‘She is the Queen of Women and the Woman of Kings.’ He had no doubt that Brekka fit that bill as well.

The trip was without incident. Since Ruhm’s elevation to a swan lord, he had been assigned his own beetle, a young blood with flaming red hair and a dash of a royale named Regir the Red, energetic son of Fork Beard. His first assignment was as driver of the covey’s carriage, and the fifteen year old seemed the perfect fit, as he bemused the ladies with his wild hunting tales and the antics of the beetles during the war.

On his way down the Shenandoah Valley, Ruhm and his ladies stopped at the various cities only briefly, but promised a longer visit upon their return trip north. His time with Brekka was magical, and Wyth and Ynys were a delight. Their gentle Chartrusean ways breathed peace into his soul. Their stay in Moby in the viceroyalty of Ala-Bamba was most pleasant. Rip had made great strides in rebuilding the city and establishing himself as a fair and competent governor. Khem had visited too, and together they conferred over the best ways to deal with the lawless robber bands who continued to stir up strife and disorder in the land. Fork Beard and his fyrd left on the third day after their arrival to escort the huge caravan of turmeric, ginger, and kenaf on its way north to the mercantile warehouses in Martinsbuhr and Hagerstown.

During the visit, Rip shared a letter from his former colleague and Prester apostle, A.P. Rockwell, now Governor of the Viceroyalty of Sylphania, stating that Sylphania was a cornucopia of resources—timber, wildlife, maple sugar, and productive farmlands. He could have never imagined the ease at which things grew in that well-watered land as compared to the waste howling desert lands of Salmalhuer.

During the last week of the Weed Moonth they traveled to the jeweled city of Charleston on one of the Dragon Lines, a well-paved road once assiduously maintained by the Pitters to aid the policing of their labor camps as well as moving the commodities over the lands of their empire. The roads were the one thing the Pitters had left that were of inestimable value, pathways of order and commerce.

Charleston was the last Pitter fortress to be captured, and represented the jewel of the south. By some mysterious force it was the only city left fully intact by the earth changes. The citizens, though yoked by the pitters, managed to keep it a hot bed for rebel ideas of freedom, equality, and tolerance, which they secretly promulgated. As long as they paid their taxes and tithes to the Yengish Dominikers, they managed to keep free of the Pitter spear points, always at their backs. This city had been the center of all seditious activities in the south lands and maintained an on-going ghost government that spread across the south lands all the way into Merry Land and parts of Sylphania during the long centuries of Pitter occupation and oppression.

Ruhm had long heard of the glories of the city, but had never laid eyes on a more beautiful place. There were large pink manses, yellow manses, white manses and columns of alabaster lining the cobblestone streets. Along the seaboard rows of mighty palms swayed in the soft oceanic breeze.

He sat clad in his red and grey cape atop his grey Hanoverian mount. Brekka was clad in a mint green silken dress, and her two bride-sisters wore the gossamer lace of Chartreusean women of status.

Upon arriving at the outskirts of Charleston they were greeted and escorted into the city by a color guard bearing Il-Alim's personal cicada banners, and summarily taken to the headquarters of Lord Il-Alim.

Hickoryans lined the streets and hailed Ruhm with rebel cries and cheers as one of their own. Herewardi Bush Masters blasted their Lurs, accompanied by shouts of "Hal Mar Mauna Alumalauna." Ruhm gave a bewildered look back at Brekka sitting in her open coach.

She smiled and translated for him; 'Hail Maid of Maids, Virgin of Virgins.'"

The procession ended at a large white mansion with stately white columns and rounded balustrades. On a squarish façade, Il-Alim stood with Ehira, Degataga, Redangus, and several Hickoryean commanders Ruhm did not recognize. Ehira wore an enormous red headdress of macaw feathers that fanned out flat to the span of a peacock's tail. The golden-haired son of Kanarus, Anghrus, stood with his nigh-mother, Sigyn. The young blood was there to receive his training in seamanship from Degataga and Redangus, the Roufytrof having singled him out as the elect of the gods in the Ea-Urth, and therefore entitled to the deference of all. His resemblence to his father, Lord Kanarus was unmistakable, but he bore the porcelain complexion of his great mother, Wilona the Fair.

Il-Alim was attired in the traditional full length cordovan leather coat and white cravat of the Herewardi gentry, but unlike most of those of royal blood, he had donned a black sash instead of the red, symbolizing his rejection of polygyny, the condition by which he received approval of his marriage to Reverend Wallenwood's black-haired daughter, Lorna.

After Ruhm helped his brides step down from the open carriage, Il-Alim came down the stairs and received first Brekka in the royal embrace, and then Ruhm.

They exchanged warm greetings and received Il-Alim's hearty congratulation on his marriage to Brekka and the bride sisters. Ruhm introduced Wyth and Ynys as his newly married brides. At first shy, the Chartruseans warmed under the charm of Il-Alim's welcome. Il-Alim looked like a younger dark-haired Sur Sceaf. The resemblance was so powerful that Ruhm almost called him Lord Sur Sceaf twice.

"It is a great honor to have you here in the south lands, my ladies. My wife, Lorna, has prepared a special suite for your comfort. She begs your pardon for her absence, but our son, Ulfr, is recovering from a broken arm and insists that his mother offer up his milk teeth to the wight of the hearth, a tradition Brekka can explain to you at your convenience." He then turned to Ruhm. "Besides aiding me in setting up a proper government, I can use you to help me decide some troubling cases. One is the matter of some black overseers from the Flar-Da labor camps who have fallen into my hands. The other matter concerns Redangus' desire to settle the large isle off the coast of Flar-Da which he has named Ah-Go-Lo-Ga after a large whirlwind that forced him landward in order to survive the storm, but enough business for now. Let me introduce you to some of our compatriots and let us celebrate your arrival first."

After being introduced to the various officers and greeting old friends, they entered a large windowed ballroom with elaborate wainscoating and huge chandeliers dripping from the high ceiling.

Ruhm was much impressed with the Hickoryan commanders while the bride-sisters doted on young Anghrus as if it was a great privilege. He overheard Brekka say, "I have heard it in the council fires of the Roufytrof that you are marked by Odhin in your youth as were Sur Sceaf, Arundel, and I."

The golden youth, bronzed by the warm southern sun, humbly acquiesced. "But no calling or commission could excel the glory of being the Virgin of Virgins, the seed of the woman."

"I beg to differ. Long Swan has prophesied that nations shall gather to you; that you will discover vast new worlds across the sea of Aegir and you shall deliver the firebrands of freedom to the lost tribes of our people in what we now identify as the far off unexplored Land of Ur-Ope."

The powerful Red Man, Degataga, fished for an answer from the rumors he had heard, "I hear Kanarus took great loss of his men in the Valley of the Stars."

Not wishing to discuss the matter before Kanarus' Son Anghrus, Ruhm motioned for them to walk over to the many paned windows.

"It was my fault. I was laid up with a wound and could not run reconnaissance for him. Otherwise we would have hewn them down like barley corn."

Ehira, the Red Man chief from the far south woods beyond the Mexus and Guatemala swung his head around, the mighty headdress giving him particularly enhanced hearing, and he gestured as though tearing something apart, "The two of ju be twin jaquars. Together, ju would have torn the enemy to shreds and not have too many losses. I am sorry jour losses."

The dinner bell rang. Stewards came to lead Ruhm to his seat next to Alim. Brekka and her bride-sisters were seated next to Sigyn on Ruhm's. After Alim gave accolades to the various honorees, he raised his krug, drank, and took his seat, whereupon he turned to Ruhm, "I've always valued your counsel, my friend of old, and I find myself in quite a quandary."

Ruhm knitted his brow. "What troubles you, Alim?"

Alim paused to allow the steward to refill his krug. "The king said we must make every effort to spare the Dominikers."

"That is right."

"Well, what am I to do with the ninety black overseers of the Fla-Da camps?"

"Have you spoken to the captives they oversaw?"

"Yes, they were for the most part black women. Said they were repeatedly raped, tortured, constantly manhandled and abused by thrice affliction of lash, fist, and cock."

"Then I would treat them the same as Pitters and put them to the blade. Where are the captives that accused them?"

"After consulting with them, I found it was their wish to join their own people in Wymouth, especially the faction that had lost their husbands and entertained some hope of rejoining them there."

"Then I suggest you deliver the overseers to Khem. He will know what to do. Besides, Sur Sceaf always admonishes that every people be judged by those of their own culture, for each culture sees through its own eyes; a bird sees the treetops, a squirrel the branches, and a mole the roots."

"That counsel is most wise, that is what I shall do."

"You mentioned Redangus wants to settle the Isle of Ah-Go-Lo-Ga. Why is that a problem?"

"Since I surrendered the privileges of royal blood upon my marriage, I do not have the authority to grant him settling privileges."

"Brekka does. I'll speak to her for you. And by the by, Brekka is to take over the stewardship of the Young Prince Anghrus. It is the will of the king. She will outline the training he is to receive and will assume the same authority as his mother would have wielded over him. Though but fifteen winters, it is the king's will that the young blood begin his selection of wives and he must be apprised that the Roufytrof has arranged a marriage to the daughter of Ilkchild. Brekka will fill him in on the details."

"Oh, which daughter of the wizard is he to marry?"

"Sunniva the Pure."

"Alas, I am but a monogamist. Were I not, Sunniva would have surely been one of my choices. She is as fair as the rays of a May sun and as brilliant as her father."

Hour after hour of sharing tales and news around festive board passed until it was time for all guests to retire to their respective rooms.

It was Brekka's conjugal night with Ruhm. Wyth and Ynys chose adjacent rooms in the suite."

Ruhm stared out of the living room window in the third-floor suite, which overlooked the Aegirean Sea and the palm lined shore. "This whole place echoes with the voices of ancient Hickoryans. Do you feel it?"

"I do. I commend you upon your perception. Your spiritual senses are becoming attuned."

He and Brekka shared a decanter of wine before retiring to bed where they expressed their fervent love for each other.

Sometime later, as Ruhm laid back on his pillow, Brekka rested on his left arm letting her fingers walk across his bare chest in some sort of song she was rehearsing in her head.

She placed her hand over his heart and said, "I shall enjoy our time here in Charleston, but the Holy Moonth opens in two days with the first sliver of the new moon. Since this is the season of atoning, we have some visits to make to all the women you have swived in the Shenandoah. Now we must make sure your reach matches your strut."

Ruhm sighed heavily. "I can tell you I'm not looking forward to that at all."

"Doing the right thing is seldom easy, but now that you've been raised a swan lord, it becomes absolutely imperative. The gods expect it if you are to continue in their favor. Just ask yourself, what would Ullr do?"

"It's just so alien to me, and to be frank with you I'm not that good at dealing with the emotions these women must have bottled up for me."

Brekka rose up and smiled into his eyes. "That's why we're a team, my beloved. Your bride-covey and I will be with you every step of the way."

# CHAPTER 5 :

## THE NORNS BRING THE HARVEST HOME

CHARLESTON ON THE BAY WAS a very liveable charming city-state. Lorna invited the bride-sisters to tea and cakes in the conservatory on the afternoon before they were scheduled to depart. It was a lovely sunlit, glass-lined room overlooking the shoreline of Soulier Bay. The room was filled with parlor palms in colorful glazed pots, along with sprays of lavender, yellow and red orchids, and large pots of red and white Amaryllis staggered around the orangery. Through the windows one could view the lush green lawn where stood a massive live oak dripping long strands of swaying silver moss.

As the ladies entered, they were heralded by the cheerful song of canaries in gilded cages along with the raucous calls of black birds, which Degataga said the locals called Caledonian crows, the delight of Lorna.

Brekka had not seen Lorna since she had wed her brother, Il-Alim, at the harrow stone on the banks of Lake Mahallah in Godeselle. The last time they spoke had been at the reception in the Stone Hall. At the time, Brekka had been full of resentment toward Lorna's father, the Reverend Wallenwood, because he had refused to allow Lorna to marry Alim unless her brother swore an oath of monogamy, thereby forcing her brother to give up his culture for another. She could not understand such rabid intolerance, and she hated Reverend Wallanwood for it. She understood that Alim's love for Lorna drove him to do this, but what angered her most was in swearing the oath he gave up all the privileges of his royal blood line, an act she equated with patricide of the worst order.

Lorna was blooming, even prettier than the day of her wedding. Proudly, she announced that she was heavy with child. "I'm so hoping for a little girl this time. Though I love him dearly, Ulfr is all teeth and horns. I have tried not to spoil him, but it's difficult because he's had no brothers or sisters for four years. And now that his father dotes on him in rough-and-tumble play, I'm constantly barraged by his ceaseless ruff-housing. Alim tells me I must not squash his maleness, but should suffer his wildness that he grow to proper manhood."

Brekka laughed. "I remember my two big brothers constantly breaking things with their stick fights and mock battles in the house. But when nigh- mother Swan Hilde was in charge of us, she would use their sticks to paddle their bottoms and order them outside to fight their battles or she would show them what a real fight looked like. Truth be told, I was often counted in those fights."

Lorna smiled sheepishly. "I must admit there are times when I wish I had bride-sisters to give me a break." She laughed. "Don't tell my father, but after spending these last four years in company with bride-coveys in the Taxus Lands, I see many more benefits to the Herewardi way of marriage than I do drawbacks. When I was a young virgin, I thought my father's religion was the only right way, but now I see his faith presumed to rob me of both reason and will, so that now I am altogether of a different mind. I learned that when one rebels against my father's zeal he first threatens and then excommunicates, and attempts to make the apostate an enemy to their family and friends. Such was not the way Christ intended, for every person was meant to be the designer of their own will." She glanced at Brekka. "Alim has never mumbled nor begrudged me for my father's zeal, and now I realize how much Alim gave up for me. But alas, we are bound by an unbreakable oath, which only father can revoke. I've approached father, but his heart is set like flint."

Brekka noted that Lorna had turned palid, not at all her usual vibrant pink. "My dear Lorna, are you feeling well."

"It's this child I carry. He seems to wrestle in me, and it leaves me exhausted."

"Perhaps some squaw root and dandelion root as a tonic?"

After they had seated themselves around a white wrought-iron table topped with ceramic tiles depicting a vivid red male and female Firginia nightingale in a holly bush, Brekka revealed with great joy that she, too, was expecting. The ladies' expressions of happiness were interrupted by a steward bearing a large tray containing a tea service and an assortment of cakes.

"I hope you like ginseng tea," Lorna said as the steward brushed aside a palm frond to set the tray on the table.

Brekka nodded. "I have favored it since I was introduced to it by Edie, the wife of the Cerulean Chief, Blufre. She calls it 'sang, and so do the locals."

As Lorna filled the pretty porcelain cups, she said, "I so envy your travels. Alim is always talking about the places you've been and the fascinating people you've met." She glanced at the two Chartruseans, and they smiled an acknowledgement. "Where are you going next?"

Brekka selected a cake from the three-tiered plate. "We're retracing our steps up the Shenandoah Valley. Ruhm intends to have extended visits in each township. Long Swan and Ysys are to join us in Roanoke. Long Swan's surveying the possibility of founding a new academy outside Roanoke at a place called Fishburne, and if I know my fa-bro, he's already there with ruler, gauge, and cannon in hand."

On the first day of the holy moonth, they set off from Front Royal for Roanoke, a two-day trip on a good road like the Pitter Dragon Line. Yesterday, Ruhm had dispatched Ugga, one of Il-Alim's beetles, to Roanoke to inform Mayor Thomas Lynch of his anticipated arrival in two days time. He also sent Uffa to Long Swan in Martinsbuhr so that he could join them in Roanoke as had been arranged.

Although the air had a hint of autumnal crispness, Brekka asked Regir to lower the top of the carriage so that the ladies might enjoy the first tinge of fall color and the pungent smell of the fermenting forest duff.

Wyth pulled her shawl more firmly around her shoulders before leaning forward. "Forgive me, Brekka, but I am still a bit puzzled. I realize the council of women has decreed that we must visit the women Ruhm has swived, but what purpose can this really serve other than opening old wounds?"

"Surely they would not want to see Ruhm again," Ynys added. "Besides, I'm not sure I would vote in favor of women who offered themselves outside of marriage."

Brekka smiled. "Tell me the truth, sisters. If Ruhm had plied his charms on you when you were maidens, could you really have resisted him? I know what agony I endured every time we were together. Had it not been for my commission from my people, I would have surrendered into those strong arms long ago."

Wyth and Ynys exchanged embarrassed looks. "I must admit I could never have refused him." Ynys nodded. "Once you step inside his circle, it's like being caught in a whirlpool. There's no way to swim away. It's a delicious form of drowning, isn't it?"

"In the Herewardi culture what Ruhm did is exactly the same as a marriage proposal. I cannot speak for these women, but I suspect they believed they would wed. Now, as his bride-covey, it is our duty by convenant to support our husband as he attempts to reverse the blows of symbolic spiritual death he inflicted with rakish delight, and which he dealt in the days of his swiving. Provided the Ur Fyr confirms it, and does not warn us otherwise, we must offer these women a place under the wings of our bride-covey if that be their choice."

"What if the ur-fyr warns otherwise?" Ynys asked.

"The All Father Woon is master of the ur-fyr and has taught that the ur-fyr is above error. They may never know it, but I was prompted by the ur fyr, whilst I slept, to send my fetch to them during their dream time, thus preparing them to receive our message."

Ynys frowned. "But, Brekka, isn't that unfair to them. Imposing on their free will?"

"Not at all. It's merely reasoning on a higher plain, spirit to spirit, soul to soul so that when we arrive they will not be able to shake the feeling that we are friends and that somehow they must have known us."

Wyth sighed. "Sometimes I think I will never master the complexities of Herewardi culture."

"Don't fret your soul. Very soon it will be second-nature to you."

"What if a lady rejects Ruhm's offer of marriage?"

"Of course, that is their prerogative, but since Ruhm chose them, I don't think there will be a problem with us loving them. However, it *is* possible they will have no palate for us. It is neither a reflection on us nor them. It is merely a cultural perception. You saw how strongly Lorna's father was opposed to polygyny. The roots of prejudice run deep, and many cultures take great delight in imposing their norms on others."

Ynys smiled impishly. "Why wouldn't they love us, every woman I meet envies us?"

Brekka frowned. "That's because most are Herewardi and recognize marital harmony. Herewardi girls start screening for bride-sisters from age eight onward. You won't find that dynamic outside our society. In fact, from what I've seen and heard, in other cultures girls are very competitive against one another over one man, a dynamic that is completely alien to Herewardi maidens. And when outlanders wed, wives jealously defend their turf much as a hen guards her own nest."

The day was warming as the sun moved higher. Vast flocks of geese, ducks, grackles, and blackbirds flew overhead. Ynys cast a glance toward Ruhm riding ahead of the carriage.

"How will Ruhm make amends if his offer is rejected?"

Brekka said, "The law only requires us to attempt to make amends. If the injured party does not avail herself of his atoning offer, then he is free of the debt. It is the same as being forgiven."

Wyth protested. "I don't think we need to worry about that. Who could ever reject a man like Ruhm?"

Brekka laughed. "Well, I agree, but we must ever remember, these women have had little exposure to what they consider our peculiar cultural practice, despite the much teaching the skalds have been doing up and down the land. I once asked the mother superior, Paloma, how she managed so many diverse cultures in her bride-covey. She said, by always listening and responding to the needs of one another. It is the duty of the husband to make each wife feel personally cherished and our duty to see to it he does."

Wyth smiled impishly. "Personally, I've only had eight days with him as my man, but so far, it's been more glorious than I even imagined."

Before leaving Front Royal, Brekka had sent a harrier requesting that Freyxus and Verushka meet them in Roanoke where the bridal council fire had decreed their atonement would begin.

They spent the night in Charlotte, a bustling Hickoryan township where they found rooms at the Albert Pike Inn, a quaint and cozy establishment known to Ruhm as a gathering place of the Rebel Freedom Fighters. Ruhm immediately sent Regir to the home of Mayor Henry Madison, inviting him and Mrs. Madison to dine with them at the Albert Pike's Inn. It proved to be a most enjoyable evening, as Martha Madison was a charming daughter of the south lands, with an infectious laugh and a honey-coated drawl. The mayor himself was only a few years older than Ruhm and had distinguished himself as a leader of the rebel fighters in the battles all along the Piedmont. He was particularly interested in learning about the Isle of Ilkchild and the lands to the west, while his wife expressed her curiosity about the Chartreuseans and how they came to have green skins.

After an early morning meeting with the mayor, Ruhm hustled his ladies into the carriage and set off for the south gate of the Shenandoah Valley. A few miles from the outskirts of Roanoke, they met their bride-sisters coming toward them on the Charlotte Dragon Line Pike.

After a flurry of hugs and kisses, Verushka said with a laugh, "Ruhm, I must tell you that last night as we slept beneath an ancient yew, I dreamed Father Ullr came to me and introduced me to all four of the women you swived. Though I could only see through the fog of a morning mist, I know that two greeted me heartily while another, with reservation, and the fourth turned her back and wept bitter tears. I know not their names, but it was as if we knew each other well by another name."

Brekka hid her pleasure. "This tells me that the spirits of these women are already being interwoven with ours by the Norns. More things transpire in the world of sleep than mortal man knows. Don't you see, this dream tells me it is likely we have known them since the dawn of the fore-world?"

Seamisch gave Ruhm a sideways glance. His first lieutenant had been progressively moving to becoming more and more Herewardi and of late the two had exchanged many conversations on the subject resulting in him revealing deeply personal details of his march into becoming Herewardi. "Well, what do you know, Ruhm. It seems like you're not the only one who has weird dreams."

"It was much more than a dream," Ruhm shot back.

Brekka gave him a questioning look, causing him to look uneasy. "What is Seamisch saying?

"I have a confession to make. At a time when I struggled to know your love for me, your spirit came to me in a night vision, more real than anything I've ever known, and the impact on my heart has never been equaled by any other experience in my life. In that night vision it became abundantly clear to me that you and your sister knights were a package, and that I could not have one without the other. Then there was the visit by the white beard who told me that there was but a small crack in the door for me to obtain your love and that if I did not act, I would forever regret it."

Brekka smiled. "Ruhm, this tells me your spiritual eye is opening. It was my fetch that came to you. Whether you are conscious of it or not, your spirit will pave the way for the women you have swived to follow their hearts. Now, as to the white beard, methinks that was the All Father come down to be a light unto your feet by emboldening your heart to become Herewardi."

Seamisch seemed to be mulling over her words.

At Ruhm's suggestion, Freyxus and Veru rode in the carriage with their sisters, their horses tied to the rear. Seamisch rode on one side of the carriage, and Ruhm on the other. After exchanging news of friends and family, Freyxus announced with obvious pride, "I should like to announce the completion of the stables only two days ago."

"Who's tending my horses?" Ruhm inquired.

She gave a devilish grin, "I've placed Donny in charge while I'm gone. Both the drogs and the fruit-eaters have nestled right in, but I confess it took some work to get the horses accustomed to them."

"Excellent," Brekka declared. "Have there been any more sightings of were-bats?"

Freyxus nodded. "While you have been gone, there have been a total of three reports of cattle mutilations in the open areas of Merry Land.

People have ceased traveling at night. Lord Sur Sceaf has ordered out hunting parties every night, particularly down in the Two Rivers area where there have been a cluster of sightings." She glanced at Ruhm and said, "Don't worry, husband. As a precaution, I have ordered that your Hanoverian and Dzungarian horses be gathered into the arena at night, and I have stationed guards. Also, Donny tells me that the drogs would stir if they sensed the presence of a were-bat anywhere in the vicinity."

Ruhm grinned. "Thank you, my darling, for looking after our interests. I can't wait to see your handiwork." He turned to Verushka. "How went your treasure hunt for the Holy Mound?"

"We did very well, my Lord. We unearthed a gandr and hring pit containing several gold and silver necklaces, numerous rings and none-too-few bracelets from the era of Hrus, but no elven jewels or relics."

Brekka noted Ruhm's puzzled look and volunteered, "A gandr is a magical staff similar to a long swan and a hring pit is where lords cast in their rings when pledging an oath to the gods. I imagine the necklaces and bracelets were the offerings of great ladies calling on the gods for aid."

"As a matter-of-fact, the gandr had the name "Ullr" etched into the staff, which El Yid told me from the looks of it that it was most likely fashioned from a unicorn whale's tusk. I intended to present it to Long Swan for his opinion, but he and Ysys had already left for Roanoke, so I left the treasures in Lord Sur Sceaf's care."

"I can imagine how excited Fa must be," Brekka said. "And nigh mothers Swan Hilde and Milkchild must be esctatic. I fashion they are pouring over the items and examining every mark on them."

Ruhm acknowledged the value of the treasure finds then inquired, "How is Loosestrife doing in my stead?"

Verushka suddenly looked troubled. "My lord, if I may say, you need to keep a tighter rein on Loosestrife. He's done perfectly well managing governmental affairs, but he is a letch in his personal life. Frankly, in my opinion, he's too involved in his *seitensprung* to be much of a man in charge."

Ruhm and Seamisch exchanged looks before Ruhm said, "I'm not sure I understand your meaning, my dear."

Brekka answered, "You know, what you Hickoryans call extra-marital affairs, the Quailor call that seitensprung."

Verushka nodded. "It seems he didn't take heed to your repeated admonishments, my lord. Perhaps it is time to give him a direct order."

"It's not my place to correct another man, but I'm told his wife, Linda, is to arrive mid month. Trust me she will swiftly put a stop to such shenanigans."

"At least in public," Verushka added.

It was mid morning when they entered Roanoake. They rode down the main street, now called Dead Horse Street by reason of all the exhausted horses of the Pitters that died there when Kanarus' troops overtook them in the exhaustion of battle. After the victory the entire town had turned out to greet them. Now they were making their way through cheering crowds once again.

As governor, Ruhm had come here with the intention of fortifying his relationship with Mayor Franklin Reedy and his councilmen. Just ahead, under a welcoming banner strung across the promenade, Ruhm was delighted to see the city fathers waiting in the middle of the street, Next to them stood Long Swan in his white robe with staff in hand, towering over his ever attentive wife, Ysys, her green skin setting her apart from the locals.

Brekka raised her voice above the good-natured shouts. "From the looks of it, you're going to have to do some politicking first before we can locate Hollyannah. I want to remind you that when we left Charlotte, you said your good-byes to Mayor Madison way too soon. My fa always insisted that's not proper protocol for these diplomatic situations. We need to keep the machinery oiled at all times for further advancement of the cause, for there are always dissenting termites gnawing at your government."

"I realize that now, my dear." Ruhm grinned at her. "I'll be sure to keep that in mind as we make our way up the Shenandoah, especially when we reach Winchester. Christian Rosenkrantz is a good man of great renown. Kanarus and I owe him so much. His influence over the mayors of the other city-states is enormous. I assure you, as he bends, so do they."

As he approached the mayor and the town council, the mayor threw his hand up. "Welcome! Welcome, General Lee. Or should I say Lord Governor Lee? You do us great honor with your visit. The whole town wants to meet you, express their gratitude, and wish you their best. We've reserved rooms for you and your ladies at the Wessex Inn. All costs on our city. But for now, we're holding a grand picnic in rough stock park, near the Walnut Grove where Lord Kanarus used to camp."

Ruhm smiled. "We'd be honored, Mayor Reedy."

Long Swan stepped closer. "I'm pleased to see you are all hale and hardy. Ysys and I are also staying at the Wessex, and I look forward to hearing about your trip, especially of the jeweled city. My major interest is in Anghrus. Did you get to spend any time with the young prince?"

Ruhm grinned. "We exchanged a few words, but he and Degataga seemed more bent on playing than training. I didn't think it my place to admonish him. Besides, Brekka assured me he would grow into his shoes as the Roufytrof has prophesied."

"That he will," Long Swan agreed. "The gods have already borne witness to me that he has been marked by the Norns. After all, who can know what runes his mother cut on his cradle?"

After a day of festivities and a congenial feast hosted by the mayor and councilwoman Donna Schaefer, who was especially interested in establishing an academy in Fishburne, they retired to the Wessex Inn where Ruhm escorted Verushka to bed, she having won the draw.

It had been decided the night before that Long Swan and Ysys would accompany Ruhm, Brekka and Freyxus on their visit to Hollyannah Horndorff. Meanwhile Wyth, Ynys and Verushka would tour the Fishburne area with Donna Shaefer in order to offer opinions on the renovation of an existing military academy that lay in ruin since the days of the Amerikans, now long since abandoned.

Upon eating a hearty southern breakfast in the inn's charming dining room, Ruhm, Long Swan, Ysys, Brekka, and Freyxus made their way to the edge of town where, according to Donna, Hollyannah still resided. As soon as he saw her house, the pleasant and stimulating memories of the times they had spent together flooded over him like a river flooding its banks. Her love had been sweet to him. It was the healing balm he had so needed at a time when he bore deep spiritual wounds from the rejection by Brekka. Holly had poured the necessary oil into his wounds and gave him reprieve from his demons, and comfort to body and soul.

Arriving at her door, Ruhm swallowed hard, glanced at Brekka who gave him a reassuring smile and took one last deep breath, drawing in the sweet scent of fermenting leaves from the garden. He knocked gently on the door. After a long moment, it was answered by a young pudgy girl around thirteen years of age dressed in a simple grey smock with a teichl covering her light brown hair, indicating she was Quailor or at least of that ilk; perhaps the race called Mennonite. She looked startled at the number of people assembled on the porch. "Yes, may I help you?" she asked with a Teutsch accent.

"Is Miss Hollyannah home?"

The girl bobbed her head. "She is, but she tendeth the baby."

Freyxus raised an eyebrow and mouthed silently, "Baby?"

Ruhm was speechless for a moment. Could the baby be his, or had she remarried? Finding his voice, he asked, "Would you tell her an old friend has stopped by and would like a word with her?"

She opened the door wider. "Please come in and find a seat." She gestured toward the open parlor door. "Who shall I say is calling?"

"Tell her General Lee has come to make his call."

The girls' mouth dropped. She was speechless as she hurried down the hallway. Considerable time lapsed and shuffling sounds traveled down through the hallway as if drawers were swiftly opening and closing.

Suddenly, Hollyannah appeared in the doorway. She let out some indescribable sound of joy and rushed to him. He barely stood up in time to receive the shock of her charge. The two embraced. "Ruhm, you came back. You actually came back!" She looked him square on with a broad smile. "I kept telling Judy you'd be here one day. Just as surely as the birds fly south, but then last September came and passed, as did dark December. By February I had given up all hope and now it is once again September, and you are here. I hope you understand your absence has made it the longest year of my life." She paused. "Forgive me I see you have brought guests. Are these your brother and sisters?"

Ruhm turned. "This is my good friend, Long Swan, High Lore Master of Herewardom. And these are my wives, Brekka and Freyxus."

Holly remained silent for a moment as her head drifted downward. "Did you say your *wives*?" She was obviously taken aback.

"Yes, Holly."

At the other end of the house a baby's cry could be heard.

Holly smiled and turned. "Permit me to go get your son, Ruhm. You should at least see him."

Ruhm stood frozen, staring at the empty doorway.

Freyxus said, "It would seem you already have a family, Ruhm."

Brekka shot him a sharp glance.

"I had no idea." Ruhm flinched at the accusation in her eyes. "Seriously, I did not know."

Brekka frowned. "This is why you don't just part a woman's thighs and run off to the next in a heated rush. Someone has to bear the burden of that birth, and the gods forbid a woman should ever have to do that deed alone."

"You know damned well I will not shirk my responsibility. You cannot think more ill of me than I do myself. I will do my best to make this right. But whether she accepts or rejects me, I will see to it my boy is cared for. I will see to it he has all the advantages that my children to come will have."

Brekka said, "I've always known that at heart you were an honorable man despite your reckless journey, but the ur fyr tells me we are not through here."

Long Swan said, "What about Hollyannah? She must have felt totally abandoned and used? How will you make that up to her?"

"I can do no more than make that my study until she says I have atoned for such a thoughtless wrong."

Freyxus said, "From the way I saw her eyes light up when she saw you that might not take very long."

Before he could respond their attention was drawn to the laughter of a baby. Holly came strolling down the hall with the small bundle. Little hands and feet were wrapped around their mother's hip. He was a tow-headed boy approximately four months of age. As soon as he spotted all the company, he turned and buried his face in his mother's bosom.

Brekka said, "He's a little shy."

"We don't get many visitors." She reassured her son by rubbing his little back. Soon the tow head's curiosity overruled his shyness. Holly handed the bundle to Ruhm and said, "Here's your son. I named him Ruhm."

Ruhm expected him to protest, took him in his arms, and instead found him looking up trustingly into his eyes with a smile as braod as the heavens and as pleasant as a rising sun. He could feel the tears slipping down his face. His emotions ran deep as he looked at the robust little fellow with strong shoulders and a solid head.

"Hello son, I'm your father." Ruhm held him and jostled him. "You named him Ruhm what?"

She laughed in her bubbly laugh. "I couldn't decide, Ruhm the Second, Ruhm Junior, Little Ruhm?"

Freyxus interjected jokingly, "How about no Ruhm at all?"

The surprise laughter lessened the tension. Ruhm smiled. "If you will allow it, he shall be called Ruhm-El."

Holly's eyes lit up. "I like the sound of that. That way I can tell him he's also named for his grandfather, Jed Rommel."

By now Brekka and Freyxus had joined Ruhm in admiring the baby. Brekka placed a finger in his chubby hand. "I think it is a very good choice of names. Now the rest of us have the challenge of finding a name that equals that."

Holly looked surprised. "I had forgotten for a moment that you had announced these ladies as your wives. I must admit I am a bit mystified. You told me you were not married."

"At the time that was true. My heart has turned in me. Since then, I have wholeheartedly embraced the Herewardi ways, and as you know they have multiple wives."

She frowned. "I don't understand. You made fun of their marriage practices when you were here. I remember how you teased about Kanarus' wives, and how Seamisch said Kanarus probably had to have his wives cast their tents on the opposite sides of the hollows so that they could not throw stones at each other."

Long Swan laughed, "I can almost hear Wilona laughing down from the heavens at that one, for she would have never allowed for such disharmony or conflict in her covey."

"And neither would our faery-mother, Brekka," Freyxus said with a laugh.

"Covey... Faery-Mother?"

"A covey is a band of wives the Herewardi call bride-sisters which is sometimes simply referred to as the sister-bond. This covey is governed by a faery-mother, almost always the first wife. In our bride-troupe, Brekka is the faery-mother."

Holly glanced at Brekka. "Yes, I remember, she's the warrior-woman who spurned you and made you so love sick."

"She is the one. I never stopped loving her, and after the war was over, the barriers between us fell like ice under a hot summer sun."

"And what about these other women? How did you come by them?"

"I've known them for many years." He smiled at Verushka. "In fact, I've known Veru since she was born in the midst of a Pitter attack. She was presented to our family when we moved to the isle."

Her voice choked, "What does this mean for me and Ruhm El?"

Ruhm dodged a little fist and then jostled the boy on his knee. "It means that I love you very much Holly, and am here to ask you to be one of my wives, if you will have us."

Brekka said, "This has got to be a shock. I know this is all so new to you, but I promise you, Ruhm's love for you is real and will not be diminished just because he loves us as well."

Holly didn't appear convinced, although she did admit that she had begun attending the newly created skaldic school. "I was so grateful to the Syr Folk Confederation for breaking the Pitter Empire and securing us our liberties that I resolved to learn all I could about the Herewardi and their ways. So far, I have been very impressed with the things I've learned about their history. But this is personal, this idea of sharing a husband. Of course, my dream has been to share the rest of my life with Ruhm, but sharing him with other women, that is another thing altogether." She shook her head. "I'm not sure I can do that, even though my father always said that a half a loaf is better than none."

Brekka smiled. "We could have expected no less, but I assure you we each will have a full loaf. It is a misconception that love gets divided in its multiplication. That's why we are here to answer any questions you may have and to assure you that you would be whole-heartedly welcomed into our covey as a full equal."

Holly was silent for a long moment. "Of course, I have questions. Right now, I'm wondering if I could possibly fit into this way of living which seems to come to you as easily as breathing. Then there is the matter that you are all so young and beautiful."

"You are definitely our equal in beauty." Brekka said, "For every question you have, we wives probably have an answer and if we don't, we've brought the lore master to give you the reasons and ways this all works so well for us and the benefits it affords us all."

Ysys stepped forward. "Because I was raised in the Chartreusean culture of one wife, one husband, I was horrified at the prospect of my man taking on other wives. But after several years of living amongst the

Herewardi, I came to understand the beauty of their ways. Honestly, I have yet to encounter a bride-covey that would have it any other way."

"How many wives does your husband have?"

Ysys exchanged warm looks with Long Swan, "Only one at the moment. But should Long Swan wish to take another, I am prepared to love her as a sister. In fact, now that the war is over, I have encouraged him to marry my friend, Sigyn."

Long Swan grinned. "I have agreed that she would be the perfect choice. Ysys has often complained that she feels a void in her life and envies the sister-bond the other wives have."

"Would you allow me an evening to think this all over? I should like to spend some time alone with Ruhm and then I shall render an answer on the morrow. If there is anything I am good at it is deciding what is best for me."

Brekka smiled, "Certainly, there is no rush for an answer."

The following morning, as she met Ruhm's eyes, Holly's expression had softened. "I can't explain it, but the moment I saw these three ladies, I felt that we had known each other for a very long time. After you left last night I prayed. I am no mystic, but it seems that I was meant to be part of your sisterhood."

Verushka and Brekka answered in unison, "We feel the same way!"

Holly grinned. "Before I start bombarding you with questions, let me fetch us some tea and treats. It is most unbecoming for a Virginian not to show hospitality to their guests."

Hollyannah felt suffused with light and joy. The wedding had been lovely, with her new bride-sisters fussing over her and meeting so many of the lead men and women of the rebellion. But the wedding night was even better than their first encounter. Ruhm was just as tender, but since he was no longer wounded, his lovemaking was far more robust and he showered her in tenderness that melded their hearts as one.

Smiling drowsily, she reached over for him, only to find the place next to her cold and empty. Dismayed, she peeked out from the sheets, only to see him sitting in the chair next to the bed with Ruhm-El cradled against his naked chest. The baby seemed utterly content with his tiny hand wrapped around Ruhm's thumb. Her heart warmed at the look of pride on her husband's face.

"I think he looks like you," she said softly, smiling.

He glanced up and grinned. "Actually, I think he looks more like my father."

She raised herself on the pillows. "Clearly your father must have been a very handsome man then."

Ruhm chuckled. "Your bride-sisters have pulled the sticks to see who gets to watch over him today so that we can have time to ourselves. Brekka is even insisting that she prepare all the meals and, believe me, she is one hell of a good cook. Her mother is Quailor by birth, and Quailor ladies are famous for their culinary skills. I'm particularly partial to her chipped beef gravy and shoofly pie should she offer preferences."

"I'll have to compare recipes with her when I move to Martinsbuhr."

"Perhaps we should make some plans." As soon as he heard his mother's voice, little Ruhm-El began to fuss. "I think he's hungry."

"He's always hungry," she said as she sat up straighter and held out her arms. "I didn't think I'd make it through the first week."

Ruhm gently snuggled the baby into her arms, then kissed him on his head before resuming his seat. The loving look in his eyes nearly brought tears to Holly's. *Finally, I've got a man with manly traits and paternal nature.*

"Ruhm, I can't tell you how happy I am that I will not have to raise our son alone."

"My dearling, from now on you will find that many hands make for light work."

"I'm already beginning to notice that." As Ruhm-El began to nurse, she said, "Our wedding was perfect. Even Judy was amazed at how sincerely your other wives wished us well. I know Brekka and the others assured me that would be so, but I admit to having had my reservations."

"I must confess I felt somewhat guilty about taking another wife in the presence of Brekka, but I realized that was leftover from my upbringing. Now, I have a much clearer understanding of the virtues of this arrangement."

She smiled. “If this week is any indication, I’m going to love it and I even think I am beginning to love my bride-sisters. Freyxus said I would have a choice of the houses that are being built. She said when she and Verushka left, the entered apprentices from the temple will keep their end up, along with the Quailor skilled craftsmen she’s employed.”

“Don’t worry. You won’t have to pitch a tent.”

She laughed as she covered one breast and switched the baby to the other. “Wyth and Ynys would like me to select a place near them.” She suddenly looked troubled. “Ruhm, I know I promised not to make a fuss about Liza if she accepts your proposal, and I won’t, but I also can’t imagine living right next door to that…woman. I’ve only ever seen her as the worst hussy that ever walked the earth and though I bore no great love for my first husband, I felt robbed by her all the same.”

“As always, Brekka has a plan. She says she can make the wolf and the lamb to lie down together without any ire.”

“I haven’t seen a carnivore yet that lived off grass.”

“In time, you will come to trust Brekka’s plans, my dear. And speaking of plans, how long do you think you will need to complete your work rehabilitating the wounded soldiers?”

“Depends on how long it takes me to train people to take over, but at least a few months and maybe longer. Yesterday at the wedding Mayor Reedy offered to buy my house to use as a hospital. We haven’t discussed price, but he is a fair man.”

“That’s my girl, always organized and at least three steps ahead of me. In the meantime, I will visit as often as possible. I’ll also send some wainers, a group of jokers from Winchester I’ve grown to rely on. They will help you pack your personal effects and furniture. Or, if you wish, we can buy new furniture. There is a mercantile interest in the Two Rivers area that is making crushed velvet furniture you’re going to want to check out. Mr. Kenneth Norton said he’d see to it my wives got his personal attention.”

“We’ll see, my love. For now, I just want to enjoy the time we have together.”

Four days after their departure from Harrisonbuhr, where they repeated the process of grafting Vicki into their covey, they found themselves entering the City of Winchester. As they made their way toward the heart of the city, now and then they passed wagons loaded with apples, reminding Brekka of the excellent hard cider called Dumpsie Dearie this township was famous for.

When they were in sight of the city of his birth, Ruhm explained, "This is a tightly knit village that is only beginning to experience prosperity again. You see that brick building up ahead? That is a brand-new school which Long Swan negotiated with Mayor Rosenkrantz to have built, and it is already half staffed with skalds, a couple Jywdic scholars, and even a Rappanock shaman. He's still marveling at the speed at which the Herewardi builders could raise up such a structure."

When they reached the city gates, they were met by a liveried messenger with the Winchester city sigil of an apple blossom over a blood rood on his tunic. "Lord Governor, I am sent by his Excellency, Mayor Rosenkrantz to escort you into the city. He is also extending an invitation for you and your ladies to dine with him and the Mrs. Rosenkrantz on Virginia fare at the mayor's residence against evening."

Ruhm thought for a moment. Now that the time was at hand to meet with Liza and then Melissa, he wished no delay. However, it was vitally important to establish a positive working relationship with Christian Rosenkrantz, especially since Christian was highly regarded by the other Virginia mayors, and Sur Sceaf had admonished keeping the mayors 'well-oiled'. Mindful of Brekka's counsel on the importance of diplomacy, he smiled and nodded. "Please convey my respects to the mayor that we would be most pleased to accept his invitation for this evening."

The messenger preceded them into the heart of the city before taking his leave in order to convey the message to the mayor whose residence was adjacent to the three-storied stone building Ruhm called the Hanley Court House. As they passed beneath the chestnut trees lining the street, yawning branches nearly touched above them, Ruhm pointed to a two-story wood-frame building with a black slate roof nestled beneath the arms of a giant sycamore. A fresh coat of maroon paint gleamed in the sunlight, and the new white trim on the eaves and shutters added a cheerful air to the façade. His mouth went dry. "That is the South River Club, the home of Miss Liza. Stop in front," he ordered Regir the Red.

After tying their mounts to the hitching post, Ruhm and Seamisch helped the ladies from the carriage. As she brushed the dust from her riding clothes, Verushka commented, "Looks like the perfect lair for a she-cat. Cozy, hidden in the arms of wide spreading trees, and resembling those buildings we saw in the Ancient Amerikan books."

Long Swan spoke up. "By your leave, Lord Governor, Ysys and I will reacquaint ourselves with Christian Rosenkrantz and his wife. I have several points I wish to discuss with him about obtaining a crew of carpenters from the North Mountain Boys to help with repairing the academy in Roanoake since our skilled craftsmen are to all be employed on the temple."

Ruhm nodded. "By all means, my Lord Lore Master, I'm sure that would be the best use of your time and talents. Get me reports on those carpenters. I wish to send Chief Hoor and Ido some builders when they finish with the Roanoke Academy."

As the buggy drove off, Wyth noted, "There're quite a few wagons and horses for so early in the day, this place does not want for business."

"In these parts, the villagers work hard, so it is tradition to break up the workday with a few ales and a card game or two at midday."

His heart skipped several beats in anticipation of seeing his wild enchantress once again. He had striven to erase from his memory the fiery pounce with her in her upstairs den, but now the feelings he'd had for her came crashing back like an addiction. A sickness passed over him at the prospect that she might even be re-married by now. Now that the time had come, he realized how much he hoped she would agree to be one of his brides. He had felt such a harmony with this woman.

"With your consent, my lord," Brekka announced, "only Frexy, Veru, and I will accompany you. We don't want to overwhelm Miss Liza with all of us at once."

Vicky craned her neck. "I see some shops up ahead. All my friends say Winchester has the best shops. What do you say ladies?"

Wyth beamed. “A great idea,Vicky!” She turned to Brekka. “Why don’t the rest of us browse for a little and return here to wait for you?”

Ynys said, “If it gets any hotter, we’ll be sitting on those benches beneath yon apple tree. Regir, would you please pull the horses into some shade?”

Brekka nodded. “Suit yourself, go shop, but be back in about an hour. In case Ruhm needs first aid.”

Verushka laughed. “As a child I had a pet lynx. Believe me, cat bites can be quite festering.”

Ruhm frowned. “Thanks a lot. I needed that bit of encouragement, Veru.”

“Don’t fret, my lord. If you could take on half the Pitter Nation, you don’t need to worry about this little Cherokee wild cat, though I hear she is quite the hisser.”

“I’d rather take on the other half of the Pitter Nation than face this fire cat.” He glanced at the young driver slicking down his red hair. “Regir, I’d like you to accompany the ladies on their shopping expedition. I don’t expect any trouble, of course, but I suspect they might need your strong arms to carry their purchases.”

The boy leaped from the driver’s seat. “It would be my pleasure, my lord. I’ve heard the girls hereabouts are of fair complexion and handsome of form.”

Seamisch stepped forward. “If you don’t mind, I’d like to visit with Uncle Zedikiah and Auntie Tilly up at Babb Mountain. Nobody brews aged bourbon better than Ol’ Uncle Zed.”

Ruhm grinned. “Bring me a case so’s I can introduce that fine drink to Rip the Prester and A.P. Rockwell that they might try it on their uneducated palates.”

As Seamisch mounted, he said, “How ‘bout I have four cases sent to your place in Martinsbuhr?”

“Good idea. As I recall, a few drinks always makes a meeting go smoother.”

Taking a deep breath Ruhm opened the dark walnut door of the tavern, allowing Freyxus, Verushka, and Brekka to precede him into the smoky interior. He shot a glance over at the corner table by the window, where Miss Liza usually sat, but now, it, like several others, had a heavy curtain pulled half shut to conceal poker games in progress. Conversation ceased as all the eyes in the club turned to his wives. The patrons seemed to be enthralled by the presence of such refined ladies in silk scarves, velvet jackets, and well-tailored traveling clothes along with their self-confidant air. None too few eyes darted at the scramasaxes the ladies wore.

When the tavern resumed in a buzz of speculation and curiosity, Ruhm looked about for Miss Liza. Behind the bar, he spied her drawing ale out of an oaken barrel. The old skinny bartender took one look at him, and then elbowed her gently. Liza turned, froze for a moment, spilled a little froth from the mug, and gazed in his direction. As enticing as he remembered, she was garbed in a black laced dress trimmed with red interior lining that showed from navel to her full breasts like the warning red shield of a black widow spider. Her face lit up and a large welcoming smile spread across it.

As Ruhm met her vermillion smile with his, she called out, "Why Ruhm Lee, what a damned handsome devil you are! Are you come to haunt my place again." It was the same sensuous voice of hers that had netted him the last time. A shiver went up his spine.

"I do declare I expected you much sooner." She stepped out from the bar and approached him in that sinuous walk that had always sent his heart racing. "Soon as I heard the war was over, I thought you'd be back earlier, but I'm just glad you're here now." She held her drink high. "Please, everybody, let's drink to our esteemed governor, the Most Honorable Custus Ruhm Lee!"

The patrons all raised their glasses and stamped their feet.

Liza set her mug on a nearby table and with no warning lunged into his arms where she planted a passionate kiss on his lips, which he full-heartedly returned with an equal verve. He felt somewhat uneasy with his wives standing nearby, only to catch them exchanging amused grins.

He realized he had not yet internalized all Brekka had taught him about the lack of jealousy and possessiveness among the Herewardi. As Liza backed away he looked into her beautiful blue eyes. The rush of desire poured into him just as it had the first time he was locked into their hypnotic gaze.

Liza ignored the women by his side. "Just give me a moment and we can go somewhere more private." Finally, she turned her gaze toward the three ladies. "You brought your sisters with you, I see."

"No." He paused to suck up his courage and brace himself. "No. Brekka, Verushka, and Freyxus are my wives."

A moment of shock passed over her face before her cheeks glowed ruby red. "These women are all your *wives*?" Her breasts heaved as she sucked in air and expelled it in a furious burst. "Ruhm Lee, you damned cold-hearted snake, how could you have done this to me? I thought we had something very special going on. You think me a woman to share my man? Why bother to bring them here, if it's me you want? Or is this just your way of humiliating me before my clientelle?"

"No, no! It is just the opposite, my love."

Brekka interjected, "You have it all wrong, Miss Liza. We've come to make right with you."

"Honey, once you've put a nail into my good table, it can't be made right."

"Liza, please, could we just find a place to sit and talk privately?" He shot a hinting glance at the curtained booth.

"Talk, no, no, no. It's not likely I'm going to allow you to taunt me with your concubines!"

Veru interjected, "You dare to call us, a holy covey, concubines? From what I've heard you're the one who acts like the frilla!"

Brekka shot Verushka a warning glance, causing her to frown.

Ruhm interceded quickly, "Liza, you wound them, you wound me. We're here because I owe you my eyesight, my very life." Ruhm looked about at the gawking faces and gaping mouths of the yeomen. "And because I still care very much for you."

Evidently not concerned that everyone was listening, she screeched, "Care for me! While I've been faithful to you, praying for your safety, sending spells out in your favor, and chasing away honorable men, who offered me their homes and fortunes, you've been giving other women everything that you promised to me."

Ruhm took her by her arm and pressed a hand to her back so as to lead her into an unoccupied, curtained booth. She twisted loose from his grip and said, "Don't touch me again, or I'll claw your cheatin' eyes out."

As things continued to spiral out of Ruhm's control, Brekka stepped forth and said in battle calmness, "Miss Liza, you misunderstand Ruhm. Give us chust an hour of your time, and you will see we have come to bless you. Not to torment you. We are most grateful for what you have done for Ruhm. Let us show you our proposal. Chust hear us out."

"A proposal, I'll give you a proposal." Liza moved at Brekka with teeth bared and one hand reaching for Brekka's throat. "You redheaded hussy, I ought to pluck that red hair out of your head right now. You--!"

Before Ruhm could intercede, Brekka had Liza pinned against the post beam with a jewel-encrusted dagger at her throat. "It is I who shall do the plucking here." Brekka pressed the blade tighter. "Unless you calm down and listen, I will strip every one of your conniving cuckoo feathers off you till you look like a plucked chicken. But if you are willing to listen what we have come to offer you, Wild Thing, I shall clothe you in the eloquent crimson of a Virginia nightingale and plant in you a new heart and help you achieve that which you have most desired."

"She twisted to get away from the pressure of the dagger's point. "And what is it I most desire."

"That which we all desire most--*true love.* And as for Ruhm, he shall be all yours as much as he is ours. Love can come in the strangest of forms. Chust hear Ruhm out before you go off so damned half cocked."

She glared at Brekka, but Ruhm noted a certain flutter of curiosity cross her face.

Ruhm took Brekka by the arm. "You've made your point, Brekka. Let me handle this from here on."

Brekka slowly released her grip, and when Liza seemed calmer, returned her dagger to her sleeve. Appearing stunned, but still stubbornly defiant, Liza rubbed her throat then gave a quick glance at her fingers as if to see if there was any blood drawn.

The room was aghast. Several of the men had risen from their seats as if to come to her defense. But a single frown from Ruhm quickly reseated them.

Liza coughed. "I did not expect such ferocity from a woman of your status," she admitted grudgingly. "You must be that lady knight he always spoke of. You don't look like the fierce warrior he described. I pictured more of a plow woman, stocky, and clanking around in armor instead of a creature of grace in fashionable attire."

His faery-queen twinkled an encouraging smile. Ruhm knew Brekka well enough to know her charm was always fantastically successful. Even when she had been a maid, she had the ability to convince every young blood who fancied her that she favored him above all. He would never forget their first meeting and the shock of vibrant red energy she exuded over him.

Brekka, ever the fire-faery declared forthright. "He has often spoken very tenderly and kindly of you. And tells me that the time he spent with you, he holds dear to his heart. So of course, we have been very eager to meet and know you. I think we will all have something to gain if you will hear what Ruhm has to offer."

Freyxus declared. "My sister speaks truly. I, for one, admire women with spirit who do not mince words and will fight for what they want. It speaks well of you that you were able to erect such a fine establishment in the contrary currents of the oppressive Pitter Empire."

Ruhm saw conflicting emotions battling in Liza's face, but curiosity won out. Liza first looked at Brekka, then back at Ruhm. "Alright, I will listen to what you have to say. " She glanced around. "Let's sit over in the corner booth. At least we can have privacy there." She motioned for the bartender to bring some wine before leading them to the booth. A visible relief of tension settled over the faces of the clientele.

The booth was an omega shaped bench that wrapped around a rustic oak table. Miss Liza sat as far away from Ruhm and his bride-sisters as the table allowed. Liza still possessed that fire and fight that made her so attractive. No man, once exposed, could ever forget the powers of her feminine guile. She crossed her arms, glared at the three of them, and said, "Alright, I'm listening."

The bartender arrived with some wine glasses and a bottle of Up-Country Wine. "Thank you, Zed, please see that we are not disturbed." The old man raised a questioning eyebrow, bobbed his head, and backed out, closing the heavy curtain behind him. Liza took the wine, uncorked the bottle and began pouring.

Ruhm waited til she had filled all the glasses with the thick dark blood of grapes before addressing her straight on. "Liza, Brekka speaks the truth. I have never forgotten you. I can see it was probably a mistake to not have come alone first and for putting you on the spot in front of your clientele. I apologize. I was just too eager to see you again. After the war when I had time to think and unravel everything, I realized that I was and still am very much in love with you. I hope you love me enough to be my wife. That's why I've come here today to ask you to marry me."

Her mouth dropped open. She stared at him. Her pupils grew bigger. She took a deep sip of wine. "How in god's name can you expect me to marry you when you are already married to *three* other women? How dare you even think such?"

"Remember the Lord Kanarus and how much you said you admired him, and how we jested about all his wives? You said, 'Of course, he wants a harem filled with weak little ninnies that bow and curtsey when he enters and then line up to satisfy his lusts. What man wouldn't? Well, I've come to learn the wisdom in the Herewardi way. It's not like anything we imagined it to be. I want you to rethink life as a Herewardi for just one day. Give it the consideration it deserves in hopes that you and I never need to part sweet company again."

Brekka leaned forward. "Miss Liza, do Freyxus, Verushka, and I look like weak little ninnies to you?"

Liza's hand went to her throat, and she turned pink. "No," she grudgingly admitted. "But it makes me wonder why you would want to share your man. Especially with a stranger you know nothing of."

Freyxus said, "You are not as much a stranger as you would think."

Brekka continued. "We Herewardi believe many of our relationships were formed before this world. During this mortal existence we are guided by what we call the Ur Fyr, what Ruhm says in your tongue is the divine spirit. We sisters have prayed and received a witness that you may become one of us and find a fulfilling life as Ruhm's wife and our cherished sister in our sister-bond. But that is only if it is of your own free will and choosing."

Verushka grinned as she added, "I am sure you will agree, as do we, that there are few men of Ruhm's stature walking this earth."

Liza glanced hard at Ruhm. "I cannot lie. Ruhm, you stole my heart." She toyed with her wine glass. "All I have done is dream of marrying you, but I never once considered sharing you. And my God, how I've wet my pillows and wept in the darkness for you." She wetted her vermillion lips with another sip of wine before shifting her attention to his wives. "You say you are happy with this strange arrangement, and that you welcome me, which goes against everything I know about women. You say you already care for me, but I have no feelings for you except resentment for coming between me and my man. I can't imagine ever being comfortable with sharing him, nor can I understand how you could be."

Verushka spoke up, "I know it doesn't make any sense to you now, because you didn't grow up in a covey with loving sisters and many caring mothers. I was raised like you until my rumspringa when I chose to become a lady knight and learned the beauty of the Herewardi way from my valiant sisters-in-arms. That is the beauty of this paradox. In sharing, you will find there is even more for us all."

Liza said, "You ladies seem genuine in your feelings. All you do and say attests to that, but I'm not sure it fits everybody. In the beginning even Ruhm thought this was all wrong."

"You're absolutely right," Ruhm said, "As you know, I fought it with all the energy of my heart, only to find out that it was the key to freeing my true nature, and after much soul-searching and prayer, and now, experience, I find it brings the greatest good to the greatest number with far fewer losers. You even told me how much you envied other women with friends and sisters. This is your chance to have that in the fullest sense of the word."

"Ruhm speaks truth," Brekka gave a genuine smile. "Let me explain this to you from a wife's point of view. You will not be lonely. But should you need time alone you will have that as well. You will have your own home and be the mistress of your own children as well as the nigh-mother to any of ours. You will have all your sisters' support in most of all you do. You will have time free to do many of the things you enjoy and like to do, but, before, had no time to do. Shop, travel, attend theatre, indulge in artistic endeavors, or just relax. You will have to give some, too. We admire your strength, your independence, and your use of the healing arts."

Liza twisted her mouth and then bit her lip before asking, "You mentioned children? Where do they fit in?"

Freyxus said, "I've just discovered I am with child, as is Brekka. I will be nigh-mother to her child as she will be to mine."

Liza said, "I'm not like you ladies, I don't enjoy the company of women as much as I do men. I like to drink, I like to cuss, and I like to beat their ass in poker. I've been making my way for so long that I'm not sure I can fit in."

"We value individual differences," Brekka said. "Each of us brings are own peculiar talents, diversity, and interests. I've learned greatly from my bride-sisters and look forward to learning from you. You must realize, as warriors we have been around men for many years. We can out cuss, out drink, and out fight most of them if the need arises. And as for fitting in, we'll be working with you to see how you best contribute to compliment us all, for harmony is the strength of any bride-troupe."

Ruhm saw Liza was listening intently, but he knew he would have to be the one to win her over on this matter. He drained his glass before standing. "Now, my ladies, if you will forgive us, I would like to spend time alone with Liza."

The bride-sisters nodded, finished their wine, and as she stood, Brekka said, "It's been a pleasure to finally meet the woman who so stirred Ruhm's heart. I welcome you to our covey should you decide to join us. And I look forward to developing a deep sister bond with you."

"As do I," Freyxus said, "and I know that our other sisters would agree."

Veru nodded. "Indeed, they would."

Liza drew back, her eyes wide, "Other sisters?"

Ruhm walked up the stairs leading to Miss Liza's apartment. The plush room, with its leather furniture, and finely turned antiques, reflected her love for good furnishings and fine plate which decorated the shelves. Rich jewel-toned drapes adorned every window. Little had changed from before. Memories of their passionate affair flooded his mind. As he walked over to the large upholstered settee covered with lamb skins, the door slammed behind him, rattling the plates in the elaborately carved hutch where she kept her green elixir.

"What did Freyxus mean by other sisters? For Gawd's sake, Ruhm Lee, how many wives have you got? Have you got yourself some sort of stud going on here?"

He was on shaky ground here. He warned himself to guard his words very carefully. After all, it had been hard enough for *him* to make the leap he was expecting her to make with very little preparation at that. "At last count, only seven."

"Lawdy me! What happened to the man I knew? You've become just like the Lord Kanarus, collecting wives like mares in a round-up into your corral."

"Honestly, I understand exactly how you feel about this, but a lot has happened inside me since we parted, my dear."

"Oh Ruhm, we'll talk about that later. Right now, kiss me and make me believe you truly love me and me alone. Then, you can tell me your story."

As his mouth found hers, he felt the sap running through his veins as hot as that first day they made wild love together on that settee. When the kiss ended, she gazed up at him with tears in her eyes and said, "I've missed you so much. I've only felt half alive with you gone. Let's not waste anymore time. As soon as I saw you standing there, I've been thinking about this moment." Her adept fingers began unbuttoning his shirt.

His heart raced. *By the gods, I want her. I want her so bad.* With a will that came from no place he had ever known before, he took her hands gently into his own to arrest their progress and said gruffly, "I want this more than you can imagine, but I am now Herewardi and it cannot be until we are properly wed. Anything else would invoke the wrath of the gods. And believe me I've already had a taste of their rod across my back."

She freed her hands and reached for another button. "But Ruhm, no one is going to know. And as God is my witness, I have not let another man near me since you left."

Once again, he captured her hands and this time gently kissed them. "Liza, my dear, I have come to learn love is far sweeter when it's not ill-gotten. I've come to learn that love has spiritual roots as well as physical. And I don't want to pollute the holy union we could have.

Her eyes darkened with rage, and as she jerked her hands free, she spit out the words, "I can see the Herewardi have really got a hold on you. I don't recall you asking me to marry you before you came to my bed." She started toward the door, but he stepped in front of her. The waves of anger and hurt that radiated from her pierced his heart. Guilt seeped into his soul—until he reminded himself that the rite and the dragon's blood had given him a new perspective as well as renewed strength to reach her heart at a level that was eternally binding. But even so, he was well aware that she had a much stronger will than he did. Nevertheless, he had to try.

"Liza, even though I knew I was being unfair to you, I wanted you more than life itself. It wasn't only your beauty that bedazzled me, but it was also your warmth, your womanly charms and your sheer grit which you hid behind some insulating mask. I knew I admired you and I knew how much I wanted you, but at the same time I was shaken and frightened by how much I came to adore you."

Some of the anger left her eyes. “But you left me believing that you would return and we would marry.”

He smiled. “And here I am, still adoring you, and asking you to marry me.”

She glared at him. “Don’t you mean you’re really asking me to get in line behind seven other wives?”

He took a deep breath. “I can’t help but believe that it must seem that way, and if things were reversed, I would probably feel the same way. Our Hickoryan culture has written it on our hearts. But I’ve come to understand that the Herewardi way of marriage is not like that at all.”

“What do you mean it’s not like that? You’re the one that holds a royal flush, while I’m stuck with a lowly pair of twos. I’m not getting into this game. All my life I’ve had to take care of myself. I’ve never been one to try and please other women. Other women have always been just an annoyance to me, a bunch of simpering weak tits twitting about in fron of one another. I didn’t even get along with my other girlfriends as a child. They were angry that I could take their boyfriends, and somehow I could never resist doing it.”

“One of the hardest things I had to comprehend was how the Herewardi women have learned to work *with* other women instead of compete against them.”

“In my experience that’s impossible. I learned early in life that sharing anything means you get less. Now I’m damn sure I don’t want to share a man, especially with a bunch of Herewardi Amazons. Maybe you didn’t notice when that redheaded bitch pricked my throat with her knife? If that’s the way it works, I don’t want any part of that. I refuse to be bullied by anyone--woman, man or husband. So, if that’s all you’re offering. Well then you might as well leave right now!”

“Of course I won’t leave. I love you, and there would be a hole in my heart the size of the Chesapeake without you.”

She walked over to the curtain and pulled it back to look into the street. “So what you are saying is, if we are to be together, it’s to be a Herewardi marriage or nothing.”

“Yes, my dear, but don’t make it sound like a funeral dirge or some sort of death sentence on the gallows. I assure you as a gentleman I would not misrepresent anything of this magnitude. I am most sincere when I say the both of us will find true happiness in this peculiar arrangement.”

"Why don't I feel that?" Her face winced with internal pain. "Ruhm, to me, it is a death sentence. All of my dreams involved only the two of us. I never pictured anyone else coming between us."

"Liza, I swear to you, my love for you is true and deep and has not diminished even a bit. I, too, had dreams of the two of us, as I still do. I beseech you not to deny the happiness we could share without a true understanding of all that a marriage such as this can offer you. Please, my dear, try an experiment before you judge wrong and sit down with Brekka and the others. Ask any question that comes to mind. Say anything to them that you would say to me. Get to know them, and I'm reasonably sure you will find them pleasantly non-threatening and friendly. Knowing them as I do, I can promise you they are eager to get to know you and show you the way that has served them so well these five hundred years."

He thought he detected a softening in her expression. "Did that flame-head mean it when she said you spoke of me to her?"

"She did. And even on the trip here, I was singing your praises. Freyxus, the blonde you met, declared that the two of you would most likely get along famously as you're very much alike in spirit."

He noticed a spark of interest deep in her blue eyes, "What about the other four?"

"Wyth and Ynys are Chartruseans and are very easy going."

"You mean the green girls we saw passing through in the Herewardi caravan?"

"Yes, I've known them for many years. They resided on the Isle of Ilkchild, whereas Vicky and Holly are both Virginians." He dared to take her hands again, and was encouraged by the merest hint of a smile. "Please, my precious darling, say you'll meet with them. Then, if you still wish to reject me on such terms, I will respect your wishes, but I must tell you, your refusal will leave me bereft for the rest of my life."

Liza searched his face with an intent gaze. Finally, she nodded. "If I find I cannot embrace this, refusing you will break my heart beyond repair."

# CHAPTER 6 :

## THE OTHER WOMEN

AS SOON AS HER BRIDE-COVEY RETURNED from their shopping expedition, loaded down with bundles, Brekka called them inside. As they crowded around the table, she explained that Ruhm had requested that they meet with Miss Liza in her residence above the tavern.

"Is this to be a vetting, then?" Wyth asked.

Brekka nodded. "It is, but, in reality, she is the one vetting us."

"What?" Ynys exclaimed, looking at Ruhm with a shocked expression. "My lord, isn't this the tail wagging the dog?"

"I suppose it appears that way, but you must understand that Hickoryans are by nature mistrustful of that which is not custom or tradition. Customs here are not forgotten. We have to approach them from their perspective."

Vicky looked puzzled. "I don't understand this vetting. You mean to judge?"

"More like getting a witness that she is one of us, just as we did with you. When it is done in the traditional Herewardi way, it is much more formal."

"It's the same with us Chartruseans," Wyth said with a nod. "I was taught to distrust anyone who did not have a green skin."

"Especially the Ceruleans, who were the ultimate taboo," Ynys added. "Since I have become friends with Jake the Blue, I realized that our fears no longer serve us."

"Brekka, remember your fa fa's wife, Clotilde," Verushka said, "and the venom she spread in that bride-covey. It became so bad that Sur

Spear had to provide a sanctuary for her and her son far enough away from the other wives so that she would not contaminate them with her fractious disharmony. If you ask me, bringing Liza into the covey could very well be a repeat of that viper's nest."

Freyxus frowned. "I have to agree. It sounds to me like she's little more than a cuckoo bird. She wants to kick our eggs out of the nest before laying her own."

Ruhm exhaled, "I admit I'm new to the machinations of a bride-covey, but perhaps what you perceive as a threat is nothing more than defensive posturing. Liza has been through the swamps and thickets of poverty and depredation but through her own cunning and craftiness has navigated successfully a terrain that would have broken most other people in her same situation. By the gods, she went from picking turnips to owning this fantastically successful establishment. I can assure you she has a very tender side beneath that protective shell. What she fears most is that she will lose her autonomy if she becomes one of many wives."

"Actually, that makes sense," Brekka admitted. "She's had no experience with Herewardi wives themselves, only the perception she's gained through the tongues of gossip that flow swifter than the Shenandoah River."

"Especially what she's heard of Kanarus," Ruhm said sheepishly. "I admit I may have tainted her perception with my own prejudices."

"Then you have only yourself to blame for painting yourself into this corner, my lord."

Brekka glanced toward the door to the right of the bar. "Obviously, we will need to depart from a customary vetting. We need to keep in mind the things that Ruhm has revealed to us about her."

Verushka spoke up. "Personally, I'm concerned about the information that Ruhm has provided about her past transgressions that run completely counter to Herewardi values. We need to make it very clear to her that she must undergo the Rite of the Veil and atone for as much as possible."

"Of course, that is part of our responsibility to fully clarify the steps to becoming a bride-sister. As always, we need to consider our own understanding and impressions, but also rely on the promptings of the ur-fyr."

Vicky frowned. "Excuse me, but I have heard you mention this ur-fyr, and I'm still not sure I understand it. Is it like intuition?"

Brekka smiled at her. "Not exactly, it's much deeper than that. It's like a voice within your heart advising you on the right course in life. Sometimes it's like a pulling of your heartstrings that won't release until you move on it."

"Oh, that I understand, as soon as I met Ruhm, against all reasoning, and despite Uncle Zeb's scoffing, I just knew we were meant to be together." She grinned. "And now here we are!"

Brekka nodded. "I urge all of you to take a soft approach and when answering her questions or responding to her criticisms, to rely on the ur-fyr for guidance in crafting your answers." She smiled at Verushka. "Especially you Veru, I know how sharp your tongue can be and how black and white you think things are. I ask only that you check yourself in this situation for Ruhm's sake. Just because something is right, it doesn't always need to be spoken."

"I will bite back my words and let my sisters do their pretty little tip-toe dance, but when we vote, I will not guard my tongue. If I think she deserves a black ball, then that is what she gets."

Brekka laughed. "Your sisters would expect nothing less from you." She rose from the table, and the others followed suit.

Ruhm also rose. "I'll escort you to her door."

"That's not necessary, my love," Brekka said. "You and Regir enjoy each other's company. Have some hot buttered rum and a spicy pickled sausage from the jar on the bar. I promise we will treat Miss Liza with respect and kindness as if she were the choicest lamb of your flock."

Brekka saw the worry in her beloved's eyes, and realized he seemed as anxious as an expectant father. Clearly, he had a deep affection for this bewitching woman, so very different from the rest of them, and thus she resolved to allay Miss Liza's fears and concerns as much as that was within the length of the cable-tow and the weal of her bride-covey.

As soon as Brekka led her covey through the door leading to Miss Liza's second floor private quarters, it was like entering a different world. For one thing the heavy walnut paneling provided insulation from the noise of the tavern below. An ornate spiral staircase led upward to a spacious landing brightly lit by a large window with diamond-shaped mullions. As soon as they stepped into the hallway, canaries in a golden cage situated beneath a lush parlor palm greeted them with cheerful birdsong.

"How lovely," Wyth remarked as Brekka led them up the stairs.

Brekka prayed silently as she climbed, *Holy Mother Freya, I ask thee for a double measure of the Elf Fire that I may truly discern this woman's heart. Bless my tongue that I speak the appropriate words and give no offense. Let thy will be done, Holy Mother of Gods, and if it is right for Ruhm, I ask that you soften the heart of Miss Liza that she will receive the truth and sincerity of our message.*

The multi-paneled door was of dark wood with oak-leaf trim surrounding a sigil of a holly sprig and berries on a plaque of hazelwood. Brekka was pleasantly surprised to find the same Talisman against dark forces that Mother Lana had carved on the hex symbol above her door. A good omen that they were sisters in the Fore-World, she decided. She gave the three distinct raps that customarily begged entrance to an occasional lodge.

The door swung open enough to reveal an unsmiling Liza bathed in a shaft of sunlight that burnished her copper-tinted skin. Brekka noted that she had changed into an elaborate dress of crimson velvet overlaid with snow-white lace of intricate design. Turquoise and silver earrings matched the heavy circlet ringing her neck. The distinct scent of attar of roses perfumed the air.

Surprise flitted over her face at the sight of the two Chartreuseans. "So it's true. You all do have green skin. It's a bit startling, but actually remarkably lovely."

Wyth smiled. "That's very nice of you to say, and may I say that you, too, are remarkably beautiful. In fact, you remind me very much of Brekka's nigh-mother, Taneshewa, who is Sharaka."

"What clan might she be? Perhaps we are related."

Wyth glanced at Brekka, who answered, "She is Bear Clan. Her father was Chief-of-Chiefs."

"I am but half blood, but my mother's people were Spider Clan. She was killed when I was but nine, protecting me from a Dominiker bent on raping me, and so I know little of my Cherokee heritage. But this much I do know, they were the freest of people." She opened the door wide and invited them in.

The inside décor was as lush and rich as Liza's attire. Brekka also noted that it was a complementary backdrop to the woman herself. The furnishings were clearly expensive; the wood treated with oxblood, but it appeared comfortable, reminding her of Paloma's distinct taste for opulence. Oddly enough, in one corner sat a spinning wheel. Next to it were two baskets, one containing skeins of natural-colored wool, the other containing fleece as black as charcoal.

The chairs and davenport were covered in sheepskin, a custom developed by the Hickoryans to keep Pitters from stealing or sitting, the Pitters having a natural aversion to sheep, and were arranged around a low table set with delicate porcelain plates bearing teacakes and dainty finger sandwiches of country ham and cheese. A crystal decanter of ruby red wine and delicate stemmed goblets sat on a silver tray.

As they found seats, Miss Liza said, "I thought another glass of Up-Country wine might put us more at ease with one another." She wore a fox-like smile. "It's Ruhm's favorite."

Brekka shot a warning glance at Veru. "That would be lovely," she said.

After the glasses were filled, Liza took her seat. "Now, my ladies, pray tell me why I should agree to share my man with you, when he tells me his heart belongs to me?"

All eyes turned to Brekka while she had eyes only for Liza. She was formulating an answer when she heard a small, still voice within, whispering, *This is Ruhm's wife.* At the same time she felt the ur-fyr burning hot in her breast. She stared transfixed for a moment, then said, "Does the sun not shine on my house as well as your house? Is not the heart big enough to love more than one?"

Liza's ice-blue eyes flashed fire. "Spare me your condescension. I am a businesswoman. You have the product I want. I will parse no words with you. Ruhm has made it clear that I cannot have him without accepting my rivals in the bargain. I find that unacceptable in business as well as in love."

"Are there not partnerships in business that benefit both parties?"

"Of course, there are, but in my experience, some partners are more equal. In this case it's seven against one. I would be the new chicken in the flock, the last in the pecking order and expected to submit or be plucked of my dignity and that I will not endure."

Freyxus leaned forward. "Lady Liza, perhaps I can allay some of your fears. We are not in any way a flock of chickens. We see ourselves as one large and harmonious beehive. Over the years we found that to maintain the harmony, we needed one directing voice, very much as it in business. In most cases this is the first wife, although not always. In the case of Lord Kanarus, the other wives chose his third wife, Wilona, as the lynchpin. In our case Brekka is the lynchpin, or what has come to be known as the faery-queen."

Liza frowned. "So you're saying she's the boss, and I would have to do everything she says?"

"For the white Christ's sake, it's not like that at all," Verushka interjected. "As the faery-queen, she merely establishes the order and structure of Ruhm's bride-covey. She's more like a mother superior. Believe me she never gets in the way of my will or reason. I honor her because she honors me."

Liza's frown deepened. Brekka rushed to clarify.

"I assure you Liza I have no will or even the right to impose capricious dominion on any of my sisters. You must understand that the Herewardi are a high-trust society. We govern our house together so that everyone has an equal voice, and all seek to complement one another."

"I suppose, if I were the faery-queen, I wouldn't mind it too much." Liza darted a smile at Brekka.

"In a way you are a queen," Verushka countered. "We each have our own house, or hive if you will, we decorate them by our own art and craft, and in that home, you will be the sovereign queen in your own home. Herewardi Law states that you will hold that home in an irrevocable trust held in perpetuity." She glanced around before adding, "If I may say so, yours is one of the most beautiful homes I've seen. Mine, on the other hand, is presently somewhere between a warrior's camp and a construction site. I shudder to think what my dear mother would think should she visit from the Spirit World." She smiled. "I would love to have your advice on how to make it more like this comfortable nest you have created."

Liza's face softened for a split-second. Brekka sensed that she had to work hard to maintain her built-in resistance to those she considered rivals.

Brekka smiled. "And not only do we each have our own home, we have total freedom to pursue our interests, whatever they be. For example, Freyxus owns and runs her own stable and stud in Martinsbuhr, and Verushka is in the process of setting up several bee yards on the orchard properties of Wyth and Ynys who have started a joint venture in the fruiting business as well as introducing the kauri Trees into the Shenandoah for timber."

"Yes, indeed," Ynys confirmed enthusiastically. "Our good friend, Xelph the Wort Master, has promised to send us some very promising scions of the best fruit from the Isle of Ilkchild and a very hardy breed of kauri trees."

"So you see," Brekka continued, "if you wish to continue running your tavern here, you are certainly free to do so. Or, if you wish to form another business, we would be pleased to assist in any way you wish. After all, the gods always reward those who seek prosperity for the benefit of the commonweal."

Ynys hastened to add, "But don't think that it's all work and no play. What surprised me most is how much fun we have together. I love my blood sisters, but I find my sister bond with my sister-brides runs even deeper."

Liza appeared to be struggling with Ynys' words. "I had only one sister and she was killed by a mountain hellhound. But I have to admit, as a child I did enjoy my grandmother's company immensely. It was a sweet time when I was a little girl. She would teach me and my sister to bake and how to extract elixirs from plants. You see, she was a mountain witch, skilled in the healing arts and a lovely woman in all her parts. There will always be a place in my heart for her."

"Oh Lady Liza, how wonderful," Ynys declared. "I, too, was taught herb lore, especially the healing herbs. Do you think we could exchange prescriptions and remedies?'

Liza actually smiled. "I'd be delighted. Do you have knowledge of the art of using needles to block pain and aid in recovery?"

"I do not, but I am most eager to learn."

"Grandmother said I must never forsake the healing arts and I must pass it down to the next generation. It is my destiny, even though there have always been religious factions that condemned me for being a mountain witch. Many are the men I saved from the green sickness. That's the one thing I could never give up. Healing is part of my nature."

"Nor should you give it up," Brekka declared. "The gods have given you a great gift. In fact, Odhin is a great healer and would be offended if you should abandon your gift. We have many wounded warriors in need of your healing potions and arts."

Over the next two hours, they sipped wine, ate the delicious cakes and sandwiches, while becoming progressively merrier. Brekka was most pleased with the questions Liza asked, and was extremely proud of her bride-sisters who showed great skill in answering. Especially Veru, who actually seemed to warm to Liza as the day wore on. Vicky spoke the least, but seemed to resonate with Liza when she declared with a beaming smile, "I'm completely new in this marriage, but what I have experienced so far has been the most fulfilling experience of my lifetime. Truly, I have been embraced by all my sisters as an equal. I assure you, you, too, will be treated with the same compassion, long-suffering and affection as you find your way along the Herewardi path."

By the time the shadows of the sycamore tree were creeping across the window, Brekka decided they had explained in sufficient detail the proper functioning of a bride-covey. Liza's attitude toward them had clearly softened. It was also apparent how deep her love for Ruhm ran. But, as if they were playing a game of poker, she had been very careful not to show her hand.

The ur-fyr was telling Brekka that one day Liza would come to be a most harmonious bride-sister who contributes greatly to the covey. But she was also forewarned that the path to oneness of the covey would not be an easy one. The Norn sisters will require a special offering from Liza before she could become one with them. Not burnt offerings or sacrifice, but an open heart and a receptive spirit.

Brekka drained the last of the wine from her goblet and set it carefully on the polished persimmon wood table. "Lady Liza, this has been a most enjoyable and enlightening afternoon. I think I can speak for all of my sisters when I say that you would be an integral part of our bride-covey. As Wyth said, there is much that you can teach us, if it is your choice to be one with our bridal troupe."

Liza's smile held a tinge of respect. "I have to say that you ladies are nothing like the women I have encountered in the past. In fact, Lady Brekka, you remind me very much of my grandmother, who was both a lady and a shaman, much as I sense you are. For she, too, was also renowned for her soothsaying."

Freyxus nodded. "You will find that Brekka is no stranger to the future."

"So, what do you see in my future, Lady Brekka?" Liza asked.

"I see you as a beautiful flower that has not yet found her perfect place in the garden. I see you blossoming in the garden of Herewardom, but only if that is your choice. One path leads to a lifetime of happiness with the man you love in a rich society of friends and sisters. The other leads to more of the same as you've had in the past. The choice is simple and the choice is yours."

Liza frowned and was about to speak when Brekka continued, "I believe that all of us sisters had a bond with you in the fore world, and that the fibers of our destinies are inextricably connected with Ruhm's distaff. However, such a harmony in marriage can only be achieved with free will. In the beehive of our bride-covey, each sister gathers her own nectar and pollen and contributes what she will in making the honey that feeds the commonweal."

Liza furrowed her brow. "Perhaps you did not know that I've been married before, and I certainly didn't find any harmony. It was so hampering. I felt caged, put on display like a bracelet on his arm, and had demands put on me that made love a duty rather than a pleasure. But when I met Ruhm, I realized he would be nothing like my other two husbands. From the first he awakened everything that was asleep inside me. I have had a taste of what life would be like with him, and it's all that I hoped marriage could be. But that was when it was just the two of us. Now you say I must choose to accept him on terms which are alien to anything I've known. All of you have been quite gracious in answering my questions, I believe, honestly. But how can I be sure that your invitation to join you isn't simply in obedience to Ruhm's wishes?"

Brekka laid a hand on her heart. "Because the spirit of discernment within me tells me you are one of us and have always belonged with us. This spirit is always true and tells me it is both your destiny and your fulfillment."

Liza glanced toward the window, saying, "I only wish I knew that in my own heart, had some sort of sign."

Freyxus leaned forward. "Trust me, you will, in time. Mother Freya never begins a work she doesn't finish."

As Brekka rose, signaling that it was time to go, Liza said, "It takes time for rain water, no matter how sweet, to percolate into dry soil. Please tell Ruhm I need time to sort this all out. Perhaps he and I can meet this evening."

Brekka took this as a positive sign. Certainly, it was no outright rejection. In fact, she respected Liza even more for giving this the due consideration such a decision deserved. "Unfortunately, Miss Liza, we are to dine with Mayor Rosenkrantz this evening. But I know he will want to meet with you as soon as he's able to."

Liza nodded. "On the morrow, then, I'll be available all day with the exception of the hours between three and six. I've promised the Swanson boys, cocky little bastards from the Two Rivers region, another game of poker. The last time they lost their entire flock of Tunis sheep calling my bluff. This time I intend to let them win the damn sheep back, but only because I can't visit this deserved plight upon their aging mother."

It was nigh unto ten o'clock on the mechanic clock, a relic instrument of the Amerikan Empire which the Dominikers had adopted, when Ruhm and his ladies said their good-byes to the Rosenkrantz's, Christian, Bobble, and Diann. Despite his angst over Liza's decision, he had enjoyed the evening very much. A natural storyteller, Christian had regaled them with tales of the heroics of the Virginia Freedom Fighters and their elusive escapes into the punishing terrain of the Rdokian Territories. The three lady knights hung on every word and expressed particular admiration for the antics of both the guerilla fighters, Rabenbrot and Hoor. They were delighted when Christian announced that he would invite the two heroes to dinner during their next visit.

As the night had worn on, Ruhm realized that Christian was particularly struck by Long Swan's powerful intellect. It was said in the Herewardi circles that Long Swan was in possession of Woon's Eye, the wisdom of All-Father Odhin. Clearly, Long Swan's stay in Winchester had won him many friends, thus paving the road for Herewardi ways and teachings to flourish there. Miss Diann had been seated next to Ysys, and, according to Ysys after they'd left for the hotel, had spent the evening pumping her for information about Ruhm's feelings for Melissa.

Ysys made it clear, "Don't worry I managed to say a lot without really saying anything of import."

The night was surprisingly balmy for September, so Brekka asked if they could walk through a chestnut grove to the Shenandoah hotel, a mere block from the mayor's residence. The breeze carried the scent of the freshly fallen leaves, and the sky pulsated with a rare sighting of what Hickoryans called the Northern Lights.

"Look," Freyxus exclaimed. "The Valkyries are giving battle to the Dark Elves."

Vicky stared upward. "Who are these Valkyries?"

Freyxus glanced back at her. "Well, my dear, the Valkyries are Odhin's shield maidens."

A puzzled look crossed Vicki's face. "Odhin is your god, correct?"

Freyxus explained, "Odhin is both our god and our ancestor. His shield maidens collect the fallen warriors and bear them on wings to Alfheim, Asgard, or Ullr's Celestial Dragoon—or what you Hickoryans might call Heaven."

Long Swan added, "Asgard is also the home of Odhin and Freya, our Heavenly Father and Mother."

The Shenandoah Hotel was a splendid red brick edifice nine stories high with accompanying columns capped in an Acanthus motif. It had been built by the Dominikers with Pitter money to accommodate their elite. After the fall, Christian claimed it as the property of the city and dedicated it to the service of the Commonwealth of Virginia. His first order was to have a mountain witch from the hills around Mount Babb conduct the exorcism and dedication.

The lobby featured plush red carpeting, walnut wainscoting and a spectacular crystal chandelier crafted by the famous glassmakers of Berkeley Springs. Ruhm had taken all of the suites on the ninth floor, which gave them access to the roof, which was particularly important to Long Swan who offered prayers and oblations to the gods every evening before retiring.

As a precaution, the mayor had arranged for two guards to be stationed at the top of the stairs as a guarantee of his guests' security. After arranging to meet for breakfast, Long Swan and Ysys took their leave. Ruhm's suite was the first one on the left where they gathered for a prayer circle. As it was Brekka's night, she stood next to him while he kissed each of his other wives good-night.

The suite was finely furnished with lace curtains and oxblood red bedstead, complete with canopy and a thick feather tick. A sturdy credenza stood against one wall, decorated with botanical prints and one large painting of Dzungarian Horses running through a bluegrass meadow.

"This is lovely," Brekka said as Ruhm helped her off with her velvet cloak.

Ruhm grinned. "I'm more interested in that krug of humming beer and the pluck pies on the table."

"How is it possible there's any more room in your stomach at all? You must have eaten at least a side of beef tonight."

"I could have easily eaten the other half had I not been on my best behavior."

Brekka took him by the hand and led him to a comfortable-looking settee next to the table. As she turned the fire of those piercing green eyes on him, she said, "After you pour us some of that mead, I wish to discuss something with you."

"Sure, anything," he said before filling the glasses and handing her one.

She took a sip, and then said, "I've noticed you've been sidestepping an important issue with both Miss Liza and Miss Melissa."

Once again, Ruhm wondered if she really did have the power to discern the thoughts of his heart. Was she indeed reading his mind? Still, she had not mentioned Hollyannah and the complications he faced. Suddenly an unsettling image of himself wrapped tightly in a spider's cocoon flashed before his eyes.

"I cannot deny that I have avoided mentioning Melissa to Liza. Every way I turn, I feel as though I'm tiptoeing through a pit of viper's, only one false step from receiving a mortal bite. If you have a solution, please, share it with me."

"My dear, dear Ruhm the only way through this is to open your heart fully for her viewing. The laws governing marriage require openness and honesty with a prospective bride. Let the runes fall where they will."

"And if they fall against me?"

"Then you must accept the will of the Norns as it has been woven. No one can stay the hand of the Three Wyrd Sisters. They spin our fates. You may be as strong as Thor, but not even he could wrestle and beat the Old Hag; for though Urth is an old hag, she is still the mightiest of beings."

"And if I don't accept my fate?"

"Trust me, my love. It never serves anyone well who dares unravel the weaving of the Norns. They only find that they have been woven right back into the very fate they sought most to avoid. So mote it be spun. So mote it be done."

Ruhm felt both anger and resentment. Easy for her to say he must risk mixing fire and ice. "First you tell me I must atone by offering marriage, and then you tell me I must do the very thing that would most likely provoke them to reject me and any prospect of marriage. How can I trust such counsel? How can I possibly risk so much? Shouldn't I hook this fish and have her at least in my boat before I tell her everything?"

"Deception in battle is often required, but in marriage, it is the death of trust. And when trust dies, love follows it to the nearest grave."

Ruhm emptied his glass and refilled it quickly before shaking his head. "You don't understand the Hickoryan way. I would lose them both."

"It seems that way because you don't have five hundred years of experience to draw upon. In order to survive, our foundation must be squared with truth and parged with harmony. And that starts with harmony and openness in the home. To ensure that harmony, nothing is more important than the vetting process. Normally, I would have formally vetted my bride-sisters, but because I, in essence, had vetted them all our lives, it wasn't necessary. With the wives you have chosen, it forces us to refit these stones so that they become part of our building. It's my responsibility by custom and law to prevent disharmony. These women must accept you for who you are of their own free will, but also must lay aside their personal differences and embrace the harmony of sisterhood and learn to love one another. Unless you're honest with them from the beginning, no structure we attempt to build will ever stand."

"Oh hell, why is the Herewardi way so damned hard?"

"Ruhm, if you would but take on the yoke of honesty, in the end you will find it the lighter to bear. And I promise you, that if these women really love you, they will find a way to put aside their hostility toward one another."

Ruhm sighed. "Very well, my love, I will put my trust in your counsel. After all, since the gods favor you, I think it wise to do the same, though I am pretty sure we're putting the cat and the canary in the same cage."

Brekka beamed him a smile that always melted his heart. "Now, my love," she said softly, "this is my night. Let's not encumber ourselves any further with any intruding thoughts."

# CHAPTER 7 :

## THE END OF THE ROAD IS NEVER THE END OF THE ROAD

IT WAS MID MORNING WHEN RUHM and Brekka joined the others in the hotel dining room. His faery-queen looked particularly fetching in her deep forest green riding gear. She looked like some goddess of fertility he had seen the Herewardi paintings of. For more than half of his life, she had been his closest friend and trusted confidante. Now that she was his wife, he felt that there was nothing he couldn't do with her by his side. Though sometimes her counsel forced him to confront very painful truths, he never doubted her love or devotion. In fact, she had always encouraged him to seek the best in life and he had found her wisdom infallible.

The breakfast was lavish, showcasing the southern cooking that Ruhm's mother had served all of his life. His wives raved over the Paw-Paw custard and Babb Mountain sausage puddin' served with piping buckwheat cakes swimming in rich maple syrup which was brought all the way in from Bedford in Sylphania.

Long Swan drank three cups of the roasted chicory root coffee with molasses, while Ysys was particularly taken with the buckwheat cakes and puddin. "Ruhm, these are the best buckwheat I've ever had. Do Hickoryan cooks add something special?"

"As I recall, Mother always added a little bit of sourdough and Indian batter."

"Indian batter, what's that?"

"Ground up dent corn. My Grandmother Schmidt even used to sing a little ditty about it. 'Buckwheat cake and Indian batter makes you fat and a little bit fatter.'"

The young buck-toothed waiter smiled, leading Ruhm to believe he, too, had a grandmother who favored the use of Indian batter.

As the ladies continued to chatter about things he considered woman talk, Ruhm grew more and more anxious about his meeting with Miss Melissa. After discussing it with Brekka, he decided that only Long Swan should accompany him to Pappy's Town Tavern.

The night before, after he had introduced his wives to Christian and his wife, Bobble, she admonished her daughter Diann, Melissa's best friend, to say nothing about Ruhm's wives. Even though Diann had promised, he was fairly certain she had at least told Miss Melissa that he was coming to dinner.

As they were finishing breakfast, Diann arrived in riding attire, bubbling over with excitement to show the ladies around the town. By request from her mother, she had agreed to lend Ruhm's wives their Tensey walking horses from her father's livery stable. The mayor had made it very clear that he was fully prepared to accept the Herewardi and their practices unconditionally. He fervently hoped that Melissa would come to feel the same way.

After the ladies departed, Ruhm and Long Swan walked along the serpentine path through the chestnut grove to Martinsbuhr Avenue, a wide tree-lined promenade through the center of Winchester. "I imagine this looks different from the last time you were here," Long Swan remarked as they strolled past a series of newly constructed shops abustle with activity. "As I continuously tell my young Skalds, personal self-interest always blossoms in a system of free and open markets, allowing all to prosper according to their personal industry and cunning."

"I must applaud Christian for adopting the honeybee for the city's business sigil. He called it the symbol of industry, and I notice that most of the establishments I've visited have incorporated the sigil on their doorknobs or on a plaque next to the door and sometimes on the apple blossom of the blood rood."

Pappy's Town Tavern was at the end of the promenade, across from Chestnut Park. Painful memories flashed into his mind of having been pounded into the mud like a worm by the North Mountain Hooligans, and then left for blind, face down in the cold mire.

"If you prefer, I can wait outside."

"God no, I need all the support I can get. I do not expect this to go that well, though I continue to hope for the best." The task felt dauntingly impossible. Melissa of all people was way too set in her ways. A fixed star in the heavens. And as for her opinion of Liza, well, even Brekka had been unable to foretell how she would react when he revealed the whole truth and she had even declared a somber warning, "You may lose this one."

With Long Swan by his side, he walked up the plank stairs, his feet growing heavier with each step. He paused for a moment for a deep breath and said to Long Swan, "It was on this very porch I met the Ancient of Days, as Brekka calls him. If I had only known who I was talking to, there is so much more I would have asked him."

"Take heart, my good man. Any visitation from the longfather betokens the noble quality of your spirit. He honored you with his presence. That is an honor denied to most mortals. And who can know in what form he will visit you next? Perhaps he shall visit in the form of a young maiden or even as some wayfaring man adrift on some back-water way."

"Right now I don't feel so noble. In fact, I am not sure I am cut out for this atoning process at all. It keeps getting harder and harder."

"If you survived atoning to that wildcat, Liza, and emerged without a scratch, this one should be little different."

"Unfortunately, Melissa has been twice burned by unfaithful men, me included, and she's nowhere as resilient as Miss Liza. Who knows, her attitude toward me may be as hard as stone by now."

As he opened the rustic old doors of the tavern, he saw Pappy, the warm and friendly proprietor and one-time friend of his father's. The tavern was abuzz with yeomen grabbing an early lunch with their wives or drinking with their buddies. Pluch the black man stood beside Pappy counting the silverware, while Pappy's wife, Edie, was pumping water into the small bar sink. Behind Pappy was a pretty blond girl around twelve years of age dropping a coin in the big pickle jar in hopes it would land in a shot glass placed at the bottom of the jar. He heard her shrill expressions of disappointment as she failed repeatedly to get one in.

Pappy, busy wiping out the wet mugs looked up to make eye contact. "Well, hell-o Governor Ruhm, I see ya come back for little Miss Melissa.

She ain't showed eyes to no body since you been gone, and them there suitors are running in and outta this place all the time with no more than the promise of a white-toothed smile from her."

The big black fellow stepped out from behind the counter and walked over to embrace Ruhm. His powerful arms expressing the esteem he held Ruhm in as he hugged. "I's sure glad you weren't forever blinded, Mr. Ruhm. Pappy, Edie, and I was right worried bout ja. Damned good thing you weren't killed by them Mountain Boys. Custus was right sorry 'bout what they did to yo eyes. Said, he never meant for them to go that far, but he raised up ten pounds of Hell he couldn't control. Trouble is, once you set your dogs on somethin', there ain't no telling what they'll do in a pack like them crazy ass peckerwoods up on Babb Mountain."

Pappy said, "Pluch, would you go fetch Miss Melissa from her place?"

"Wait, Pluch," the young maid cried. "I'll fetch her, Pappy; she will be so happy Ruhm has come back."

"No, L'il Charlotte, you stay right here till your mother gets back from her errands. Won't do for her to arrive and you not be ready to go."

She pouted.

Pluch put on his hat and took off through the door. Pappy motioned at the young maiden with his head. "Remember Melissa's niece? She loves her as her own. Sun rises and sets on that child. Hard to believe anything that pretty can come out of Ol' Custus Duff, ain't it?"

Ruhm laughed. "Sure as hell is! He's as surly as a dusty old cave bear with a burr in his craw. Had a stranger pass this way the other day, name of Gordon Swineheart or something like that. Said the Herewardi aren't no different than the Pitters were. I done told him that he should be fixin to hit the road after he finished his drink 'cause that was just one downright lie if I ever heard."

As Pappy leaned over the bar, he asked, "What's it going to be like now, Governor, now that the Pitters are forever gone?"

"A lot better, I assure you. We have big plans for prosperity. Virginia will once again be an old dominion of its own. All the taxes and tithes you were pressed to pour into the Pitter Empire will eventually be returned to you."

"Ya hear that, Edie? Ain't that somethin' special? Neber heard tell of a gov'mint givin' back to the folks, no neber in my life."

"Me neither, but it sure will help." Edie smiled her eyes bright with curiosity. "Gov'nor, who's the tall white fella standing next to ya?"

Ruhm turned and said, “Forgive my bad manners. Meet Master Long Swan.”

Pappy said, “I heard tell there was one of them Elvish looking fellows come to town, staying over at the Rosenkrantz mansion. People be sayin they ain’t ever seen a man know more about things than you, Master Long Swan.”

Long Swan coughed. “It’s my responsibility to teach and instruct in government, philosophy, and ancient lore as well as to encourage tolerance amongst the various tribes.”

Ruhm grinned at the formality of Long Swan’s reply. Clearly, the man was uncomfortable with praise.

Pappy smiled. “I done heard you had Mayor Rosenkrantz build that fancy school. It’s right pretty. Miss Charlotte got ‘cepted there. Folks ‘round here are damn glad there be schoolin’ again. We ain’t neber sent our chillin to Pitter schools. They were all lies and no teaching.”

“Nice place you have here, Landlord,” Long Swan deflected. “What would you recommend for drink?”

“Dark ale, beer and Dumpsie-Dearie apple wine. Dark ale is about our best bet. But if you like something even harder, we carry the tiger sweat of late.”

“Keep the tiger sweat for now,” Ruhm replied quickly with a warning look at Long Swan. “How about two ales?”

Pappy drew a krug of mulled ale, set it before Ruhm, and was drawing the second when a stout yeoman at the other end of the bar shouted out, “Another two whiskeys down here, Pappy.”

“Hold your horses, Shorty,” Pappy shot back. “Only got two hands.” He winked at Long Swan. “Man’s got a peg leg and the other’n hollow. Ever day he does his best to fill it to the brim.”

Long Swan chuckled. “Good for business, I imagine.”

“It is that,” Pappy replied as he reached for a jug on the shelf.

Ruhm swallowed half the contents of the krug in one gulp before turning his back to the bar. He put one foot on the rail, his attention all focused on the door. After taking a more moderate swallow, Long Swan followed suit with a silent grace he had long admired.

“Relax, Brother, I can feel the tension of your muscles coming through the bar.”

“Hard to do when all my past sins are stampeding through my mind like a herd of longhorns.” Ruhm had gulped down the rest of the strong ale and was about to ask for another when the door opened, flooding the taproom with sunlight. Melissa walked in with the outline of Pluch close behind her. He was sure his heart stopped. Certainly his breath caught in his throat. She was lovelier than ever, clothed in a soft blue dress that hung down to her feet but expressed the pleasant curvaciousness of her hourglass body so well. Her cornflower blue eyes were filled with joy and focused solely on him.

Pappy belted out, "Didn't I tell you he'd be comin back for ya Miss Mely? I done told ya, he would. Ain't no man could forget ju."

The room went dead silent. Ruhm even thought time had stopped and, for an instant, there were only the two of them. Slowly, as if she wasn't sure her eyes were telling her the truth, she walked within an arm's length of him. Pappy, Edie, and Pluch stared like spectators at a play in silent expectation.

"Melissa, you are lovelier than I even remembered."

Her eyes filled with tears, and her smile trembled. "Oh Ruhm, you made it back to me alive! I was so worried about you. No word from you, and only evil reports of monster bone crushers and those horrible eaters from the skies. Then, after weeks of bad news, word of victory finally came, but the words were empty on my ears, because there were no messages from you. I thought you dead. I grieved and mourned. Then by the autumnal equinox, just as harvest had begun we heard tell we had a new Governor, a man called Ruhm Lee. I knew then you were probably caught up in the affairs of state and were too busy to come, but how I wish you would have at least sent some word that you hadn't forgotten me. It was too painful to bear. The silence near killed me. I almost fainted when Diann told me you were coming to visit her Father, and though she invited me, I thought it best to wait upon you."

L'il Charlotte blurted out with a huge grin. "So that's why you've been fixin' your hair ever which way and primping in front of the mirror, Aunt Mely. Why don't you kiss him?"

"Hold your tongue, Miss Charlotte."

Ruhm felt a stab of guilt. "The end of the war consumed a lot of my time, but I was not able to come until I had completed my terms of service to the Syr Folk. Besides, I've recently had a great epiphany that completely turned my world upside down and has set my life on an altogether different course than I had ever planned."

Melissa framed his face with her hands as she studied him with a disbelieving gaze. "I prayed for you every night. Sweet Jesus, how I prayed you'd be safe and come back to me. We parted on too sad of a note. I swear I buried my heart that day, thinking you'd never return, but my heart was an amadou, always nursing a tiny spark of hope you would perhaps return to me." Oblivious to the watching eyes, she pulled his face to hers, went on tiptoes and kissed his lips. Her soft lips brought back all the feelings of warmth and attraction he had previously felt towards her, and in that moment he knew he could never stand to lose this devoted of a love.

The townsfolk applauded. A couple of the cowpokes whistled. Melissa pulled back with a blushing face. "I'm sorry; I didn't mean to embarrass you."

"You didn't embarrass me at all, but first, I should like you to meet my friend," Turning while attempting to contain his joy, he said, "Meet Lord Long Swan, Master Netter and Wizard."

Long Swan genuflected, took her hand, kissed it and raised it to his forehead as a sign of honor. "It is a great pleasure to meet you, my Lady. Ruhm has told me much good about you."

"Lord Long Swan, the pleasure is mine. When I attended the ribbon cutting for the academy, I tried to make my way to you to thank you and your wife, but the crowd was too pressing on you, and I didn't want to add to your discomfort. I've heard many tales of your good works and teachings in the village. Everyone speaks very highly of you and the miracle your wife has wrought in teaching the healing techniques of the green people. Please thank her for me. I can't tell you how thrilled we are that Miss Charlotte got accepted at your academy."

"Actually, the girl was most impressive. Miss Diann has graciously taken her and her friends on a tour at the moment, but perhaps all of us can meet for an evening repast at the Shenandoah Hotel."

"I'd like that very much."

Long Swan placed his empty krug on the bar. "And now, I must excuse myself, for I have an appointment to meet with a group of Skalds fresh out of the academy from Moon Door and newly arrived to take up teaching at the Academy here." Once again, he took her hand and placed it to his forehead before taking his leave.

Melissa watched as the white-robed wizard exited. "Your friend emanates a kind of light I've never experienced before in other Herewardis, or anyone else, for that matter."

Ruhm smiled. “Amongst the Herewardi, he is considered a holy man.”

She nodded. “And now, why don’t we go over to our favorite niche and do some catching up. I want to hear everything you’ve been doing. Mayor Rosenkrantz says all of Virginia adores you as their native son.”

Melissa led him to their booth under the window, followed by L’il Charlotte.

“I want to hear, too,” the girl insisted.

Ruhm smiled and tugged gently on one of her long blond pigtails. “Not this time, little one. Your auntie and I have much to talk about.”

“I’ll be very quiet.”

“Ruhm is right, dearling. You can visit another time.” She shot a glance at Pappy who called out, “My little stillpot, you come on over here. I got a feelin’ there are some lucky coins here just waitin’ to win you the pot.”

Reluctantly, the girl returned to the bar.

As they slid into the booth, he couldn’t help feeling it was a holy place. He had shared so many endearments with Melissa at this table and so enjoyed the company of Pappy, Edie, and Pluch, often laughing together into the late hours of the morning. As he gazed out the diamond-paned window at Long Swan heading back to the Hotel, he thought back at the day when Woon’s Raven stood at this self same window and grokked a stern warning to him. Of course, he had no idea what it meant at that time. It wasn’t until much later when Brekka explained its true meaning; that the gods had always been right there in the very midst of everyone if one only knew how to see them.

Melissa appeared puzzled. “Why are you staring out the window so intently?”

“Just watching that large raven perched on the sign.”

“Oh, that crazy bird with the golden eye is always hanging around here. Sometimes, it even follows me home. I was afraid at first, but now I think it was someone’s pet that’s just looking for a friend.”

Ruhm leaned back, took a deep breath, and plunged in. “Melissa, I wish to apologize for my wrongful behaviors before I left for the final battle. It was uncomely of me to have ever behaved in such an ungentlemanly manner. I have never been as confused of mind and heart as I was at that time in my life. But, nevertheless, my behavior was inexcusable. I only hope you can find it in your heart to forgive me.”

Her smile was gentle. “Ruhm, be at peace; all that is behind us. All that matters is that we are together now and we never have to think of that brazen hussy again. I knew you had just left the love of your life, and I know how hard that is to rebound from, but now just being with you is like having a healing balm poured into my heart. I hope you are feeling the same."

"Oh, sweet Melissa, you are such a jewel. My love for you runs as deep and endlessly as the Shenandoah."

"Ruhm, I decided long ago, if I can't have you, I don't want nobody else. No man is perfect so I don't care if you're a flawed rake you're still heads above most men."

He felt a lump come to his throat. "Mely, I have never forgotten you, and my heart ached like a whipped puppy because of how we parted. You didn't deserve that. More than anything, I want to marry you."

Her eyes lit up with so much joy that he hated to proceed. "Oh, Ruhm--," she broke off.

He held his finger to her lips for silence. "But there are things you need to know before I ask for your hand. Things you have to consider most carefully—and, maybe even things that make me too flawed for your company, and if not, they will likely be agonizingly painful and dreadfully bitter to swallow."

"Ruhm, I know how war can twist a man. I know you must have trauma and shock sickness from all the killing and losses. I am willing to take you no matter how many scars and nightmares you have to wrestle with. Together, we can heal each other's souls."

"Oh my dear it all goes deeper than that."

"What could possibly stand between us after what we've both been through?"

Gazing into Melissa's trusting eyes, he realized how much it would hurt telling her the truth. Suddenly, he hesitated to say the words. Only the grok of the raven drove him on. He took her by the hand. "Melissa, remember the woman I said I loved when I first met you?"

She nodded. "Why yes, certainly, that Lady knight, Brekka. How could I forget? You told me how much it hurt you when she rejected you. She left a deep wound in your heart, the same as Paddy had done to me."

He resolved to be direct and frank. "Yes, I mean Brekka, the king's daughter."

Her smooth brow furrowed. "Are you talking about the high priestess of Heredom, the one people never tire of talking about, like she's a goddess or something out of the heavens. Many are the stories that circulate here about her magical powers and skilled sword. I took great comfort in remembering that she's the one you said you were through with."

He took a deep breath. “Yes, I did say that. At the time I believed it, but now I realize I was lying to myself. I was punchy and resentful of her. I was too hurt to realize that she had no choice but to send me away like she did. I had become a thorn in her side.”

“Pluch heard rumors from Leroy that she’s gotten herself married. Pluch said he thought the boy had a crush on her, but the boy regretted she got married to some Herewardi, I hear of considerable status. Pluch said he couldn’t get the man’s name.” She squeezed his hand. “I hope that didn’t hurt you too much.”

Ruhm realized that this was just getting more and more painful. The Ur-Fyr burned in his chest that he was doing the right thing and that everything would work out according to some grand celestial plan, but that did not mean he would win her heart and will. He was still learning how to interpret these inner messages, but this one felt absolutely right. He tried to choose his words carefully, realizing anything he said would be like hitting her over the head with a mason’s mallet. “Pluch heard aright; the Lady Brekka did marry. She’s married to me.”

Melissa jerked her hand free. She seemed aghast. Her face twisted with lack of understanding. “But…but I don’t understand. You’re Hickoryan to the core, not Herewardi!”

“Actually, I have chosen to be grafted into the Tree of Hereward and I underwent the Rites of Passage.”

Had someone poured molten steel on her head, she could not have looked any more pained. Storms of emotion paraded over her face and eyes like melting wax. Her hands began twisting her handkerchief into tight knots.

“Oh dearest Mely, don’t look at me like that. I knew this would be hard for you to accept, but if we are to be together, you have to know the truth in its entirety.”

She stared square on at him. “You mean there’s more to tell? And how in Christ’s holy name could we be together?”

He nodded in hopes of gaining some tiny hope of a positive cue. “Like Kanarus, I have adopted the practice of having more than one wife. I am a polygynist.”

Melissa brought her scarf to her mouth as if to prevent a cry or perhaps a scream from escaping.

He rushed on. “I know it’s a lot to take in. Believe me, it is a difficult bridge to cross if you are not Herewardi. Please, just give our love a chance.

All I ask is that you speak with my wives this one time and hear them out that you may know there is still a way for our love to flourish." *By the Gods why did I just say that? I moved too fast? I should have waited!*

She blinked hard at him and said, "For God's sake, Ruhm Lee! Exactly how many wives do you have?"

"Currently, I have seven."

In a faint voice she almost choked, "Seven."

"Most of them have traveled here with me and are very eager to meet with you."

"But Ruhm, you and I had a pledge. Now you are telling me you've broken it seven times."

Ruhm interjected. "On the contrary, I consider that pledge most sacred and I've come to keep that pledge not break it."

"I don't even understand. How in God's name, is that even possible?" She paused as profuse tears ran down her face. "Please, tell me, how is that even possible. I'm not Herewardi, and I don't want to be. I worship the White Christ and no Heathen God."

"You don't have to be Heathen in your belief of God. You only have to be in Herewardi marriage practices. You can stay as Hickoryan as hickory wood. All you have to do to be grafted to me is to agree to their practice of multiple-marriage and belong to my bride-troupe."

The rosy color drained from her cheeks until she was as pallid as a corpse. "This is all too much for me to take in right now."

"The High King Sur Sceaf has seven wives. Only three of which were Herewardi. Even Brekka's mother is Quailor."

"And they all get along?"

"I can honestly say very well. It's a happy family. Just as my wives all delight in one another's company." He put his hand over hers to calm her nervous twisting of the dainty linen. "And that is why I want you to speak with them. I know you have many questions. Brekka and my wives can answer any of your questions far better than I ever could. Try to understand this. I've probably already botched it, but God, I love you with all my heart, Melissa."

Melissa looked down at his hand covering hers. "I love you Ruhm. I've confessed that to my own people who constantly tell me it won't work because of your unbridled lechery. I don't believe that, but it just seems like you're constantly stepping on my heart. Every time I turn around you've kicked it in another direction. I don't know if I can take it anymore. Why should loving you have to be so damned painful for me. Shouldn't you bear some of the pain?" She sighed, shook her head, and then looked up at him. "If your long absence has taught me anything, it is that I could never enjoy life with another man. It's got to be you or nothing. Now that I've seen you again, the thought of never being with you is almost more than my heart can bear. This is not the way I pictured your return at all and I don't know if this community can take this without me being the football of all their gossip and snide mockery."

"You will be cocooned in a safe society with me even if this community rejects or mocks you. Tolerance requires us all to shed our old skins. I love you, Mely, and all it would take for us to be joined as man and wife is for you to just say yes."

"I desperately want to say yes, but I just can't. Not yet. It's against everything I've been taught. For Christ's sake it's against everything that you've been taught. God, I hope Brekka can explain it to me in a way it feels right, but for now, it feels so, so wrong and I have to believe I am going to say no in the end, even if I have to go down to the grave with a broken heart."

After Melissa agreed to meet with his wives, they said their good-byes to Pappy, Edie, and Charlotte, and then he escorted Melissa from the tavern. As Ruhm and Melissa walked along Martinsbuhr Avenue, he noticed Pluch was following a little distance behind. Melissa turned to see what Ruhm was looking at and said, "Oh, don't worry about Pluch. He has to shadow me. Since our city has opened to free trade, every merchant from Jimson to Balmor has been stalking me, thinking to dissuade me from a single life. A few have been very persistent and some perhaps dangerous. That's why Custus hired Pluch and some of his Mountain Boys to take turns watching over me. I hope you don't mind."

"Why should I mind? They're protecting a valuable treasure of mine." He squeezed her hand for reassurance as they made their way through the meandering path leading to the Shenandoah Hotel.

The low grokking of the golden-eyed raven overhead let him know Woon was encouraging and supportive of him. Still, his courage was somewhat abated by the task before him, but he would press on in his cause. He found himself angry that the culture he grew up in had placed them in such a small box that at one time had grossly restricted his growth.

The hotel featured an enclosed courtyard that included a bower of honeysuckle and comfortable tables, chairs, and benches. To his surprise, he spied his bride-covey sunning themselves around a large table.

"See those ladies under the Tree-of-Heaven? Those are my wives. That is my beloved covey."

Ruhm could feel Melissa's fingers squeezing harder on his arm as they approached the staring women, every one of them looking like angels for their beauty. "Ruhm, damn you, I hate this. I can't even believe I'm considering doing this. If I turn and run please don't follow."

Brekka looked up from the persimmon she was nibbling on, and a smile broke across her face. The others soon spotted Ruhm and Melissa coming toward them. Pluch stationed himself at the entrance to the courtyard and pulled out a knife to begin whittling an elm stick.

"My ladies, please let me introduce you to a woman I fell deeply in love with. This is Melissa Duff. Melissa, this is Brekka." Then consecutively he indicated each one of his brides with his hand, "Freyxus, Verushka, Vicky, Ynys, and Wyth."

"Os Frith, peace and prosperity to you, Lady Melissa," Brekka said with a welcoming smile. "Please join us. We were just discussing the things we saw on the tour with your friend, Miss Diann, a lovely young woman we've already become quite fond of. By the way, she sang your praise most exuberantly."

Melissa seemed caught off guard by the friendly faces and warm greetings. "Diann is like another sister. After my parents were taken away by the Pitters, her parents were most kind to me. Diann and I were always together, the Sisters of Mischief."

Ruhm drew up an extra chair and the ladies made room for Melissa around the table, he offered to send a waiter to refill the crystal wine decanter that was almost empty. "What a great idea!" Verushka answered. "Wine loosens the tongue and gladdens the heart, and I have a feeling we're going to need it here today."

Melissa had seldom taken to the habit of drinking wine in the afternoon. Usually she was far too busy. These days she avoided spirits and wine altogether, as they tended to make her heart bleed and tears to flow. For more than a year, she had grieved Ruhm's absence and regretted the harsh words of their last meeting. In all those months she had hoped for his return but feared she had driven him away forever. But when her gaze fell upon Ruhm once again, all of that was forgotten and she knew it was her destiny to be his wife.

Now she was forced to decide if she could accept him under the terms he proposed. She had no doubt he loved her as much as she loved him. He claimed he loved these other women as well, but how could that be? At one time, her total focus had been on Paddy and her love for him, but Paddy disappeared like a fallen star when Ruhm entered her life in the form of the rising sun. Because of that love she now found herself among a cluster of beautiful, and charming women, having to decide if she would live this kind of life, a life alone, or a life with some grimey yeoman rather than this fine cut of a man that Ruhm was. From the intense scrutiny they so aptly tried to disguise behind friendly conversation, she realized they were in fact trying to get a sense of how she would fit into their circle.

As she and Ruhm were walking toward the hotel and this meeting, she just knew she would dislike, maybe even hate this Brekka woman who no doubt occupied first place in Ruhm's heart. How could it be otherwise, the woman was of perfect breeding, educated beyond anything Melissa could acquire, and on top of that she was drop dead gorgeous and held in the highest of esteem by everyone that knew her. According to Leroy and the other Lazy Jokers, this war woman was the most marvelous, beautiful, accomplished, bravest, and fiercest woman they had ever met. How can I possibly compete with such a perfect entity? Melissa thought.

But now, seated next to her, she sensed from Brekka none of the guile and jealously she usually felt from rivals. *Of course, why would she feel even an ounce of jealously when she had won the prize? She had it all, and yet obviously she was willing to share him. How could she ever grasp the meaning of this strange practice?*

From the way Brekka directed the conversation and how she spoke with such inherent authority, it was clear she was used to being in charge. After all, she was the daughter of a king whom all acceded was the greatest of kings. That is what surprised Melissa the most, that this woman radiated a humble and endearing demeanor. Try as she might, she could not detect the slightest hint of arrogance, and she could not hate such a choice soul. It was like looking upon the Christ in femine form.

Melissa had been in and out of the tavern since the age of nine when her parents had been rounded up and sent to a Pitter labor camp. Pappy and Edie had adopted her sister, and brother, and her, raising them as their own. Far too often she had witnessed the mistreatment of Pappy, Edie, and Pluch by rude customers, especially Dominikers putting on airs. Early on, she had judged a person's character by the way he or she treated those serving them.

So when the waiter came with the wine, she was quite curious to see how Brekka interacted with him. To her surprise, Brekka treated the young man with what felt like genuine warmth, engaging him in conversation, and even introducing him to her, using his name, Johnny Ray Jones. From the young man's reaction as he served each of them, it was clear he delighted in serving Brekka the most.

*Damn,* she thought, *I'm beginning to like this woman.*

After the waiter departed, Brekka turned to her. "I've only heard Ruhm speak the deepest and fondest affection for you, Lady Melissa and I can see he has in no way exaggerated your exquisite beauty. I wholeheartedly welcome you to our covey of brides should you desire to be a member of our covey and into the ancient bond of our sisterhood."

"Miss Brekka, I confess I have not yet said yes to his proposal. There's so much I have to think about, particularly how this kind of marriage actually works. Ruhm said you would explain it me."

"With pleasure, and please feel free to ask questions. This is not a schoolroom and I am no schoolmar'm. My sisters and I understand fully how great the cultural distance between the Hickoryans and the Herewardi is and we shall attempt to bridge the chasm between those two cultures so that you can feel as comfortable with this peculiar practice as we do, and thereby secure your man unto yourself."

Vicky grinned at her. "I know what you're thinking because I had the same angst about this. It felt like I was on trial, but honestly, this is more about you understanding us."

The fierce-looking woman called Verushka leaned forward. "Don't worry, Miss Melissa. Brekka made us leave all our weapons in our rooms."

Melissa was taken aback, until the laughter exploded. "Please don't take Veru seriously," Brekka said with a grin. "She's hard-shelled but tender hearted. In truth, you'll never find a more constant friend and sister."

The long blonde next to her quipped, "That's very true, but don't get between her and apple strudl or you're sure to be dead by nightfall."

Melissa found herself laughing with them and wondered if these ladies were using humor to put her at ease.

"Let's all refill our glasses before we begin."

Melissa glanced down and realized she had emptied her glass without even knowing it.

For the next few hours Brekka explained the intricacies of the Herewardi system of marriage. After two hours or so while Melissa simply listened, she asked, "Well, isn't there lots more jealousy and contention with all those women vying for one man's attention?"

One of the green ladies declared, "Surprisingly, Miss Melissa, there is less. I have seen far more jealousy and contention among my own people than I have ever seen among Herewardi women."

Melissa found their soft green complexions quite alluring and realized she would love to know more about these exotic Chartreuseans. Diann had told her they were very gifted in making love potions as well as making dead plants come back to life.

"Forgive me if I'm being impertinent, but how does this kind of marriage work in the bedroom?"

Vicky grinned. "You're not being impertinent, just practical. I asked the same question. After all, you only have to look at Ruhm and your thoughts go in that direction."

"You see," Brekka said, "it's all done rather orderly. We draw colored sticks corresponding to the day of the week. On your day and night, Ruhm is yours alone. However, you can trade with a sister or purchase her day if you both agree. During that time of the moonth this can be most convenient."

"I'm wondering if any of you have ever felt unsatisfied with this, well, you know what I mean, the rationing of affection?"

"Not in the least," the long blond answered. "When your cup is full, it's full and there's always more in the jug."

She noticed several nods and smiles from the others. Brekka declared, "I am the faery-queen of this bride-covey. We govern our house together so that everyone has an equal voice and all seek to complement one another, harmony being the key to all successful coveys."

The other green woman spoke up. "I promise you, Miss Melissa, "I've never felt any loss of my husband's love or attention. There are some things a man could never understand. But when we are with our man, he is our man alone."

Melissa took a moment to absorb all she'd heard. "I think I would be willing to live in a multiple marriage with Ruhm. Not because I have chosen this lifestyle, but because I have chosen Ruhm. The rest is a necessary imposition I somehow must learn to cope with. When I first heard of the Herewardi practice I was aghast. I said, 'Never.' But that was before I met a man like Ruhm, a man that strums the depths of my soul with his words. And when he speaks love to me, I feel it in every part of my body. He's changed the whole equation. And I've heard much about the Herewardi from Diann's father, who holds them only in the greatest of regard. He says they are an honorable and fair people, if anything can be said about them."

"That's very comforting to hear, but don't ever think we are a perfect people. All of us have flaws of one kind or another, and sometimes they are amplified by our way of life. But almost all of us keep the Forty-Four Laws set down by our great longfather, Howrus, who prophesied, 'If you keep the Forty-Four Laws, the Forty-Four Laws will keep you.' To this day the Roufytrouf has striven to inculcate those laws into us."

Melissa smiled. "Well, then, I should fit in very well, since I certainly have my flaws, jealousy being one of the worst."

Brekka reached into the upper right-hand pocket of her riding jacket and pulled out something pink. "I assume you recognize this," Brekka said.

Ruhm took Melissa's hand as he poured a glass of wine. "I could never bear to live without you, Melissa." She knew she could not live without him either. He touched her at levels and in ways no other man ever had, and these other women were no longer frightening to her. She had talked with Mayor Rosenkrantz on several occasions, and he described their strange marriage practices in glowing terms and his wife gave confirmation of the same. Cultures were different like that. The Rdokians married at age thirteen and the Babb Mountain Folk were known to marry cousins, and the Yengish in the north were often known to not marry at all, but to only cohabit with one another. How is this Herewardi marriage practice any less honorable? She wondered.

Suddenly she looked closer on the scarf. "Sweet Jesus, that looks like the scarf I put in use to mop up the blood when I bopped Ruhm in the nose for being with that hussy of a Mountain Witch, Liza." She studied it for a moment, turning it this way and that. "Wait a minute I didn't hit him that hard. This has way too much blood on it."

"True, not all the blood is Ruhms. Some of it is mine." She touched the half-moon scar above her eyebrow. "He staunched my wound when the Pitter commissar stabbed me in the eye." She handed Melissa the scarf. "I want you to take this to be a bond the gods have ordained between the two of us."

Ruhm carried the glass of wine over to Pluch and offered it him while they conversed.

Melissa eyed the scarf in her hands, "And a bond with Ruhm." She smiled nervously hoping she had found acceptance. "So what has to happen next? Do you take a vote on accepting me?"

"For my part, I already think of you as my sister." Brekka glanced around the table. "What say you, sisters?"

In unison, as though accustomed to the question, they answered, "Yeah, verily yeah!"

Tears came to her eyes. She found it difficult to believe that these accomplished women so readily accepted her.

"I…I don't know what to say, other than I would be proud to become part of your Sisterhood or Sister Bond. But, because under the law my brother, Custus, is my guardian-protector, I have to ask his permission to marry. He's in Front Royal delivering a herd of cattle and he's not returning for two days."

Brekka beamed. "Your prospective bride-sisters are indeed thrilled that you intend to become one of us, normally there is an eighty-eight day waiting period. As haligawaecca I can suspend that requirement. Still, Herewardi Law requires that you give a formal written proposal to your husband to be. Once there is a formal proposal and free-will acceptance, I as haligawaecca, will perform the Rite of Marriage according to our custom. The details are not important now, but I know you'll want to know how that works."

Freyxus offered, "It's a bit overwhelming, but it is truly a beautiful ritual which you will find deeply inspiring."

"Frexy speaks true," Brekka affirmed. "Now, if you don't have any more questions, why don't we leave and send Ruhm to you to hear and receive your answer in private."

# CHAPTER 8 :
## DOUBLE JEOPARDY

**RUHM DID NOT EXPECT THAT** Melissa would so readily agree to join his bride-covey. It came some what as a jolt. His wives delighted in giving him the news that Melissa had consented to be grafted into their sisterhood. He had to suppose that the great contribution the Herewardi had made to the victory over the Pitter Empire had introduced a new age of tolerance and acceptance of different cultural practices. Before sending him out to the garden, Brekka gave him a quick overview of all they'd discussed. "I explained about the Rite of the Veil in the Secret Place, but only in general terms. I leave it to you to explain the details of the Daleth Tent and just what that means for proper marriage. We also discussed the absolute necessity of completing the atonement process under the requirements laid down in the Forty-Four Laws."

"Did you mention Liza or Holly to her yet?" She smiled as if she thought he had. "Well, she knows you have another wife from Roanoke that she has yet to meet, but I did not mention Miss Liza. I've done enough of your dirty work so I leave the rest in your hands."

Ruhm sighed. "I knew it was too easy to be true, but of course I must tell her about Liza. This will be like setting my hand into a bag of fighting cats."

"Stay calm, and be yourself and that way you'll get more purr than hiss." Brekka gave him a kiss and a gentle push toward the door to the garden where Melissa was waiting. "Remember, you created this mess and our gods expect you to attempt to fix it. Marriage must be built on the stone of truth."

Stepping into the garden, he saw that Pluch was still on guard outside the gate, but the garden area was deserted save for Miss Melissa. As he approached, she sent him an inviting smile, and didn't give him a chance to even say a word before she blurted out, "The answer is yes, Ruhm my love. Yes, yes, yes! Who do I write the letter to that I may be your bride? "

"I don't know what to say. That is the sweetest music to my ears I've ever heard. Just write your petition and hand it to Brekka. By the gods, Melissa, just the thought of living without you is like having a severed limb."

"But there is one more river to cross, as Pappy would say. You must know that by Hickoryan Law, I am obligated to ask permission to marry from my Father, and in this case, I must ask Custus. Undoubtedly, he will say no, but since I've come to my majority, that is really only a formality."

"My dear, I can understand why you would like his approval. Would it help if I went to Custus myself and formally asked for your hand?"

"I don't think that would be a very good idea. He has no good opinion of you, and if he finds out you have more than one wife, he will never give his permission. He's just too fixed in his ways to ever change. His father was a gad about, so I think that's why he hates you so much. He was always the one that helped put his Mother back together again. Something a young boy should never have to do?"

Ruhm thought for a moment, "Probably accounts for his hatred of me. In fact, he wrote a scathing letter to the king about me. I'm sure he still holds that same ire. It may take some time to get around it."

"Oh, Ruhm, I fear more than ever he despises you. When he heard you had become governor, he flew into a rage. He kept shouting, 'Not my governor'."

"If you're so sure he will say no, then why even bother to ask him?"

"It's expected in proper culture. It's a courtesy I owe him for his adopting me, but in any case I will marry you come hell or high water."

The thought made his heart swell with joy. He could hardly wait to hold her in his arms once again. "I hope it will be that easy, but I fear not. I pray to the gods he won't try anything foolish again, because by Tyr, I'm past tolerating his insolence." He held out his hand. "Let's take a walk in the orchard and talk, shall we? There's another even more pressing obstacle that we must surmount, and I fear it may prove a wedge between us if I do not tell all. Unless we're absolutely honest with each other, there's no foundation for a lasting marriage."

She put her hand in his and rose. "Of course, I will listen, but I truly cannot imagine that anything can come between us at this point. I have given you every piece of my heart, and I can never take it back. Nor do I want to."

Ruhm was intrigued by Melissa's mouth. Her pleasant and joyful expressions were a striking feature that no other woman possessed. They swung each other's hand back and forth as they strolled beneath the sweet-smelling apples hanging heavy on the winesap trees.

Melissa glanced up at Ruhm with an endearing look. "You know, I really believe I will come to greatly love the Lady Brekka. She is cut out of the stone of truth. No mincing of words, she's not pretentiousness, she's just so natural. Just who is she?"

"She has that affect on most people. There's a feeling like she is from higher realms."

Melissa glanced behind. Pluch was still trailing at a comfortable distance. "I can't say the same for Verushka, though. Whenever she talked, I expected her to draw her sword at the same time."

Ruhm smiled. "She puts on a tough front, but once you get to know her, you will realize that's simply a shield to protect her tender soul."

"We'll see about that. But, Freyxus now, is very sweet. She was easy to figure out. She's beautiful and also earthy in her likes. Vicky seems likable enough, has quite the head on her shoulders, but favors the simple things in life; children and horses. Holly I don't know, but you say she's very endearing. The two green girls fascinate me and were very engaging." She glanced up once again. "Though I have heard they bear flesh colored children."

"That's right. Their skin color is not in their seed code; it's induced by special herbage that they make into an elixir and drink. It's called nyrth-ka." Ruhm took a deep breath. "In all fairness it's time for me to tell you about that last obstacle I mentioned. There is yet one more woman I have asked to be my wife."

Melissa stopped in mid-step. "What? Who for God's sake? And why didn't you tell me all of this in the first place?" Then flippantly added with a half laugh, "Oh well, what's one more, cheaper by the dozen they say. Right?"

"I do not do this to play with your tender emotions, but what if I was to tell you it is Miss Liza Martin the Halfblood. I knew it would be too much for you to swallow so I held off telling you until I felt it was safe and the time was right."

"Oh, Ruhm, stop it now. For sweet Jesus' sake, I had forgotten that hussy. Quit trying my patience and stop jesting with me. It's hard enough the change of heart I had to make without your tormenting me with such horrible jokes."

"But it's true, my love. I jest not, and I would not tease about something this serious."

Melissa jerked her hand free, and her blue eyes flashed a paralyzing cold fire that caught him in mid step. "By God, Ruhm Lee, that hussy is the last person on earth I could ever accept. I can't believe a great Lady like Brekka would approve of the likes of her in her covey. She's a worm in an apple."

Ruhm sensed the storm was just beginning to brew. Silence hung in the air heavier than the weighted branches they strolled under.

"Never," she shouted. "I will never share my man with that brazen man-stealer. Arggh! You make me so damned angry, dumping this on me at the last moment. If you had told me this before I met with Brekka and the others, I would never have agreed to become your wife."

"I'm sorry you have such a low opinion of Miss Liza. She's the one who saved my life from your crazy ass uncle."

"Sorry? You should be. Bringing up the name of that trashy bitch rips an old wound wide open again. I thought I had forgiven her, but honestly, I can't think of another soul I hate more than I hate her. If the Devil was a woman, that Jezabeel would be it."

Melissa sank to the ground and began to weep into the pink blood-stained scarf. Ruhm placed a hand on her shoulder in an attempt to comfort her, but she swiftly threw his hand aside. "Damn you, Ruhm. First you asked me to walk a mile with you and I walked two. Now you ask me to walk through hell itself. How in God's name can I agree to live with such a conniving serpent ever in my sight? She's probably happy as hell that I'd be yoked to her."

Feeling sick, he half whispered, "My dear, it is required by the atoning process that I make it right with Liza."

"Don't treat me like a fool, Ruhm. I know you were with her every time you came to town. You fell for her bewitchment like every other man, and wouldn't let her go, even if you had to."

Ruhm snorted. “It is true I fell for her. I truly fell in love with her.”

Melissa hissed through her teeth. “How can you say you love me, knowing how much I loathe that Jezebeel? Knowing how much pain she caused me. How can you say you love her and me at the same time? Christ Almighty! We are as different as day and night. I can’t look upon her without my heart turning to stone, and I would feel the same way about you every time you left her heated bed.”

“Honestly, Mely, I don’t understand it myself. All I can say is I love all of my wives in very different ways. According to Brekka, this is the way it’s supposed to be. She has met Liza and she said that she sensed a very different woman under that brazen veneer. I’m not excusing anything we’ve done together or the things she’s done to slander you. I’m just asking you to weigh Brekka’s opinion of her and listen to that small voice within yourself, the Holy Spirit.”

“The Holy Spirit would never tell me to yoke myself with an out right whore.” Melissa looked up at him with tear-filled eyes. “This is all my fault. I told Custus I would walk through fire for you, and now, by God, I am walking through a river of fire and any which way I turn I am seared by pain.”

“I wish you wouldn’t think of it that way, my love.”

Suddenly, her expression changed. “Have you told her about me?”

“No not yet.”

“Well, that’s at least one relief. Once you so much as mention my name, she will fly into a rage and boot your ass out the door faster than a Nu-Yalk pedlar. I know her, and she’s too damn proud and selfish to share a man with me. Ruhm you know there is no greater hatred than the two of us have for one another.”

“What if you’re wrong? What if she does accept my proposal?”

Melissa stared at him. “Well, then I damn well will accept you, too, because this time I’m not going to lose my man to her, of all people.”

# CHAPTER 9 :

## A MIRACLE COMES ON THE TOOTH OF A SERPENT

RAEDS-ELF'S LOG: IT IS THE 24th day of the Holy Moonth in the year 608 HSO as reckoned by the Herewardi Calendar. (This season is also known to the Herewardi as the Third or Golden Cup.) Be it known that this is the thirteenth moonth of the administration of President Chise.

*I am Raeds-Elf, daughter of King Kanarus of the White Mountains and born to Raedella's hearth. I am also first wife of Chise, former chief of the Chiricahua Apaches, now president of Panygyrus, who calls me Hehewuti meaning Warrior Mother Spirit in his language, as I was once a lady knight under the Lady Brekka. I have persuaded Chise to keep a scribe, as the Herewardi do, so that our posterity may know of our struggles and works in the Ea-Urth.*

*After Chise was elected president, he appointed me as prothonatory scribe to the Office of the President. Within a few moonths, we fell in love and married.*

*This entry into the Official Record of the History of the Government of Panygyrus chronicles the Battle of Mys-Ra-Im in the Flooded Lands North of the City-State of Wymouth, a place of robber bands and lawless outliers. I base this account on a dispatch delivered to the president by one of Governor Custus Ruhm Lee's silver harriers. Herewith is a summary of the cause and outcome of the battle between the miscreants and outlaws seeking to displace the honorable governor, Khem of Wymouth.*

*According to Governor Lee, the Virginia Cavalry led by Loosestrife, the Bush-Masters of Il-Alim and the Black Corps under Deputy Governor Amanuel first disoriented the encampment of the miscreants at a place called Blue Springs in the dark of night through a curious means. Alim's men carried matchboxes of crickets against their warm bodies, the chirping of which masked the sound of their swift approach on foot. Once the rebel cry to attack went out, the forces of Amanuel and Loosestrife, under the command of Governor Lee came smashing in against the sleeping enemy in a pincer movement, resulting in the near annihilation of the miscreants. Due to careful planning and the successful surprising of the robber bands and conspirators, the Allied Forces suffered only a few major injuries. As chief judge, Amanuel had the survivors of the conspiracy put to death by blood and iron.*

*President Chise offered congratulations to the commanders and their forces for their swift and efficient response to those threatening the peace of the nation. He also praised Chief Justice Amanuel of Wymouth for uncovering the conspiracy to assassinate Governor Khem in order to gain control of the fort at the mouth of the Mys-Isys River. The leader of this conspiracy was a Dominiker whore-master and pharmacologist by the name of Prestonius Gooden, who was the first to taste the bitter steel of Amanuel's axe. The president ordered every sovereign state to maintain a standing order. "Let it be known throughout Panygyrus and all its sovereign states that an attack on one is an attack on all for 'We many Races are One'."*

After the slaughter of the outliers, Ruhm spent two days at Khem's bedside as he recovered from wounds, discussing measures to eliminate other robber bands known and unknown throughout the Flooded Lands. Ruhm suggested employing Rabenbrot and his Rdokian guerrillas as mercenaries, thus freeing Khem and Amanuel to employ their own soldiers to better secure their borders, a suggestion readily approved by both Khem and Amanuel. Also offering their approval was the

Wymouth Council of Women co-chaired by Khem's wives, Anne and Margot in consultation with Cathy Coffee, the president of the Society to Aid Labor Camp Survivors.

Satisfied that Khem was in good hands and well on the way to recovery, Ruhm departed the Flooded Lands with Loosestrife and the cavalry. Once they reached Roanoake, he parted company with the others in order to spend a few precious days with Holly and Ruhm-El, while Loosestrife took the cavalry on to Martinsbuhr.

Holly was delighted to see him, as he was to see her again once she secured the sale of her estate. Even the baby gurgled a laugh when Ruhm took him into his arms. After a night of robust loving, Holly revealed that Mayor Reedy, an old friend from her childhood who had protected her from the unsolicited advances of many Dominkers, thought he would be able to amass the money to buy her hospital by Nutcracker Evening—or, at the latest, Christmas, which meant they could be together as early as the Christian Saint John's Day and the Herewardi Yule.

Most of their time was spent playing with Ruhm-El or enjoying each other's company as man and wife. During that time, he told her all that had transpired in Winchester. After he revealed the conflict between Melissa and Liza, she surprised him by encouraging him to be patient.

"The world changed drastically after the war was over. We're all going through a period of mammoth adjustments, especially in the way we interact with others. Like my father always said, 'When a snake begins shedding its skin, it goes blind for a day or two until it is freed of its old self.' When Liza stole Heinrich from me, I hated her for a long time—until I realized she had actually freed me of my much unhappiness. Why I clung to it, I do not know and cannot tell. I understand when you explained how the Herewardi require amends for past sins, but honestly, Liza has no need to apologize to me. Indeed, I should thank her."

Ruhm smiled. "That's very magnanimous of you, my dear, but Liza needs to do this for her own sake. It's also mandated by the Herewardi atonement process."

"Then I shall accept her apology. I don't know Melissa, but if she loves you as much as I do, she'll put aside her anger and disgust in order to have you. I've always held that light is stronger than darkness."

He opened the gate leading to her small orchard to allow her to proceede. The weather had turned warmer, reminding him of the days of his youth called Indian Summer. "You don't know how much I want to believe that, but Brekka has taught me light and darkness, good and evil are of equal strength, and that it is in balance that we conquer. Besides, you didn't see Melissa's expression when I told her about Liza. The look on her face tore at my heart. I hated myself for putting her in this position by my actions. Brekka swears All-Father Odhin has charted this path for me, so I must needs believe it will ultimately be for the benefit of all. Even so, it wracks my soul with pain and anguish."

"Oh my dear Ruhm, it hurts me to see you in such agony. I know how deeply you love and how sincerely you regret hurting her so. But think of it this way, from what you've told me, Melissa has been so sheltered that she has very little experience with other cultures."

"That's very true. Even I, who was exposed to the Herewardi and other cultures from a young age, had a deep-rooted prejudice against many of their practices. And that almost cost me ever so dearly." He kicked an osage orange fallen from her hedgerow, sending it rolling down the path. Suddenly, he remembered his aunt telling him that if he broke open the bumpy yellow fruit, a witch would spring out and carry him off to Babb Mountain where she would cook him in a kettle of paw-paws and acorns.

Holly said, "I might have felt the same way as Melissa had I not been living in a town that was the crux of so much trade and travel. I met many different people from many different lands. I heard of the Herewardi from many peddlers and merchants that crossed this way. At first, I didn't believe the tales of the freedoms they enjoyed in their lands. But the tales were very similar. Some praised their way of life, but many others cast aspersions on it." She smiled. "I must admit most of the criticisms had to do with how men could have a bevy of wives. Though I hate to say it, I fear winning Melissa to your way of marrying may be too difficult, considering she would have to overcome her deeply felt resistance toward a woman who exemplifies all she has been taught to consider abhorrent, or maybe even sinful. You came back to me when I was resigned to never seeing you again, though I secretly hoped you would. Besides Freyxus explained to me how their Fetches were actively preparing our hearts for what was coming when they were dream fasting. I for one know something prepared my heart so that when you arrived with your brides it was not altogether a shock. Perhaps, it will take a miracle, but then, miracles do happen."

This was the second time he'd heard the word "miracle" in reference to Melissa. Long ago, his mother had used that word when talking about escaping the reach of the Pitters. But they had made it to the isle from less happy lands safely, and they had eliminated the threat.

Suddenly, he felt emboldened. He was determined that, somehow, he was going to reach Melissa. *By Hereward's sword and shield, I am so glad the gods have blessed me with this woman.*

"Holly, you are a jewel amongst jewels. You heal my soul as well as my body."

Before she could reply, he scooped her up into his arms. He laughed at her little squeak of surprise and carried her back into the house, heading straight into the bedroom.

Soon he forgot everything but her.

The trip from Roanoke to Winchester could be accomplished in one long day of riding. But since one of his beetles, Ugga, had broken a rib after his horse had been shot out from under him during a confrontation with robbers and villains, Ruhm decided to make the journey in two days to ease the boys pain.

On the morning of the second day he sent Uffa ahead to give Brekka and the bride-covey news of his pending arrival sometime in late afternoon, and that Ugga would require some medical attention. True to his word he and Ugga rode up to the Hotel against twilight. As soon as he walked into the lobby, he was surrounded by his ladies. To his great delight, both Brekka and Freyxus had blossomed into full-blown pregnancy. Soon Ruhm-El would have playmates.

After he hugged and kissed each one in turn, and watched as they gave Holly the kiss of sisterhood on her forehead, Brekka linked her arm with his. "Sisters, let's allow our dear husband some time to refresh himself from his travels. My lord, Freyxy was fortunate to draw the stick for tonight, but I have had the porter bring the big copper tub you prefer to my suite so that you may soak your road-weary bones for as long as you like. Vicky has charmed the chef into preparing all of your favorite dishes for a family dinner in the private dining room at a time of your choosing."

"I had to teach the chef how to make the apple medlar pie just like the one the cook at our inn made for you that first time you visited," Vicky promised, "you're gonna love it."

Ruhm grinned. "Perhaps I should go away more often if this is to be the way I'm welcomed home."

"Diann told us about these Bulgers in the Village of Inwood who make wonderful beechwood furniture. And when the mayor heard we were planning a trip there, he gave us a letter to give to a man named Glen Miller, who gave us a jug of beech flavored whiskey which could raise the dead," Veru chimed in.

"We intended to sample it, but his wife warned us to only take a tiny sip at first. Said it was famous for making the hair on your arm stand straight up. So we decided to let you take the first sip."

Ruhm laughed. "Ladies, you do spoil me, and I admit I'm just about the happiest man on the face of the earth when I'm with you."

The suite was like an oasis, with sage green walls and large windows overlooking the apple orchard. All was as he remembered save for an abundance of potted plants of all shapes, sizes and colors. "My dear, this reminds me of those glorious gardens we used to stroll through in Ele-Anor-Ness."

"Exactly, they are a gift from Lord Duif to Wyth, and he requested that they be planted in the summer garden of the temple when it's completed. His messenger said that Siwell is eager to spread the seed code of these plants across the entire face of Panygyrus, though some are tender in their seedling stage and will require great care the first winter."

Ruhm unbuckled his sword belt and dropped it onto a chair. "I've seen most of these before, but I don't recognize those really striking ones with all the colors and patterns in their leaves."

“Siwell marked those as priority, and even sent an apprentice botanist to tend to them on the journey. Wyth said they are called coleus and begonia, but Xelph has labeled them harlequin mint and faery swirls. I love them.”

She was interrupted by a knock at the door. Two stewards stood there, each carrying two buckets of steaming water. “My lady,” one said, “you asked to be informed when Dr. Vogel arrived. He is downstairs in the reading room tending to Lord Ruhm’s aide de camp.”

“Thank you, Philip.” She turned to Ruhm and smiled. “I shall return shortly, my love.”

While the stewards emptied the buckets into the tub, he shed his clothing one layer at a time. By the time they left, he was naked. The water in the oversize tub was steaming hot and perfumed with cedar oil or was it cypress oil? Just as he was sinking down in the chest-high water, Brekka returned to report that Dr. Vogel had determined that the fall had not only cracked several of Ugga’s ribs, but had also gotten a displaced one that was threatening to pierce his back. “He intends to ease it back into place before rewrapping his chest. I also invited Ugga and Uffa to dine with us tonight. They look a lot skinnier than they were when they left.”

“Thank you for your thoughtfulness, my darling, as always you are so concerned about your charges. The boys deserve a pleasant evening after living rough in a soldiers’ camp for two months in the most punishing country under the sun.”

Brekka folded a towel and placed it over the rim of the tub’s high back. Resting his head, he sighed. “By sword and shield of the Mighty Wake, this is heaven.”

“Ruhm, last night I traveled in the Faery Realms where I was instructed by Mother Freya, Queen of the Faeries in how to bring back the magic of yore to this generation and to fulfill the prophecy which says that in the latter days all the kingdoms and religions of the Ea-Urth would come to drink from the fountains of Heathendom. She told me that the Seed of the Woman would reveal that the secrets of Heathendom have lain hidden in plain view for all people to drink from for eons of time, and now they shall see that all religions and kingdoms are mere borrowings from Heathendom. For the first shall be last and the last shall be first.”

“Freyxy tried to explain that prophecy to me and taught me that Heathen means hidden in plain view, but I can’t quite comprehend it.”

"For example the Christians' Christmas came from our Yule as did the Jywd's Hannukah. It goes on and on through all our holidays of May, Eostre. the Solstices, Halloween, and endless more all the way back to ancient times when the priests and kings of the north vowed to keep the holiness of the elves forever hidden until the day the entire Ea-Urth would be flooded with light and righteousness so that all nations might see eye to eye. The day is shortly at hand when the magic of the Gods of Osgard will dwarf the sciences of this world and usher in a glorious age of prosperity and unprecedented growth both individual and collectively."

She leaned down, brushed aside his thick brown mane, and kissed his forehead. "My love, it is so good to have you back with us again and I shouldn't make this a teaching time. We missed you terribly, and of course, lifted our voices up in prayer for you every night. When word came that you were successful and safe, we made special offerings to your guardian, Frey."

"For which I am very grateful. And now, pray tell, how have my beloved wives fared in my absence?"

"Very well, as you see, you are going to be a father of a multitude before the next Cup of Light pours out in the Golden Days of Summer. Freyxy and I will most likely deliver in Albiespiene, and Veru may be close behind."

"If all goes well, Holly will be there to midwife you. And I'm sure Ruhm-El will be happy to have brothers and sisters close to his own age."

"How are Holly and Ruhm-El? I'm sure they were thrilled by your visit."

"They are doing very well, but eager to join us at Mount Heredom as soon as that is possible. I discovered while I was there that she too believes in miracles. And she feels that her god directed her to us."

"I would suppose that to be true. After all, the gods of the various nations must live in some kind of harmony in the Nine Kingdoms. Otherwise, there would be constant war."

She handed him a bar of soap and a sponge and, as he began lathering the soap, she said, "I thought of all of you everyday and wondered how you were occupying your time."

"In truth, we've all been rather busy. I've received frequent reports of the progress being made on the temple. There have been some setbacks, particularly in the shipment of materials. The quarrymen have found a new vein of marble in a place in Merryland called Piedmont that they swear is the finest they've ever uncovered. So Sur Child ordered the quarry men to cease work until he could examine the samples for strength. Hoor reports that he and the fellers cannot meet the quota set by Sur Child for yew wood beams without additional help. It would seem skilled fellers and sawyers are in short supply. I've managed to locate a number of Hickoryan sawmills who specialize in juniper and hickory woods to assist him. It will cost more, but if we are to meet the deadlines set by Sur Child, we will need to use juniper for some of the beams."

"My dear, you amaze me. Nothing seems beyond your ken."

"Well, I have to do something with my leftover warrior energy. Otherwise, I fear I will be challenging my sisters to mock battles. Veru has poured her warrior energy into writing a history of our travels since we left the Isle. Wyth and Ynys have been all over the area collecting seed stock from paw-paws and persimmons. They've also dug up and potted saplings of pecan, hickory, walnut and butternut trees. In fact, they've amassed so many that we've had to rent a space behind the hotel for them. Fortunately, they're dormant, healed in, and won't need much tending."

"Good thing I appointed Russell Ezra Smith to be minister of tree-crops. He has been determined to diversify the crops in all parts of Virginia. His last report to me was about his conversations with Xelph on developing osage orange and buckeyes into edible crops for humans." He soaped one arm, then the other. "I can't wait to hear what Freyxy has done with her warrior energy. Hasn't started any wars with the locals, has she?"

"Believe me, if she didn't have drogs and her stable to worry about that might have happened. In fact, she has made several trips back to Martinsbuhr already to check on them and your Dzungarians. And she got that shipment of Wiener Tumblers from Hans Gemelhausen. You would not believe the velocity of those birds. She plans on taking a drog up to watch them perform from above."

"That's got to be a beautiful sight. How are the horses doing?"

"Your horses are well tended, and she returned with all praise for Donny, and even announced that she's going to import some wisent stock from the Isle to arrive here no later than the Green Cup of Spring. Also, I should warn you, she brought back several large sacks of mandrake apples that she collected in the Dehaven Forest just beyond Bender's Wood. I suspect she has plans to ply them on you tonight."

He grinned. "I look forward to that, but believe me she won't need to employ their love magic."

Brekka smiled. "I sense you are right. But be warned, Wyth and Ynys are both fascinated by their reputation as a sexual elixir. Be prepared both will probably feed you an apple delicacy on their nights."

Moving her chair to a spot behind the big gleaming tub, she began running her fingers through his long hair, combing out the wind-whipped tangles. "Lean forward, my love, and close your eyes. Your hair is in dreadful need of washing."

Feeling lazier by the moment, he obeyed, bracing himself for the deluge of warm water to come. With water dripping from the long strands, she began massaging lavender perfumed soap into his hair.

"Have you been visiting with Miss Liza and Miss Melissa during my absence?" he asked drowsily.

"Of course, we have."

"Does Miss Liza still have bees in her bonnet over Melissa?"

Brekka laughed as she poured water over his head a second time. "From what you had told us before you left, we expected those two were going to need a calm-down period. In fact, we expected them to be like two hissing cats in a gunny sack clawing at one another's throats."

"Are you saying they went at one another tooth and claw?"

She laughed again. "Not exactly, indeed to everyone's surprise, they have become the best of friends."

Ruhm sat straight up splashing water over the tiled floor. He twisted around to stare at her in disbelief. "Don't play with me, Brekka. This is serious stuff. I love both of those women."

"I am being serious, my love. It seems your patron god has helped the Norns weave this good fate."

"How did this possibly come about?"

"Well, you know how Melissa dotes on her niece, L'il Miss Charlotte. It wasn't two days after you left when Charlotte was helping Miss Melissa rake the leaves in her garden and uncovered a nest of copperheads. Before Melissa could snatch her away, she was bitten five times."

"Oh no did she possibly survive?"

"At first, we were sure she wouldn't recover. Even Dr. Vogel said he'd done all he could do for her, but he didn't think she would make it. Pluch ran to Miss Liza's to get some magic herbs, but when Liza heard what happened, she grabbed her medicine bag and ran straight to Melissa's home. Melissa tried to send her away, but Liza insisted she could save the child's life. Reminded her of how she saved your eyes. And she did."

"The woman is a healer."

Brekka began drying his hair with a towel. "It turns out Miss Liza apologized for all the ugly things she ever said or did to hurt Melissa. And Melissa was so thankful to her that she accepted the apology and then to everyone's amazement, apologized to Liza for spreading hateful rumors about her. It took a little time, but because Liza visited L'il Charlotte every day to minister additional medicine, Liza and Melissa got to talking and even laughing together. I'm told many of the jokes were at your expense."

"How do you know all this?"

"Because Miss Liza actually asked for help and advice from Wyth and Ynys, and of course, as usual, they reported all that they had observed."

Ruhm twisted around to look at Brekka again. "When you told me to expect a miracle, I couldn't believe you, but by the gods, this is no less than a miracle."

"The elves can weave night into day if they choose. But you have another serpent in the garden to deal with. In this case it's her Uncle Custus. According to what Miss Melissa told us, he not only refused to give his blessing, but when she told him she was going to marry you no matter what, he flew into a rage and swore to do everything in his power to prevent it even if that meant killing you. He has a murderous spirit in him. Perhaps a Dark Elf."

"We cannot be tolerant of the intolerant. If he raises one hand against me, I will lay him in the dust. I hope it doesn't come to that, but if needs be, I will send him on a journey from whence no traveler has ever returned."

"It is the way of the Os-Syr-True, those true to the teachings of Os, that we must always extend a warning to any natural man before we destroy him. I remember Fa wrestling with his conscience about what he should do about Fromer Muckenschnabel's constant meddling and intolerance. As I recall, he debated whether he should slay the self-righteous prig, banish him from the isle, or simply endure his incessant heckling and leave it to the gods to render judgment as they saw fit. He meditated on his dilemma until the Ur-Fyr told him to fight him if he fights. In the end, because he considered himself exempt from the safety instructions issued by the Roufytrof concerning wilderness areas unsafe to human travel, Fromer was gored to death at the foot of Mount Elflohana by a golden takin."

"I've tried to learn to understand that still small voice within me, but honestly, Brekka, I can't tell whether I'm telling myself something I want to hear or if the words come from the holy gods and elves."

"Don't worry? The more you listen, the more you will be able to discern. There are so many voices that you must eventually learn how to tune some out and listen only to the true ones."

"I just wish to God Mely didn't have to go through this. Perhaps that's what angers me the most."

"It isn't only Mely he's hurting. Li'l Charlotte and her mother are in tears over his ceaseless rantings. Mely says it's gotten so bad that Custus' wife leaves Li'l Charlotte with Pappy and Edie most of the time. She's even threatened to leave Custus if he ruins Mely's happiness. But from all I've heard, her threats have fallen on deaf and stopped up ears. Even after that threat, he still came to the hotel looking for you, and he brought along a half-dozen surly looking mountain men, one or two who would make Pluch look like a child. When I told him you were gone and would be away for some time, he left a message we can't decipher the meaning of, but he said you would know."

"What did he say?"

"He said, 'Elm hateth man and waiteth.' Does that make any sense to you?"

Ruhm sighed. "By Christ and all of his holy elves, I'm afraid it does. It's a Babb Mountain expression. It means he plans to hang me from an elm tree no matter how long it takes."

When Ruhm and Freyxus left the suite to go down to breakfast, he found that his bride-covey, Long Swan and Ysys were already seated. After a hearty meal, Ruhm prepared to excuse himself. The night before, after dinner, he had sent Uffa to Melissa's home, asking her when it would be convenient to meet. She had sent back word that she would be at Pappy's Tavern all morning and that she had a special surprise for him.

"If you will excuse me, I have an appointment to keep with Miss Melissa at Pappy's Tavern."

He placed his napkin on the table and was preparing to rise when Brekka declared, "My Lord, Freyxy, Veru, and I will accompany you."

"If you don't mind, my ladies, I would prefer to meet with her alone. We have much to discuss, and it would probably be more comfortable for her to meet in private."

"We don't intend to interfere in your personal matters, but we intend to have your back." Veru's cheeks dimpled in a teasing grin. "Besides, we've taken to having a cup of Dumpsie-Dearie every morning. It's surprising how much energy it gives us."

"By all means have your Apple Wine, but there's no need to have my back, as you call it."

"On the contrary," Brekka said. "Odhin would not have intervened when Custus and his Babb Mountain Hooligans blinded you, had he not recognized that Custus was interfering in his plans for you. It is within his power to smite Custus dead, but he often prefers to allow conflicts such as this to chisel off your rough edges in order to make you into a perfect ashler."

"Ashler or not, I don't need the protection of my wives, especially when they are expecting my children. I can handle Custus on my own."

"Of that we have no doubt," Brekka replied. "But what about those Mountain Hooligans he's likely to bring with him."

"Brekka is right," Long Swan interjected. "The Ur-Fyr bears witness to me that Custus is a rabid dog and must be stopped before he destroys the peace of this community. This is a man who knows no law, but his own will. Remember, this is not just about you. In a broader sense this is the type of intolerance we have pledged to permanently stamp out, not through compulsion, but through confrontation. So whether you like it or not, I, too, will be accompanying you to Pappy's place. And if nothing happens, then I will have had my fill of that black beer that I've taken such a hankering to."

Ruhm realized he had already lost this battle. Generally, it was not wise to reject the counsel of the lore master. "Well, I can't argue with that."

When they reached Pappy's Tavern, the front was filled with the usual mix of horses, wagons and carriages. To his surprise, he recognized Eliza's grand carriage with four matched black steeds parked in front, the horses' tails swishing back and forth. Her driver, Efrem, raised a hand in greeting before returning his attention to the mane he was currying.

"I hadn't expected to face both women at the same time," Ruhm admitted. "This is not how I foresaw this meeting."

Long Swan grinned. "In cases like this, I have learned to trust in the weavings of the Norns, and particularly Mother Urth who is full of surprises both good and evil."

As soon as they entered, he quickly spotted Melissa and Liza at the corner booth playing cards together. Liza gave him an impish look, "Ruhm Lee, you handsome devil. Sit yourself down here. I'm teaching this Gawd forsaken virgin how to play poker."

Ruhm laughed as he slipped into the booth next to Melissa. "I hope you didn't lay any money down, Mely, because if you did, you just gave it all away."

"Of course she did." Miss Liza said, "If a body don't pay, she don't learn. It's simple as that."

Melissa winked at her new found friend. "Besides, Ruhm, she let me win a couple of times." She gestured toward the small stack of chips at her elbow.

Liza began to deal out the cards, her practiced hands moving swiftly. "So, did you round up any more wives from those outliers I hear you beat down yonder?"

Ruhm gave a hearty laugh. "No, the women I saw mostly resembled lizards; scaly skin, matted hair, and not a whole set of teeth amongst the entire lot."

"Oh Ruhm, that's unkind," Melissa murmured.

"Not unkind, just truthful. They are sorry wretches. Living the life they did, most of those poor unfortunate souls were barely scratching out an existence in a hardscrabble land that's so wild that not even a cat can slide through the thick brush. Girls age quickly there. At twenty, they looked fifty. I felt sorry for them, especially the poor little urchins hanging at their skirts. Oh God, their faces still haunt me. We gave them what goods we could spare, and Khem promised to do what he could to help them out with a quota of gators."

Finished dealing, Liza glanced toward the bar. "I see you brought reinforcements." She waved in their direction. "Surprises me that you ain't heard how Mely and I turned the axe over and smoked the peace pipe."

"I heard, but I had to see it with my own eyes." He grinned. "My father always said that women are like weather. Never can tell if it's going to be sunny or stormy, where they came from or where they are going."

Liza laughed. "Well now, you're going to have your hands full when Mely and I teach our sister-wives how to conspire and connive against you. Aren't you?"

"Don't listen to her, Ruhm. Her hiss is far worse than her bite."

"Now, Mely, don't give up all my secrets." Her devilish grin suddenly froze on her face, and the color drained from her cheeks. "Damn," she whispered, staring at the door opposite.

Ruhm turned his head to see what she was looking at. There, framed in the doorway stood Custus Duff and three of his huge Mountain Ruffians."

"Ruhm Lee, you damned whoring scoundrel!" he belted out, his face dark as a beet and red with a seething rage. "We heard how you knocked up that poor gal down in Roanoke. Heard you have a mind to make my sister a damned Heathen too. Turn her away from the White Christ. Have her bowin' down afore them false gods and the demonic spirits of the woods. They be gods not known in these parts for a long time. I done told you in clear terms I won't be standin' fer it."

Melissa threw her hand down on the table, stood tall and declared firmly, "Custus, I know you're trying to protect me, but you've already interfered way too much. Let me live my life as I see fit. Why can't you understand that nothing you say can make me stop loving Ruhm."

"Hush, Sis, you been bewitched by this swiving snake doctor and his bevy of witches on his coat tails."

Melissa's face went red with anger. "How dare you call them that, especially after Miss Liza saved your daughter's life. Now get out of here and leave me be."

"Sorry, Sis," Custus Duff said. "I can't let this go. Our family's honor is at stake." He stalked across the bar room to the booth, raised his rawhide riding crop and slashed Ruhm across the face with a loud crack.

Ruhm's head snapped back. Melissa screamed. A gasp went up from the patrons. Behind the bar, Pluch grabbed the hickory club from under the counter. "Hear now," Pappy shouted. "There won't be none of that horse shit in my place. Custus Duff, git your sorry ass out of here afore I have Pluch take that there billy club upside your knucklehead."

"Don't worry, Pap. I'm just challenging him to a proper duel like our pappies done many times afore." He turned to Ruhm. "If'n you be any kind of a gentleman, you will accept this here challenge."

Ruhm ignored the stinging from the welt on his cheek. "Do you really want to face a seasoned warrior accustomed to fighting to the death? If you insist on pressing me, I will not hold back."

Custus sneered. "I done had my taste of war, too. We beat them there Pitters at Bunker Hill if'n you 'member. And now I'm fixing to bus' you up."

"So be it."

Custus turned around and left, his bruisers following him out. Ruhm turned to Melissa who had tears running down her cheeks. "I'm sorry, Mely my love, but this has to end here. I don't plan to be looking over my shoulder for the rest of my days."

"Oh Ruhm, please, isn't there another way? No matter who wins, I lose."

"I wish there were, but when he struck me, he left me no choice. If I refuse to fight him, he'll still find a way to attack me. No, I must put an end to this." Ruhm took her head between his hands and kissed her forehead before heading for the door.

"Cut that peckerwood bastard no quarter, Ruhm," Liza called after him. "Man's been needin to be taken down a peg or two for a long time now. He's a drunken lout who acts like he's Holy Moses handin' down the Law."

As he opened the door, he could hear Liza behind him comforting Mely. "Don't you worry none now, my little kitten. Ruhm will set this score right."

Outside, he paused to glance up at the sign, hoping to spot Woon's ravens, but to no avail. Clearly, he was on his own.

Stiffening his spine, he walked past Liza's carriage and out into the street where he was soon joined by Long Swan and his wives, followed by Melissa, Liza, and a steady stream of patrons from the bar.

"You were right about Custus, Brekka," he said. "I pray Woon is on my side, because I have a feeling only one of us will leave this place alive."

"Don't worry, my love," she murmured. "Freya's wings are spread over you. She has promised me that you will give me many children. Her words never fall to barren ground."

"I agree with Brekka," Freyxy told him. "The man is a bully without a spine. Most likely used to fighting unseasoned warriors. Show him the mettle that won many a battle for us."

It was nigh on to midday, and traffic was sparse on the dusty street. As though prearranged, two of the mountain corsairs split off to halt traffic in either direction.

Standing with the remaining ally, Custus stuck a wad of chewing tobacco in his mouth, chewed, then spit into the dust of the road. "I spit on your grandpappy's shadow, Ruhm Lee. Choose your second. I choose Ron Terschander here as mine."

"And I choose Long Swan as mine. As the aggrieved party, I have choice of weapons and I choose the sword."

Custus sneered at the lore master, who appeared far from threatening in his long white robe. "Just like you to choose this inflated elfman in a dress. Hope he has some balls under all that purdy white cloth, but I doubt it."

Unperturbed by the insult, Long Swan walked out into the dusty street and with his staff, drew a large circle. His commanding voice boomed out, "Contestants to the rink."

Both contestants stood at opposite ends of the circle. Spectators lined the perimeter, jostling for the best view behind the ladies. Pluch and Pappy stood apart. Gradually, the growing throng grew silent.

Long Swan glanced at Brekka and the other ladies. "May I beg a scarf from one of you ladies?"

Freyxus removed her swan scarf for Long Swan to take. "At the drop of this scarf the two of you shall commence fighting to the death. If you are wounded to the point you cannot fight, you may either surrender or have your second take your place. If you have the opponent in a position of imminent death, you may show mercy at your own discretion as well as set the terms of your payment for redemption. Agreed?"

Both he and Custus nodded. Miss Melissa cried out, "Please Custus, don't do this. I'm begging you for Charlotte's sake."

Brekka took her by the arms. "Calm yourself, Melissa; Ruhm shall soon divest him of all metallic substances and put an end to this silly sense of enmeshment your brother has in your life."

Long Swan held up the scarf. "Custus Duff, are you ready?"

Custus drew his sword, slashed it through the air and called out, "Damned straight, I am. Y'all watch while I gig this no-account bastard like a frog."

He then turned to Ruhm and asked, "Custus Ruhm Lee, are you ready?"

Ruhm drew his sword, touched it to his forehead and answered calmly "I am."

Long Swan dropped the scarf, and then swiftly stepped back out of the rink.

With a roar, Custus charged and swung wildly. Ruhm parried, diverted, and instead of slicing Custus in two, Ruhm gave a solid punch to the gut with the butt of the sword. The man doubled up in groaning agony.

"That's for having your hooligans beat me senseless."

Custus rose from the dust, shook himself like an enraged fighting cock, and charged once again, Ruhm parried, ducked, and then flat bladed him across the kidneys. Howling in pain, Custus danced around the rink fluttering like a chicken with a broken back. "And that's for almost blinding me."

Custus' face bulged in anger as he gritted his teeth and ran once again against Ruhm's skilled sword. This time Ruhm kicked Custus' foot out from under him and, as the man fell to the dust, Ruhm brought the tip of his blade to Custus' neck just enough to draw blood and make him aware that there was no escape from his cunning blade.

Long Swan shouted out, "The call is yours, Ruhm. Death or mercy?"

Melissa screamed out, "Mercy Ruhm! Show mercy for my sake."

"Master Long Swan, is it not now within my power to set the terms of mercy?"

"It is."

Ruhm pricked the throat further sending a look of shock across his fallen opponents face, then gave a stab to the heart that merely pierced a quarter of an inch and then with the pommel of his sword hammered

Custus on the head so as to cause excrutiating pain, but neither to kill or make him unconscious. He had done this to allow Custus to realize that he had brought the man to the edge of life and now Custus would have to make the choice.

The bully's eyes swam with pain. "Custus Duff, hear me. My terms are these. If you agree to allow Melissa and I to marry and never to attempt coming between us again, then you shall live to be a daddy to that sweet Lil Charlotte, and I shall forget the evils you intended me. Agreed?"

Custus glared, tobacco juice running down his chin as he mumbled out, "Agreed."

"Say it louder, Custus, that all may witness, this was honorably decided this day once and for all."

"Agreed!" he strangled out, "Gawd dammit, I said, agreed!"

Long Swan helped Custus Duff to his feet and Ron Terschander helped him to his horse. His friends also mounted, and the four of them rode off out of town. The crowd clapped their approval.

Ruhm withdrew his sword and returned it to its sheath before smiling at Liza and Melissa now standing side-by-side. "Now, my lovely ladies, by the gods, let us hie to Mount Heredom where we shall be wed."

Pappy, Edie and Pluch led the cheers. All but a few in the crowd joined in.

"When will ya'll come back, Ruhm?" Pappy asked.

"We'll be back at Yule for Rosenkrantz's Ball."

# CHAPTER 10 :

## ROSENKRANTZ'S BALL

THE VAULTED CEILING OF THE ball room of the Shenandoah Hotel was bedecked with boughs of holly, ivy, and the feathery branches of yew that contrasted boldly against the sage green walls. Three walk-in fireplaces were ablaze with long fires made of a base of hickory and one long yew log atop it, broadcasting warmth throughout the room while a cold hoar frost settled on the naked branches of the apple orchard beyond the frosted glass of the windowpanes.

In the center of the room stood a towering yew tree decorated with red and white glass balls and misseltwig. Mayor Rosenkrantz had gone to great lengths to accommodate his Herewardi guests with a grand farewell ball patterned after their customs.

Brekka squeezed Ruhm's arm as he admired the great care to get every decoration right. "It would seem that Ol' Rosenkrantz knows every nuance of our culture. He is a rare asset indeed, a jewel among the Hickoryans."

"As a leader in the Resistance he had to know his allies well. He's apparently opened the ball to everyone within riding distance, but in all likelihood those open skies, hoar frost, and only a sliver of a moon will keep most people near their hearths on this evening."

"Ruhm, what your people call Christmas is a very holy time for us. It is symbolic of the passing of the king energy where the Ur Fyr goes from one generation to the next. It's a time when we rehearse all the travels and hardships of our forbearers as far as our Folk Mouth stretches. A time to reflect as the king disappears for three days under the Cup of Darkness, and a new king rises and leads us into another future."

Ruhm had been listening intently when his thought processes were interrupted by the entrance of Custus Duff, his wife, and daughter. None of Custus' usual rabble attended him, which gave Ruhm a sigh of relief.

It was clear the man was uncomfortable and clung to his wife and daughter like they were his only security. He let go of his daughter's hand who ran over to observe the large decorated tree. Taking his hat off, he bowed at the neck and declared. "Custus Ruhm Lee, I am come to bid you and my beloved sister-niece a farewell and to offer my heart-felt apologies for all the wrongs I did ja."

Custus' wife smiled on when Ruhm observed Melissa cover the distance from the serving table to his side as swiftly as a mother hen. It was easy to see her hackles were up. "Custus Duff, don't you come here to cause me anymore trouble. I've had it up to here with your shenanigans," she raised a hand to her nose as if to stifle a cry. "Just leave us alone."

She said it so emphatically that Mayor Reedy's attention was drawn away from Freyxus and the room grew as quiet as a funeral dirge.

Ruhm laughed; "It's alright, my dear, don't fret your gizzard. Custus has had a change of heart and was just apologizing and wishing us well."

Mely's mouth dropped open and her face reddened. The people resumed their conversations and soon Mely was able to speak again.

She looked Custus over, carefully eying her sister-in-law as if to ensure this was no trick. "Cus, it just ain't like you to apologize for much of anything. How came you to this sudden change of heart?"

"T'was on the day Ruhm won the duel." Custus said, looking to Ruhm with a nod. "I was so pissed off I went storming down Babb Mountain Trail when I come upon an old traveler sitting aside the road like he had all the time in the world. He looked like he was on the other side of a hundred years old but fleshed out like a man in his prime. He were dressed like that Long Swan feller, only in a green hooded robe, stead of white. Went by the name Ullr, so I knew he's likely one of them Herewardi elf-men. But that din't make no never mind. No, it din't, Sis. Cause I found out I had a right strong likin for this here man, like it were my daddy come home from the grave." Custus choked back a tear. "The old feller said, you look bereft and troubled, let me give you the comfort of my counsel. You know, t'weren't like me to listen to nobody, but I was speechless and my heart burned in me while he spoke. For a while as we walked the trail side by side, I was soon tellin this here stranger ever'thing 'bout me I could think of. Finally, as we crossed that Salamander Creek I told him bout Ruhm and how the man had set my whole world on its head."

Ruhm's attention was peaked. When Custus mentioned how his heart burned with each word the traveler spoke, Ruhm remembered the same experience when Father Odhin spoke with him. Personal experience had taught him how involved and real the Herewardi gods were. No untouchable spirits without parts or passions, but real flesh and blood beings, up close and personable, yet awesomely formidable, and steeped in the everyday lives of their children. Had not Brekka said, "Expect miracles. Once Mount Heredom is reclaimed the rebirth of the gods will begin in earnest."

He perceived Melissa could tell he was moved by Custus' tale. "Do the Herewardi have a god named Ullr?"

Brekka declared, "Ullr is the weardean god who sits on the throne of the All Father in his absence and oft acts in his stead." She acknowledged Custus Duff with an improving nod. "He is one of our more ancient gods."

"So, you see Sis, that old feller gave me cause to repent. Set my heart on a whole different course and showed me how you made the right decision by fixin your sight on Ruhm. I just want us to be like we used to be again. God knows I love you and far's I'm concerned, Ruhm is now family."

Mely hugged her brother and kissed him. "You sour old Cus. I knew you'd come around. Just didn't think it would happen til Hell had frozen over."

After some jovial jesting and sharing of coon-hunting tales, the three of them shared some humming beer and promised to get together for a wolf hunt at the end of the Mud Moonth. Custus was just beginning to describe a hunt in which he treed a black panther when Ruhm caught the familiar sight of a band of young Sharaka warriors at the door. It was Degataga, followed by Redangus. When he saw a shock of the blondest of hair pass through the door behind them he realized Anghrus was accompanying them with his wolf pack. Yet even of greater surprise was the lady accompanying Anghrus. As her head turned so he could see under her riding hood it became evident it was his beloved Hollyanah.

"Excuse me Custus, don't think me rude. One of my wives has surprised me with a visit."

He greeted Hollyanah with a bracing hug and a warm kiss. "I didn't expect you for at least another week, and in this weather. I do marvel."

She unfastened her hood and removed it from her head, letting her reddish-brown tresses cascade over her shoulders to frame her rosy cheeks.

"Well, Mayor Reedy was able to secure the funds to purchase my house early. But he was fearful of me being burgled with all that money until he learned that Degataga was accompanying Redangus and Anghrus to Marinstbuhr, so he explained the situation to them and they readily agreed to get me here under guard of their band of Sharaka warriors."

"Why would they be coming to Mount Heredom? What business do those boys have in Martinsbuhr?"

"It seems quite a bit. First off, Anghrus received a mandamus from the Roufytrof, I believe he called it, to report to Long Swan for education, training, and to receive new directives from the lore master. Redangus is here because he has petitioned Chief Chise for a charter to the new island kingdom he discovered, and he wants to get the legalities worked out."

"You mean the tropical isle he found off the coast of Flar-Da during the war?"

"I believe so, the large one. He was granted a charter so that the isle can be colonized and settled under Sharaka and Herewardi rule, but comes for advisement."

"If his charter was already approved, why does he need further advisement instead of engaging in kingdom building?"

"Long Swan has to record it and give him a certified charter before its official. Least that's how he put it to me."

Ruhm considered the wisdom in such then asked, "And the Young Prince Anghrus, why has he come?"

Degataga declared. "Long Swan sent a mandamus for him to come to Mount Heredom where during the winters the wizard will teach him the depths of the Forty-Four Laws and the runes, and during the summers I am to teach him to be a sea cock capable of traveling over the Swan Path to the Lost Kingdoms of Ur-Ope. There are great prophecies and expectations placed on this young prince. The Roufytrof has even made provision for him to travel from Annapolis to Nu-Yalk so that El Yid can train the young blood in pirating, and parkour."

"I have seen this sort of thing before." Ruhm said, "It's how it went with Brekka. The Roufytrof groomed her vigorously from her youth. I do not envy Anghrus the grueling tasks they shall set him to."

Degataga frowned, "Why ever not? The braid heads adore his every move. His father commands a great kingdom, and he is privileged to sit and to drink the teachings at the feet of Long Swan just as I sat at the feet of Onamingo. They seek to make him a complete man fit for the demands of the gods. How else could he complete his odyssey to Ur-Ope?"

"My experience is that the Roufytrof exerts enormous pressure on those they groom for a commission. He will be taken deep into the forty-four runes. Besides, Rhoda the Hag told me ample tales about the monstrosities and trans-humans that once plagued Ur-Ope in the last days of the Amerikan Empire when all the kingdoms of the Ea-Urth collapsed and the gods rained ice and fire down on them. Methinks it will not be an easy thing they require of the lad. The god's only know what he will find in those forsaken lands, and he is still little more than a tender lack beard."

Degataga declared, "A smooth-faced boy he is, but his thoughts are those of a bearded and wizened man. Nay, even more than a man. He is of king's blood. Some say nigher Odhin's blood than anyone else living. I have never had a more worthy student, and our hearts have been melded as one. When he comes of age the two of us shall become blood brothers forever."

"I shall look forward to getting better acquainted with the two of you and with Redangus the Sea Wulf, should you all be sojourning long in these parts. But for now, please, help yourself to the festivities and I shall delight in the company of my wives."

As Degatoga eagerly sought out the food table with his compatriots, Brekka returned with Ruhm-El in her arms, while Hollyannah and Judy still stood with their eyes transfixed on the magnificently bedecked yew tree with a white bearded image of Odhin atop it. The Roufytrof had announced through the mouth of Long Swan that the Mound of Heredom was projected to be completed within seven years.

# CHAPTER 11 :

## THE DEDICATION OF MOUNT HEREDOM

KING SUR SCEAF HAD RETURNED to Godeselle with his retinue where he would set the affairs of the Isle of Ilkchild in order and establish the governance of the Seven Kingdoms now that Mount Heredom was to be restored. Those seven years passed swiftly as he set the affairs of the isle in order. Many of the Hickoryans and Quailor had left for their former lands, leaving vast allotments and areas open for re-settlement. The isle was left in the hands of the Herewardi, Sharaka, Ceruleans, and Chartreuseans. During that seven years all the city-states across Panygyrus strove to perfect their governments and assert their sovereignty with well defined borders and appropriate laws to reflect the individual needs of their cultures, religions, races, and tribes.

Now Brekka had been much busied by the establishment of the Herewardi sanctum atop Big Springs in hopes that the old gods might find place to rest upon their visits to the Ea-Urth. Ruhm had built the Land of Virginia into a republic that was the envy of other tribes and nations.

Brekka planned the arrangements for the high king to return from the Sacred Isle in the West for the dedication of the Heathen temple atop the Holy Mound. This mound had been held in enemy hands for nearly six hundred years in what the lore masters had taken to calling the Age of Proving.

Brekka was overwhelmed with excitement and expectation at the return of the high king. Like a wet blanket on a fire it had rained nearly every day in the Moonth of Bird Song, causing the great rivers and small streams to rise to full capacity. But on the twenty-first day, the sun awoke in its full glory and poured the Green Cup of Fertility and spread the spring sky like a celestial canopy over the lands of the fertile Shenandoah. According to Brekka, the god Frey had cast his smile upon the Big Springs. More important to Ruhm, his bride-covey was now able to complete their preparations for the Time of Interpolation, or as it was better known, the Fifth Sabbath, composed of the first five days of the Moonth of Albispiene.

The House of the Gods on Mount Heredom at Big Springs had finally been completed after seven years of intensive labor and much sacrifice. Those years had been a busy time, with Ruhm straddling his role as governor of the Virginias along with all his duties as husband and father, while Brekka presided over the Herewardi See and oversaw the many capital projects and infrastructure from the Sacred Mound.

Much had changed since Brekka, Long Swan, and Sur Child had laid and set the cornerstone. The confederation had made great strides in solidifying the diverse states and tribes under the leadership of President Chise and his Circle of Chiefs. One of the first acts of Chief Chise had been the removal of the offensive statue of Amerika's first emperor which was removed from the Holy Lands of the Black Hills while Washington and Jefferson were permitted to stand as a memorial for the Hickoryans, and as a special tribute to their Virginia compatriots and as a grant of a special dispensation from the Red Tribes. The tropical island off the coast of Flar-Da known as the Isle of Redangus was the newest city-state to join the Red Nations.

Despite the best efforts of the city states' militias, robber bands continued to plague the middle and northern reaches of Panygyrus. Most of these outlaws were renegades from the ranks of one-time Dominiker sympathizers, those without family or communal ties, and those driven by greed, crime, and lack of skills to earn a civilized living.

Godeselle on the Isle of Ilkchild continued to be the Jewel of the West, and just as Sur Sceaf had scryed during the first days on the island, its prosperity had spread to the city-states on the western coast of Panygyrus. Frisco and Citriodora once again bustled with trade, their ports swelling with merchant ships from as far north as the Land of the Snowmen and as far south as the strongholds of the Moxo. Of the many merchants involved in the shipping trade, the most notable and successful were Turtle Duck and his many sons as well as the fleet of Sonny Ridelli. Adding to the family's prominence and influence, Turtle Duck's daughter, Penelope had recently been democratically chosen as the Lady Mayor of Citriodora where she infused the city with new verve and vigor.

The stronghold of Witan Jewel was now governed by Sur Spear's son, Godwin the Wise, and had become a center of the woolen and silk industries. And to this, wines of the Umpqua vineyards, particularly those produced in Hrusburg, were considered the finest vintages and came into great demand across the face of Panygyrus.

Since peace came to Panygyrus, the Haligryft on the North Umpqua River had become a popular place for Herewardi pilgrimages, as had the great column of the Irmunsul farther upstream. Over the years many pilgrims had attested to receiving visitations from the Herewardi gods, some even saying they had seen the soul of Hereward the Wise and Watchful, and none too few Red Men had described meeting Thunder Beings and Manitous in the woodlands of the vicinity and at the Elk Spirit Crater. In addition, many visitors had reported hearing elfish singing and heard mournful songs for the fallen arising through the portal of the stone column.

Shug Moss and his son Seth, Governor of the Columba Nations had re-built the port cities on the Columba River. King Kanarus and the Chiricachuas established plantations of date palms throughout the Arid Zones and down in the Taxus, just as the Chartruseans on the Isle of Ilkchild continued developing vast new varieties of fruits that could grow in a wide range of climates.

In the southlands of Panygyrus, city-states surrounding Wymouth had taken to calling the Lieutenant Governor Amanuel "King Cotton" because he had collaborated with Siwell and Xelph to develop white, green, and brown cottons that did not cross-pollinate, leading to the increased production of fibers that needed no dying. Another benefit was the elimination of allergies to the dyes that seemed to proliferate in such hot climes, thus giving thousands relief.

Now firmly established in Martinsbuhr, Ruhm's family had expanded rapidly, both in wives and children. His latest brides were the twin daughters of the lord mayor of Annapolis, Cornelius Shipley. Both Florence and Lucille were expecting soon to add to his flock of twenty-seven children.

During the Constitutional Convention it had been agreed by all voting members that, since Mount Heredom was deemed the most sacred and Holy See of the Herewardi Kingdoms, the mount itself, along with the Big Springs and five square miles of surrounding grasslands and woodlands would be ceded to the Herewardi in perpetuity. As such, it was recognized as a sovereign entity of the Herewardi Nation and not subject to the rule of law of any other governing body under the heavens.

As High King of the Herewardi, Sur Sceaf had appointed Brekka as queen of the Principality of Mount Heredom, equal in all manner to all the kings and queens of Heredom. As both queen and haeligawaecca of the Holy Herewardic Priesthood, she wielded great authority and power throughout Heredom and began to teach the godly magic of yore to approved initiates and skalds. Sur Sceaf had returned for the dedication and also for the anointing of Ruhm as a Herewardi king.

Brekka's official residence was the Great Hall atop Mount Heredom, not far from the temple. Fashioned from giant hickory and juniper timbers, the hall boasted three stories of spacious and elegant rooms fronted by wide balconies. The bottom two stories had been designed to facilitate Herewardi council fires and the formal entertainment of official visitors from throughout the various constellations of Heredom, while the third story served as Brekka's private residence. The year before a separate wing had been added to house guests and dignitaries in preparation for the dedication of the temple.

On the day that the silver harrier, Heardwin, had brought word of the pending arrival of the high king and his royal entourage, Ruhm walked out on the top floor balcony of the hall. It was a great honor for Ruhm to be hosting the high king, therefore Brekka had hired additional staff to satisfy every whim of her father, her mother and her nigh-mothers.

In the six summers that had come and gone since that fateful fall of the Pitter Empire, all of the constellations of Herewardi city-states had contributed their wealth, time, and talents for the benefit of establishing Mount Heredom, which, in the days of Hrus-Syr-Os, had been known as the Enclave of Nornbuhr, a vestal coal of the flames of liberty. This interpolation was not only to be a rendering of their accounting for the wise use of those resources, but also a time of great celebration and offerings up to the gods.

Under a dispensation granted by Long Swan, most of Sur Sceaf's royal rrain would be housed in the bastion which now served as the headquarters of Ruhm's fyrds and cavalry along with the temple guard. After the ceremonies, many of the attending dignitaries would have to return to their various city-states and lands of origin, but Sur Sceaf and his wives planned to stay on for an indefinite period of time.

Though Ruhm often visited Brekka at the hall, he made his official seat of government at the governor's house in Martinsbuhr. His other ten wives had chosen to build their homes on the southeast corner of the principality near Freyxus' farm. As Long Swan had always taught him, fairness did not mean sameness, so each home reflected the wishes and needs of the individual wives. Indeed, it was a common teaching among the skalds that egalitarianism was at the root of all strife and forced people to grapple for specks instead of enjoying the benefits of prosperity in contentment as the gods had ordained.

Ruhm took a deep breath of the fresh air that was perfumed with the stimulating honey-tinged scent of hawthorn. Patterned after the splendid Temple of Godeselle on the Isle of Ilkchild, the temple rose like a large white dome on a green mound. It reflected an ethereal pink in the sheen of morning light, with its two protective wing-shaped pylons ensconcing it. Standing in the bluegrass sward between the pylons was the golden obelisk waiting to be raised into place on the fifth day of the Five Days of Sabbath.

The gold plating encasing the marble obelisk was being given its final polishing, and the last of the forty-four runes in the flame elfabet were being graven upon it. Once in pride of place to the east of the temple, its shadow would fall between the two wings or pylons of the temple on the first day of the Cup of Light, the longest day of the year.

As Ruhm watched, a wagon piled with bunches of cut flowers in all sizes and hues from the Arden District of Martinsbuhr rumbled up the incline leading to the oblong courtyard. Before the driver even stopped, a bevy of housemaids emerged with empty baskets soon to be filled.

All along the road from Big Springs to the hall, dynastic banners displaying golden bees, red hoof-prints and green Eyes of Howrus had been raised and now fluttered gaily in the morning breeze. Ruhm had stationed green beetles at strategic spots along the Winchester Pike to give notice of the passing of the royal caravan. As soon as word came that the train arrived at the Runic Menhir at Pikeside, the order would be given to all guests, greeters and musicians to take their places. If all went as planned, the king would arrive precisely at high noon.

The door behind Ruhm opened, and Brekka emerged, still attired in her diaphanous dressing gown, and her hair a tousled shimmer of copper framing her face. "What a perfect day for the king's arrival!" she exclaimed as she joined her husband at the railing. "He was here for the laying of the cornerstone. Wait till he sees the might of the marble structure."

"My dear, every time I look at that temple in the early morning light, I discover another aspect of it, so let me commend you on your selection of Sur Child as your master builder."

Brekka hummed a smile. "He is every bit as great a builder as was his father, Muryh, who was the most revered of all Herewardi master builders. Everything from the laying of the foundation to the final stages has gone smoothly according to plan, with only a few minor exceptions."

"Such as what?" he ran a finger through a stray ringlet and over her ear.

"Well, for example that horrible delay in the marble shipments from the quarries of D'If. That man is not only a genius he has accomplished what most believed was the impossible in the five-year time frame demanded of him. I think the king will be pleased."

Brekka slid a slender arm through his. "He has done well enough indeed, but I must give much of the credit to Arwena, his faery-queen, as well as her bride-covey, and all those strapping sons who labored to the very end at his side chust to make it happen."

"Well, he does have an army of Sons, that's for sure, but why so great a mystery about the private commission from your father? I can't begin to tell you how many times I've been asked what Sur Child is building behind the canvas walls in the yew grove. It's become like a crying baby in the night. I just want to punch the next person that asks me. Even the Lazy Jokers have tried to discover the secret, but Sur Child's sons drove them away."

"If you're asking me if Arwena has confided in me, the answer is no. She claims that when Fa gave Sur Child the commission, he swan swore him to utmost secrecy. Try as she might, she has not been able to weasel it out of her husband. One thing she did say was that the piece was personally designed by Fa, to be a true masterpiece and a crowning work of art atop Mount Heredom."

"If anyone could have gotten Sur Child to break a confidence, it would have been Arwena, she's as curious as any woman and just as conniving as my lovely Brekka. Apparently, we have to wait like everyone else until the opening of the Golden Cup at this Autumnal Equinox. By your father's decree, its hood shall be pulled back and it shall finally be unveiled to all eyes."

"It's not like Fa to be so secretive. Besides, you'd think as haeligawaecca, Fa would have at least confided in me."

"Over the years it has become all too apparent that no man makes much progress without the support of his wives. I want you to know that I owe everything I am to you, my dear. Because of your wisdom and example as faery-queen, the House of Lee increases in beauty and prosperity daily. I admit I had my doubts when you and Freyxus described how a covey could work in harmony, but I have come to see that it, indeed, enriches every aspect of our lives." He smiled down at her. "Nothing short of herding cats can be likened to it."

Brekka smiled. "Women, even though many initially resist, really do crave and need the kind of sisterhood found only in the deep bonds of the bride-covey."

"I yield to your superior wisdom, my darling." He leaned over and kissed her. Even though he was supposed to be staying the week at Liza's, she had yielded her time so that he could support Brekka in this moment of greatest need when her family arrived.

Brekka and the sister-brides had been preparing for this celebration for months. Brekka, in particular, was beside herself for joy. Because of their experience with pleasing guests, Melissa and Liza had been accorded the honor of orchestrating the Grand Festive Board to be held on the fifth day of Albispiene. Wyth and Ynys were in charge of seating arrangements according to rank and prominence, with one exception. By Sur Sceaf's command the young Prince Anghrus was to be seated at the king's right hand, not only because he was representing his father, Ruhm's own dear friend, King Kanarus, but also because, as rumor had it, he was to be presented a commission from on high, to be officially bestowed upon him by the Roufytrof's anointing on this occasion.

Freyxus and an army of milkmaids in their colorful dirndls had gathered May knots, peonies, and irises for the tables. Additionally, Freyxus had arranged for a day at the drog stable where Donny would demonstrate what an asset the drogs had become, and the Lazy Jokers would put the proud Dzungerians of the Rdokians through their paces in the show ring. Rabenbrot offered to contribute a special appearance of his famous troop of Rdokian Cossack Dancers, and a Quailor choir of girls was to sing the song, 'Praise to the Lord, the Almighty, the King of All Creation.'

Hollyannah and Vicky had planned the performance of a child's play, having heard the king very much enjoyed them. And at Brekka's request Forsetti and Ka-Luna had come over from their cabin in Benders Wood two weeks earlier to prepare to stage a passion play portraying the trials, tribulations, and triumphs of Heredom from the time of Hrus-Syr-Os until the present to be held in the amphitheater next to the springs. Ruhm's Cherokee wife, Dawning Duck, Daughter of Degataga, whom he affectionately called Ducky, had arranged with gardeners to provide fresh bouquets in all the guest rooms and to see to it there would be nosegays for the ladies on a daily basis.

On the first day of Albispiene, the first sabbath day, the traditional Procession of the May Queen would take place on the promontory during which the May Queen and her attendants would be presented. Guests and dignitaries had been invited to participate, followed by a carnival on the green with tournaments, games, refreshments, music, and dancing.

Brekka had managed all with the efficiency and good humor of a general. She had set up a room to house the Young Prince Anghrus in while he was to undergo his last stretch of spiritual instruction from her. The young blood had indeed become as a son to her and she loved him as she had loved his mother, Wilona. He represented a continuing bond with her.

Ruhm, himself had obeyed her request that there be every desirable wine, ale, bee-ur, and liqueur in stock, along with the best cuts of venison, buffalo, wisent, and beef, not to mention Sur Sceaf's favorite, hare and quail. To this end he had kept the huntsmen, ranchers, and butchers working dawn to dusk. Now, to both Brekka's and his relief, all was in readiness.

In the tradition of the Herewardi, the festive board would be filled with celebrations, conviviality, pounding feet on the earth in the praise of dancing, and the passing out of accolades and honors under the the ancient sumbel of toasts and boasts. Long Swan was to hand Sur Sceaf his completed leather-bound history of the time between the Fall of Heredom and the Rise of Pitterdom--or as he called it, the Post-Human Era before the Rebirth and Arrival of the Gods from the Stars.

"Well, my dear, I believe we've done everything we could have to prepare for the royal cortege; with the exception of one last thing that I believe you neglected."

Brekka looked at him in alarm. "What is it?"

"Your husband needs one more kiss of encouragement to get him through this day. I honestly think the planning for the king's visit is more exhausting than the preparations for battle."

"Me too, but it'll be my pleasure to kiss the man who is my tower of strength," as she circled his neck with her arms and leaned into his lips.

After Ruhm and Brekka had left the balcony, they bathed, and dressed in their finest, while droves of Quailor nannies marshaled the older children into a downstairs parlor, ready to sing a Herewardi greeting song they'd been practicing for weeks.

As soon as the last beetle arrived with the news that the king's party had reached the Menhir of Hereward, Brekka and Ruhm joined their bride-covey in a prayer circle in Brekka's private quarters before going downstairs to greet arriving guests and dignitaries.

As they stepped out into the courtyard, the sun was directly overhead and they heard the first horns from the approaching caravans of the king sounding through the dell. The lurs immediately gave answer, the deep droning sound echoing off the mound like an approaching thunderstorm.

Brekka's nannies shepherded the eight eldest children outside and into position to the right of Ruhm and their mothers. Once they had made their bows and curtsies to the king properly rehearsed they would rejoin the other children in the nursery. Eyes dancing with excitement, Brekka exclaimed, "They'll be here soon. It's almost time for their arrival. I can hardly wait. It's been way too long, and I want to hear firsthand how Zschamillah, Arundel, and all my friends on the isle are doing."

Eldir, Brekka's oldest asked in his usual loud tone, "Muti, is my mofa here yet?"

His Brother, Ruhm-El said, "He's my mofa, too."

Hollyannah smiled. "No, my dear, he's your nigh mofa. Remember how I told you your fa fa and fa ma live far away on an island in the big deep and wanted to be here but could not suffer such a long journey. One day soon, perhaps as soon as next year, Long Swan will take you to the isle to see them."

"Me, too," cried Sassia-Faxa, blue-eyed daughter of Freyxus whose blond hair was as thick as three rovings of flax. "Mama says I don't have a mofa on account of those awful Pitters."

"That's because the bad men pulled his guts out while he was still alive," Eldir explained with little-boy relish.

Sassia's face crumpled. "That's not true, is it, Mama?"

Before she could answer, Eldir protested, "Is too true. I heard Uffa say it to Ugga."

"Hush, all of you," Ruhm commanded in a stern voice. "This is not a day to talk about sad things."

As Ruhm took his place in the foreground with Brekka, his heart began to beat faster. He was eager to see his king and rub shoulders with his former comrades in arms, and he knew Brekka was eager to see her parents and siblings once again. It's all she talked about since Yule. They had always been such a tightly woven family. He had been disappointed that ill-health had prevented his parents from making the long and arduous journey across Panygyrus, and he resolved to make time to visit the Isle at the end of the next winter along with Long Swan and his son. They would take the sea route to Elves Island in the Taxus and from thence overland to Urford where they would be ferried over the Aurvandilean Sea to Godeselle, the heart of Herewardom.

From his vantage point on the mound, he marveled at the number of people gathered on the promontory just to watch the king's caravan pass. It appeared that, just as he and Brekka had done, most of the spectators had dressed in their finest, and the mood was joyous.

Troops billeted in the bastion lined the parapets the landing, eager to pay tribute to the legendary warrior-king, Sur Sceaf. Just as Long Swan, his bride-covey and his elder children arrived to join them, the lurs sounded once again.

A scout shouted, "Here they come. They approach from the south!"

With his white hood, Long Swan shaded his eyes against the sun.

"From what I can see, you couldn't crowd even one more person onto that promontory. I know my brother well enough to know he would have preferred to come quietly, but if no one else were here, the very trees would have clapped and shouted for joy. See how the white horse and swan banners hail his arrival. Now there is a king. It seems everyone wants to welcome the king."

"Just as it should be," Ysys said.

When the final three times three blasts of the lurs was sounded, Ysys, with a wiggling toddler in her arms, and the rest of her bride-covey joined Brekka's bride-covey. Sur Sceaf's cortege rode up the mound in their coaches marked with a white crest splashed with three crimson drops of blood, symbolizing the King of Three Bloods. At the ramp of the bastion where they were to be billeted during the visit, the fyrds and the rest of the caravan split off.

As the notes of the lurs faded, the sounds of Sur Sceaf's approaching fife and drum corps could be heard in the lead. An instant later the procession came into view, swan and magnolia banners flapping their welcome in the breeze, and Sur Sceaf's twelve silver harriers leading on prancing white steeds. Next to come were the musicians in their vivid red, white, and blue uniforms, followed by the three coaches of Sur Sceaf with his royal bride-covey, several baggage wagons, and the royal guard.

As the regal caravan made its way past the spring on the way to the hall, the crowd's excitement mounted. Shouts and cheers followed them in a wave of sound. After heralding the king to his destination, the harriers and fife and drum corps made a circle and headed back to the bastion.

As soon as Sur Sceaf's royal coach pulled up beside the landing, Ruhm, Brekka, and Long Swan stepped forward. A footman came forth to open the door of the carriage. The king was the first to present. His hair and beard had greatly whitened since they had last met, contrasting dramatically with his deeply bronzed skin. The laugh lines at the corners of his still brilliant green eyes had deepened, as had the worry lines across his brow. But he still boasted the same robust frame and proud carriage of a much younger man. It struck Ruhm suddenly that Sur Sceaf now very much resembled the ancient one who had saved him from certain blindness. But then, why not? Hadn't Brekka taught him that the House of Hrus-Syr-Os was directly descended from Odhin during his various sojourns on the earth.

"Os-Frith, my lord and king," Ruhm said before taking the king in the royal embrace. As he did so, he felt the rock-hard muscles of a warrior ripple beneath the leather surcoat.

"Os-Frith," Sur Sceaf replied, "And Waes Hael!"

The king turned and helped Paloma step down. Dressed in a form-fitting blue silken traveling gown, Sur Sceaf's faery queen was still lovely at sixty-four winters. Though her golden hair had turned platinum, her face showed remarkably few signs of aging. Her eyes were as blue as cornflowers, her complexion as creamy as a magnolia blossom in first blow and as always, she exuded grace, elegance and dignity, the perfect complement to the innately regal king. Here was the queen.

She took a deep breath and gazed upward at the temple surrounded by ancient yews and menhirs. "At long last our seed has regained the Holy Mound. It was a great leap of faith to ever believe this day would happen."

Brekka smiled up at her father as he addressed her. "My dear, when you first received your commission, it was like an arrow to my heart. Even though I had all faith in your abilities and courage, I feared you would become another page in the History of Herewardi Martyrs and not live to enjoy the fruits of your faith or the fruits of your womb. The gods have been merciful and preserved you as their favored one."

Sur Sceaf leaned into Paloma to say in a low voice, "My dearest, you were always the rudder on my ship. Even though your bride-sisters helped row, you were my guiding force. When I was at my lowest ebb, you always found a way to restore my faith."

Paloma blushed as she stepped aside to hug first Ruhm and then Brekka, Ysys and Long Swan. Turning once to the carriage, Sur Sceaf extended a hand to assist Lana in navigating the step. As soon as Lana alighted, she took Brekka in like embrace.

Ruhm was extremely fond of Brekka's mother, Lana, who also seemed ageless. Her burnished red hair was still luxuriant, lightly graying only at the temples. The resemblance between mother and daughter had become far more pronounced. Teary-eyed, she held Brekka at arm's length.

"Thou wast always such a beauty, my dear. I honestly never thought to see thee live long enough to have children, and now thou hast three. I am so happy to see thee once again. I do hope we get to stay a good long time with thee this time, because I can't stand living without my sweet ginger girl."

Brekka leaned into her mother's ear. "Don't tell Ruhm, but I think there is a fourth on the way."

Lana's face lit up. "I know thy father has said we will probably wait until next year to return to Godeselle, and if the gods' will it, I will be here to midwife my grandchild. Oh! Pray it is so."

"Mother, nothing would make me happier. If it were up to me, you'd never leave. Who has Fa put in charge of the isle in his absence?"

"Lord Alfeah. Fa has come to lean on him quite heavily in recent years and is full of praise for his achievements and administrative abilities. But thou knowest Alfie, he would much rather be in the breeding stables and round pen than as he put it, 'Untying the knots of disputes between ministers and disputers of borders.' He detesteth the legal harangues of governing."

"That sounds like Alfie, alright."

As Lana turned to Ruhm to hug him, Sur Sceaf slapped Ruhm on the back. "Your turn to get splashed in tears, Ruhm," he let out a hearty laugh.

"I appreciate the warning, my lord, but I've already been baptized many times over by wives and children, and even Sur Child on an occasion or two when the marble was delayed coming out of D'If."

"Sur Child has done so much for us here and, of course, on the isle when acting as his father's apprentice. And when he became a master builder, he created grand structures in Ele-Anor-Ness that perfectly complemented the traditional Hyf. Clearly, he bears the mark of his father's seed code." His expression turned thoughtful. "I remember when he was scarcely old enough to toddle how he followed his father around, collecting chips of stones as he went."

Although Lana's eyes brimmed, she managed to restrain her tears. "Thou art truly a tower of good looks, Ruhm Lee. I can see why my daughter fixed her gaze on thee so young. It comforteth my heart that thou art now my son. And I would feign meet Brekka's bride-sisters. Truth be told, the unusual mix of her covey has provided much chatter everywhere we've been. From all accounts, thou hast saddled thyself to a whirlwind."

Ruhm laughed. "I'm certainly never bored. And I'm beginning to think my darling whirlwind enjoys producing little whirlwinds to add to the chaos I'm already in."

Lana grinned. "Chust how many little ones dost thou have?"

Ruhm felt a rush of pride. "I have twenty-seven, thirteen strong sons and fourteen of the fairest of daughters in the land. We've arranged for you to meet them this evening before dinner at a party in the nursery playroom."

"How lovely! There's nothing I love more than to be surrounded by little elves and faeries."

"I promise you it will be loud."

The party was indeed loud, and at times, even raucous, especially when the two eldest boys, Ruhm-El and Eldir carried on the battle between their wooden soldiers into a huge glass fish tank in the solarium adjoining the children's playroom. Water soon covered the boys, their cohorts, the floor and anything else within splashing distance before Anghrus' newly married brides mustered the nannies to restore order, leaving the fish cowering in the corners with shell-shocked eyes bulging at the fright.

Sitting between her mother and father, Brekka shook her head. "Honestly, my bride-sisters and I have tried everything short of hobbling those wildlings to instill manners and company behavior in them, but as you can see, they are still more wild than tame."

Laughing, Sur Sceaf glanced at Lana with a twinkle in his eyes. "My dear, doesn't this remind you of the time I came home to find Ary, Alfie and our sweet little Brekka in the kitchen feeding their pet lambs the apple pies you had spent all afternoon baking?"

Lana laughed. "Oh heavens to Betsy, Surrey, I had forgotten all about that. It took me a week to get the odor out of the floorboards. I finally had to scrub them down with lye and vinegar and follow up with lavender oil."

The joy of being with her parents again brought the warm radiance to life Brekka had missed in their absence. Since they had arrived, she had found herself thinking about her childhood at Namen Jewel and then on the Isle. Such happy times they'd been. "You made me and Alfie and Ary do the scrubbing," she teased. "I remember telling Ary that the smell of that awful mix was much worse than sheep manure."

Absently rubbing the old wound in his broad chest, Sur Sceaf suddenly looked thoughtful. “You know, my dearling, the only regret of my sixty-four winters is that I was too often away from home and missed so many evenings like this with my wives and children. Now, as I sit between the Green Cup of the Big Dipper and the Golden Cup of Light in the presence of my beloved daughter and her posterity, I am filled with gratitude to the gods that I may experience joy and rejoicing with my children and their children. When a man has as many wives and children as I do, he experiences loneliness seven-fold when parted from their company.”

“Mama said you may be staying for up to a year. I can think of nothing better than to have my children and nigh children come to know you and your wisdom as I and my siblings were privileged to do, Fa.”

His sudden smile erased years from his sun-weathered face, reminding her of the king at the height of his power. “And I can think of nothing better than to witness the ancestral fire rekindled atop Mount Heredom. We have come far.”

As haeligawaecca, she felt a keen urgency as well as a driving compunction to ensure that that ancestral fire burned bright and that the culture of her people might once again flourish in the Ea-Urth.

“My dear, it was so thoughtful of thee to invite all of thy brethren and sistern and their families to this dedication. Many are the number of excited letters from those east of the Mys-Isys River. Hast thou any inkling of how many plan to attend?”

“At last count, we’ve received 72 acceptances, and regrets from six, who for various reasons aren’t able to make the trip. Ary and his bride-covey plan to break their journey in Wymouth to visit with Khem, Margot and Anne, and their children. Khem and Amanuel will then travel here with Ary. And you already know about the letter Fa sent to Dak asking him to bring Redelfis, Going Snake with him. Last I heard they plan to arrive either tomorrow or the next day. Then, only yesterday, a harrier arrived from Il-Alim saying that he will do his best to be here in time for the dedication ceremony, but Lorna is heavy with their sixth child and is having a hard time, so he may have to stay home to tend her.”

“Have you told Ahy?” Lana asked, glancing across the toy- and-child-littered floor where Taneshawa sat singing a gentle Sharaka chant rocking Vicky’s newborn, Alfbert.

Brekka nodded. “I know she was disappointed, but she said she understood.”

Ahy glanced in their direction, as though sensing she was part of the conversation. She said something to Vicky, kissed the little black-haired boy on the top of his head and handed him back to his mother before rising. She smiled quizzically as she walked toward them.

“Why do I think you were talking about me?” she said as she slipped her arm around Sur Sceaf’s shoulders.

“Because we were, dearest,” he said, taking her hand and kissing it. “As always, I was remarking on how beautiful you looked holding my newest grandson.”

“He is a darling,” Ahy replied. “And you know me I can’t resist cuddling any baby I see.”

Brekka smiled. “Actually, I was telling Fa and Mama about the message we received from Il-Alim.”

Taneshewa’s expression sobered. “I plan to send a message to him, telling him not to risk leaving Lorna, and that after the festivities, I will come to him, should Lorna need a mother’s comfort and aid.”

“Dost thou not remember when Milkchild was carrying her last little one? She had many bouts of false labor, sending us all into a flurry of anxiety. We took turns staying with her to ensure that her household ran so smoothly she had no need to worry.”

“I do remember. I was carrying Il-Alim at the time, and Paloma refused to let me take my turn.”

Lana nodded. “And now Milky’s baby, Jemima, is the mother of four of El-Yid’s brood.”

“That’s true. But even so” Ahy’s brow wrinkled, “I worry. There are dark omens in the night sky and it worries me evil forces begrudge our happiness.”

“Of course, you do, my love,” Sur Sceaf told her. “And if you feel the need to travel to Charleston, I will gladly go along with you.”

# CHAPTER 12 :

## THE LORD OF THE FOREST AND THE SPRINKLING OF THE MAY QUEEN

FORSETTI WAS READY FOR THE day. It was the first day of Albispiene. As he adjusted his robes the parade began with a flurry of trumpets, the full-throated rumble of the lurs, and the pounding of drums. Forsetti and Ka-Luna led the procession. Dressed as the Lord of the Woods in multiple colors of green, his head was crowned with antlers and a garland of magnolia leaves so that he resembled the God Tyranus in his entire earthly and woodland splendor.

Ka-Luna, on the other hand was honored as the Queen of the May, a sylph-like beauty in her gossamer white dress and a crown of May flowers that fit her brow like the eildon trees on the mound above. The young maids followed them, tossing May knots and sprinkling blossoms in the wake of the Mother Superior of All Faeries, Freya, whom Ka-Luna was meant to represent.

As the parade advanced with the fifers and lurs, the white-hooded Long Swan escorted the green-gowned Ysys representing the Goddess of Fertility, Yster. They were trailed by a train of children dressed as bunnies and ducks passing out candies and egg-shaped treats to the children along the parade route.

The next to come was Little Doe, attired in beautifully beaded white buckskin, representing the Lady Redith, who was of Sharaka heritage and whose memory was much venerated by all. Both the Herewardi and Sharaka cheered and shouted; "Hail, the grand seeress! Hail the Lady Redith! May her memory endure forever."

Jake the Blue's son, Jethro, and Siwel's son, Strepto, were dressed in puckish green tights and pointed green shoes symbolizing the arrival of the woodland spirits of the season who would sprinkle magic and the chemistry of love throughout the wild lands until the sun climbed to its full height on the sides of the north on the Day of Light, still over a moonth away.

Forsetti's heart was full of the season. As lore master it cheered him to see so many peoples in their festive attire and playful moods on this holy holiday in the Merry Moonth of May. Elmer and Jake, both blue-skinned Ceruleans, were sitting with Mendaka and the chiefs. Forsetti's eye caught on the commanding form of the tall dark robed form of Raven's Tongue, next to the yellow-haired Xelph and his dark-haired wife, Face-Of-Stars.

As the parade made its serpentine path through the crowds he discovered Mangus Coloradus and Zoot with their wives and children. Upon cresting the promontory, they were greeted by Forsetti's father-in-law, Ilkchild with three of his wives and the romp of ottermen consisting of both dogs and bitches. These trans-humans were breath taking to look upon insomuch that he had to turn his head to break the transfixed stare he was locked in. Their sleek muscular physiques and the almost human faces and craniums gave them a look of refinement nature usually reserved for those of royal blood.

It was easy to see from Ilkchild's expression that they represented the choicest prize of the wizards many achievements. Not only was he a wizard maker, but clearly his work with the ottermen placed him in the category of a beast master after the order of Zschamillah, whose expertise Ilkchild had relied upon in their considerable taming and training.

Ilkchild motioned with his turning serpent wizard's staff for Forsetti to draw near. "Hail and well-met, my beloved Ka-luna, and my favorite student, Forsetti. Stand ye with us and suffer us to hear all your doings up and down through these eastern lands of Panygyrus. Nothing is so rich as tales and experiences given from mouth to ear. I have sent many pigeons out throughout Panygyrus, and it has done my heart good to hear their reports of success into their various fields of labor."

"Hail, Mighty Wizard." Forsetti took Ilkchild in the royal embrace. Then he gave each of Ilky's wives a genuflection while touching the back of their hand to his forehead. "It gives me pleasure to report your teachings have guided me well throughout my commission here. I think you can be proud of our achievements."

Ka-Luna did likewise to her father and then curtsied to her mother and nigh-mothers. “Oh Father, we can’t wait to report all we’ve accomplished, and there are so many questions we wish to barrage you with, but we don’t want to ruin this moment with you.”

“Hush child, I’ll not hear of it. You ask whatever your blessed heart desires and my heart shall dance in the light of your countenance I have so yearned to see for nigh six winters.”

“By the gods, it is so good to see you and mother again too, but I’m dying to hear about the ottermen. Your letters have enflamed us with pressing questions about them. What’s the story?”

“Well, first off, this bevy is made up of all master swimmers, and who ever mixed their seed codes, I am convinced, used human donors with the brightest of minds. I never thought to be an advocate for transhumans, but these creatures force me to re-think the matter. Their speech is remarkably musical, and they’re capable of thinking just about anything we are capable of, which makes them beings more than creatures, whereas, Xelph has to contend with constant sophomoric attitudes from his wyrm kats. I, on the other hand, can discuss advanced lore with my romp of ottermen.

“Ever since they were discovered on the peninsula of Moon Door by Hari the Fisherman, I have been invested in teaching them our language and testing the limits of their intelligence. It dawned on me what an important role they might play in our ventures at sea, aiding both the military and the merchant ventures. In point of fact, I sent out several of those best gifted with speech with Hari and his fishing fleet, and they were able to warn him not to draw in the nets, as a shark wyrm was lurking directly below their ship. Having had personal experience in the bowels of a shark-wyrm, I shudder to think what havoc that monster could wreak on a small fishing vessel. Such a warning alone attests to their value.”

“If I remember Xelph’s story correctly, he said the wyrm-kats were as vicious as panthers before he managed to tame the kittens. Was it the same with the ottermen?”

“Hari said they were confrontational, showing their teeth, but when Hari turned his back on them and showed no fear or aggression, they slowly calmed, and their unbridled curiosity took over from there. He was amazed that they seemed to be trying to communicate in some form of language similar to the chortles of a cavy. On his many return visits, he left scraps of fish near their cave. Once, he inadvertently hit one of the males' splat in the face with a piece of fish, causing its companions to chortle some laughs. That's when he realized they understood humor just as well as we do. It was about this time when Hari came to me, and I went with him to their cave and planned expeditions to study them in their natural habitat. It didn't take me long to decide that they could be trained as well if not better than the wyrm kats. I began a correspondence with Queen Zschamillah for her skills as a beast master, and she suggested I contact the hags at the Citadel to find out what they knew of these creatures. Apparently, they have an archive of the beasts and creatures the Amerikans had engineered."

"I'm sure you've noticed," Forsetti declared, "The Hickoryans are both intrigued and spooked by them."

Ilkchild smiled, reached down and swung his wooden leg around with the help of his right hand. "Well, they do take some getting used to."

Forsetti looked over at the lodge of otters. They walked in a tight kit without an apparent order, their necks and heads darting and occasionally diving as they interacted as curiously as a playful bevy of otters in a stream. He could barely make out the musical tones of their speech, but definite strings of sentences were discernible.

"What kind of problems have you run into with them?"

"Nothing really serious, maybe, the occasional stolen fish, the pollution of drinking fountains by over energetic swimmers, and their pestering questions about anything new. But I can tell you this much, they must only be corrected through positive means. Any other means and you have an enemy until you make it right. They have a very high moral code of right, wrong, and fairness. By the gods, they live by the law and they die by the law. So teach them right and honor this credo and all goes well."

Seeing Ilkchild's leg was aching as witnessed by his fidgeting on and off his good leg, Forsetti asked him, "May we invite you to our home in Bender's Woods so that you can give your leg a rest?"

"We'd be delighted, but in all honesty I have a lot of business I need to conduct with Long Swan, Sur Sceaf, and Brekka. Be assured, we'll have plenty of time together. I want to visit the place called Paw Paw. The records say it is where Hrus took refuge and hid our people from the

Pitters. My hope is to find the lost scriptures purported to be buried there, The Bok of Os and the Poetic Eddas of Baldur. Besides, we're staying til the Elven Fair and won't take the journey back to Moon Door until after the dedication of the temple and its surrounding mound, forest, and menhirs. Let's get together after all the celebrations and formalities."

Going Snake was smoking the pipe as he sued the Manitous for their guidance in his being raised a war chief. On the second day of sabbath, representatives of the Red Nations held a pow wow on the promontory opposite the Mound of Heredom. Just as the Herewardi celebrated the first five days of the sabbath, the Red Nations gathered to celebrate the planting of the Three Sisters—corn, squash and beans. They, too, held games and races and contests of bravery as well as performed traditional ceremonial dances, and the presentation of the Booger Dance was to be held on the third day.

As with all pow wows, this had a serious portent as well—in this case, the settlement of the Isle of Redangus South of Fla-Da, a joint Herewardi-Sharaka venture. In addition, of particular import was the raising of a thirteenth chief to join the Circle of Chiefs serving as advisers to President Chise—in essence acting as a flying buttress to the building of the Nation of Panygyrus.

Going Snake was to be raised as the new chief of the Sharaka and many were the dignitaries who had come to honor him. In addition to the Circle of Chiefs were President Chise and Chief Zoot, Sur Sceaf, Arundel, Zschamillah, Ruhm and his bride-covey, Xelph, Face-of-Stars, Khem, Anne, Margot, Amanuel, Raven's Tongue and Yellow Horse were in attendance who would all assist in the establishing of sovereign laws for each individual tribe to ensure home rule and application of customary laws.

At sundown, Going Snake left the I-Ni-Pi Lodge made of tulip tree saplings and covered with hides and blankets in the reeds and cattails near the Elf Waters. He had fasted and prayed for the customary three days in the makeshift sweat lodge, wherein he had heard the voices of ancestors long dead who showed him in a vision the future of his people.

Waiting for him when he emerged was the Circle of Chiefs arrayed in the finest of ceremonial garb of their diverse tribes. He had known almost all of these revered leaders since his childhood. In point of fact, Chief Zoot of the Apache had been even younger than he was when they first met at Godeselle. After the Apache youth had been freed from Pitter captivity by Starkwulf and Hartmut Hegele, he went on to rule the Apache Lands at a young age, until his appointment as president of all of Panygyrus placed him as the head of all nations.

The pow wow was held on the promontory of Big Springs just across from the Mound of Heredom. Foot races were taking place near the Elf Waters when the chiefs called for the presentation of Going Snake in order to deliver him into the hands of the spirit chief for remaking and proper marking.

Going Snake was honored to have his father, Mendaka, and his beloved mother, Little Doe, along with his brother, Redelfis, and sister, Moon Waters, in attendance at this most sacred ceremony. O-Lum-Ane, his newest bride from the Rappahannock Tribe sat with his bride-sisters and Too-May the Wolf, his most recent father-in-law, all of whom were chewing leaves of rabbit tobacco to elevate their mood.

White Moose and Chief Roaring Waters of the Buffalo Nations stood in the Circle of Chiefs at the pow wow. Raising both of his hands to the sinking sun, buckskin fringe waving in the breeze, White Moose intoned with all solemnity, “I call upon the Thunder Beings of the Four Winds to welcome a new brother and chief to this Circle of Chiefs, the representatives on Earth of the Grand Council in the Sky.”

Drums beat over the Elven Waters as flaming arrows rose in an arch through the darkening skies and extinguished themselves in the Big Springs.

As acting spirit chief, Mendaka was attired in his full shamanic regalia. He unwrapped the ceremonial pipe fashioned from carved juniper wood, filled it with sacred tobacco from a pouch at his waist, and lit it with a paw paw brand from the campfire. He inhaled, held the smoke for a moment before slowly exhaling and using his free hand to waft the smoke over his face and head as one would lift a veil. He then passed on the pipe to White Moose who repeated the ceremonial breath. When all had taken their turn, Mendaka emptied the ashes at Going Snake’s feet.

"These ashes symbolize your rising from the losses of your life to the exaltation into the Society of the Thunder Beings."

White Moose motioned for the attendees to move up to the promontory past numerous campfires illuminating the columns of sycamore along the road.

Redelfis and Redangus stood at Going Snake's side, preventing him from moving forward. Since he had been instructed not to speak, he stared straight ahead, his heart thundering in his chest in anticipation.

Finally, at a signal from Mendaka, Redelfis and Redangus took him by his arms and led him up to look straight into the painted face of the spirit chief standing between two pillories, signifying that the Thunder Beings have led him to the destiny of his choice.

"Going Snake, is it of your own free will that you accept this honor and all its attendant labors?"

"It is both my will and the will of the Thunder Beings."

Mendaka took out his smoldering bundle of artemesia and smoked Going Snake thoroughly, allowing the sage scented serpentine smoke to twist about him and impart him with the necessary ritual purity.

Redelfis then stepped forward to secure Goin Snake's right wrist to a pillory while Redangus did the same to his left. After he was thoroughly bound, Mendaka dipped his raven wing into a saucer of owl and serpent blood, and then sprinkled the blood with three swishes of the feathers about Going Snakes neck and shoulders, leaving him properly anointed with their spirit fetches.

Mendaka pulled out his sharp black obsidian knife and cut an owl hieroglyph on Going Snakes right breast. Going Snake bit back the pain, and though he winced, he dare not cry out. This was followed by the carving of a serpent hieroglyph on his left breast while the spirit chief intoned, "From your heart and your mind you shall rule your people, and from this day forth you shall be chief over the Sharaka Nations from the rising of the sun in the east to the setting of the sun in the west and upon all the isles of the deep of which your people go forth to inhabit."

Roaring Waters began his song Wah-Kan-Tanka while O-Lum-Ane cut Going Snake's bindings and staunched his blood with ashes of sacred sage.

Going Snake embraced his brides one by one and then addressed his people with his pronounced vows, "I promise to be a circuit-riding chief, and to visit all my tribes and people in their season. We shall be one in war and peace, in poverty and prosperity. Let the spirits of the ancestors sing a new day for us."

# CHAPTER 13 :

## THE TRIALS, TRIBULATIONS AND PASSION OF THE LONGFATHERS

FORSETTI'S HEART POUNDED WITH EXHILARATION. As one of the youngest lore masters it was beyond unusual that he had been chosen to choreograph the Passion Play. Few had ever been afforded such an honor. Most were written and choreographed by either Long Swan or Ilkchild—and once, by the scholar, Heimdal. When Long Swan asked him to do a play of the longfathers he and Ka-tune had already been throwing some ideas around on the subject. He had given his all to making this performance the most memorable.

He chose the Opequon Heights where high cliffs overlooked the meandering stream and meadows below. The Heights were framed on three sides with mixed deciduous hardwoods to give the privacy the actors would need for rehearsals so that no prying eyed spoilers could give away the presentation and thus dilute its desired effect. Guards were posted at all points of entry so no one could pass or repass without his specific permission. This passion play was to serve as an eternal tribute to the chain of the longfathers from Hrus-Syr-Os all the way up to Sur Sceaf.

A large square area was marked off. It served previously as the camp of El Yid and his dragooners during the campaign against Hryre Seath. Long benches of walnut and oak logs surrounded the center area that would serve as a stage. The field was in full flush of blue grass salted with sun yellow dandelion and blue pimpernel.

The chimes sounded three times three which served as the signal for silence and full attention. Forsetti gave his wife a confident smile as he took center stage gripping his hazelwood staff, denoting his office of a lore master. "Youth of Herewardom, even though you have witnessed the Sabbath Passion Play for as many green cups as you young bloods and maidens can remember, I want you to know this one will be done very differently. It will mark the beginning and end of the Herewardi struggle against an evil force that plagued our race and other noble races for over five hundred years; that damned nearly resulted in our extinction and the reduction of humankind into mere drones of the state.

"Young bloods, it is my hope you do not use this time we have here to flirt with the maidens, and they with you. You owe it to your ancestors and to your king to put aside every aspect of your lives for the next three days so that we together may deliver the best performance we are capable of. Many generations shall pass before you see another king the likes of the High King Sur Sceaf. One day you will be telling your grandchildren that you performed before him. I hope when you do that you say it with pride of knowing you had performed your best."

Uffa elbowed Ugga and three maidens behind them giggled.

"I don't have to tell you I have the authority to dismiss anyone who's not prepared to treat this subject matter with the utmost of reverence. Please, I invite anyone to leave this very moment if their heart is not fully in this solemn endeavor."

Uffa gave answer, "Forgive us Master Forsetti. We will put away our loud laughter and light-mindedness. We just needed a few moments to get into the spirit of the occasion."

"Then I shall proceed."

He surveyed the young bloods and maidens sitting around the log benches, their faces eager to participate. This was indeed the crème de crème of Herewardom. He walked into the exact center point of the stage gripping his hazel rod and pointed it directly at Anghrus.

"You! Your name is Ang-Hrus, is it not?" The girls giggled causing him to flush red as he walked toward center stage.

Forsetti pictured him as a king and thought to himself, *This could very well have been how the young Hrus-Syr-Os looked.* The young blood's thick shock of hair bounced in harmony with the spring in his feet. Forsetti caught the flirtatious glances coming from the maidens who knew most of the young bloods, but Ang-Hrus was new to these wolf packs. Though his promise had been made known in council fires and in the tournaments, this was the first time most of the maidens were able to see him up close. It was clear they were very much interested in currying his favor.

"You shall play the role of Hrus-Syr-Os."

A contagiously wide smile spread over his alabaster white face and ruddy cheeks. The maidens cheered and the young bloods gave half-hearted claps. As the young blood took his place next to him, Forsetti, he swung his hazel rod in the direction of Uffa before calling out. "You three maids, come here." As they made their way, stepping over the log benches, they stood next to Anghrus and looked at one another with questioning looks.

Ka-Luna joined them at center stage and sized them up for a moment before choosing the tall brunette maid in a beige smock. "Forsey, this one will do well in representing Urth. What is your name, my dear?"

"I'm Eahlswith, Haakon's daughter."

Ka-Luna smiled at her. "Good breeding, my dear. You're perfect for the role. You shall play the role of Urth." Then turning like a Shepherdess choosing only the best of stock, she pointed with her hazel wand at the ginger maid. "You shall play the role of Verdandi. What is your name?"

The lass boldly declared, "Gondul, daughter of Cumra."

"Cumra the Wise, is he not the one who taught philosophy at Moon Door?"

"He did."

"Of what hearth are you?"

"Ringhilde's"

"Many were the classes I had with Ringhilde." Turning to the last of the maidens, a tall blond with fishbone braids, "And you, my dear, what are you called?"

"Morkere, daughter of Aelfgar."

"Well, you shall play the role of Skald, youngest of the Fates." Then addressing the braid-heads collectively, she asked, "Maids, I ask you, can you give your heart and soul to these roles?"

They answered in unison, "Yes".

Forsetti stood for a few moments studying the maidens and thinking they were just perfect for his intent and effect.

"You fine young ladies shall be the Norns. Take your role seriously, for the Wyrd Sisters do not allow themselves to be mocked, and they reward those who do them honor. Let's begin. You three shall start the play. It will open with you gazing into the mirror of a large cauldron from which you shall scry the birth of the Herewardi Nation." She looked to her husband as if she was just struck by inspiration of some sort. "Forsey, we've got to devise a way to produce smoke coming up from behind them."

He caught the waving of Ugga's hand out the left corner of his eye and acknowledged him with a flick of the finely tooled hazel rod.

Ugga cleared his throat. "Master Forsetti, we can dig a trench behind the Three Sisters, fill it with hot coals and then cover it with wet leaves and artemesia. You have smoke and spiritual essence all in one."

"Yes," Ka-Luna shouted, "we must give their presence an air of other-worldliness."

Forsetti gave a reflective nod before acknowledging, "You're right Ugga, that idea works."

"We will have to make some wattle-weave in front of the trench, so that no one can see the source of the smoke."

"Alright, I can see this is starting to materialize very well," Ka-Luna said. "Now, you maids come with me. I'm going to teach you your lines over a cauldron I've had placed in the wood. While I work with the Norns, Forsey will work with the other role actors."

As the maidens trailed off with Ka-Luna, Forsetti turned his attentions back to Anghrus. "Ang-Hrus, are you ready to take upon you the Spirit of Hrus-Syr-Os and learn your lines?"

"Where do I start, Master?"

"We'll work that out as we go." He looked over the young bloods and remaining maidens very carefully. Using a Hickoryan expression he called out, "Laws-a-massy-me! You," He pointed at a lovely red-haired maiden at the Ur Fyr's prompting. "Come here my dear."

As she approached he knew this would be the perfect actress for the role of Brekka. His heart breathed a sigh of relief. "You are Leofsi, daughter of Godgifu. Are you not?"

"Master, I am."

"You will play this role well. My bones burn in me from the witness the Ur Fyr is giving me. You have no idea how I agonized who could play such an important role, and here you are delivered to me by the hands of the gods." Once again, he looked over the crowd and announced, "After the first scene with the Wyrd Sisters on top of the mound, what we shall refer to as the Nornbuhr, the lamps will be shaded with red shields, then the white lamps and torches will switch over to the yew bower."

He called upon his personal silver harrier, Heardwin; a bull in a young blood's body. "You shall represent the militia that Hrus-Syr-Os gathered under his roof in preparation for the coming fall and collapse of the Amerikans. You and all the green beetles present will show the militia leading the Herewardi kith and kin into the caves just as the Wyrd Sisters scryed and warned them to do."

"Caves!" Heardwin exclaimed with a look of puzzlement on his face.

"It'll just be a dark back drop, but we have to show them carrying food supplies, gold, and weaponry inside. You will hunker down there while the storm of nature and the burning stars pass over." He swung swiftly around to the benches on the west and called out, "Ealdfrith, you shall represent the philosophers and scholars of history, mythology, and languages that Hrus first gathered to build the Herewardi Enclave in the days when the fyrds were little more than a mere militia.

He motioned for another harrier of his, a short stocky built young blood with a sideways speaking mouth. "Aethelmaer, you will represent the Ex Chequer. You will be attired in a tattermallion just as Hrus was wont to have all his money-men attired in, for no one suspected that such poorly clad wayfarers were transporting the massive wealth of the Herewardi Enclave from place to place."

Using his hazel rod, he assigned each of the remaining young bloods to portray the succession of kings and other important characters of Herewardi history, including the lady knights from Myra-El to Brekka, and especially those pivotal figures during the reign of Elrus and the Golden Age of Enlightenment with the Elven Folk deep in the heart of the Taxus.

Finally, Forsetti pulled a stack of papers out of his rucksack. "Come and get your lines. I realize that it would normally take a sennight to learn them, but I'm only giving you two days at most. Every one of your roles, whether as warriors, philosophers, or wayfarers are critical to portray how the Founding Fathers were Os-Syr-Tru to the man. Yes, they were true to the living gods of Ancient Wessex, the Golden Branch of the Saxon Race from which we are all sprung. They gathered on Nornbuhr at great sacrifice and untold labor to raise a temple, an academy, and an enclave of safety from a swiftly degenerating civilization that had utterly forsaken truth and honor, and at a time when most peoples spurned the roots of their origins. It was their goal to build a new tribe and they swore oaths to promulgate the inalienable rights of every people to sovereignty, liberty, freedom, and tolerance. And it is precisely atop Mount Heredom, originally called Nornbuhr, where they held the ensign of freedom up for every folk, kindred, tongue, and people and offered a chance to take up the Sword of Righteousness against tyranny, censorship, monoculture, and oppression while at the same time preserving the teachings of the ancients who had long ago slept in the dust, but still shone in their writings and archives.

"I want you to feel your roles as deeply as the deepest wound you ever felt. Whether it was with sword or broken heart it was gotten. Get into the scene your longfathers lived in. Eat it, breathe it, feel it! First imagine the extreme political unrest in which every man's hand was against his brother, and minorities were extinguished as easy as one throws a sack of kittens in the river for drowning. Hearts grew cold. Laws were given no substance. Every branch of government was up for hire. That society collapsed under its artificial, unnatural, and imposed norms.

"Now, imagine in all this turbulence the night skies began to be lit by burning stars shouting their warnings of the pending judgments coming on swift wings of lightning. We'll have flaming arrows to represent them. The sun gave off great waves of heat, and the entire Ea-Urth in her anger shook like the leaves of a quaking aspen tree. Volcanoes spewed out rivers of lava across the face of the lands. Mountains fell and valleys rose. Seas heaved themselves beyond their bounds and men's hearts failed them. The sound of the bones of the Ea-Urth breaking could be heard in all lands and on every continent as the whole world wobbled for balance like a drunken man aboard an unsteady ship. With the arrival of the burning stars, the forests were set aflame, roof tops incinerated, and many lands drowned in the floods that ensued.

"But Mother Holle would not leave the Os-Syr-Tru without hope. She guarded her people like a hen guards her clutch in the cleft of a rock, under Mount Heredom, one of the chosen sees of the Norn Sisters. The rest of the gods cast nets of protection over the Seed of Odhin, that they should live to fight the rising evil of the Pitter Empire. Thus were the Herewardi conceived and born into the conflict of the age. Thus were all the other good and upright peoples such as the tribes of the Red

Man and the Quailor preserved to become the one-day inheritors of this land, for the gods had ordained that the true of heart should one day inherit the Earth."

He took a deep breath, hoping these young bloods and maidens grasped the importance of portraying the trail of suffering and sacrifice their longfathers gave that this generation might dwell in peace, possess free agency, and freedom of thought and movement.

Uffa walked up next to him, his face a slight wince, a sad affect.

"What is it lad?"

"Master, I am the last man, and I have no role."

"Oh, but you do. You have the greatest role of all. My good man, you are to play the role of the High King Sur Sceaf."

# CHAPTER 14 :

## THE ERECTION OF THE GOLDEN OBELISK

IT WAS THE FIFTH DAY OF Albispiene, the last of the five days of the Herewardi Sabbath. During these five days unmarried maidens with no promise of marriage were permitted to enter the woods and mate with the princes of the land without any fear of censure or recrimination from the community. Offspring from these woodland liaisons would be ascribed the respectful surname of Ev'Rhettson or Ev'Rhettdaughter and be entitled to full legitimacy throughout the commonwealth of Herewardom.

In the nine days since Sur Sceaf and his party arrived, there had been a steady stream of his relatives, friends, and comrades in arms come to pay homage to Sur Sceaf the Man and to celebrate the raising of the obelisk. It seemed as though every waking hour was filled with family reunions and festivities of one sort or another.

Since Sur Sceaf's arrival, the guest wing of the Great Hall was bursting with the families of his children and their children. He delighted in the robust conversations the he was having with his grandchildren. His wives were equally occupied, especially with the youngest of the family. As he remarked to Paloma, the nursery had become the noisery with all manner of cries, gurgles and laughter, but it was the place that most delighted the king's heart.

Despite the aches and pains from old battle wounds and his days slogging through steaming swamps and frozen wastelands, he found himself revisiting the happy days of his youth when there were always several babies running through the house. Now those babies were chasing babies of their own. But along with happy memories came a grieving for all the fallen warriors who had not lived to see their posterity prosper in peaceful times. Remembering the loss of Jackie Doo deeply saddened him as did Aethelstan and so many other good friends and comrades. He thanked the gods that the Pitters and Vardropi were no more.

Now, as he donned the attire of Herewardi gentry, he recalled the long list of ceremonies he'd attended throughout his life. The first had been the occasional lodge he attended with his Quailor grandfather, Ludwig von Hollar and Starkwulf of Zamora, during which his fafa, Sur, anointed Ludwig into the kingship, declaring him to be a direct descendant of the God Ullr and therefore, also of royal seed. Afterwards, he had gone so far as to inquire how Sur had known that Ludwig was a descendant of Ullr. He would never forget the expression on his grandfather's face when he declared, "By the stones, my boy, by the elven stones. Someday, when your eye is open, these stones will be a lamp unto your feet in an otherwise very dark world."

Then, there was the Great Pow Wow in Di-Ahman when, after his victories over the Pitters at Frink Glen and Irminsul along with the betrayal of Walker Pig and Yggep, the revered Sharaka Shaman, Thunder Horse, named him the Bravest of Braves. It was at the same time that he and Mendaka were put through the rites of the Sun Lodge, making them blood brothers in the Red Nation. But the one event that truly defined him was the day in the Shepherd Hall in Witan Jewel when the Roufytrof in solemn assembly appointed him above his accomplished and decorated older brethern to meld three divergent nations into one confederation.

He would never forget the look of pride in his father's eyes when he read aloud the Commission of Divine Suzerainty. Nor would he forget the shock on his many elder brothers' faces, with the exception of Pyrsyrus and Long Swan. It still saddened him that his brother, Melyngoch, had openly expressed his anger and displeasure at the decision, but he had not impugned him, because Melyngoch's mother had filled his mind with vain imaginations as to his status in the family hierarchy. Nor had she brought him up in the Os-Syr-Tru religion, so he did not know to call upon the gods of his fathers or any other gods for that matter. A man without a god is no man at all, only an empty jar of flesh.

It had turned out to be a glorious spring day for the ceremony. Sur Sceaf wished his father and mother, Redith and the Thunder Horse, Ludwig and Rus-Syr-Hrus could be there with him to see the culmination of their valiant efforts.

The first act of the first emperor of the Pitters, Augustus Syth, had been the destruction of Mount Heredom. In those days when Syth had witnessed the pulling down of the obelisk, a slab of marble had exploded upon impact, sending a sharp projectile of stone into the emperor's head, resulting in his immediate death. From that event on, the entire vicinity of Mount Heredom was believed to be cursed by Herewardi wights, and the following emperor decreed the area to be off-limits to Pitters, essentially creating a no-man's land where even Hickoryan shepherds often feared to tread.

The new raising of the obelisk signified the renewal of the Kingdom of Os in the Ea-Urth and the restoration of the Lost Word of Hrus-Syr-Os. Sur Sceaf was humbled to be present to witness this memorable day. To his surprise, when he had visited Rhoda the Hag in the bastion, she had declared that for the first time she began to comprehend the significance of all that had transpired during the last five hundred years. She had admitted that she now believed that there were operative spiritual forces at play in the affairs of man that she had heretofore simply dismissed as the folkish lore of the unscientific.

Just as Sur Sceaf was tying the red sash of the Royal Bloodline about his loins, Brekka arrived to escort him to the mound. "Are you ready, Worshipful King?"

"Oh yes, my dear, I am ready."

"All is in readiness on the mound. So many people have gathered to do you honor and participate in this event that you couldn't slide a scramasax between them if you tried. And now, your chair begs your presence."

"Though inheritance and deeds have placed me as Father of Kings, I count my greatest deed the rearing of you, my dear. Let me remind you that it was your spiritual connection that brought all of this into fruition. None of this glory shines as brightly in my heart as you do, beloved daughter of my heart."

Beyond the hall the hawthorns were in full blow, and the box hedges were bright green. The sun shone brilliantly in a nearly cloudless sky, save for a single silver cloud which several had come to recognize as a prelude to the presence of Odhin or one of the chief gods. A soft cedarn breeze caressed the grassy mound where the Elf Waters had flowed in purity since before the time of Hrus-Syr-Os, as if appointed by the gods to witness this day. And the multitude drank of its healing essence.

Large long trestle tables stretched out in multiple lines on the grassy field in which the obelisk laid supine and gleaming in the sunlight. The benches were so crowded that there was little elbow room at the tables, yet the mood was festive. As soon as the crowd caught sight of Brekka and Sur Sceaf approaching, cheers crescendoed from the top of the mound to the valley below and all around. Like a rising wave on the deep, the crowd rose up until all were standing.

Sur Sceaf was deeply moved by the show of respect as he took his place in his appointed seat in the center of the top table. As haeligawaecca, Brekka had carefully chosen those who were seated with him: the king's men and lady knights, old friends and comrades, men who served alongside him throughout his numerous campaigns with courage and distinction.

Blood-Brother Mendaka sat to his left, while Big Brother Pyrsyrus was on his right. It warmed Sur Sceaf's heart to see so many others at the table as well; Juan Carlos de Sajones, A.P. Rockwell, El Yid, Long Swan, Ilker, Starkwulf and his beloved sister, Va-Eyra. Seated at tables directly in front were his wives and family, as well as Ruhm, Khem, Pluch, Rosenkrantz, Reedy, Loosestrife and Seamisch. Directly behind them the next king of kings, Arundel, sat with his comrades, including Yellow Horse, Redelfis and Going Snake. Appearing distinctly nervous in such august company, the newly commissioned Anghrus sat in the place of honor to Arundel's right. Though this clearly was a celebration of the holy rebirth of Herewardom, the reverential mood was accompanied by the high spirits of May. In fact, many of the celebrants wore the green in honor of the Green Cup which constituted the Big Dipper's spring phase and the pouring of green over the land.

Sur sceaf had just exchanged greetings with the king's men when the lurs commenced humming, announcing the imminent erection of the obelisk, symbolizing the Lost Word or the most fertile component known amongst the Roufytrof, the Godhi, and the Godija.

When the sound of the lurs died into silence, Brekka, attired in the priestly aubergine robes of the haeligawaecca took her place in full view before the obelisk. Beneath her hood her thick copper mane cascaded in ripples all the way to her waist.

Raising both hands to the heavens, she cried out, "O mighty Aesir and Elven Fathers of Old, we raise this golden shaft in your honor, and call upon you for your blessings over this mound, that from this place your word and your law may go forth to bless all the nations of the world. That your word may be understood in the Wessex Tongue as it is on Ea-Urth and in Heaven and that your law may gain the favorable acceptance of all who hear it. Lowering her arms, she turned to Sur Child and nodded.

"We of the Royal See wish to give praise to the man, Sur Child, son of the grand master, Muryh, and all due appreciation to the master builder for his unexcelled art and engineering skills that both designed and created this magnificent temple and obelisk. With this deed, the Herewardi may sit crouched upon this hill like a wisent bull and not be moved. Firm and established is this beautiful House of the Gods, from which the cries and prayers of our people may now be heard and answered."

Sur Child stepped forward, impressive in the traditional white tunic and bonnet mitre of a master builder. His gold breastplate was encrusted with jewels representing the Seven Houses of Herewardom. A red and white tessalated apron of a master mason circled his waist.

At a signal from the haeligawicca, the master builder ordered his masons and craftsmen to slowly pull on the creaking ropes, so as to raise the great golden obelisk to a living perpendicular by means of a lewis. Slowly and carefully the golden monolith with its pyramidal crown rose. When fully seated, the glistening shaft cast a long shadow directly between the two wings of the House of the Gods, The Aesir and the Vanir.

Sur Child turned to four, two-ton perfect ashlars each set in a cardinal direction, and announced, "These four cornerstones once sat here atop Mount Heredom marking the original corners of the Temple of Hrus-Syr-Os, and were located by Lady Brekka through her scrying. Each bears a rune carved and painted by the hand of Hrus-Syr-Os himself, representing the Four Cups of Heaven in their season. Touching each in turn, he intoned, "First the Green Cup of Spring. The White Cup of Summer. The Golden Cup of Autumn. The Black Cup of Winter. Together the runes spell the first initial of the four Ur Gods; Seth, Isis, Osiris, and, Nephthys."

In a booming voice, he repeated the initials, pausing between each for emphasis. "S. I. O. N."

A cheer went up when he finished. When the sound faded, he continued, "The memory of these ancient deities is so rooted in the Folk Mouth that not even the lore masters can plumb their depths. Now that our temple has been resurrected, these revered gods have a place to plant their feet once again."

Sur Child turned and walked up to Brekka, genuflected and said, "Lady Haeligawicca, with your permission I have one more task to complete."

"Granted, Master Builder."

As he rose to his feet, his son-in-apprenticeship, Unn, handed him an object wrapped in scarlet velvet. Sur Child then proceeded to cross the green sward to the high-table. He bowed his neck. "My lord and high king, you see before you on Mount Heredom the fulfillment of your grand vision. Here stands a beacon of light, liberty, and tolerance to all mankind. According to your decree it shall also stand as a warning to despots that the Dragon of Tyranny, should it ever present in this land, shall be slain at its gates. And, now, it is my great honor and privilege to present you with this mason's trowel, a symbol of spreading harmony among the Seven Nations." Slowly, he unhooded the velvet swaddling to reveal a golden trowel encrusted with the same seven jewels as on his breastplate.

As Sur Sceaf took it into his hands, he felt an instant connection. Upon examining it more closely, he noted the runic spell engraved into its surface. The letters were patterned after the Ancient Futhark Saxon Runes and proclaimed a blessing for the rising generations.

Sur Sceaf rose, and in his deep voice said, "I thank you, Master Builder, for the untold labors and contributions you have made to the Seven Kingdoms of Herewardom, carrying on in the same tradition as your visionary father, Muryh, whose sermons of stone shall outlast us all. And now, the Roufytrof has spoken. You shall go forth to the Isle of Redangus to serve the newly chartered territory of the combination Herewardi-Sharaka Nation in the same way that your father served the Syr Folk on the Isle of Ilkchild."

As Sur Sceaf resumed his seat, a cheer rose from the throng, reverberating over the Elf Waters and as far as the promontory, followed by a burst of laughter as a grinning Sur Child offered a flamboyant bow before heading back to the obelisk.

Sur Sceaf grinned, saying loudly for many to hear, "Methinks, Sur Child, in your heart, you are more jester than builder."

"Nay, my king," Yellow Horse volunteered. "Thou art comparing a plodding ass to a racing steed. Methinks the man should stick to building!" Another wave of laughter surged over the crowd. Ever the one to have the last word, the jester rose and gave an even more elaborate bow, earning another wave of laughter and applause from the appreciative crowd for his flamboyant manner.

Brekka waited for the laughter to trail off before raising her arms for quiet. "In my capacity as haeligawicca, I declare that The Kingdom of Os is returned to the Ea-Urth. Henceforth, the Aesir, those who from above to Ea-Urth have come, shall be frequent visitors and advisors here on the mound. In the ancient tongue *Eluma Enish*; as above, so below. Now, let us put the formalities aside as we celebrate the culmination of the Fifth Sabbath. Let the festivities begin!"

While the serving stewards brought out tray after tray of meat morsels, fruits, baked delicacies and humming beer, the Godhi swiftly erected a May pole on the green sward, festooned with streamers, flower garlands, and ribbons. Godija, the priestesses, bearing citherns, began the call for the gods to attend, and then musicians with their dulcimers, fifes, sitars, and drums began playing a lively tune. Eagerly, young women in colorful dirndls grasped the ribbons and circled the pole, until it was interlaced with ribbons of all colors. Spirits were high, especially among the unmarried maidens and eager young bloods of the princely lines. One-by-one, the maidens slipped into the wood, followed by the young bloods, and it was known in the Folk Mouth that the gods often attended the dallying in the greenwood, that the God Seed might increase in the Ea-Urth and the old blood return.

Pyrsyrus turned to Sur Sceaf with a devilish glint in his eyes. "Did you ever wonder if some of the babies born of these five nights of yore might bear your stamp?"

Sur Sceaf shook his head. "I've always bowed to the Council of Women and their sacred obligation to record and keep sealed the Book of Sireship as is their holy duty."

"And yet, oft time's blood will out. In fact, I have no doubt that the lass Ethelwyn, daughter of Hethwyn, bears the stamp of my seed code. Even Swan Ray remarked that she bore a strong resemblance to my eldest daughter, Halifaxi. Nothing gave me greater pleasure than the day Aethelstan took Ethelwyn to wife." He leaned closer and lowered his voice, "Before she passed into Valhalla at the hand of the Pitters, I always saw to it that she received a special gift on her birthday."

Sur Sceaf blinked his surprise. "Are you saying that Freyxus is your grand-daughter?"

Pyr nodded. "According to custom, I've never been able to publicly acknowledge the connection. I thought her slain in the arena in Frisco along with all the other captives, but when I discovered she had survived the arena and was in Stonyford, I asked my comrade Athelred to keep an eye on her and inform me of any of her needs."

"Aha, you're the one who anonymously purchased the steed, Lightning Strike, from Aelfheah and had it delivered to her. We all thought her benefactor was one of Aethelstan's old war buddies, but the price was so dear, we couldn't think which of them would have had that many solidi." Sur Sceaf grinned at his Brother. "Hell, Brother, I could have equipped an army with that amount."

"True enough. I knew Aelfheah would grant me a special price, but I dared not bargain directly, so I had to use Karl Throckmorton as my agent."

"Do you think Aethelstan knew of his wife's sireship?"

"I believe so, because Aethelstan once told me that Hethwyn claimed that her woodland lover had to have been a god in human form because he was so long of limbs and superbly made. And as you know, he always called me the Woodland Giant; his way of hinting without revealing."

"What's for certain is there is no narcissism in you."

They laughed.

As the day wore on, Sur Sceaf exchanged gossip and reminiscences with his comrades over a delicious repast and thirst-quenching beer. A golden light filled his being with the warmth and love he felt amongst his old comrades, his lovely band of wives, and the multitude of grandchildren weaving in and out of the tables.

As the final rays of sunlight bounced off the tip of the obelisk, it appeared to burn like a giant candle, betokening the time of nocturnal festivities was to begin. Musicians played their hearts out whilst Ka-Luna as the May Queen was paraded up the path of the mound to be joined in a dance by Forsetti in the role of the antler bedecked Tyranus, who gave his right hand that the evils of the world might be bound for a season.

The setting sun cast a long shadow that gradually engulfed the shaft of the obelisk. When it was completely engulfed, lurs blasted the final call for hopeful maidens to slip into the dark of the wood for the Fifth Sabbath Tryst.

"Appears to me there are more maidens than ever this Fifth Sabbath," Mendaka remarked.

"Tis true," Starkwulf commented. "So many young bloods gave their all during the Holy War. It'll be a long while until balance is restored."

"Still, what better occasion than the Feast of Ev'Rhett to commemorate these fallen warriors cut down in their prime that their seed may go forth in proxy for them throughout the Ea-Urth."

After a time, the trilling of many fifes issued the final summons to Robin Goodfellow and his Puckish band of lusty brethren to take to the wood in high spirits.

Leaving the young to their frolicking and dancing in the night wood, Sur Sceaf and company moved into the Great Hall where Ruhm had arranged for the honors and accolades Banquet. On the way, Taneshewa caught up to her husband. Weaving her arm through his, she whispered, "It's the Fifth Sabbath, and you're all mine tonight. When you're asked to speak, my love, remember to keep it short."

"Definitely, my love, but I have no control over my long-winded friends." He smiled into the warm glow of her eyes, and thought for a moment he could hear her thoughts of love in his heart.

Sur Sceaf and his wives entered the formal meeting room which had been transformed into a woodland bower, with garlands of ivy, colorful porcelain pots of robust acanthus foliage, vases of irises and paeonies of every color, as well as May knots and misseltwig hanging from the heavy hickory columns.

"Oh my," Ahy exclaimed with an expression of amazement lighting her dark blue eyes. "How lovely. This morning as I passed by, Wyth and Ynys had just begun on the bare bones of the hall, and look at it now." But Sur Sceaf had eyes only for his dear wife of over thirty years. On the edge of fifty winters she was even more beautiful than the day they married. Her long raven black hair gleamed like purest onyx in the soft hews of the candlelight, and her gilt-tinged skin was still smooth and soft to his touch. The mere thought of which made his body to stir.

Just as the remainder of his covey joined the two of them, they expressed the same appreciation for the attention to detail in the transformation of what was usually a formal hall with stark furnishings more suitable to council fires and the conversations of visiting dignitaries.

Freyxus separated herself from her bride-sisters and came forward. "My lord and ladies, welcome! On behalf of Lord Ruhm and my bride-sisters, I wish to express a Merry May and a Happy Albispiene to all. We are delighted and honored to have you here during the celebration of the Faery Moonth and only wish you had been here during the celebrations of the Pink Moonth."

Paloma smiled warmly. "On behalf of my lord and bride-sisters, I thank you for the hospitality you've shown us. And I must tell you, Freyxy, we can't wait to ride one of your drogs." She turned to grin at Milkchild, who raised her eyebrows. "Well, most of us that is!"

Milkchild excused herself, "Actually, Freyxy, I get dizzy just approaching the edge of a cliff. I think I'll watch the suicidal antics of my more reckless sisters from more solid ground. After all, like my father the Rabbi always told us children, never climb higher than you're willing to fall."

Sur Sceaf chuckled. "And yet my dear Milkchild is always eager to explore the sunken cities of the Amerikan Giants, the deeper the better in hopes of answering the many questions of how they lived."

"Ah, but I'm always rooted to the Ea-Urth, my love."

"That you are dearling."

Freyxus grinned at Milkchild. "Then you must meet Rhoda the Hag, who has vast knowledge and memories of how the Amerikan Giants truly lived. She's already told us truly remarkable things. Like men going to the moon and to the Red Planet of Tyr where she says some of the Amerikans may still live not having been exposed to the earth changes."

The ladies laughed, but Sur Sceaf believed that Rhoda had spoken truth.

"Rhoda has spoken of many astonishing things," he said, "but I must caution you to pass anything you learn through Long Swan before revealing it to others. The Roufytrof is determined to seal off much of this knowledge to prevent a replication of the technology outpacing those who would use it improperly, so that it does not turn and rend us to pieces as it did the Amerikans. We must always keep in mind the warning of Elrus that the Dark Elves take great delight in placing sharp knives in the hands of us mortal babes."

More and more guests streamed in, rapidly filling the tables and benches until it seemed the walls could no longer contain them. "I believe I'd better show you to your places before we all get trampled," Freyxus urged. "If you would please follow me to the high table, Brekka has arranged the seating, and you'll find place cards with your names on them."

"My lord, I need to have a word with Brekka before joining you," Paloma murmured. Affectionately, she touched his arm before scanning the crowd. As soon as she spotted Brekka and Ruhm near the door welcoming the new arrivals, she headed their way.

"Is something amiss?" Freyxus asked anxiously.

Sur Sceaf shook his head. "Don't mind her, Freyxy. Paloma and my sister, Va, have been clucking over me since my wounding at Wymouth. If they'd had their way, they'd still be spoon-feeding me in my sick bed."

"I disagree, my love," Swan Hilde countered. "You were the worst possible patient. We had to slip you poppy tears without your knowledge to keep you from ruining all of Va Eyra's brilliant work. If you recall, Dr. Shanks told us that you shouldn't have survived such a serious wound so near the heart, and credited Va-Eyra with saving your life by using the poppy tears and the crucial removal of the arrow that sat so close upon your heart that you stood but one knife blade away from the door of death."

"Ah, now I know why I had so many visions of mythical proportions. It was the poppy tears that made me so idle. What you fail to understand my dear is that a man of my ambition will die sooner from idleness than he ever would from an arrow to the heart, even if it were dipped in yew oil."

Swan Hilde shook her head and whispered just loud enough for him to catch it, "Stubborn as a Witan Jewell ass and as bull-headed as a wisent caught in rut." They wended their way to the table. "And to think I married that reckless rogue".

The high table had been placed on a movable platform directly opposite a stone fireplace large enough to allow a man to walk into it. A cheery applewood fire burned in the grate, adding to the mouth watering scents filling the hall.

Shortly after he and his wives were seated, Ruhm escorted Brekka and Paloma to the high table where they took their places; Paloma to his left and Brekka to his right, with one empty seat between them. At a nod, Ruhm continued to the fireplace where he mounted the raised hearth.

Puzzled and more than a little curious, he leaned toward Brekka and asked. "My dear, do you not wish to sit next to your father?"

She smiled. "Of course, I do, but this evening I've arranged a big surprise."

Before he could quiz her further, Ruhm declared in a thunderous voice, "Friends, family, Herewardi, and fellow landsmen, we are gathered here to offer up our gratitude to a man and a king to whom we all owe our freedoms and comforts in this life. But before we open the floor to comments, permit me to introduce to you a most distinguished guest, fellow warrior and dear friend to us all and most especially to Sur Sceaf, come to pay homage to his lifelong friend, our beloved High King of Herewardom." He looked toward the double doors in the rear. "Now it is my great honor to present to you, the president of Panygyrus, Chise."

The doors opened and a cadre of Apache braves marched forward, followed by a tall and imposing Red Man attired in brain-tanned buckskin heavily adorned with beads of turquoise, red, black, and white.

Sur Sceaf couldn't have been more surprised, particularly since he knew all too well the pressures of governing such a new and thriving confederation entailed. Turning to Paloma, he whispered, "Did you know about this?"

"I confess I did not know the president was coming." She glanced past him to Brekka. "This, I believe, is the workings of your red-headed girl and her clever husband."

Brekka laughed. "Mother Paloma is right, as always. My dear husband takes his role as governor of the Virginias very seriously, and is eager to enlist the president's stamp of approval of his plan to promote trade of tobacco across Panygyrus and other nations. But he also thought the appearance of President Chise would be a fitting finale to this special Fifth Sabbath celebration. I must tell you, Fa, Chief Chise was very eager to participate in honoring you, and even canceled a planned trip in which he was negotiating trade agreements with the Mexus."

As the newcomers approached, Sur Sceaf quickly rose to make his way around the table so as to meet his old friend halfway. Chise was now a heavily muscled, dignified man of nearly forty winters, but when he grinned, Sur Sceaf saw the image of the skinny boy of eight or nine Winters who'd just been rescued from captivity. He and his twin brother, Zoot, had been taken under the wing of the Wose, just as he had been.

"My lord if you would but loan me a few pence to buy sweets with today I would gladly make you another dream catcher on the morrow."

Sur Sceaf burst out laughing. "As I recall, you must owe me at least twenty dream catchers by now." They shared a bear hug. The audience exploded in cheers and whistles as Sur Sceaf and Chise seated themselves side-by-side at the high table. The president's braves took seats at the table with their good friends Mendaka and Zoot, Going Snake and Redelfis.

Ruhm waited until the audience settled once again before inviting, "Who will drink a hail and a toast with me to our lord and king, Sur Sceaf?"

"I will drink a hail and a toast to my blood-brother and king," Mendaka said. Dressed in beaded buckskins, he stood to proclaim, "Since our boyhood, Surrey and I were always the best of friends. In the many moons that followed, that friendship only grew stronger and stronger, surpassing the bonds of death which must surely one day overtake us all. Always, my blood-brother fought the good fight. In war his heart never failed him even in the face of the mightiest of enemies."

Many rounds of applause followed with frothy mugs raised and people yelling out, "Hear! Hear!"

It struck Sur Sceaf then that instead of presenting awards to others, he was to be the guest-of-honor. He resisted being publicly praised, not because he felt unworthy of it, but because he detested being the center of attention for long periods of time; yet social grace required it of him. Though he sat tall and alert, he was actually wearied to the bone by the day's activities.

Mendaka got a devilish grin on his face. "Of course there was a time I saw fear come over Surrey's face. But it was not in the throes of war. No, not at all! It was when he tried to win the hand of my fiery niece, Ahyyyokah Taneshewa." The hall burst into laughter. "I have never seen a soul so sorely tried as his was when he wrestled to win her heart, but he only managed to dig himself a deeper and deeper pit. I never saw him so anxious, not even when I pulled him out of a Pitter crypt, where they sought to make him their slave by scourging him and placing him under the rock of oppression and took him deep into the Valley of Death. Fortunately we found him, on the threshold of death in time enough to rescue him, and through the ministrations of Queen Va-Eyra she was able to restore him back to life once again until he was tenderly tended by his sweet wife Lana who showered him with her nurturance. Few there be who survive the pit, but the trial of the pit was nothing in comparison to his struggle in winning the heart of Taneshewa. Sur Sceaf, you will forever remain my brother and dearest friend in this life as well as the next."

Shouts of Waes Hael went up from the banquet hall as the company stamped their feet on the floor, clapped, and raised horns of hop and malts. Stewards stationed at each table rushed to refill horns and krugs to overflowing. When it quieted down once again, Ruhm asked, "Who will be next to drink a toast to our lord and king?"

President Chise rose to his feet, his mead horn held high. "I am come to give honor to a man I value more than any other in this world, save my father, Mescalero. I know that you Herewardi call him the Hring King, so this day I wish to honor the man my people call the King of Three Bloods by presenting him with this ring, which was forged by Abel Moses, an Apache- Quailor elfsmith personally schooled by Govannon the Alchemist." He held the ring high. "It bears a diamond representing his Herewardi Bloodline, a ruby representing his Red Man Bloodline, and an emerald representing the Quailor Blood. Let us all hail the Hring King of Three Bloods; showing that not only Nature, but the gods sought to weave our destinies all into one."

Horns and krugs were raised and drunk, followed by shouts of acclaim and praise, while a young Apache ring-bearer offered the ring. Sur Sceaf slipped the heavy, jewel-encrusted ring onto his finger.

Chise continued, "It is my wish to be as wise and fair a leader as this great king. Few there are in his position who willingly surrender power to ensure the future of a confederation."

Cheers and shouts filled the hall, lasting for several moments. When, at last, the hall was quiet, Sur Sceaf rose to thank his old friend. "I shall wear this with pride and gratitude. I cannot express adequately how deeply I will cherish it."

More cheers followed while stewards replenished the drinks. "I will be next," Pyrsyrus declared, rising to his towering height. With drinking horn brimming from the froth of mead raised, he boomed out, "I drink to my younger brother, who was always so filled with the light of intelligence since his youth. Insomuch that at age twelve I told Father, 'this brother is touched by the light of the gods. He can already scry hidden objects and plumb the depths of secret knowledge. Though he is wild, he possesses a grasp of law and strategy like no other brother I have trained.' Father took note and sent him along with Long Swan to the academy at thirteen, since the two were the perfect compliment of one another. Many times as a young blood he proved to be a cunning warrior against the enemy, and at seventeen in the Battle of Frink Glen he pulled off one of the most strategic defeats of the Pitter legions ever witnessed in the annals of Herewardi History since the days of Herald Godwinson. I have been honored to be his elder brother all these years, and knew from a very early date that he possessed the favor and love of the gods in double measure."

Numerous hails went up from the crowd as a well-groomed Starkwulf made his way to the hearth. "My dear friends and countrymen, I was a lone lost man, a mere Wose, filled with sorrows of living alone in the woods and deserts of this world, scorning the company of men when a young man of fifteen winters made it his mission to follow me up and down from place to place in an effort to improve his crypsis. For several years, he was the only human contact I ever had. After the Battle of Salem, in which his grandfather was killed as a result of my ignorance, I swore to be this young man's guardian protector. At the time I did not know it would lead me out of my sorrow, heal me of my grief, and place me in the arms of his sweet sister, Va-Eyra, the Desert Queen. I owe so much to you, Surrey, and like Mendaka, we will part for a season, but I think our paths will weave together throughout the eternities to come when Odhin sends us out of Valhalla with new swords and new worlds to conquer."

Rounds of applause and cheers went up as a tall blond figure made his way to the hearth and raised his horn to a toast of praise. "I am Ilker, the Lost Son of Taxus, who had the marvelous fortune to begin the offensive against the Pitter Empire in these latter days. Untimely as my attack was, it prepared the way for Sur Sceaf to plunge into the Taxus Lands, and once we were reunited, I realized he was the Anointed One of the Gods and not I. He was the one to carry out the mission I had so longed for. Once I came to know the works of Sur Sceaf, it did not take long to know that he operated under divine favor of the gods that love us, for his brilliance lit our way against an unconquerable Empire and brought it down into the dust of our feet forevermore." He turned his head and spit on the floor signifying disdain for tyranny, as did all the warriors present.

"Hear! Hear! O ye! O ye!" the people shouted as horns and mugs were raised to the ceiling once again.

A dashing black caped man with a sharply delineated mustache, a dark royale running the length of his chin, and two peyos framing the corners of his black hatted head walked up to the hearth. "I will drink to the king. Most of you know me just as El Yid, for I am a Jywd, but my true name is Zeru-Herewardi. My mother was Herewardi, and my father you will know as the Rabbi Amschel. As a very young boy, my uncle, Sur Sceaf, took me under his wing. He made me proud to be a Jywd but taught me all the cunning of a Herewardi warrior with a sword at my side and a fast horse beneath my ass. Early on, he set his hand to grooming me for the restoration of my people, and encouraged my love for the sea despite my father's many protests, and did it by appealing to everything I liked, while assuaging my Father's fears. He saw to it I was trained as a seaman and sent me on forays with Uncle Pyrsyrus that soon earned me my own ship and a host of Jywdic pirates to train as all my friends and classmates from the shiva joined me. I am here to drink to the king and to give him the gratitude of our newly formed Kingdom of Jywdah in Nu Yalk."

Thunderous applause went up from the crowd. But it did not take long until the hearth was occupied by a large Black Man. "Most of y'all know me as Khem, Governor of Wymouth. As a young man I followed Surrey out of the Quailor settlement of Salem, and we became like family as I traveled about with him. His boys and I became like brothers. At that time, we Blacks were few and far between, particularly out in the west. We weren't even sure any others existed. Once a few more Blacks were discovered from the Mys-Isys Labor Camps, Surrey suggested to me the pressing need to found a Black Nation. He is the rootstock of all nations here present. It was something I never thought to see, but here I am, some thirty years later, and we are fast growing, our numbers increasing daily. All thanks to Sur Sceaf."

People stamped their feet and cheered, as person after person rose to praise Sur Sceaf, including Hartmut Hagele and his wife,the beautiful

Lady Mendaho, Juan Carlos and his Apache wife, Tree Song, Chief Zoot, and numerous others.

When it was clear all who had wished had spoken, Sur Sceaf rose, raised his arms for silence, and declared, "Men and women of Herewardom, I thank you for the great honors you have bestowed on me. But I am nothing more than the peg your glories hang from. Now, with your indulgence, I have several important announcements to make. First off, King Arundel will have the Signet Hring of Kingship over Herewardom, and from his throne will go forth the law unto the Seven Kingdoms. Lady Brekka shall rule the priesthood as Haeligawicca here at the House of the Gods, from which the word of the gods will go forth and the ancient lost wisdom of long ago shall return. While I am sojourning here it is my intent to bestow kingship on Ruhm."

The Virginians shouted out their approval with rebel cries.

"First Lieutenant Seamisch declared we must get the two houses of Congress to grant him a special dispensation to be a monarch while he is occupying the Governorship of Virginia."

Sur Sceaf acknowledged he would need the approval of the Republic of Virginia as part of the due and lawful order. It would be a mere formality allowing Ruhm to operate in both the world of the Hickoryans and still practice the laws of Herewardom.

"Now, I wish to declare a new star has entered the Royal Constellation, for the gods have shown me in vision that the young Prince Anghrus shall inherit the Ancestral Medallion. I have conversed in great depth with the Roufytrof, and they have confirmed this as well. Tomorrow night, at the twelfth hour, I shall confer upon Anghrus his commission and anoint him for his holy calling to launch a voyage. He is charged to locate the Jewel of Ullr in the far-off distant lands across the Aegirean Sea in the Lost World of Ur-Ope, still unknown to us at this time, save only in the Folk Memory."

There was much cheering and shouting as Merri-Doo, Ugga, and Uffa of Anghrus' wolf pack heaved him high on a shield and did three perambulations around Sur Sceaf's table. After Anghrus was returned to his feet, Brekka stood. "As Haeligawicca, I hereby confirm the calling and election of Anghrus by the Roufytrof. I have sent a circular dispatch to the Seven Kingdoms of Herewardom requesting their time, talent, and materials in support of his mission. I have also sent out letters to the nations of the confederation to contribute what they can to the benefit of his explorations that will waylay the dark powers that are yet unknown, but which we know from our seeings in the stones and from Rhoda the Amerikan, for there are dark and benighted powers seething on the other side of the seas which we must prepare for. Again, as Haeligawicca, I would be remiss if I did not give honor to my father. All the freedoms we enjoy, all the sovereignty and self-rule, all the prosperity, freedom, and liberty we have, is because of you." She turned and looked him square on with tears running down her cheeks. "Because of you, the confederation is, and I am."

# CHAPTER 15 :

## THE WELL OF URTH AND THE WINDOWS OF HEAVEN

THAT EVENING, AFTER THE ACCOLADES of sumbel had all been given, Brekka sensed all was not right with her father. She recognized the signs that something was deeply troubling him. The Confederation of Panygyrus had enjoyed nigh six years of remarkable peace and a continuously growing prosperity. Indeed, it had been pronounced a cozy time with no great strifes and only petty robber bands to extinquish, though rumors circulated that the robbers were forming alliances. Some bone crushers occasionally wandered out of the woods, and several gyrlocks had been shot out of the evening skies, but all and all prosperity was pouring forth its bounty and times were cozy. Those with complaints were drowned out by the prosperity and freedoms most were enjoying. Only the lawless, the fanatically religious zealots, some few Dominikers, and robbers had any disaffection for the confederation.

Every city-state had tales of bumper crops, full granaries, and an increase in their flocks and herds. Yet it seemed to her that her father sensed that something was amiss. Since her childhood, she had learned to recognize the signs that something was troubling him—his wrinkled brow, a pulsating muscle in his temple, an occasional vacant stare, as though he were trapped in thought, and far removed from the company at present.

She had looked for signs of concern amongst his bride-covey, but if they knew anything, they gave no indication, save for Paloma's request at the beginning of the banquet that Ruhm not keep the high king up all night drinking. Still, she couldn't shake the feeling of uneasiness within her own bosom. Once the formalities of the banquet concluded, she accompanied her father and Taneshewa to the door. But before kissing him goodnight, she drew him into the night and asked, "Fa, what troubles you, man?"

"Nothing troubles me that I would care to discuss tonight, especially, with my beautiful wife lying on my arm. There will be time enough tomorrow. Thank you for everything this evening my dear. We shall address your concerns on the morrow."

He kissed her before he and Ahy were swallowed by the mist rising from the Elf Waters, leaving Brekka alone to ponder why, at a time of reunion and rejoicing, was her heart still so filled with an underlying turbulence, storm, and concern? What was this dark shadow that fell over her spirit like the sound of a distant dark wolf when one is all alone in the woods at night? Looking out the window of the hall, she saw naught but the thick mist that had engulfed the mound.

She had to get herself to prayer. She had to call upon the Gods at Tor-Illi for clearer sight. While her husband made joyous boasts of days gone by with his comrades in the hall, she made her way back out into the dark of night with no more than a lantern, and soon discovered her way into the Ancient Yew Grove of the mist shrouded mound where she called out to the All-Father and the All-Mother for further wisdom and light.

Raising her arms above her head til they nearly reached the first branches of the Never Dying Tree, she cried out, "Oh Gods of Osgard hear the words of my heart as they flow from my tongue."

She wrestled within her soul to make connection, reaching for the heavens a second time. "Is there no help for the king's daughter? Oh Freya and Woon, have you shut the heavens against me in this my hour of need?" She paused for answer as she lowered her arms. She sighed before raising her arms skyward for the third time. "Is there no help for a daughter of the Aesir?"

A crack of loud thunder was followed by heat lightning which rumbled over the Sacred Grove and burned in the sky like Ancestral Fire. The entire yew tree lit up in a pure white flame. Her eyes were immediately drawn to the two figures standing in the air before her. The first figure she quickly discerned was mighty in brilliance and appeared very much like Woon, only she sensed he was much older.

He introduced himself. "I am Ullr, who answers the prayers of all of my children and this is my beloved wife, Holle." He indicated to a female figure of equal magnitude standing at his side.

Brekka was speechless before she could formulate a plea. She had expected to encounter Odhin and Freya, but she sensed at a deep level these were the most ancient of gods. She stumbled through her explanation. "I, I, I am come to call upon the gods for further light and knowledge."

His lips did not move, but she heard him, as well as the woman beside him. All three minds had melded before the words came to her. "You want to know what troubles your father's heart, and what the great evil is you are sensing."

Without her lips moving, her heart answered. "Yes."

Ullr glanced at Holle, and then declared in loud thought, as if to address her every need and concern, "Odhin and Freya have placed us in charge of the Aesir. They have appointed us to sit in judgment upon their thrones while they are off visiting their other worlds and creations and wandering with the inhabitants thereof to take measure and to weigh the hearts of their offspring. We have come through the Rainbow Bridge as soon as Fair Heimdall heard your prayers and alerted us to your supplication."

With little warning, but with complete comprehension, wings sprung from the backs of Ullr and Holle. Soon Holle handed Brekka a set of what appeared to be the wings of a Thunderbird. "Place this gyrfalcon hame upon your shoulders, and together let us fly to the four corners of the Ea-Urth and we'll show what is, what is to come, and what evil thy father hath scryed."

She helped Brekka into the hame, stepped in front of her and raised a finger to her lips. "As Haeligawicca you may know these things and prepare thy people for the dooms that are coming, but not a word of it to anyone save only the Roufytrof, so as to influence them for the good."

Holle's wings spread wide and her mind instructed Brekka how to do likewise.

It was not altogether different from riding a drog, except they were capable of speeds surpassing the flight of an arrow. They were over the mountain coves of the Rdokians in a flash as they hurled in a tight kit above the Oheo Valley and crossed the Mys-Isys River. Brekka could focus on any detail below her and chose to see the mighty cities of the Buffalo Nations at will. It seemed the gods let her mind guide them.

They flew above Salmalheur and darted down to Witan Jewell then over the Aurvandilean Sea. She looked hard upon Godeselle and in an instant every aspect of the city was revealed to her mind's eye in a greater degree of consciousness than she had ever known before.

Soon she was hurled to Ele-Anor-Ness and many choice memories appeared in colorful beauty and detail. Very pleasant memories of her and Ruhm in their youth paraded through her head in vision after vision. What power this hame had to allow her to travel through time and space at will, she could not grasp.

Ullr revealed, "If we had wanted to, we could have gone to the precise event of you and Ruhm dallying and gathering coquitos in the jubea plantation. Just know that with this hame, the event will always be there for you to return to.

She blushed at her flirtations with Ruhm while on a hunt. She decided too many of her secret and intimate thoughts were being shared, and she thought to divert her guides by heading to Moon Door where, in less than the blink of an eye, she saw the beautiful Marbled City of Wizards in all its splendor, and could even see Ilkchild lecturing his newest stall of young wizards, including Ka-Luna and Forsetti before they were married. It was as if she was standing right before them insomuch that she wondered how that the River of Time could be ever so present and one was at liberty to go anywhere forward as well as backward at mere will.

Ullr declared, "From here on I shall light the path and show the way and show you the things your father was shown, that his troubles shall be made yours."

They turned north and west from Moon Door to cross the vast expanse of the Aurvandilean Sea until they came to a stretch of lands that ran from steppes to mountains.

Holle declared, "It is the vast land of the Russ. It is called Russland."

Brekka looked with her inner eye, which came to her as easy as looking with her outer eyes. She beheld tall men, powerfully built, of blond hair and fair of complexion, setting to sea in boats under the aegis of a dark wolf. She was brought to understand that they were men of war, hungry, and determined.

Ullr declared, "These are the lost seed of Odhin, fallen under the sway and spell of the Dark Elves for too many generations, determined to loot, pillage and plunder. Behold their abominations."

Suddenly, a collection of the most frightful of beasts appeared before her vision. First came powerfully muscled creatures that blended the body of an ape, the head of a vampyre bat, the claws of a badger and eyes as red as the flames of Hell. Holle called them Hellhominids marching by the thousands into ships beyond number as Holle told her that the Russ are also master seamen, but were kept from saling to Panygyrus by the many encounters with the Kraken and the shark-wyrms.

Next came pack after pack of Fenris wolfmen with bull-like muscles bulging under their coarse shiny black fur and features like those of a werewolf— yellow eyes, long grizzly-like fangs and claws, shiny wet noses and pointed ears. In her mind's eye she was given the knowledge that they had the ability of rudimentary speech. As she observed, she noted that they were obedient to every command of their Russ overseers as surely as sheepdogs obey their masters. She knew in her heart that the design of the Russ was to ravish Panygyrus with their beastly shock troops and shucks. These Shucks were not unlike the dog men she had seen in the wild lands of the north during her battle with the Vardropi. But the dog men she had encountered were self-willed and lacking in speech.

Long Swan's teachings came to her. "The Dark Elves swim through the Ea-Urth to extinguish light and raise up dark powers against us. They are entities that seek the destruction of all that is beautiful, good and light and provide inspiration to perform dark works. Beware their cunning and deceptions."

Ullr waved his hand before her face and the vision was gone. Now, they soared higher, and with exceeding speed passed over lands numberless to man until they came to what her heart told her were the Lost Lands of Ur-Ope.

As they crossed various bounds Holle declared certain names; Germania, Scandanavia, Enki-Lahn-Tiy-Ea. "All these lands are in the possession of Odhin's seed, begotten by his many shield maidens and placed under the protection of the Great Northern Woods. There is one amongst you, the son of King Kanarus of Wilona's hearth, whose spirit name is the Deep-Minded One, but whom you know as Ang-Hrus. He it is you must admonish to take to the seas, and I shall give it into the heart of the Lore Master Long Swan to set the Young Blood Anghrus on a quest to locate the Hring of Ullr, which shall empower him to drive back the giants, the trolls, the Dark Elves, and the Hatetadons; creatures and people which always seek to break down the boundaries of the peace of Odhin's seed, our national enclosures, and to extinguish the Ancestral Fire of our people. Above all, remember the West Saxon Tongue is the tongue of freedom by which all nations of the Ea-Urth shall be set at liberty for it is given to no other tongue to do so. Therefore, cultivate it among the inhabitants of all lands; perfect and purify it. It is the greatest weapon we have bestowed upon mankind since the operative runes acquired by Odhin for his offspring and their betterment. The tongue of Wessex has been ordained as the leaven of nations to bring down the haughty and to lift up the meek and holy."

Holle explained, "We do not show you all the lands under the heavens at this time. Only those your generation will encounter." She pointed to the far south where they came upon a dark and benighted people, Corsairs of desert heritage, who traveled upon camelids under the sigil of a scorpion. "Acting unknowingly at the behest of the forces of darkness, under the swords of compulsion and tyranny, they first subdued their own people before going forth to crush the will and cultures of other tribes. Through the doctrine of submission, the tool of Dark Elves which were perfected in other worlds, they brought the inhabitants of their land into bondage to the will of the Pale-Dark Elves. This is that which the Council of Gods has strictly declared to be the enemy of all free peoples. It is the same pattern of evil employed in all worlds, by agents of the Dark Elves, some who sell their souls for gain, others deceived into collaboration by dark devices and secret combinations."

Ullr declared in a powerful thought, "Behold the Hatetadons. They are the children of hate, and there is no light in them at all. They are wholly under the spell of the Dark Elves and are currently being held in check by the Ashanti-Boer Alliance."

Immediately, an image appeared before her of powerful Black warriors, who inhabited a large land in the south, and she saw also a nation of White Men, lovers of freedom, liberty and self-determination. These two nations were sworn together to hold back the tyrannical expansionist designs of the Hatetadons.

"The alliance is good, but its boundaries will not hold, for the time soon comes when the Hatetadons shall spread to the lands north and to the lands south to sorely plague all the peoples on their borders with their unrighteous dominion. The foot of the Hatetadons shall be on the necks of many kings, both Black and White, increasing misery, torture, and oppression in all its forms, ultimately leading to a mighty war of Ragnarok and the Twilight of the Gods. It is then that the Deep-Minded One, the Anointed Son of Aesir, shall take up his calling and election to go forth on his white horse conquering and to conquer. He it is that shall break the scourge of the Hatetadons and utterly extinguish them by the Sword of Righteousness, for the gods shall lay them to the edge of the sword and bring upon them a consumption that is overwhelming with justice. But only if Ang-Hrus lives true to the Osyr."

As they traveled ever farther to the south, Brekka was astounded at the beauties and beasts inhabiting the Great South Land. "I see so many different lands; jungles, savannahs, and deserts. Oh look, what in the world are those mounds that look like giant pyramids?"

"Those are the marvelous works and wonders of the First Generation of Gods, attesting to their works in the flesh in the Ea-Urth."

Holle clarified, "Thinkest thou ye have seen many lands and wonders? I tell thee, Brekka, Daughter of Sur Sceaf the King of Three Bloods, before thou art of many days, thou shalt behold the gardens of the universe in the gyr falcon hame, and live to record the wonders of a thousand isles in the seas of the night sky in the Holy Archives at the Great Temple on Mount Heredom where thou shalt seal it up for the viewing of the Roufytrof only."

After a swift flight back along the coastal lands of Ur-Ope, they came upon the majestic land of Enki-Land-Tiy-Ea. She could think to call it naught else, and, besides, through the mind-meld she could feel Ullr and Holle's great love for this land above all others. "Hear now, Haeligawicca, we must alight in the Holy Grove where lies the Sacred Hring of Ullr that ye may mark its placement and map it for the Deep Minded One, who alone is destined to wield its force and tame its power and subdue the Dark Elves under his foot in this world evermore."

As they circled for a while above the most beautiful emerald land that she had ever seen, Ullr said, "Behold, Enki-Land-Tiy-Ea. This was once a great isle but has since become one land and rejoined Germania of Ur-Ope during the Ea-Urth changes. The seas were driven back, and it became one with the Fatherland. At one time the connection between Enki-Land and Germania bore the name of Doggerland. In times dark to man this was a gathering place for the sons of men where they were instructed in the ways of Heaven until we determined to veil the Holy Well from the profane, and covered it with a veil of the waters of the sea and thus, placed sea wylfs to watch and guard over the Great Well of Urth. Now, after its' unveiling by the Ea-Urth changes, it is guarded by mazes of deep and dense forests of beech, oak, hawthorn, and yew until such a time that the Deep-Minded One obtains its prize. This will ultimately bring about the return of the gods, faeries, and elves to dwell among men, as well as the restoration of nature's glory, where plants, trees, mushrooms, man, and beast shall grow to their full potential and vigor. It shall be an age when the lifespan of man will equal that of a yew Tree. All sickness and disease shall be banished. All the Seeds of Odhin shall be redeemed and see eye-to-eye. Once again, the Gods of Herewardom shall sit on their thrones on the sides of the north and the nations of the Ea-Urth will say, 'See, let us go up unto the Fair Ones and learn the ways of the starry heavens and of the gods who from Heaven to Ea-Urth do come."

Soon, they were hovering above a large beech grove. In the grove Brekka beheld a stone well of ancient design from which the very ashlars sang the praise of Mother Holle. The forest about her was filled with faeries and beings of light that joined in the song. She could not entirely make out the language they sang in, but it was hauntingly alluring, and the song seemed to speak of the great treasures that were laid in the depths of the well.

There was a dome of light which prevented mortal eyes from seeing this grove, perhaps because the well contained sacred objects of power and glory which existed before the foundations of this land and all the creations of this globe. She knew these powerful spiritual beings guarded forces unknown to the mind or heart of man, but they were soon to come into the hands of the sons of men at the appointed hour in the future, after they had developed their spiritual maturity and powers. Thus, the barriers of the heavens could be lowered for them.

As Ullr led them down through the branches to land a few feet from the Primordial Well, Holle said with great reverence, "Behold, the Holy Well of Urth."

Brekka leaned upon the huge perfectly fitted stones and gazed upon her reflection in the deep dark water below. Soon, she felt a powerful vibration humming through her. At the same time, a commanding female voice inquired, "Who goes there?"

Brekka understood in her heart that it was indeed Urth, the Oldest of the Norns, who spoke in a voice that was both old and youthful in one.

Ullr replied, "Tis the Seed of the Woman who shall groom and prepare the Deep Minded for his appointed mission."

"Then let her behold the sacred trust of this Holy Well, an honor few mortals have been granted, for the wells of the universe are guarded against the greedy eyes of mortal man and Dark Elf alike, that their usurious hands may not lay hold of its timeless treasures. Worthy art thou, most favored daughter of the Osyr. Indeed, the Seed of the Woman is worthy to behold these powers of fertility, creation, and longevity kept safe in the Treasure House of the Gods, contained in this most Sacred Well. Behold, the very Navel of the Ea-Urth."

Ullr placed his right hand over Brekka's face. Her inner eye beheld a jeweled Hring of sun-infused gold with ancient runes of power written in its interior surface. Immediately, the Ur-Fyr told her that the hring was created before time and had not been forged in this world, but was star metal from another world more ancient and advanced than this one.

"He who possesses the hring shall judge the nations. This can be none other than the Deep Minded One, Ang-Hrus, Son of Kanarus, favored of the Gods and of Woon's Daughter's hearth. That is provided he prove worthy after being sorely tested and tried, as are all who are chosen. It is written in the runes, and it is written in his seed code, but since the Laws of the Gods grant free will to mortals, even if he should prove worthy, it shall be his choice to accept or reject this grand commission. Again, by the Laws of the Gods, all that would be a blessing unto him shall turn into a cursing which shall invoke the scorn and wrath of the gods. But should he accept, he will come with his japer and together they shall come through the furnace of affliction to take up his throne which hall shall never lack for seed to sit upon the Throne of Hereward, but the gods' love and longsuffering endures forever."

Another, more youthful, but equally penetrating, voice came from the unfathomable depths of the well. Brekka assumed the voice belonged to the Maiden Fate, Skald. "We Three sisters spin Os Frith to the rising king, the Young Prince Ang-Hrus, whom we hid under the hand of Red Knife and thence through many masters until he was passed and raised to the sublime tutelage of the Seed of the Woman that his grand commission could be fulfilled. All hail the rising king." This was immediately echoed by the faeries and the sylphs in the surrounding wood echoing "All hail to Ang-Hrus."

After spending considerable time listening to the voice of Urth, who in her great wisdom, instructed Brekka in the vital duties and responsibilities of a haeligawicca, Brekka soon understood in her heart that she was to choose the japer who was to be Anghrus' right hand man. She was overwhelmed by a compulsion in her mind's eye that this jester advisor was essential to serve as a counterbalance to the princeling's obvious pride and cocksuredness. Immediately, the image of Merri-Doo, grandson of her dear mentor, Jacky-Doo was emblazoned on her mind.

It was made clear by Urth that it was Brekka's calling upon her return to use all the powers of her office, position and considerable prestige to persuade the other leaders in Panygyrus to make available all necessary resources Ang-Hrus would require in order to ward off the great evil that was purposed to come upon him. She would wait til the morrow when her father came to the council fire to divulge what she needed to reveal and to ever conceal, for it was not meant to be known to any, save only the Roufytrof and only when thoroughly tiled, secured, and beyond prying eyes and ears, so that no Dark Elf should discover their plan or design.

She looked at Ullr and Holle, who by some unknown prompt, nodded, and she knew it was time to leave. Sweet songs arose out of the well as they took to the air. With a turn of her head, the gyrfalcon wings lifted her up next to them where they flew across the Great Aegirean Sea and soon started their descent for the Yew Grove atop the Sacred Mound of Big Springs.

Holle smiled and said, "Keep the gyrfalcon hame; learn all its uses. You will see it can transport you through time and space as needed, but it is to be employed by none other and must be locked in the crypt of the temple."

"I thank thee for answering my prayer this day. I thank thee for the gift of the hame, Holy Mother. And, most of all, I thank thee for making clear the vision which the gods had imparted to my father through his scrying. The matter has weighed so heavily upon his soul. Now I may share his burden and give him the hope you have shown me this night."

Ullr spoke once again. "Be warned. Ang-Hrus must make his calling and election sure, for if he does not fulfill the ends of his seed code so as to thwart the Dark Elves, the whole of Panygyrus and its freedoms will be once again plunged into chaos, blood and horror such as existed in the day of the Pitters. Thus has been the fate of other worlds before this, when men of the mould yielded to the sinister persuasions, temptations, and enticements of the Dark Elves, who are not of our seed code, but are alien life forms from darker realms, lacking altogether in love, compassion, or mercy. Few and evil are the days of mortal man, and throughout time, many have succumbed to the temptations and allurements of the Dark Side. Witness how quickly the Tree of Liberty withered under the ill care of the Amerikan Giants. Only through the endless labors and courage of Sur Sceaf were the Dark Elves ultimately overcome throughout Panygyrus. But as with all mortals, the King of Three Bloods must pass the baton of kingship to another and one day answer to the crowing of the Golden Rooster in Valhalla who sends forth his summons sharper than a two edged sword. Now, Anghrus, as the soon to be anointed possessor of the Golden Medallion of Hrus-Syr-Os, has been set apart and sealed for a commission to ensure the security of Panygyrus, but, like the commission given to your father, under the Laws of Suzerainty, the fulfillment of that commission rests solely in his hands."

The next night after the feast, the moon was a silver-white sliver in the dark star-studded sky. Whistling ducks and spring peepers sang in chorus, joined occasionally by the melancholy hoot of an owl. The night air was filled with the smoke of applewood fires drifting through the feathery yew branches like gossamer blue curtains atop the Holy Mound. Dark shadows of the surrounding menhirs fell upon the grounds like the footprints of the gods. At Sur Sceaf's bidding, Brekka, Long Swan, Arundel, and Anghrus had gathered for the calling and anointing of Anghrus for his grand commission.

Long Swan, acting in his official capacity as high priest and prothonatory scribe of the Roufytrof, wore the white gold-trimmed swan robe of a lore master, while the other men were dressed in the usual Cordovan leather tunic, white silk shirt with cravat, and red sash of the Blood Code. In honor of the occasion Brekka had donned the flowing aubergine robes of the haeligawicca.

Though this was far from the pomp and circumstances of a formal ceremony such as Sur Sceaf's anointing, Long Swan deemed it to be in the interest of prudence that, not only must the official calling, election, and anointing of Anghrus be held immediately, but that it also be held in secret in order to keep this secret knowledge from the dark entities of the Nether Realms and their sinister workings for as long as possible.

After the participants formed a circle beneath the yawning branches of the Ever Living Tree, Long Swan raised his swan staff and intoned solemnly, "It behooves us to offer up a prayer to the gods before we set the lad apart and anoint him to this solemn and holy calling. Brekka, would you do us that honor?"

Brekka nodded, raised her arms high, and cried out, "Oh Holy Ullr and Holle, hear the words of our mouths."

The fellowship repeated the words aloud.

"Grant unto us this power to bestow on this young prince all the rites and keys pertaining to his sacred charge as appointed by Urth, the greatest of the Norns."

A warm wind lifted the branches of the old tree as the fellowship said in unison, "So mote it be!"

Sur Sceaf was amazed at Brekka's degree of spiritual awareness and suspected this was the reason the gods had granted her greater access to their actual presence on Ea-Urth than most of the godija and godhi. It merely confirmed to him that his dearly beloved daughter was indeed highly favored by the Osyr.

Long Swan ran his hand over the top arch of his staff. "My dear Lady Brekka, it would interest me to know why you called upon the Old Gods rather than our Holy Mother and Father as is the usual custom."

"Noble Long Swan, yestereve, after sensing that Father's heart was much troubled I called upon the gods for comfort and enlightenment. Here beneath the Tree of Ygg-Yung, I was blessed with the divine presence of Father Ullr and Mother Holle, who are in charge of this world and its heavens while Odhin, Freya, and his other wives make their rounds to their other worlds, which their seed inhabits by the millions. These Old Gods have gifted me a gyrfalcon hame, and together we flew faster than a bolt of lightning, whereupon I was shown many lands on our sphere heretofore known only to the scientists of the Amerikans."

"Unto what end, my dear?" Sur Sceaf inquired.

"I was prompted by the Ur-Fyr to seek answers in order to confirm the validity of why your heart seemed so troubled. In answer to my pleas, the gods granted me a visitation in which they showed me the same vision that had been revealed to you, but with further clarification."

Long Swan handled his staff as if he could hardly contain his eagerness to hear more. The young prince stared wide-eyed as he adjusted the Suebi knot at the side of his golden head of hair.

"Pray tell," the lore master asked, "what did Ancient Ullr show thee?"

"He showed me several wars going on between numerous tribes. One was the Ashanti-Boer, a combined alliance of Black and White Nations fighting against a most dreadful and tyrannical nation called the Hatetadons. The Ur-Gods declared that the Black and White alliance would hold the Hatetadons at bay until the times appointed when a king of the Herewardi would rise up to challenge them; at which time they will over the wall of the Aegirean Sea like another deadly plague of rats upon Panygyrus. At that same time, a fierce menace shall also come from the West by a warlike people akin to us and called the Russ. May the gods save us from the wrath of the Russ, for they come with the most abominable of forces to ravish Panygyrus. They bring with them the offspring of Loki. Fenris wolfmen like in appearance to the dog men we encounter from time to time in the mountains, and certainly in the North Lands."

Sur Sceaf murmured aloud, "And as we have learned nothing short of elf steel and fire can bring them down. Weapons of iron are useless against these naturally armored trans-humans."

Long Swan leaned on his staff and pulled off his hood as though to hear well. "Does such doom have any redemption? Brekka, did you see more?"

"Oh yes, Lore Master. Holy wonders! I beheld our salvation lies in the depths of the Well of Urth." Looking directly at Anghrus, she said, "Anghrus, you are to find and wield the Hring of Ullr. It is a deed woven long ere this world had air or water. And in the age before Ea-Urth, you were appointed as a spirit and one of the brightest stars in Odhin's quiver at a time when you were called the Deep-Minded. It shall be for you a quest, and when the hring is obtained, our enemies will melt before it like frost before a hot sun. But, mind you well, you shall go through a furnace of affliction and temptations before you may obtain this jewel of power. Loneliness and a traitorous journey await you."

Sur Sceaf's countenance lifted, "You speak right, Daughter. My heart was troubled. I only had vision of the evils the Dark Elves purposed against us. I was visited by the War God, Tyr, who told me that our salvation would lay in the deeds done by the Young Prince Anghrus, whose fate hangs by but a strand of a spider's web. But he had not revealed to me the power of the hring and of its forging in some other world."

Brekka added, "There was something else Ullr and Holle impressed upon my mind."

Sur Sceaf leaned closer. "What is it, my dear?"

She turned toward Anghrus. "It is known that you and your fathers are filled with vanity and pride. Your very seed code screams it."

Anghrus nodded.

"To this end, the gods have deemed it necessary for me to appoint unto you, the jester Merri-Doo, who is to be the counterbalance in your great quest. When you are going in full stream of your heart, take heed to the words of Merri-Doo as you would to the nose of your own favored hound when hunting."

"Quest?" Long Swan inquired curiously.

"Yes. Anghrus is to take a fleet of ships and warriors across the Great Deep of Aegir and seek for the hring in the land of Enki-Land-Tiy-Ea."

"Ah, yes, the island nation Rhoda called Eng-Land."

"Yes, but it is altogether different from the land she remembered. It is still in possession of the seed of Odhin, but the gods have pushed back the seas that separated it from Germania and heaved it up out of the deep to make it one with the land of Ur-Ope."

Sur Sceaf turned from her to Anghrus. "Son of Kanarus, since first I heard of your heroic deeds as a man-child, when you so bravely overcame the venom of rattlesnakes and stopped the mouths of mountain lions to survive the hardships of prolonged thirst and the deprivation in the Great Desert, I knew the gods had already forged you for some yet unknown greatness. Lad, I was little older than you when I set out on my military career under the tutelage of the Wose. Sit on this rock at the base of the yew and let me bless and anoint you with the holy yew oil, that you may lead us safely over these menacing hordes of trolls that the gods have fore-shown us."

At a nod from Long Swan, Arundel stepped forward and bowed his neck to his father. "According to your decree, most High King of Kings, I surrender this Ancient Medallion of Howrus to the newly anointed king, Anghrus. With it goes the rites and honors of lifting and forming the Kingdom of Enki-Land-Tiy-Ea." He removed the glittering medallion from around his own neck and turned to Anghrus who had just arisen from the lichen-covered rock at the foot of the Ever Living Tree. As Arundel slipped it over the new king's head, he declared, "Worthy is the Deep-Minded One to rule and reign over the seed of Odhin in our ancestral lands. What the gods have placed in your hands, no mortal man can remove. Remember always, you have been anointed to be the shepherd of Odhin's seed. Though thy sheep are scattered in the wilderness, weary, worn, and torn by tyrants who oppress, they will recognize their shepherd's voice when he arrives and will gather under the ensign of Heredom which thou shalt raise high unto them. So mote it be."

All present raised and lowered their arms, declaring three times, "Waes Hail, Anghrus!"

As the participants walked back to the hall, Sur Sceaf drew close to Brekka and put his arm around her shoulders. "I thank you, my bright and shining star. My soul can now rest easy in the knowledge that the mantle has been bestowed by the gods upon Anghrus' strong shoulders."

Brekka smiled up at him, her eyes bright with love. "So true, Fa. Now you can take joy and rejoicing in your seed. And those who love you will take joy in your countenance."

During the summer moonths that the High King Sur Sceaf assisted his daughter Brekka in setting up the temple with the proper furnishings, the decorum of its guests, and the proper handshakes, grips, and tokens for admittance, Governor Lee was called upon for assistance down in the southern lands. The Hickoryans that had not yet entered into organized city-states called for help in eliminating the monsters, the tyfons, and the gyrlocks that plagued them and their herds.

Ruhm reflected on his march into the west of Tensey to hunt a roving band of tyfons who were ravishing the livestock on the large plantations there. Il-Alim's man, Donnerschlag, had provided and had waited for Ruhm to arrive with the beast stoppers, gas bombs, in order to kill the monsters without unnecessary loss of life or limb. The efforts to eliminate the beasts by the locals using their bows and spears resulted in a great loss of life and thereby greatly reduced the male population of the Land. This in turn brought the prowling robber bands in closer and emboldened them to make in roads into cattle rustling and molestation of the countryside.

Ruhm, along with Donnerschlag had easily dispatched the monsters with the beast stoppers they brought. The communities of West Tensey and the Mys-Isys Regions expressed their gratitude for eliminating the beasts, but then sued for help against the robber bands whom they were unable to repel from their wild areas. The tales of mayhem and robbery so infuriated Ruhm that he and Donnerschlag set out on a campaign and launched a hunt for the robber bands.

The people of the Mys-Isys Region had reported that the robber band that ravished them was upwards of three hundred, but as Donnerschlag did his scouting he discovered that many more robber bands had come to join the original invaders. Ruhm had only brought a cavalry of twenty-four and Donnerschlag his band of twelvers. No accurate count of the enemy had been taken, but Donnerschlag postulated it was upwards of five bands, and therefore in the area of fifteen hundred to two thousand robbers. Donnerschlag could tell by their direction that they were heading for the Wedgewood Plantation Region just outside the boundaries of Ophir.

It was determined that the loss of cattle from this plantation alone would devastate the economy of the region and result in collapse of the surrounding communities, thus placing a burden on the surrounding city-states. There was no time to send for reinforcements and both Ruhm and Donnerschlag agreed the best course would be to strike the enemy swiftly and thereby convince the robbers that the Hickoryan forces were greater than they had antipated.

After a day's ride Donnerschlag located the robber camp in the vicinity of the small village of Flora. As the enemy camp was bedding down for the night Ruhm launched a direct slaying foray down the center of their camps thus stirring up a real hornets' nest.

The robbers were angrier than hell, but Ruhm had taken a healthy slice out of their forces, thus compelling them to build bonfires and tighten ranks. But Ruhm had not chosen to fight them there where his meager forces would be completely vulnerable. Instead they rode some twenty miles off to some high ground of their chosing from which they would engage the enemy.

Donnerschlag commented that although the stone outcroppings provided protection, they had no water, and if they waited for the enemy's hounds to find them out, and stayed for the fight, then they would likely lose their horse flesh and be compelled to drink horse blood to stay alive.

Ruhm was torn. He loved his horses as much as his men. But he saw no way out of this sacrifice. These people and their cattle needed and trusted in his deliverance, and if they did not engage now, the robber bands would only become more emboldened. He noted that there were no reports of robber bands in the whole of Ophir anymore. Khem had rooted them out of those lands permanently. That is what needed to happen here. To leave would have resulted in the total ravishing of Wedgewood, and this community was simply too valuable to let fall.

In the distance, the cry of the enemy hounds could be heard. His far seer, Indigo, grandson of Pita Blufre was his eyes. He announced, "The hounds are on a bee line for us. We're likely to git hit in less than a fortel of an hour."

"Thank you for that report Indigo." He secretly wished he had brought the wyrm cats with him, or at least a larger detachment. He upbraided himself for not having brought a greater fighting force. With the wyrm cats he could have easily dispatched the hounds and then played attack and flee, attack and flee until the enemy host was worn down, but there was no fleeing those hounds. The stand had to be made. The sacrifice of some of his best horse flesh had to be committed, and this was not going to be a guaranteed victory by a long shot. Even in a victory the losses would be high. It wasn't long before his reflection was broken by the hounds in a full cry. The comfort was in knowing they had led the enemy horses and hounds through some punishing brush, and he and his men were rested and ready for the fight.

When the enemy was within range, Ruhm ordered three volleys of arrows, and the robbers all along the lines fled back in disarray, revealing that they did not understand military decorum. Hounds were fallen; horses were screaming and kicking, many running off with arrows in their necks and rumps.

The battle recommensed and burned hot throughout the daylight hours, only to subside with the setting of the sun. The enemy withdrew for the night. As the crickets began to sing, Indigo spoke to his pack leader, Donnerschlag, "My lord, if you wish, I can do reconnaisence in the enemy camp. My skin is dark and is not easily seen in the night," he being blue-skinned and of the Cerulean race.

Ruhm knew Indigo was supposed to return to Winchester with him where his bride, Lucy, was to meet him with their child. "I don't know Indigo. I don't want to lose you."

Donnerschlag interjected, "His fate is already spun by the Norns. If you compel him to stay here he may endure a worst fate, and he is the best at cyrpsis. I recommend we send him."

Ruhm was still not accustomed to the Herewardi's absolute trust in the concept of fate, and he had a hard time swallowing this line of reasoning, but realized he was now Herewardi, and thus tried to trust in their implicit belief in fate. "Very well, do what you can, Indigo. That which would be of most value to us is for you to some how cut their mounts out from under them."

The Blue Man gave a broad smile, "That will be an easy matter, Governor." He pulled what looked like a sack of grain off his hip.

"Grain?"

"It's yew seed, General Lee. A few of these sprinkled in the feed, and there won't be a horse standing in the morning."

"I hate the thought of killing horses, but by the gods, it will put our chances at surviving a lot higher. So be it."

"It shall be done, my lord."

Ruhm slapped the Cerulean on the back and he disappeared into the field before them.

By the time the Morning Star, Earendil, had risen, Indigo returned to report, "Won't be so much as a neigh to be heard in that camp today, and I managed to punk several of the band's leaders."

"Well done, Indigo," Ruhm acknowledged. "I fear if we are to make the most of our water, we are going to have to save our piss for drinking. Comrades, prepare yourselves for a long fast." He had contemplated the loss of life this battle would cost before the sun set this day and it had robbed him of sleep all night. *Oh holy gods who love us, deliver us this day from the evil blades of our enemies, and show thy infinite ability to bless in the face of adversity.*

The robbers awoke in a rage. They were not used to not getting their way. They had assumed they walked into a fat and indefensible land only to find that they had met their match in a measely band of Herewardi and Hickoryan warriors. They hurled themselves into the battle like frothing rabid dogs to be hurled back by shield and buckler followed with thrusting short swords. The battle raged fiercely, when about noon the enemy was just beginning to make their first inroads. Donnerschlag lost three men, and Ruhm six. Ruhm's men were excellent cavalrymen used to battling in the saddle. The moves of infantry were not as well known to them, but they still far surpassed the enemy in their haphazard slicing.

Several of Ruhm's men bound their own wounds on legs and arms from unshielded arrows. No sooner had the enemy begun to make inroads than they sounded a retreat. This came as a shock and an unexpected boon. Never had a bugle retreat sounded so sweet. He simply had no idea why the enemy would sound a retreat and not press the advantage they had gained. He sent a young scout, John Wilkerson out on the field to ascertain what the cause of the alarm was and why the retreat. The lad came hastily back and reported, "My lord there is a large host approaching from the rear. They bear the banner of a black cougar on a green background."

"Praise the gods, it is the legions of Ophir."

The lad tilted his head, "You mean the Blacks?"

"None other."

It did not take the Ophireans long to sweep the field. Their commander, Amanuel, rode up on his mule.

"Commander," Ruhm said, "you are a wonderful sight this day. You just saved our asses. In the name of the gods, how did you know we were here?"

The large Black Man gave his winning smile,"In point of fact we did not. Willi Howard of the Wedgewood Plantation sent his scout, Ken Creel, to report a large band of robbers were about to plunder their Anghus herds. When we arrived to their aid, it was easy to track the robbers here."

"I pray I shall be able to repay your help someday."

"Well, you saved us from hunting them down. We've got a lot invested in these herds. We purchased three thousand head on futures alone. It's my hope you'll return to Wymouth with us. I'm sure Khem will be delighted to see you. He would love your company."

"As I would his, but as you know I am currently entertaining the high king, and must hie back to Big Springs forthwith to the wedding of the Young Prince Anghrus and the Princess Sunniva. But first I have to negotiate a timber sale with Hoor at Paw Paw. So please give Khem my heartfelt gratitude and tell him how pressed I was. I shall take my leave forthwith."

"I have heard there is much invested in this Anghrus; and they say Sunniva is as fair as the rays of the sun and as bright of intelligence. Please take a moment to repose. Have some Muscadine and Scuppernong wine before you depart."

"By the gods that would be most kind of you. We could use the refreshment."

Indigo chided, "Its better than drinking piss." They all laughed.

Ruhm's reflection on the last fortnight floated away like a cloud on a windy day with only the warm smile of his Black friend remaining for an instant. He called a rest at the fork in the road to Babb Mountain and realized he was less than a holler away from Winchester and his beloved wives, Liza and Melissa.

"Gentlemen, let us pitch camp for the night, and on the morrow we will arrive in Paw Paw to negotiate the timber sales with the Rdokians."

The next day they doubled their pace and were riding into Paw Paw at least two hours before their appointed meeting with Hoor. It took another hour before a scout was able to locate Hoor in the woods and announce their early arrival.

The leather faced man took off his hat and nodded a smile at Ruhm. "Governor I did not expect you so soon or I would have had some vittles waiting for you. I'll see to it you get some nice country ham and a little 'shine.'"

"I'll pass on the shine. Salted pork suits me fine."

"The misses will get you some dandeleon wine. Something tells me you're here for business and have something more pressing to do besides drinking with an old friend."

"You are most observant, my friend, I have neglected my wives, and also have a wedding to attend. I've been gone over a fortnight."

"Nothing beats the feeling of going home after a long journey. Many were the times I pressed through brush and blizzard just for a night or two with my family before heading back out to war. I am familiar with the feelings of a wanderer's heart."

"So are you ready to get down to business?"

Hoor looked at him with a raised eyebrow, "I'm ready to do some dealin', but I should warn you, there's a man here says it would be better if'n we did business with him. He says his company don't require us to leave half the timber standing, But it seems his major complaint is that you guys will Heathenize us and destroy our worship of the Blood Rood which we Rdokians hold most dear."

"This man you speak of, is he here now and where does he call from?"

"Feller said he was from the Isle of Ilkchild, a place he called Hockney, but was born at Two Rivers and has returned to his home there."

"Was his name either Etzel Grubs or Gordy Swinerd?"

"That's right, Swinerd was the name. He be tellin the folks that living under the Herewardi is worse than livin under the Pitters."

Looking the leather faced man straight on, Ruhm asked, "Is this what you believe of us, Hoor?"

"Of course not! I have proven you Herewardi in days that are past. T'weren't hard to see this Swinerd was full of greed and malice. Wanted to undercut you and cast awful aspersions on your folk. I told him, ain't you heard we live in a confederation now and our president is an Apache. We enjoy more peace and have self-rule and ain't ever felt more free."

"Is he still here in Paw Paw?'

"He is. I invited him to the timber negotiations. When my wife heard him speak at the town hall, she near likely was gonna split his skull with a rollin pin had I not took it from 'er. She gave him an ear full. Said there ain't no Rdokians would ever betray their friends, cause we don't never switch horses mid stream. I tell you truly, we don't forget our friends, and we have a hell of a lot to thank Lord Arundel for. There was no hope in any land afore you Herewardi came, and I told him straight up that I didn't care that you all had kings and queens and a hundred wives each; That it don't make no never mind, because by God and the Holy Blood Rood the fruit that grows on that tree is the sweetest I ever et. And that's a fact. The Herewardi ain't never done naught but good to me and mine. Far as I'm concerned the Devil can just have the rest."

Anghrus decided he would take the road less travelled. He veered to the east to cross the Opequon River, and traveled many miles until he came upon Cat Haven. He had heard the Lazy Jokers talk about how much they enjoyed this area and something powerful was drawing him to it. It could have been the Jokers descriptions of the place being a hide out from which they had wreaked havoc on the Pitters or the descriptions they gave of the hunting and fishing in the area. At any rate he was compelled to spend a day there, and then after he had fully satisfied his curiosity he would pick up the trail to Winchester at Wizard's Clip on the Opequon and go straight to Liza's home to meet his new bride in an arranged marriage.

Her name was Sunniva, daughter to Ilkchild, and from all accounts a truly bewitching beauty of insurmountable wit and wisdom as well as a blade master at the Academy of Moon Door. She had come via the Monastary of Leakey down in Taxus where she received her religious training under the greatest of skalds and godija. He was proud of his heritage, but there were times it became a pain in the ass. Too many seemed to want him to be a man overnight, but there were still boyish moments he longed to snatch, and this moment in Cat Haven was one of them. He would fish, run around naked through the forest glades and scream and yell with all the abandon of a moonstruck Wose.

A small swift flowing stream ran out of Cat Haven and into the Opequon. He drank from a nearby spring only to spew the waters out, the sulphar taste lingering for some time on his tongue. "What the Hell!" The old shaman Red Knife had always espoused the virtues of sulphar water. Out of deference for his friend he swallowed a few swigs before wiping his mouth and wading up stream in just his loin clout whilst he tossed his sack of clothes and tools over his shoulder and scouted out a good fishing hole. As he walked farther upstream he turned rocks and collected helgramites from beneath them. He even managed to trap a few minnows in the canary grass.

He watched several trout, spotted a large mouth bass, a couple blue gills, and an eel swam into the nearby bank. This was the place he could be free of all the encumberances of protocol, courtly manners, and the ever expectant teachers and guardians he was forced to hear. He felt as free and wild as Cernunos, the God of the Wood. He sat upon the grassy bank and watched hummingbirds drinking from the yellow tubular blossoms of the touch-me-nots lining the bank. He remembered his Lazy Joker friends had said there was nothing more beautiful than the thousands of lights coming from the glow worms that lit the banks of this stream in the night.

It wasn't long at all until he had hooked a few wigglers with his fishing line. He placed a willow branch up through their gills. He had watched a large golden trout playing on the outer current of the stream where it wrapped around a rock and after the third cast he hauled it to shore. His lips smacked with anticipation. Now he needed to build a fire and cook the mess of fish up. Then he would do some exploring, for the Jokers said a group of hunters had found some Heathen gold along this stream, objects shaped by intelligent hands, but of which no one could discover a use. The men carried the strange objects of gold and silver back to Bunker Hill, but found that the objects lit up in the night and they all suffered high fevers and nausea. They so feared a wight had cursed the treasure that the next day they hurried it back to where they found it and swore they would never return.

He began digging a U-hole for cooking the fish just as Red Knife had taught him. His small shovel struck an object when he was about a foot down. He tugged on the object which felt like slate. Finally, he took his scramasax at his ankle and pried the slate loose. It split off from the bedrock below into a flat sheet which he eyed carefully. Embossed on the surface was a perfect imprint of a fern. It was a fossil from the time when the land was wild and covered with trees.

He smiled as he slipped it into his sack. His bride-to-be would cherish it. It was said of her that she knew all manner of wortcunning, the knowledge of plants. He dug another hole about ten inches away from the previous one when he once again struck bedrock. Now he must join the two holes from the bottom so as to complete the U and build a fire in one side of the hole.

As he plied his scramasax to tunnel from one hole to the next he used his fingers to carry away the loose soil when he felt what seemed to be a thick root about the size of his wrist. He tugged at the root or whatever it was until he felt it give and he dragged it up to the surface. This time he felt the root vibrate and feared he may have trapped a bee or velvet wasp between his hand and the object or worse a nadder-viper. Suddenly cool green beams of light began emitting from the object he held in his hand. Upon closer examination the object was about ten inches long and the light it shown was luminous like faery-fire or that of a lightning bug or a jack-o-lantern mushroom.

This was certainly no mushroom, and the metal the object was made of was not any metal he had ever seen. He had worked with his fair share of metals at the alchemist's forge with the greatest of wizards, and this metal was unlike anything they forged. It had the ability to shine as brilliant as the sun one moment and then as soft as a green moon the next.

Looking with increased curiosity he now descerned curious runes and swirls he could not read. They were similar to the elfabet, but different, more refined, and unknown to his generation. He held it up in wonder for perhaps a fortel of an hour. This was a find. Perhaps a gift he was meant to find, and there was no wight guarding it. But if a gift, was it anything more than a jewel? What were its origins, its history? It came to him slowly that he had dreamed of finding this jewel and it felt like he had been there before. He immediately felt a sense of ownership, and then drew it to his bosom and declared, "Mine!"

But would he own it or would it own him. Perhaps it was a tool of some Dark Elf and it would consume him or alter his thoughts so that he would no longer even know himself. He decided there would be a fouler feeling if this was such.

He decided it was a treasure and that it was a good thing. The skalds had told him that Mount Heredom had a connection to Cat Haven, but he hadn't listened that day. He continued to stare at the column with its remarkable magical lettering from top to bottom as if its maker wanted to convey some advanced message or knowledge. He yearned to know their meaning. Was the lettering Elvish, Vanirean, or Osgardean?

For a while he had forgotten how hungry he was, but young bloods seldom forget hunger for long. Quickly he got into his ruck sack and pulled out a piece of vellum with the Poem of the Wayfarer written upon it and wrapped the cylinder carefully in it before placing it back in the sack.

He then set about getting the fire going by stuffing sticks in one side and lighting the other side with a flint and a piece of amadou mushroom.

The fire began to take on a nice glow from the air flowing through the U-hole. He cleaned and skewered the fish, his mouth watering and his lips smacking in anticipation. He reached into his ruck sack for a small box of honeycomb which he placed on a nearby rock. He knelt down to blow the fire hole and add more hickory faggots. As he commenced puffing, he caught a glimpse of two bare feet before his eyes, followed by a melodious female voice.

It so alarmed him that he fell backwards into a supine position looking up at what he could only characterize as a flawless virgin, perhaps thirteen to fourteen winters.

"May I join you?" The faery-like creature asked. "I have a bag of berries and a bag of mushrooms, if you are of a mind to share with a fellow traveler?"

Speechless, he scanned the paw paw grove and the butter nut trees, then looked up the narrow stream. Where had she come from? This was certainly no wight and no Dark Elf. Red Knife taught him there was always a confused or dark feeling if a Dark Elf approached you, but all the same they could cunningly deceive you and confuse your normal logical processes.

Every feature of hers was in harmony with the others and she was most pleasant to look upon. Her voice was only what he could imagine elven speech to sound like and indeed it bore the same tones he remembered his mother singing to him when she put him to bed in the Apache Lands of the White Mountains.

"What is a young virgin doing in these woods all alone? Have you no sense or fear? Or are you touched with madness?"

"I certainly have no need of fear and I have oft traveled this trail from Big Springs through Cat Haven to Wizard's Clip, and thence to the short-cut through Mosby's Wood. I've never been accosted by man or beast, troll or Dark Elf."

"Well, I'll be scared for you, because no maid in her right mind would ever make such a journey alone."

She laughed a musical laugh that sounded a lot like the trickling waters in the brook beside which they sat.

Frustrated, but extremely intrigued, he said, "I should like to know the short-cut through Mosby's Woods, maybe you could show me." After all, if the poor girl was to prove to be mad he felt it was better to play along with her and then see to it she would be claimed by some well-meaning guardian.

"I'll show you. It is the way Major Mosby and his Grey Ghosts used to ride."

*That is it. She must be mad. How could this mere maid know the ancient history and Mosby's Raiders?* "Please sit with me and we shall share. Here you have the trout."

"I think I've found a dear friend in you."

"Why do you say that?"

"You gave me your best fish didn't you? That speaks of good character."

"Very well, let's have some of your berries and put a little honeycomb with them."

She sat with her back against a hickory sapling and nibbled daintily at the fish, which she  chased with a couple black raspberries followed by a bite of honeycomb.

He stared at her inordinate beauty, at the same time half chastising himself for the desire to seduce her, though he knew he wouldn't. "A young woman of your attractiveness would make an easy target for a man less gentleman than I am."

"Oh, you are a gentleman are you?'

"By that I mean I am Osyrtru."

"You are Herewardi and I expected no less."

"Still there are vile enough creatures that prowl this land. Like murderers, rapists, corsairs and the outcasts of all societies."

She made a distinct mocking, "Psst! Do not fear for me. Would you be off or from?"

Her bravery excited him. "I've been in training and am off to Winchester to fetch my new bride in an arranged marriage, but I am quite sure I shall love her."

"And you know this how?"

"It's very easy, I love almost all women. Besides it shall be a royal wedding and I have heard her to be both smart and pretty."

She laughed so pleasantly he paused to take it all in. He was more and more drawn to this maid and began wondering if maybe she was a woodland faery or nymph of some sort, maybe even of Elvenkind. "Have you no kith or kin in these parts?"

"Kith, kin in these parts, well, yes, I suppose I do. As a matter of fact they're all over the place." She gave her musical laugh once again. It wasn't an insane laugh, it was something indescribably endearing.

He had to smile at her. She awakened a brotherly sense of protectiveness in him. He had to admit, despite the utter queerness of their meeting he found her absolutely irresistible and delicious company to be with. *What would Sunniva think of me traveling in the company of someone so attractive? For that matter what would Lady Brekka think, who is both my nigh-mother and Sunniva's chaperone and protectoress. All well, I'm not about to send her into the dark wood alone. I owe her in the name of all woman kind to extend to her what ever protection she needs, even if she is so damned fool hardy.*

"I suppose you know I shall have to tell my new bride that I was your protector through the wild."

"Oh, don't bother, I will tell her I was your protectoress."

He had to laugh. By the gods she was spunky and comical. As they walked along together he noted that she was barefoot and only carried one bedroll. It wouldn't do for them to sleep together so he would have to build a long fire to keep her warm in the night.

After they passed Wizard's Clip and greeted a few strangers of Hickoryan extraction on the road to Bunker Hill they decided they could make it to Mosby's Wood by nightfall. When they arrived they found the hot embers of a previous traveler near a large old oak backed up to a locust grove. He extended the fire, while she made them some mushrooms wrapped in elacampine leaves, and they bedded for the evening.

Tree crickets commenced their songs and the dark canopy of the heavens soon spread over them. As he hauled several large logs over to the fire he stated, "you know, I didn't catch your name."

She looked over the fire at him. "I am known by many names. Just call me Dawn."

After telling various stories to one another to pass the evening he found himself admiring her. She was delightsome to converse with and well versed in ancient lore. He enjoyed her company so much that he wished they had farther to travel together. As he stared across the fire at her in silence her face seemed to transform into that of his mother. "Mom, is that you?"

He didn't mean for those words to blurt out like they did. Fortunately she did not respond. His hope was that she had not heard, but momentarily he felt she was transfigured into his mother, and he wondered if the mushrooms and the elecampine hadn't done something to his perceptions.

Dawn smiled and once again her face resumed their usual structure. She began speaking in a melodious tone, "You are a valiant young warrior—the pride of the god, Baldur. You have to shoulder so much more than other young bloods of your age. I can see you are the hope of your bloodline." She paused as if to draw a picture of his face so focused on his eyes was she. "You loved your mother very much, didn't you?"

The words extended down through his ears and into the core of his heart like the proboscis on a butterfly. He could not help but let her drink of his deepest feelings. "As a matter of my heart, yes I loved her dearly. Perhaps my eyes were just playing tricks on me, but for a moment you appeared to assume her visage." He shook his head to make sure he had his proper senses about him. He had never experienced anything like this. "How is it you can know so much about me?"

"I have been amongst the braid-heads of Herewardom and heard them speaking of a young prince who has come to the east under the advisement of the Roufytrof, one favored of the gods, perhaps even a son of the White Goddess. That is all."

"This would tell me you are Herewardi."

"More like the Herewardi are me." She laughed teasingly at the paradoxes she presented to him.

The enigma of this girl just got to be more and more confusing, but then he also felt like he knew her. He had to get to know her better. "It would suit me very well to become better acquainted with you, Dawn. I am booked at the South River Club and I am sure accomadations can be obtained for you. You can meet my nigh-mother Brekka. If anyone can untease your being, it will be her. For none see better than she."

"I would like that very much with the charge that you do not encourage your attraction for me any further than that of friends. I perceive your heart contemplates me a bride, but friends alone we shall always be. You shall find no wife here, even though I know I am purely of your liking."

Was she playing hard to get? How did she know he was attracted to her? He had to laugh so as to break her bluntness. "And why not?"

"Because a different Fate has been spun for you and I that does not include the romantic fantasies your horny young mind is currently contemplating."

"Oh, so now, the maiden is a seeress and reads the hearts of men."

"Such is not unheard of among those of my race."

"And of what Race of Herewardi are you?"

"The First!"

"So you are of the First Nation?"

"I didn't say that."

"I'm not sure what tribe you are, but if you feel the need to be cunning and evasive then suit yourself. I believe you have caught me in the net of the Sire Sheaf, and I don't have time for their riddles nor do I wish to fish through your indirectness. Your company has been charming, your wit stimulating, and it's made my journey pass swiftly. I hope it does not offend you, but I think we should turn in for the night."

It seemed the morning came in the blinking of an eye. They were up and on the road before the first rays of the sun had pierced the East. They passed through the north gate of Winchester and were immediately slung into the traffic of wagons and buggies heading to market with trains of pedlars and pilgrims coming into the city. It was but a slight jaunt to the South River Club and Inn. It baffled him that the South River Club was on the north end of town.

Upon entering the tavern, Anghrus offered, "May I buy you a drink before we seek accommodations?"

He waited an answer as she studied the listings on the black slate board. She turned with a mischievious smile and said, "I'll have the panther sweat."

"No, no, no! It is made from powerful herbs and decoctions that would make a young maid such as you cry, weep, maybe even get lustful."

"You horny boy, is that all you ever think about? Where's your hospitality, I want panther sweat."

"Alright, alright then, but I shall have to say I am your guardian or you won't get it."

The lanky bartender made his way down to them and said, what'll it be young man?"

"Two panther sweats" and just as the bartender began to protest, he added, "and I am her guardian."

"Suit yerself. Ain't no law says a young blood can't have a drink with his fiancé. I swear she looks even more pretty today than she did yesterday."

Anghrus wrinkled his brow and thought the old fool was probably mistaking her for someone else. The bartender turned, and his skinny hand searched for a bottle of green hue on the back of an upper shelf. As he returned with the elixir, he reached under the counter and then plopped two cannons in front of them. Have at it?" He opened his hand for payment.

Anghrus reached into his pant pocket and pulled out two coins freshly minted with the image of an eagle owl of Virginia on the front. "Pardon me just one moment sir, would you know the whereabouts of Miss Liza Martin?"

"She's upstairs with the Lady Brekka." He gave a puzzled look before stating, "I thought that's where ju came from. She's preparing a young bride from the isle. I thought it was the lass here, lessen I be erring."

"That would be my fiancé."

"They would be awaitin you up thayrr. Would you like me to fetch them down heayr?"

"That won't be necessary. We'll show ourselves up after a drink or two." Anghrus was bemused that Dawn launched right into sipping the green elixir with much relish. First she had placed her finger in the liquid and sucked the contents off it before she gently sipped and then swished before swallowing. She laughed that beautiful laugh that was loud enough to catch the attention of several yeoman and a bar maid or two.

"It's delicious. Everything I ever heard about this drink is true. It's a masterpiece." She swirled the green contents in her cannon and then swiftly swigged it down.

Anghrus gingerly put the cannon to his lips and drew the contents across his tongue. It had the cool bite of sage with an exotic trail of herbs unknown to his palette. Suddenly the cool green fire lit his body from head to toe in an all encompassing warmth that caused a feeling of radiant coziness to settle into his being. "By Thor, that's some good stuff."

A nearby bar maid offered Dawn, "Go easy on that stuff sweetie, or you'll be kicking your nickers off before he gets you to the wedding bed."

Defiantly, Dawn slugged down another shot and retorted, "I'm just drinking for the pleasure of it. It will not affect me in any way."

"You're a sassy little tart. I was only offering some good advice."

"And for that I thank you, Trish, but I am not like you. I did not drink it and kick up my heels for a few pieces of silver."

The bar maids mouth went agape. "Why, you little hussy! Who told you my name and where did you hear that crazy story?' She began to assume an aggressive posture before the bartender said, "You don't want to go there Trish. They be Miss Liza's guests."

The bar maid backed away only to have Dawn follow up with another insult. “No you don’t want to go there, Trish, because you wouldn’t stand a chance against me, but I meant you no harm, only wanted you to know Johny will be coming for you within two weeks with a proposal for marriage.”

The bar maid looked utterly surprised as did those standing nearby. She turned to Dawn and asked, “How do you know such things?”

“I see things. I hear thoughts. I know things.”

The bartender seemed to be creeped out. “Just so you youngins know, I rang Miss Liza’s bell. She’s been ‘specting you.”

“Well, Dawn, we mustn’t keep our hostess waiting. Shall we?” Anghrus rose up, re-corked the bottle and hooked Dawn’s arm to lead her out of the bar.

As they exited the bar they took the stairway to the upper floor where a doorman announced their arrival. Dawn tugged at the crook in his arm. “Please, allow me to introduce myself to the Lady Brekka and say not my name I gave you.” She laughed. “This should prove quite interesting.”

“Honestly, you are a bundle of contradictions. Normally I would not honor such a request, but I go along with this one for your sake.”

Miss Liza was the first one to greet him with a hug. Her raven black hair emitted the rich scent of rose perfume. As they entered the living room copal incense burned near a vase of cut daffodils and daphne. “Oh Anghrus wait til you meet your bride. She’s got the same color of hair as you, eyes as green as emeralds, and she’s smart as a whip.”

Dawn followed him into the room. He had not introduced her because she requested she present herself. Liza gave him a turn of the eye as if to rebuke him for his lack of etiquette. Instead she acknowledged Dawn with a bow at the neck.

The Lady Brekka caught his eye from across the room. She wove an arm through the young Lady Sunniva’s and escorted her to meet him. Upon approaching him he was impressed with her well-fitting light green gown that displayed her feminine form to advantage. She had long blond hair and a gentle, almost child-like face. As he began surveying her features he was suddenly taken aback at her clear resemblance to Dawn. Is this a cunning trick? Could she be a twin? Has Dawn merely been testing me? And if a twin, will I be expected to wed both? That is a prospect I am not at all opposed to. He no sooner made his observation than Dawn went before him to introduce herself.

First she introduced herself to Liza and smiled, "Miss Liza, I'm just a traveler who had a chance encounter with Anghrus at Cat Haven. I'm on my way to Paw Paw and could sure use the accommodation tonight if you can see fit. He said you might be able to put me up."

Liza was speechless. Presumably, it was from the almost identical appearance of Dawn to that of Sunniva. Brekka had a very quizzical look on her face before she imperatively stated, "Of course you can." Then looking to Anghrus said, "But who is this young lady?"

He remained silent, because Dawn had said she wished to do her own introductions.

Dawn blurted out, "I am Dusk. Anghrus and I became fellow travelers through the Wizard's Clip and Mosby's Woods."

Liza finally found the words to say "See you not the likeness, Brekka? These two maidens could pass for twins."

He now knew this was no trick by Brekka's design. Nor was it known to Sunniva who looked on in utter amazement, as if she had just witnessed her spirit exit her body in some out of body experience.

Brekka appeared to be calculating and summing up the situation. "I mark their likeness. Methinks Ilkchild plays us. He was ever the trickster, and he has sent us Sunniva's Twin."

"By my troth, my lady," Sunniva exclaimed, "I know her not and know not how to know her. She is ever bit my own image. See, she bares the same scar on her neck that I have, won through a stick fight with my younger brother Markwood at the Bacon Day Fair. Verily, I know not how this maid comes to look like me."

Dawn responded, "Alas, the Queen of May stirs oft the blood of youth. Perhaps we sport the same father?"

"But the scar," Sunniva placed her fingers to her neck to mark it.

"I acquired it in my travels. Ladies, I shall impose on your good kindness no longer than to gather what I have come for and to protect what is my own."

Anghrus held up the bottle of green elixir, "Anybody for a cordial?"

Miss Liza declared, "Sure, the occasion is ripe for celebration. That liqueur is of my own making. It is fire for the soul, oil for the tongue, and ease for the heart. I say what better way to get to know your bride-to-be."

Sunniva went to the walnut cabinet and procured the necessary cannons. Anghrus poured, and everyone partook as he told of his strange encounter in the woods with Dusk and his discovery of the curious cylinder.

Brekka suggested he show it them. Unlike when he found it, it no longer emitted light. Brekka studied it closely. "The writing is of ancient origins. It is Elvish and from the time when elves and gods enjoyed this world without the encumbrance of the quirks and contentions of pestering mortals. I should like to take this implement into my study and get a more thorough reading on it. The elves buried it in Cat Haven for a reason. You were meant to find it, and we are going to discover its use."

Dusk smiled, "True to form. Lady Brekka thou art a genius. It is no wonder the gods so highly favor you and Anghrus. You too have found their favour, for no Elvin artifacts have been found since the days of Elrus the Wise."

Sunniva spoke up, "Husband, my Father said I would be pleased with you, but I thought him merely to be comforting. I see now you are favored and you are certainly handsome as a bullfinch and quite pleasing to my heart."

"What did your father say of me?"

"That you were the son of a goddess and the hope of the Baldurean Bloodline and both wise and brave, though I know not how he should know such things, since you are no more than a young blood and were never known to grace the academy."

Dusk threw her golden hair back, "Not all wisdom and knowing come from the academy. You must never make that mistake. Indeed none too few idiots have passed that way and fill the river of knowledge with their damnable trash.

Sunniva was quick to retort. "My father prides himself on producing the best scholars and wizards in all of Panygyrus."

Dusk held up her hands in a halting gesture. "You take me wrong, Sister. My statement in no way reflects upon your father's skill. It's just that not all apply their hearts to seeking out wisdom, and way too many merely muddle through their schooling in an idol stupor more suited to an ox or an ass than man. The Academy of Moon Door has attempted to rectify this and has produced some of the finest skalds of all ages, both male and female."

Brekka seemed to be pondering heavily the words of Dusk.

Sunniva observed, "You are a very opinionated maid for someone of such tender years as myself, I wonder you should speak with such authority."

Dusk smiled, "Wisdom is not owned by the passing of years, nor by sex, neither by rank, nor by wealth. I apply my heart as deeply as I can and live in every moment. Knowledge is power when governed by wisdom."

"Well, said, Dusk," Brekka remarked, "I regret that most of my youth was spent learning the art of war. Had it not been my calling, I should have liked to have spent more time at the academy on the cliffs of Abandon by the Sea."

As the day waxed on Anghrus marveled at Sunniva's wisdom and beauty, and found her to be most pleasing, despite it being an arranged marriage. History had shown that many of the greatest pairings had been arranged marriages. But this was the first time he believed it.

Dusk and Sunniva had sat together and conversed freely like the best of friends. He would catch Sunniva listening intently and then look up at him with a warm smile. When Dawn, or as she now chose to be called Dusk, joined in open conversation, she shot questions to everyone present that would cross a skalds eyes. When she was presented with philosophical questions it was remarkable with what ease she addressed them, and that to everyone's satisfaction.

Miss Liza had nine cats. All were Havana browns, mahogany in color with forest green eyes and as sleek as Belgian hares. It was well known that they had no tolerance for anyone save Miss Liza, and they went to great lengths to avoid petting from anyone. However, these cats clustered near Dawn and vied for her petting, even over that of Liza's.

Liza shook her head, "If that ain't a strange sight. No one has ever been capable of petting my cats. How do you do it, Dusk?"

"I have a way with cats. All cats are drawn to me."

"I don't understand it. They take to you like catnip."

"Nothing short of magic, if you ask me." Brekka declared, "Not a one of them has ever let the rest of us approach them."

Conversations and games went on into the evening as Anghrus found himself more and more fascinated with his cousin, Sunniva. He was pleased the Roufytrof had linked them to be husband and wife, and was now anticipating the wedding bed and the years ahead.

Everyone had one last cordial before Miss Liza showed them to their rooms. Dawn had announced that she had some pressing business to attend to in Paw Paw at the House of Ido, and that she needed to depart early in the morn. The company wished her well and invited her to stop in anytime she was in the vicinity. Anghrus was forced to admit he found her as pleasing as Sunniva, but she made it perfectly clear she wanted no romantic attachment at all.

The room Miss Liza assigned Anghrus was decorated with the most ornate of cherry wood furnishings, with displays of bone-plate porcelain in the hutch. The walls were painted a rich, carmine-red with an almost purplish hue. His bedstead had two dragons circling one another and had a large soft feather tick spread over it. He availed himself of a hot bath that the servants had drawn for him and laid back to look out the black mirror of windows framed by heavy maroon drapes. While he soaked his bones in the penetrating warmth of the copper tub, his mind went over his sojourn there in the Virginias. Everywhere he had gone he had been afforded the best of treatment and hospitality, but there was always the added burden that people expected more of him than he was capable of delivering. When he had trained under Il-Alim in crypsis he had sensed how much more the master expected of him than he was able to perform. Then Redangus drilled him at sea in a crash course of seamanship. El Yid insisted he repeat the training in parkour until he felt he would rather die, only to realize that Yid would suffer nothing but a proficient to leave his ship. The only way out was through. *Why did everyone expect so much out of me?*

He yearned for his days gone by with his Apache Master, Red Knife. Red Knife was always so patient and permitted him to develop at a natural pace. It's true that none of his recent masters had ever said a word to him about his failings, but their body language communicated frustration with his slow progress.

Now he had come for his spiritual training under the Lady Brekka who was his assigned guardian and protectoress. She was no less demanding and indeed, it was her that pressed him to get a bride-covey going, that his seed might go forth on the Ea-Urth in the advent that some great evil befall him. He might be killed or never return from the scheduled journey to Ur-Ope. Though scheduled, the precise date of departure was still not made known. Brekka said he would depart when the Ur Fyr burned in his chest as well as hers. Not a day before, nor a day after.

Soon he would be married to Sunniva. He contemplated that with delight. She fit the bill of everything he loved in a woman. She was possessed with that same grace as his mother, wise, beautiful, and feisty to the core. Though her figure and attractiveness pleased him greatly, it was her wisdom that drew him. She was deeper than most girls he knew. Once, when alone with the Lady Brekka he had described how he felt an unexplainable draw to Sunniva even though he didn't know her and Brekka explained that blood calls to blood and that royal blood always seeks its own. Its attraction is planted in the seed code. She further explained to him that in the beginning the gods colonized the Ea-Urth with tribes which they ordained should be eternal, but the Dark Elves always seek to scatter and confuse the tribes so that they may be masters of the tribes of man instead of being nourished by the gods. The Dark Elves cultivate confusion so they can control mankind and steer them away from the glory which would otherwise be theirs by inheritance.

She had explained that tribalism, which she also called nativism was the supreme order of government in the heavens and must also one day be the same on Ea-Urth. The Dark Elves seek to twist and pervert nativism so as to destroy the tribes and impose an unnatural monoculture over all the lands under the heavens so as to rob all tribes, races, and nations of their noble birth rights, and distinctions, and leave them slaves to one government, as if no tribe knew what was best for itself. As the Grand Wizard Elrus said, the entire Ea-Urth can only become one when they first become many.

The nations became so mixed up and confused that the gods were forced to give them the laws of confederation in preparation for the more perfect form of government the heavens live by. The Lady Brekka explained that it rests upon the unborn to re-establish the heavenly order on Ea-Urth as it is in Heofonum. She said his marriage to Sunniva represented the efforts of the unborn materializing in this world so as to prepare the way for the advanced generations to come. Indeed, it was possible, he already loved Sunniva. He pondered where that love came from. *Do bonds really take place before this World of the Mould?*

He broke his hypnotic ponderings and finished his bath. Whilst drying off he hefted his balls and said, "Soon you will be able to empty your contents into a most lovely vessel." He towel dried his hair, combed it out and then tied on a new loincloth bearing the Eye of Howrus on it, the right to wear such was reserved only for those of royal blood. He blew out the candle lantern and then pulled back the blankets and lay upon the soft bed. Miss Liza's reputation for comfort and luxuriance was deserved. He pulled the soft feather tick over his shoulders and watched the lace curtains flutter in the gentle breeze as he drifted off to sweet sleep.

The first thing he felt upon awakening in the dark of night was heaviness upon his chest. Upon opening his eyes a tall dark figure stood at the foot of his bed. He sought to speak, but his tongue was bound. A sickening feeling filled his stomach like he had swallowed wormwood. Icy eyes devoid of mercy or humor looked sinisterly down on him. The shrill voice of a woman knifed the air, punctuated with cat like screams. Writhing forms entered his bedchamber through the walls like the black smokes of Hell.

As the dark figure moved toward him the timbers of the bed shook and a stifling tide of darkness moved over him like the Angel of Death. Without explanation he felt himself being levitated up to the ceiling. The entire bedchamber trembled like it were a quake, insomuch that the fine porcelain rolled out of the hutch, shattering on the floor.

He had no idea what was happening, and his heart raced as rapid breaths escaped his lungs. He didn't know what the approaching dark being was, but he understood at every level it was bent on destroying him. His arms would not move, he could not speak and laid utterly paralyzed.

With all the strength he could muster he called upon All Father Odhin in his heart. Explosively the name of the All Father burst from his mouth and he fell back to the bedstead below, but the darkness was still pervasive. Cold hands took hold of his limbs once again and he could feel their malice intent. In the blackness, a beam of light burst through the opening door enough to see that Dawn was standing in the threshold of the door. Like a glowing coal, light emanated from her, and she transformed from being a young maid into a mature woman before his very eyes.

The dark horde attempted to pull him away from her like a wolf dregs its kill. Dawn spoke with more authority than he had ever heard, "Stop in the name of Odhin, ye dark fiends of Muspelheim. I command, no fiend shall lay hands upon this lad again throughout time and all eternity. So shall it ever be. Release your hold this very moment or I shall cast a spell over you from which no being can recover."

Like dark smoke flying out of a chimney the howling dark horde of demonic shades fled uttering croaks and cackles like some hellish nightmare. All went silent. The only light in the room was emanating from Dawn, which gradually subsided until she resumed a maiden form once again.

Soon Brekka, Liza, and Sunniva came running through the door with their candle lamps lit. Liza's face was filled with fright, "For God's sake what were those awful sounds and tremors all about?"

Sunniva said, "See, you are naked Anghrus, cover yourself."

He quickly pulled his loincloth over his man parts. Then gathering his wits he said, "I have suffered some sort of demonic attack," he looked at the broken porcelain then continued, "It was an attack from the Spirit Realms. My tongue was bound, as were my limbs, I could not give utterance no matter how I struggled, and I was hefted up to the ceiling by dark creatures whose cold hands were hell-bent on destroying me."

Dawn declared, "It was the Dark Elves. For this reason I came to join Anghrus' journey at the Haligryft at Cat Haven. It was to protect him and to properly instruct him in the artifact he now possesses."

Brekka replied, "I know of no Haligryft at Cat Haven?"

"You will find it soon enough, Haeliggawicca. It will be revealed to you."

Anghrus reflected upon what she said, "You mean you know the use of the jewel shaft I found."

Dawn smiled, "Yes, it is a gift from the gods you were drawn to discover. I will return one day to teach you its proper use."

Brekka looked Dawn square on, "I know thee now! Thou art the Mother of Heaven. Thou art Freya come to us in this maiden form."

Anghrus remarked, "Why, of course, you are Dawn and Dusk, the Beginning and the End. You are a shapeshifter and the Queen of Heaven, for none other could strike such terror in the Muspili save only one in possession of the fire of Heaven. Thou art an Ur-Faery."

"Blessed are you Brekka and Anghrus for flesh and blood have not revealed my identity to you, but the Ur-Fyr within you has. Now, it behooves me to ponder in what guise I shall assume when next the three of us meet at the Pink Moonth of Anghrus' wedding."

# CHAPTER 16 :

## THE WOLVES ARE AT THE DOOR

LONG SWAN'S LOG: IT IS *the twenty-first day of the High Holy Moonth of Autumn, one day before the Herewardi celebration known as the King's Day. The Year is 614 H.S.O.*

*From the Fifth Sabbath to the harvest, Sur Sceaf has remained here at Mount Heredom where he had the ancient menhirs, barrows, dolmans, and henges improved and the box hedges and topiary on the mound trimmed. He has caused the planting of many forests of hawthorn, magnolia, yew, and oak trees throughout the land of the Holy See.*

*Additionally, he and Brekka uncovered some golden plates called the Bok of Os hidden inside a stone box that lay within an ancient marble pillar buried in brambles, briers, and ivy. Also found within was a brass tube containing the Table of Osirean Geometry inscribed on a double interlocking pyramid called the star tetrahedron which was fashioned from an emerald. Upon this jewel was written the divine laws of numbers, measures, weights, and the geometry of the Elven lords of olden times come forth in the beginning of days to bless mankind.*

*The table is being reviewed by the Roufytrof and Sur Child and will be used in all future building projections. In days past, famed Master Builder Muryh had proven many of these principles, but this remarkable find added to the fund of knowledge. Of greater import was the fact that it revealed the law of levitation, which, when mastered, will allow for far greater works of architecture. When shown to Rhoda the Hag, she was astonished beyond measure, and revealed that the Amerikans had never reached such an advanced level of science, and such would have been the envy of all the engineers of her day and age.*

*This evening, the High King Sur Sceaf presided over the council fire in the council chamber of the great hall, Ruhm and Brekka's home overlooking the Elven Waters of the Big Springs. As the spirit master, Sur Sceaf called upon me and Paloma in private, to receive his last will and testament. I am to read it in the closing meeting on the morrow during the royal moot to be held at the setting of the sun. In addition, as was the custom of his forefathers before him, he committed into my hands his personal journals, which I am to enter into the Hall of Records and Archives of Herewardom.*

*This holy council fire on the morrow is to be held for the benefit of the royal family and the Roufytrof only, as the matters to be discussed are still to remain secret at this point. Furthermore, Sur Sceaf announced, that like his father before him, he will now assume the role of weardean, and will be taking up permanent residency in a lodge near Bender's Wood and would not be returning to Godeselle. To no one's surprise, the mantel of high kingship will fall upon the shoulders of Lord Arundel who will rule the Seven Kingdoms from the Stone Hall in Godeselle.*

*After our private council, Sur Sceaf took the floor and announced to the family that after tomorrow's council fire, he will unveil the long anticipated artwork which has been sculpted by the master builder, Sur Child, and he declared that it would be the capstone of his life. This created a lot of stir as to what masterpiece stood veiled on yon mound. Many believed it was to be a repository for the Holy Books, but Sur Sceaf has shown Paloma and me what lies beneath the canvas shroud, and we are bound to secrecy.*

*I have been much consumed in the teaching of the young king, Anghrus the Deep-Minded. I have schooled him in the principles of good kingship and the proper duties of a monarch. Let it be said that he has diligently applied himself to learning and soaks up information like a forest absorbs rain.*

*Sur Sceaf spoke at length to the royal family and discussed the importance of building filial devotion for one another, as one of the Forty Four Laws implores. He addressed his wives, Ruhm's wives, Uffa, Ugga, Unn, Forsetti and Ka-Luna, and Merri-Doo on the importance of preparedness and the need the gods have impressed on his heart for the fortifying of the gates of Panygyrus against an enemy that only a select few are even aware exists.*

*Finally, he charged all present to ever strive for the welfare of Herewardom, that the Ea-Urth may not ever again give place to the evil schemes of men that once polluted it with corrupt governments and sciences raised up for gain and force rather than the welfare and common weal of the people and the individual tribes.*

*The council fire ended with Brekka's address wherein she praised Sur Sceaf for the nations he fathered both in body and spirit. The meeting was closed in due and ancient form.*

The Golden Cup of Summer was pouring out its final offerings. The summer moonths were filled with good works and plenty of uplifting activities, as the king inspired everyone to greater efforts at elevating civilization. Finally the High Holy Days had arrived. It was a glorious day for the mushroom hunt. The air was crisp and carried the rich scents of the forest floor. The older children rushed ahead, while Ducky and her bride-sisters helped the smaller ones to discover their share, and by mid-afternoon, the collection bags and baskets were nearly full.

Ducky blew her hunter's horn, the signal for the children to assemble at a heavy-laden osage orange tree next to the stone gates where some of their parents had gathered to collect them.

During the nine days of the Elven Fair preceding the King's Day, so many events, games, tournaments, meetings, council fires and moots had taken place that no one, man, woman, or child could do anymore than choose to be at a fraction of them. Each day had brought another special event or showcased some Herewardi custom for the improvement of the commonwealth.

The harvest celebration had been a tremendous success, prompting many in the audience to tears. Arundel and Zschamillah had sat next to Sur Sceaf and Swan Hilde, and Ary noticed that his father, too, had been deeply moved.

Due to the number of children and maidens wishing to participate in the Day of Harvest, dancing around corn sheaves and pumpkins had had to be conducted in shifts. To occupy the children Brekka had conceived the idea of a mushroom hunt led by new bride-sister, Ducky, who had been educated in the identification and uses of mushrooms by her shamanic mother, Sun Mover, of the Spider Clan.

It was a perfect day. A burst of shouts and laughter came from the direction of the deep forest, followed by the rustle of grass and the pounding of feet. Ruhm-El and his pack of older boys hurled walnuts and osage oranges at one another before Freyxus, Verushka, and Hollyannah corralled them.

Arundel and Zscha arrived at the gates just as the boys and their antics came into view. Ary grinned at his childhood friend, Redelfis. "Redi, it's a damn shame we didn't have access to those osage oranges when we were training as young bloods. We could have cleaned house on Haakon's wolf pack."

Redelfis laughed. "True, but as I remember, we did well enough with acorns, walnuts, and haws. Haakon has never really forgiven us for capturing his flag. After all, he and his wolf pack were two years older."

Zscha lifted her eyebrow at Ary. "Such tales are best not told to our children, my dear. They get into enough mischief on their own."

Going Snake's wife, Bithia, shot a look at her husband. "Sound familiar?"

Going Snake laughed. "My sweet, as my father told my mother when my dog, Fur Puller and I knocked over her cooking tripod one time while chasing a rabbit, 'Today's ruffians are tomorrow's warriors.'"

Bithia wrinkled her brow, "But there are no more wars to be fought. The empire has been crushed and the confederation runs as smoothly as a kit of pigeons."

Zscha shook her head. "Since I first encountered Ary, I have tried to grasp the warrior culture, but it still eludes me why we must always settle our differences with teeth and horns."

Redelfis smiled. "Lady Queen, would that the good always triumphed, but more often than not, that is not the case. For nigh six hundred years evil repeatedly defeated us, driving us to the ends of the Earth. I still think it a miracle that we triumphed over the Pitters at all. If the Thunder Beings had not been with us, I'm far from confident we would have ever prevailed."

The gaggle of boys raced toward the gates, jostling one another for the lead. As they neared, it became a contest between Ruhm-El and Ary and Zscha's Son, Dov-Elf.

"Mom, I found a goblin's fart in the woods!" Dov-Elf shouted as the two boys ended up in a panting tie.

Zscha frowned. "Dov-Elf, Mommy has told you I don't like such coarse talk."

Ary suppressed a laugh. "It's not what you're thinking, my dear. A goblin's fart is no more than a puffball mushroom."

"And I found ten chanterelles!" Little Sylphae plucked a large salmon-colored mushroom from her boxwood basket and held it up for all to admire.

Ary's mouth watered at the mere sight. He was glad he had brought Zschamillah and the kids with him to witness the temple dedication and the the various honors, including his elevation to the high king, soon to be confirmed by Brekka and Long Swan in the age-old tradition. Even more important was giving his children the opportunity to mingle with their cousins. During the five moonths since the dedication, he had relished the time spent free of administrative and executive responsibilities. The balmy weather was revitalizing and the natural beauty was restoring his soul.

Zscha had expressed her Joy, not only to have him all to herself, but relishing the time to catch up with Brekka on their new lives free of the war and the struggle of former days.

*What a queen she is!* Ary thought as they walked down the pike toward the Great Hall. There was not one bone of guile in her entire body. Somehow, she had managed to dovetail her culture with his as seamlessly as if it were made of one material. Her bride-sisters loved her, her people worshiped her, and he adored her, even more now than when the two of them first sparked their relationship in the crater during their tumultuous seventeenth winters.

He loved the way she walked, the way she praised his youngest son and her tender affections for little Redithel, hair as red as her mother's, and eyes as green as fresh leeks.

Happy is the man that finds a good woman. He had found many, and this one was their shepherdess. While she walked with Redithel holding her hand, she used the other to reach up to ply her fingers through his mane of hair. "Oh, Ary, I can scarcely believe the difference in Brekka.

Remember how she struggled with her emotions when she was in the crater. How she was torn between her womanly emotions and her high commission to serve her people. But now, she seems deeply satisfied and joyous in her life with Ruhm. Now I can hardly believe how the warrioress has truly taken to domesticity."

"Indeed. I had doubts that one not of royal blood would be worthy of her, but Ruhm is all that I could have wished for her and more."

"And she to him."

It did Ary's heart good to see how deeply Zscha and Brekka loved one another at a spiritual level.

After a few more steps, she said in a somber tone, "Ary, have you not noticed the countenance of your father of late? He has the king's look, the same as I sometimes saw in my mother when she was wrestling with some kind of threat to our people. I can't help but feel something is troubling him deeply."

"Why, no my dear, he is always in deep thought. He's probably concerned over the Hickoryean response to Ilkchild's strange ottermen. I tried to persuade him to leave the trans-humans on the isle, but Xelph and he insisted on showing Ruhm and Brekka how he's shaped them into his very own Praetorian Guard. When I confronted Ilkchild, he declared he received inspiration from the God Baldur speaking out of Hell that he was to bring this romp with him, and that Brekka would know of their use."

"Since they've taken over the marshes near the bastion, they've become objects of extreme curiosity. Yes, Brekka has put the marshes off limits for their safety and the safety of the gawkers, but more and more I'm hearing complaints that they are free to catch all the fish, turtles and crawdads that they wish."

"But no salamanders, efts, or newts," Ary reminded her with a grin. "After all, they are sacred totems to Herewardi jesters."

She shot him an exasperated look. "I'm surprised that Mayor Rosenkrantz hasn't issued a protest."

"Well, I did have to explain to him that they pose no threat and that the citizens of Moon Door consider them part of the scenery. I explained that after Ilkchild had found the ottermen in a cave on the North Peninsula, he took to raising them like they were his own children, enlisting your help from time to time with their taming and training."

"And Rosenkrantz's response was?"

"He thought it brilliant that they could swim and overtake an enemy ship in an instant at sea."

"How would he know that?"

"I told him about the Mexus Pirate vessel that attempted a foray over Moon Door. On Ilky's command, the ottermen sent those bandits whimpering back home with their tails between their legs. They are most likely telling stories of being attacked by sea wylfs."

Dov-Elf tugged at Ary's arm. "Fa, Skeeter promised to teach me and Ruhm-El how to swim as fast as he can in the marshes."

Zscha shot Ary a look. "When did he say that, Dov?" she asked.

"When I was visiting with Uncle Ilky and Auntie Hava last year there was a night I had an awful dream that the ottermen were after me, and Auntie Hava told me they would never hurt me. She asked me if I wanted to meet them, and I said yes, but only if she came with me. They talked funny, but they were really nice and offered me one of their oysters. That's when Skeeter promised he would teach me."

Ary ruffled his Son's hair. "Just like the wyrm kat your Mo Fa and you played with last night."

"Chloe's funny, and when I, Eldir and MoFa play grass beast, she can make herself look really scary. But she's not as scary as MoFa's dog, Bergere. She *really* scares me, because she has a big mouth and big teeth and Eldir says she could take your head off in one bite."

"But you know Bergere and Chloe would never hurt you, don't you?"

Dov-Elf nodded. "Can I take my basket to the cook now? She's promised to trade us cookies for 'shrooms."

"Of course, Young Prince, but you may have only three cookies."

The boy raced off, his brown curls bobbing with each step.

Ary smiled. "Where were we? Oh yes, I can see now, the ottermen will prove most useful in the future, particularly when we take to the seas to find Ur-Ope. I suspect that's why Ilky is eager to give them to Brekka. He wants them to come under Anghrus' hand."

"Oh husband, such talk scares me. Is there not enough trouble for us in building up the waste places of Panygyrus that we must send our children off to lands at the ends of the earth?"

He loved the passion she had for those causes she believed in, but he also understood she was of provincial bent from the long isolation of her people, and that she still very much feared the foreign or strange.

That night when the children were tucked into bed with their cousins in the Great Hall, he looked forward to a romantic toss in bed with his green-eyed queen. He enjoyed the lifting spiritual oneness they possessed all of their marital life. Each time seemed as new as the last.

While her bride-sisters had accompanied the children on the mushroom hunt, Brekka had remained behind to oversee the preparations for the royal moot scheduled to be held later that evening. In the Herewardi tradition, a royal moot was held each year during the Elven Fair to honor the kings and queens of old. This moot had special meaning to the extended family since the king of kings himself would be in attendance and deliver his State of the Bloodline Address.

Her eldest child, Eldir, was of an age now to learn courtly demeanor and protocol, so she kept him nearby at all times, and indeed, took him with her when she went to the shrine of Wilona to offer morning prayers and oblations. On the walk up to the dolman, Eldir had insisted upon collecting yew fronds to lie upon the altar.

With the ferny fronds in his small hand, he said, "Sister Wilona, it is I, Eldir. I brought you a pretty yew twig, because Mama says you speak through trees. Please watch over me and my brothers and sisters, my mama and my nigh-mamas and my fa and my mo-fa and mo-mo Lana. And don't let the coyotes get us, like they got my little hen, Betsy, and ate her guts out."

Brekka hid a smile. "That was a very nice prayer, Eldir. I'm sure Sister Wilona loves this branch, and I know she will protect you from the coyotes."

She took his hand, and together they walked down the cobblestone path. "Oh, look, Mama, there's Mo-Fa sitting under the Ever Living Tree. He's going to teach me how to fight with sticks, like the big kids do."

"I think Mo-Fa has forgotten that tomorrow is the King's Day and he will likely be very busy. But I'm sure he'll keep his promise somehow."

"No, Mama, he said that 'cause it was the King's Day, he gets to do whatever he chooses, and he said he wanted to spend time with me cause I'm his favorite future king."

"Well, if Mo-Fa said that, you can be sure that's what he'll do." She snickered inside knowing full well how special Sur Sceaf could make each grandchild feel.

Suddenly, the sun disappeared, its rays blotted out by the massive swarms of migrating grackles covering the sky. The air was filled with the raspy *chack-chacks* of their song as they passed over.

"Look, Mama! It's a dragon up in the sky."

"It does look like that, doesn't it? But it is just a flock of grackles flying into the arms of the sun to some special place in the Sun Lands where they feed during the winter."

"How come the chickens and the guineas don't go with them?"

"Probably because they are too fat to fly that far," She ruffled his thick reddish-brown curls. Now, run along and feed your chickens and bunnies while I have a talk with Mo-Fa."

"Okay, and then I can have some of Nigh-Mama Wyth's anise cookies?"

"Yes, but only two."

"She said I could have four, but don't tell her."

Brekka hid a smile. Her son was just like his father, always pushing for more, "Only two, my little neanling. Tell Cook Elsa I said it was alright."

She watched Eldir skipping down the path and cross the lawn toward the stables where the children's pets were kept. Shifting her gaze toward the yawning yew, she thought about the many times she had sought out her father's advice and comfort, especially on the War Road. He was always her advocate, whether it was protecting her against the wagging tongues of the village magpies or a blood-thirsty grizzly about to rip open her rib cage. In his prime he had been a magnificent figure of a man, everything a king should be. Even now, he exuded dignity and strength, though she couldn't help noticing that like the scars and hollows of the ancient yew, the battles and stresses of his long life had drained some of his essence.

As he turned to see who was approaching, a warm smile crossed his face. "Behold the Shield Maiden of Odhin has come to set an old man's heart at ease."

"Waes hail and Os Frith, Fa. Happy King's Day."

"That sassy sister-bride of yours, Miss Liza, has promised to bring me some of her green liqueur when she and the others return. You know Lana and Faechild have taken a great liking to it."

She laughed. "Ah, now I know why Mama and Faechild sometimes act like giggling maidens when cutting flowers in the garden."

He smiled and patted the bench beside him. As she settled herself, he said, "It warms my heart to see my wives still delighting in each other's company." He slipped an arm around her shoulder and drew her tightly. "And it does my heart good to see my daughter, the haeligawicca, shine the light of the gods to the nations, but even more so, I am pleased to see her finally drinking from the cup of happiness that had so long been denied her. For many years I grieved the personal sacrifices you were called upon to suffer that you might fulfill your calling as a lady knight. I watched you go forth from childhood to warrior princess without partaking of the natural fruits of youth by wedding the man of your dreams as your sisters were privileged to do. Your mother and I suffered with you. But now when I see the love between you and your husband and his bride-sisters, I am at last at peace. It is recorded in the Psalms of Elrus, '*Unto those from whom much is required, much is given by the gods. Hope deferred maketh the heart sick, but when satisfied, it is the Tree of Life and they shall feast upon the Apples of Idun.*'"

Tears came to her eyes. "Oh Fa, that is what I've always loved about you. When I asked for bread, you never gave me a rock. When I asked for a fish, you never gave me a serpent. Every gift you ever gave me was precisely tailored to address my needs at that moment."

His emerald eyes gazed into hers for a long moment before smiling gently. "Perhaps, then, you will tell me what is troubling your soul?"

She frowned. "Nothing that we need to discuss today. After all, this is the King's Days."

"This king has always been able to detect when his daughter is troubled. Our hearts are too intricately interwoven to keep secrets from one another. Just as you sensed that I was troubled, I sense a stir in the deep river of your soul."

She debated with herself, but finally decided to seek his counsel. "As always, I can keep nothing hidden from you. Since the Fifth Sabbath I have done little else but ponder the meaning of my journey with Ullr and Holle and the things I was shown. The land of Ur-Ope had a very different shape from all the maps Rhoda the Hag has shown to us. I fear the information she has given us concerning who might be allies, and who might be our enemies is as out of date as her knowledge of the geography. We may be up against enemies much worse than any we have yet faced."

Sur Sceaf nodded. "It is as the stones declared to me. I was shown a large land mass surrounded by water on three sides. I saw throngs of dark-hued warriors spilling over the wall of the Aegirean Sea in black-sailed ships on course for Panygyrus under the banner of the scorpion. But I know not when this will occur, when it does, the threat will come first from the east. Still, I was much encouraged by your report of the counter measures of the Black and White Alliance in keeping this menace in check, but for how long only the Osyr know, for it was not revealed to me by Father Odhin."

Brekka replied, "I sense that it will be long enough for Anghrus to obtain his divine gift. Moreover, I got the distinct impression that the Nippons far to the west could be a valuable ally to Ary in the battle against the Russ, if Ary could but engage them. We must ever be mindful that the Russ are also of Odhin's seed and our responsibility will be to break the teeth of their Fenris wolves and then raise them as equals by teaching them who they are and what their great heritage truly is. They know not that they are led by Dark Elves though I'll wager you many of them sense it."

Her father glanced toward the hall. "Yes, it is the will of Odhin that we redeem them from the influence of the Pale Dark Ones. If I were Ary, I would send out an exploratory expedition of our finest warriors and negotiators to treat with these Nippons. I've spent much time thinking about the the fair young lad, Anghrus. I understand full well the strength of the dark forces of these corsairs arrayed against him. He will need all the help and support he can get. Yes, it would be of great benefit if Ary is able to forge an alliance between the Syr Folk and the Nippons and others to force the Russ into a two-front war. And it should lift your heart to know that I recently received a missive from Chief Ehira of the Moxo, telling me that he has already met with ambassadors from the Land of Nippon who came upon his shores to express the wish to open trade with them. He has told them of us and is working on sending their ambassadors to Godeselle."

"Have you told Ary?"

"I have. He tells me he intends to follow through on this."

She sighed. "We have so little time to prepare Anghrus for his mission. Fa, do you sense that we are sending a child into a wolf's den with little more than a slingshot for defense?"

"I understand your concern, but I am comforted knowing that the gods have chosen him and therefore, we can only commend his spirit into their hands. But I must admit I often think about Kanarus and the cascade of feelings besetting him. His son is soon to embark for an unknown world fraught with unknown dangers. A world, according to Rhoda, that was once filled with poisons, vicious monsters, and trans-human demons such as the skin walkers, the were-bats, and the bone crushers that we had to defeat." He smiled sadly. "You were even younger when the eyes of the Roufytrof turned upon you. We did all we could to make straight your way, but still, there came a time when you had to fly with your own wings. Soon, Anghrus will fulfill the measure of a covey of wives and must spread his wings for Ur-Ope, and I can only pray he is as equal to the task the gods have set for him as you were, my dear."

"I remember the day Aelfy and I were practicing staves, and I actually beat him for the first time. I thought it was just fun and games, until Aelfy pointed out two wizards from Stonyford who had been watching our game. He said that not even Ary had been so tested. 'Don't know what it is, Sis,' he said, 'but you're not like the rest of us. And whatever it is that they came to see, I'd say from their expressions, they liked what they saw in you.'"

"And you came to me later to ask if there was something wrong with you." Sur Sceaf squeezed her shoulder. "That night I wept in the dark because I knew by your seventh winter that I had begotten a true warrioress, and that in the unfolding of time, you would be singled out by the Norn Sisters for great deeds. I feared then that such a Fate could only mean a hero's death."

"There were times, Fa, when I envied my sisters as they seemed so free to dance through life, following the safe paths, while I was always bruised, battered and torn from training or frustrated by the failure to master a new weapon or strategy. Sometimes, when I thought about the expectations of the Roufytrof, feelings of powerlessness overwhelmed me and I have no doubt Anghrus must be feeling the same way."

"Indeed, he is. We've had many talks since his anointing. His doubts are as numerous as grains of sand, but his heart is stalwart and shall hold course. I'm an old man and my ideas might be old-fashioned in the eyes of such a young man. You, on the other hand, have a powerful connection with his mother, Wilona, that transcends time, and which none of us can match. Not even his father. You can be to him what Redith was to me. Your wisdom and experience can light his feet in a very dark world. And I know how much he admires you. He's even told me that he believes his mother speaks through you to him."

"It is true; there is a spiritual bond between the three of us. In many ways, he seems as much a son to me as does Eldir. I will do all I can to prepare him to fulfill his grand commission."

An otherworldly smile lit up his lined face, and a serenity glowed in his eyes. A lump came into Brekka's throat. This man was beyond comparison, as a leader, as a friend, as a husband to her mother, and as a father. Her dear, dear father. How she would miss him when that inevitable day would arrive when the Valkyries came calling for him.

"I love you, Fa," she said before kissing his cheek.

"And I love you, my dearest flame faery." He hugged her close before releasing her. "And now, I must take up the staves against your firstborn. I hope he will be gentler than you were with me. After all, I am far past my prime."

"Never, Fa," she declared as he stood up. "To me you will always be a god on Ea-Urth."

On the morning of the King's Day, the twenty-second day of the Holy Moonth, Brekka mistakenly overslept. The royal moot had gone on well past midnight, and by the time she had said good-night to her father and the elders of the Roufytrof and the ladies of the Council of Women and made it to her bed, she was exhausted. When she finally opened her eyes, she immediately glanced at the window opposite her bed. Sunshine streamed through the gauzy curtains to splash a golden streak across the intricate pattern of the carpet. A slight breeze teased the vivid red, pink and white blossoms of the potted geraniums on the wide windowsill, a deliberate reminder of Redith's beloved dooryard garden.

Knowing she faced a busy day, she quickly left the warmth of her bed. As she passed the open window, she heard Eldir shouting from below, "Fee, fee, bumble-bee, you're in free!"

Seconds later, her father answered, "Don't give in so easily. I'm in the kitchen. Come find me, if you can!"

She smiled. Many times she and her siblings had played the same game with her father. When she and the twins were the youngest players, he always managed to leave his foot sticking from wherever he was hiding. At the time, she didn't realize that he was making sure she always won, a courtesy he did not extend to her older siblings.

Ruhm had spent the night with Verushka and their children and, since the king's feast was not scheduled until sundown, he was not expected at the hall until mid-afternoon.

Brekka planned to briefly consult with the hall's head cook, Betty Dyck, a bustling treasure of efficiency and culinary talents who ran the kitchen as well as her Fa-Mo Mahallah had once done. For the past week, the maids had been cleaning every corner, polishing the hickory floors and black walnut furniture, cleaning the windows and setting up the tables in the council chambers, complete with her finest plates, D'If crystal, and silver.

The ground floor bustled with activity, with servants going about their chores like bees in a hive. In the kitchen the cooks and scullery maids worked elbow-to-elbow, their cheerful conversation reminding Brekka of the days of her youth at Namen Jewel during special occasions, especially when the Chiefs of the Sharaka would come for their annual visit. From the age of four winters, her place at the table was always between the sisters Redith and Sagwi the Hag.

"It all smells wonderful as usual, Miss Betty," she said as the rosy cheeked cook turned in her direction. "I assume all is under control."

Miss Betty tucked a stray silver curl under the blue and white bandanna that she wore whenever she cooked. "Everything is in order except for the delivery of the two sides of wisent. It's been hanging for a full week, but the head of the abattoir promised to have them here by mid-afternoon. Just barely enough time to cook them properly. And, oh yes, there was enough of that cocao from those hardy stock trees you planted out of Ele-Anor to make some huge batches of the drink the children all love."

"I'm sure everything will be delicious as always." She turned to leave before turning back. "Miss Betty, would you please make sure that an extra decanter of Miss Liza's green liqueur is placed on the table where I've seated Chief Mendaka and Little Doe. The King wishes this as a special token of his affection and honor for his lifelong friend."

"Of course, Lady Brekka. Anything else?"

"No, I'll leave the dinner in your capable hands. Oh, and do you know when the floral arrangements are scheduled to arrive?"

"According to the schedule put up by Lady Vicky, Mr. Cresswell is to be here directly."

"Very good." She glanced around. "Have you seen the king and Eldir this morning?"

Miss Betty chuckled, and several of the cooks giggled. "I have indeed. Pardon me for saying so, but the high king and Eldir have been like two puppies racing around underfoot all morning. Last I saw of them, they were heading off like two foxes toward the council chamber."

"Oh no. I'd better shoo them out of there before they make a total mess."

"Well, my dear, you know men and boys, always romping and roughhousing, trying to impress us lady folk when we're fussing over the niceties of life."

As Brekka walked into the council hall, she was shocked to see the barrel of conjugal wands had its contents of painted sticks scattered about the floor like a game of pickup sticks. A couple of wands sat at the far end of the large hickory council table.

She shot an angry glance around the room to assess the mess her father and son had made in their horse play when her eye caught Chloe the wyrm-kat, crouching in a dark corner off of the large fireplace as quiet and still as a gargoyle.

It startled her enough to make her catch her breath. "Chloe, what in Hell are you doing in here? Go to the kitchen if you want some milk."

The she-cat turned her head in her usual aloof manner and revealed, "Sur Sceaf and man-child, want me to play grass beast. I chase them and they fight me with swords and wands. Sur Sceaf make mess. Not Chloe."

"For the gods' sakes, doesn't he know you have kittens to feed and tend? You know very well I don't allow for play in this room. Honestly, Fa is as much a kid as Eldir. Chust look at this place. It's a damnded mess and the king's feast is to be held here this afternoon."

Brekka gathered the colorful wands and put them back in their barrel by the hearth. She tossed a log on the fire, and as she turned a look toward Chloe, she thought it mighty queer that Chloe showed no signs of swollen or lactating breasts.

She paused. "Chloe, is your milk giving out? Your kittens need to suckle for at least another six moonths."

Chloe covered her breasts with her arms. "Kittens fine."

"Well, it's none of my business, but if you're going dry we could get you a goat to nurse your kits on."

"Chloe not dry! Top Cat said Chloe wait here. Play more with Top Cat and man-child."

Brekka was startled by the strange way the kat stared at her, *Like she's stalking me.* The thought crossed her mind, was Chloe suffering from the pregnancy madness? Brekka knew outlander women who had suffered from it, a deep depression that made them behave abnormally after a birthing. Maybe that's why Chloe looked dried up.

As Brekka broke eye contact and stepped back to grab another log, she noticed Chloe's hands were as black as if she had stuck them in a coal bin. A quick glance at the wooden floors told her that Chloe had not tracked coal dust across the floor. She breathed a sigh of relief. *What was Fa thinking by roughhousing in the council fire chamber?*

"Chloe, why are your hands so black?"

"Chloe go in barn where ottermen talk to Ilkchild. Ottermen see Chloe. Chloe afraid, run away. They not like Chloe. Chloe trip, fall into ink vat. Get hands black."

Brekka shook her head. "Did Long Swan shout at Chloe?"

"No, Long Swan not there."

"You're very lucky, then, because Long Swan is very particular about his ink. He makes it himself. And the otter's will never hurt you as bad as Long Swan if you mess with his ink."

"Chloe sit here on hearth. Not move. The king, I mean Top Cat, come soon."

She noticed an almost imperceptible snarl at the corners of the kat's mouth. It was not like Chloe to behave in any way like this. She was always like a playful child and very close to being a member of the family. Certainly, the wyrm-kats had become a frequent attraction at the springs and around the house and they had always deported themselves very well.

Just then, Giles, the hall's head footman appeared in the doorway. "My lady, Lord Uffa wishes me to tell you he has returned from this morning's hunt with Bergere, just as the high king has ordered, and requests admittance."

"Tell him to enter and have one of the maids bring him a little repast and some of that ale from the Up Country. And Giles, Sur Sceaf will want them to bring Bergere an ox bone to gnaw upon." She glanced at Chloe still sitting oddly motionless. "Also ask Miss Betty to bring Chloe some red meat, raw, and warm milk."

"Very good, my lady."

Turning to Chloe, Brekka suggested, "Chloe, you can pet Bergere, but all playing and rough housing has to go outside. No horse play, cat calls, or caterwauling. You got that?'

"Chloe hear good enough."

The footman saluted, turned about face, and went to lead the guest in. Chloe showed none of her usual excitement when she announced Bergere was coming. Usually the kat loved Bergere. As a matter of fact, under normal circumstances she usually bounced off the walls when Bergere came over for a little rough and tumble play. All the wyrm-kats loved Bergere. Especially, since the dog was so agile at running down wild pigs for them to feast on.

Little time had passed since Giles left to when Uffa presented at the chamber door dressed in red surcoat uniform, gilded sword, and polished boots. Bergere wagged her tail beside him.

"Waes hael, Lady Brekka."

"Waes hael and Os-Frith, Uffa. How did you fare on the hunt?"

"Very well. Bergere ran three of the wolves to ground and enjoyed doing it."

"By any chance did you bag the two wolves the temple ground guards heard last night. The report said one was pure white, the other jet black?"

"No such luck. The three we bagged were all grey."

She nodded. "Actually, from the size of those two that the guards saw, I suspect they were Woon's wolves, and if so, no arrow, sword or spear can bring them down. Neither can any hound, not even Bergere. In the past, such visitations have occurred around the eve of King's Day. We shall see if they return tonight."

Uffa looked thoughtful. "I've heard that Woon's hounds can bite through steel and not even fire can touch them."

"Such sightings have always been an omen of good for our people from the time of the migration of Elrus. It has come down through the Folk Mouth that when Elrus' people were surrounded by Pitter legions and had determined to sing their swan songs they spotted two wolves, one white and one black. On the morrow when they awoke, the legions had disappeared."

Brekka reached down as Bergere came up to her for an approving pet. Her father's favorite, she was the get of a beauceron also named Bergere given to him by Chief Elmer of the Ceruleans and sired by Oberon, Chief Pita Blufre's favorite hunting dog. Beauceron was a name from the Frankish tongue. Bergere was known for her unusual size and athleticism as well as her docile temperament and above-keen intelligence. As Brekka ran her hand along the soft black fur of the dog's powerful back, she admired how the dog's fur shone like polished onyx and her clearly defined red socks set her apart as unique among all the hounds of the Herewardi, just as the white body and red heads of her faery hounds marked them as distinctly Herewardi.

Two serving maids arrived, one bearing an ox bone that Bergere accepted with an anticipatory 'woof". A platter of raw meat and a bowl of warm milk for Chloe. She also had the other maid carried a plate of warm bread and cheeses, and a krug of dark Up-Country ale for Uffa to quaff his thirst with. Dressed in a well-filled out dirndl, the girl earned an appreciative grin from Uffa.

Without warning, Bergere's hair rose on her neck and a vicious growl came out of her throat. The dog assumed a hunting posture, her teeth bared and her fierce gaze fixed squarely on Chloe, who assumed an arched back and attack position by the fireplace. Before Brekka or Uffa had time to intervene, the dog covered the distance between herself and the wyrm-kat and leapt with mouth wide open to rip at Chloe's throat.

The wyrm-kat let out an unearthly panther-like scream, followed by something that sounded like the slowed down roar of a bear as the powerful hound's jaws clamped down viciously on the wind pipe of its throat.

"Merciful Tyr! Uffa, help me get them apart!"

Even as Brekka rushed across the floor to restrain Bergere, it was too late. The powerful bitch had Chloe by the throat in such a death grip no one could break it. Bergere was chomping down, and shaking the wyrm-kat like a terrier does a rat, disregarding all commands.

Brekka slapped a cupped hand on Bergere's back and shouted, "Los," the command for release. But instead of releasing, Bergere clamped down even harder and the kat screamed cries Brekka had never heard any animal utter. Suddenly, Chloe's black hands and her head began to alter their form and turn into a dark mist. Chloe's image changed like a facial reflection when a pebble hits the surface of the water. An eery form moved like dark smoke up the chimney as if it had a mind of its own and with a loud scream like that of escaping gas from a roaring wood fire it departed up the flue.

Brekka stood dumbfounded as the last tails of dark mist wisped up the chimney, leaving an other-worldly chill running down her spine.

The maids stood frozen, mouths agape. The pitcher of ale lay shattered on the floor.

Uffa exclaimed, "It was a Dark Elf, my lady. A damned shape-shifting Dark Elf! The spawn of Hell!"

Brekka took time to assimilate his words before nodding her agreement. Bergere came to her side and she stroked her back vigorously. "Good girl! Good girl, Bergere!"

Bergere ran back over to the chimney and barked up at it as if to say, 'And stay away.'

"Good girl! You knew it wasn't Chloe, didn't you?"

Turning to Uffa, she said, "We have to purge the council fire today. Those Dark Elves have not bothered us since the fall of the Pitter Empire. Some big change is at hand and they must know it."

The terrible thought crossed her mind that this Dark Elf had come to do harm to one of them. With no further thought given, she dashed back to the kitchen guided only by motherly instinct. As she burst through the kitchen doors, she yelled, "Has anyone seen Eldir?"

# CHAPTER 17:

## CROSSING THE RAINBOW BRIDGE

ALL EYES TURNED TOWARD BREKKA and Uffa. "Eldir. Have any of you seen him?"

Miss Betty looked alarmed. One of the cooks, Bakrulah by name, continued to stir her pot while pointing with her head at the food larder. "In there, my lady. He be roughhousin' with the king."

Brekka and Uffa raced to the larder side-by-side. When they squeezed together through the door, she stopped dead, her heart pounding. A terrible weakness came over her, and her knees threatened to buckle. Uffa caught her before she fell to her knees.

"Oh no, oh no," she whispered. "It's too soon. The Lady Paloma warned us his old wound in the heart was cutting his time short. It's chust too soon"

Sur Sceaf lay on his side on the floor with Eldir sitting beside him, shaking his arm. "Come on FaMo, wake up. Wake up. Quit playing dead. You can come in free."

She knelt down. Somehow she forced the word past her constricted throat. "My darling, the gods came for FaMo. His heart has given out and he is being carried up to Valhalla."

The boy looked up at her with a quizzical expression. "But, Mama, Forsey says you can't get to Valhalla unless you die with your sword in your hand. FaMo keeps his sword in a special chest at his cabin. He showed it me and said it was a great troll slayer. He let me hold it and it was really heavy."

"That's true, but not all swords are made out of metal. Some swords are invisible and some are called by a different name. Long Swan's sword is his pen. Sur Child's sword is his trowel. My sword is my breasts and womb. Each bears the sword of his or her own office that serves the commonwealth best. Someday, you will be able to grasp that our sword is our gift or as Elrus put it, 'our spirit is our sword'."

Still shaken, she placed her hand next to her son's. Reaching for her father, the moment her fingers touched his cold arm she could feel death's grip was upon him. Not even the most horrific aftermath of a battle had affected her like this. She had seen many faces of death, but as a warrior, she had forced herself to be detached. This was altogether different. This was her father, the man she had been sure would somehow transcend mortality.

Uffa placed a gentle hand on her shoulder. But instead of comforting her, it only gave her permission to cry. She took Eldir in her arms and rocked while she wept aloud. Her mind continued to work and plan, but she could not give utterance. Only sobs and groans issued from deep inside her. She wanted to tell Uffa to get the wives that they might prepare and dress the body of the king for the Herewardi Burial Ritual. But she was incapable of choking out any word save "Uffa." Helplessly, she waved her hand toward the door.

Thankfully, Uffa took her meaning and went to fetch Sur Sceaf's bride-covey. Brekka squeezed Eldir to feel his warmth and the insurance that he was still in the bud of life. After considerable time rocking her Son in her arms and crying, Eldir patted her cheek. "Don't cry, Mama. FaMo has gone over the Rainbow into the Summer Lands."

She wept again and kissed him on the head. Soon she was joined by the king's wives. Paloma entered first, and in her usual dignified manner said, "Sisters, your lord, king, and husband has left for the Halls of the Fathers on High." Lana knelt and wrapped her loving arms around Brekka.

Taneshewa let out a wail of anguish and threw herself on his body. After considerable weeping and wailing, she looked up at Brekka. "Did the king leave a message?"

Brekka shook her head.

Taneshewa turned to Paloma. "I thought all high kings knew the appointed day of their death. Surely, he must have shared that with you."

While the other sisters attempted to console each other, Paloma declared, "Heavens to Tyranus! My gods why have you forsaken me?

It is too soon. How can I ever bear this grief? My beloved husband the king is dead. He was my buckler and shield." A muffled howl came from deep within her chest before she pulled herself together and forced herself to be composed. She wiped away her tears and at first choked on the knot in her throat before declaring, "Sisters, hear what message the king confided in me. He made me swear to not speak a word of it, though I accidentally let a word of it slip to Brekka. First off, he regretted leaving us all, but the old wound, near his heart had been slowly working the destruction of his mortal frame, and was greatly weakening him day-by-day. Secondly, he has designated Lord Arundel to receive the scepter as the next high king; though all here knew that would be the order of things.

"Last night he walked with me upon the Holy Mound, where we met with the All-Father and his two wolves in the dark of the yew wood. The All-Father, the Father of Fathers, Our Everlasting Father, and the Prince of Holiness told the king he would come for him before the Feast of the Winter King. Thus, you see it is so, and all things have been fulfilled which the Norns have spun."

"Why didn't you tell us so that we could say our good-byes?" Shining Moon said through her sobs.

"It was the king's wish, and I could but honor that."

Brekka's throat tightened in a sobbing knot. She could no longer cry, but only whimper as Lana wept on her shoulder, while Faechild gathered Eldir in her arms. Taneshewa began chanting the Sharaka song of parting while the other wives, save for Paloma, wept in chorus.

Paloma said, "Believe me, my dear sisters, I share your pain. I only hold my grief until I have fulfilled the wishes of my husband upon his death."

Brekka squeezed out the words as she took Paloma's hand to comfort her. "We all see thy pain Mother Paloma and we are so grateful the king entrusted you to reveal his will. We want you to know that we all will support you in whatever you request."

"Thank you, my darling Brekka. I needed that vote of confidence. Inside, I grieve over our parting with our man. But be assured, we shall all, one day, be rejoined in that eternal circle of familial love from which no darkness from beneath nor from above can separate us."

Sur Sceaf floated on the ceiling above the kitchen larder. As he directed his sight below, he watched Eldir as the boy continued to goad his body into play. A keen awareness overtook him and moved him to pass through walls like they were silk curtains and into the council fire room. He spied a Dark Elf perched by the fireplace, disguised as a wyrm-kat. He was about to rebuke the fiend when he saw Bergere had already detected its deception and was moving to protect his family. After Bergere's jaws clamped down on the demon's throat, it had no choice, but to reveal itself or flee. It fled out through the chimney in its ethereal form, shooting a frightened glance at Sur Sceaf as it passed.

Sur Sceaf attempted communion with Brekka, but she was too distraught to detect his presence. He followed her to the kitchen and then to the larder. And though he sought to comfort her as she wept over his body, she was soon to be joined by his bride-covey. His heart was moved in anguish at their suffering. He felt no pain, but any attempt to comfort them only caused them to express greater grief, so he backed off in his spirit body and watched as Taneshewa fell atop him wailing. He was about to embrace her when he felt a hand on his shoulder and heard the distinct voice of his own father, Sur Spear.

"Sur Sceaf, my beloved son, turn away from this place of wrath and tears. Your mortal trials are now over. From henceforth, you shall eat from the Tree of Life in the exulted company of the gods and the elves."

As he turned he saw his father, the All-Father Woon, and Muryh the Master Builder, come as a quorum to guide him home. Woon beckoned him and, as he approached, it was like leaving a dark room for one filled with brilliant light. Woon took him in the royal embrace and said, "Come with us, thou good and faithful son. Thou hast been Os-Syr-Tru over a few kingdoms. Now I shall place thee as lord over many kingdoms. But for now, the time for refreshment and rest from all your mortal cares is come. Trouble thyself no more for the cares of the children of the mould. In good time thy wives, thy children, thy kith and thy kin shall all be restored to thee insomuch that not one hair of thine head will be lost."

Paloma had sent Uffa to summon Long Swan, Forsetti, Ilkchild and Arundel to the Great Hall. One-by-one, they had arrived, and with the exception of the lore master, to a man, had expressed shock and dismay at the sudden shift in the orbit of the kingdom. Even though Surrey had prepared Paloma for his passing through the veil, she still felt as though a part of her had been torn to shreds. Yet, she managed to summon the strength to remain composed by promising herself that after the internment, she would allow the floods of grief to overtake her. She would retire to some distant ghost marsh to wail, weep, and keen.

While Ilkchild and Forsetti gave way to tears at the sight of the body, Long Swan and Ary remained stoic. Clearly, Long Swan had long prepared himself for this day. Knowing her son, Ary, as well as she did, Paloma knew that although he was suffering as grievously as was she, he was following her example, very much as she had followed her own mother's behavior upon the death of her father, Malcolm the Great.

Though spacious, the larder had grown crowded with the arrival of the men. Eldir glanced up at his mother, his face wrinkled in confusion."Mama, why are Ilkchild and Forsey crying?"

Pale and teary eyed, Brekka replied, "It's always sad when someone we love must take leave of us."

"Are they going to take MoFa to Valhalla now?"

"No, MoFa is likely already on his way to Valhalla. We are going to get his body ready for its journey to his dolman. Remember when I told you that a dolman is a door to the heavens?"

"Like Wilona's?"

"Exactly. And I've told you how often she visits me when I pray at the dolman. When you find yourself missing MoFa, you can go to his dolman and pray, and a channel will be opened for you to be heard, for our wights guard our tomb."

Eldir brightened, his large gray eyes filled with the faith of an innocent. "Will MoFa visit me? Will he play with me again?"

"I have no doubt, my love. I know he will watch over you in his many visitations. You will find him at your side during a hunt or on a mushroom foray. Should you ever encounter a bear or a troll he will strengthen your arms. Should the trials and tribulations of this world befall you, he will be there to proffer you counsel and uplift you on the wings of hope. But now, we must find your fa." Reverently, Brekka kissed her father on the forehead before getting to her feet. "Mother Paloma, please feel free to request the assistance of my servants and staff. In the meantime, I'll begin arrangements for the formal announcement and the royal lying-in-state."

"Thank you, my dear one. Your fa has left instructions that he wishes to lie beneath the Ever-Living Tree."

"Then I shall make it so." Brekka extended her hand to Eldir, who leaned forward and kissed his grandfather on the forehead.

"FaMo, tell the gods to let you come back to see me a lot." After scrambling to his feet, he took his mother's hand and they walked into the kitchen where Miss Betty and others were heard expressing their own grief. Every face was drenched in tears and sad eyes.

Holding back her own sobs, Lana bent over Taneshewa. Speaking softly, she said, "Dear Ahy, it is time now we go to prepare our husband for his final journey."

"When we were at dear Lorna's funeral, Surrey promised Il-Alim we would return in the spring to reinvest him with the Red Sash of Royalty." She choked a sob. "Poor Ily. First, he loses the love of his life in the throes of childbirth, and now I have to tell him his dear father has departed into the west."

Swan Hilde knelt beside Lana. "Darling Ahy, it is required that the bride-covey prepare the king's body, but if that is asking too much of you, we will understand."

Taneshewa looked startled. "No, you're right, Hilly. I must be there. Surrey would expect that of me." She tried to rise, but her knees buckled. Ilkchild was instantly at her side and used his good arm to help her stand.

"Ahy, great was Surrey's love for you," he told her in a nurturing tone. "He never tired of telling me of his devotion to you."

She offered him a shaky, tear-drenched smile of gratitude before attempting a smile. "Forgive me, Sisters, for my weakness. Surrey was always my stay in life. I will now honor him by doing my duty."

While the men bore the king upon a litter into one of the upper chambers, Paloma delegated tasks to her bride-sisters in preparation for the ritual washing and anointing of the king's body with the required spices and ointments and in the prescribed order of the ritual.

Efficient as always, Brekka had summoned the ritual embalmers from the House of the Dead located in an underground chamber of the temple to perform their services, which included the removal of the king's heart to be enshrined in a golden reliquary.

Once in the upper chamber, Paloma asked Ary and Long Swan to cut off Surrey's clothing and remove his boots, but to leave his loin cloth in place until the maids bringing the water and soap had departed. She nearly broke down at the sight of the many scars that marked the trail of his sojourn through the Ea-Urth as both a king and a warrior. She recalled that when they had been first married, his body was as unmarked as a marble statue. But now she could mark each battle that he had fought by tracing the tracks of wounds across his body.

*Oh, my sweet Surrey, although I rejoice that your mortal suffering is over and you shall now bear no more afflictions, this parting is bittersweet. I shall miss you dreadfully and for a very long time.*

At her direction, censers containing precious copal incense given as a gift from Mendaka and Little Doe were lit, filling the room with their resinous scent. Paloma's brides sister each took up a position alongside the bed in the order of marriage, with Paloma anointing his head and Taneshewa at the feet. Taking up sponges and lavender soap, they lovingly bathed and dried the body with the finest chamois cloth.

Paloma then broke the seals on alabaster jars of spikenard, myrrh, and the requisite funerary spices. After mixing them with yew oil, the bride-sisters let down their hair and used the long thick strands to anoint every inch of the body after the manner of prescribed burial of Herewardi royalty.

In silence, the sisters wrapped Sur Sceaf in the finest linen swaddling cloth, leaving his noble face uncovered for all to see. They then crossed his arms and bound them on his chest, before wrapping him in his kingly robes.

Unbeknownst to all but Paloma and Long Swan, Sur Sceaf had also commissioned Sur Child in secret to fashion sarcophaguses for himself and his bride troupe from the trunks of ancient yew trees personally selected by Sur Sceaf in the forest of D'If. Since that time, Sur Child and his trusted apprentices had been painstakingly hollowing out the trunks one-by-one until the interiors were silken smooth and displaying the rich grain of the holy wood.

The Quailor master carver and artisan, Horst Gimmelhausen, had been personally chosen by the king to carve the lids, over which Sur Child was to add thin plates of beaten gold. At the time of the king's death, Sur Child and his select crew had completed four of the eight sarcophaguses—Sur Sceaf's, of course, and three others chosen in no particular order so as not to tempt the fates, as it was believed. Upon inquiring, Paloma found that the three included her own, Milkchild's, and Taneshewa's.

After Sur Sceaf was placed in his sarcophagus by Uffa, Ilkchild, Forsetti and Arundel, Paloma placed a sprig of misseltwig tenderly on his crossed arms to ward off all evil. Arundel then stepped forward to place a hickory flail in his father's right hand, the symbol of justice. As he stepped back, Long Swan stepped forward to place a shepherd's crook in his right hand. Striped in red, white, and turquoise to represent the colors of royal blood, light, and truth. The crook was the symbol of mercy.

At Paloma's request, Long Swan led the company in the dirge, "The Passing of the King."

And then it was done. The last duties of the wives were finished. The king was clothed for passage into the Celestial Realm.

At the rising of the sun on the following morning a hundred and forty-forty snow-white pigeons with whistles attached to their tails were released into the cerulean sky, followed by three pigeons dyed blood-red, emblematic of the King of Three Bloods. In Herewardi tradition, a royal death was always thus announced to the inhabitants and dignitaries of the land.

Word passed quickly, from house-to-house, person-to-person. Soon the streets were filled with men, women, and children wishing to offer homage to the departed king. During the night, under Brekka's orders, announcements had been posted on message boards in Martinsbuhr announcing the order of events open to the public as well as giving directions for the positioning of families, tribes, and distinguished visitors. Harriers and circuit-riders had sped to outlying villages bearing similar announcements, which town criers spread far and wide. Rangers lit spirit fires and fanisks atop surrounding hills as beacons to the gods.

Paloma, as queen of queens, had laid out the funerary ceremonies, procession and wake in accord with the archival instructions for the burial of the king of kings as relayed to her by Long Swan in his capacity as prothonatory scribe.

After Paloma and her bride-sisters had prepared Sur Sceaf's body and placed it in his sarcophagus, they and any member of his family or close friends who wished to attend, formed a prayer circle in the great hall council chamber. The godhi and godija sang hymns and dirges interspersed with prayers from Long Swan representing the Herewardi and Dr. Shanks speaking for the Quailor. All culminated with a full-hearted Sharaka burial chant conducted by Mendaka and his family.

In accordance with the Herewardi Law of Two Witnesses, Sur Sceaf had made it known to Paloma and Long Swan that he wished to lie in state beneath the Ever-Living Tree instead of the customary site of the Urth Room in the temple. He had confided in Paloma that the stone bench beneath the lacy canopy had become one of his favorite places to sit and reflect, a place where he'd experienced many revelations and communications with Odhin, lesser gods, the Holy Elves, and other familiar spirits.

Tears filled Paloma's eyes as she revealed, "One day, as we sat together under its hoary branches, he took me into his arms and told me how much he cherished me every step along the way from virgin to matriarch, and that he particularly appreciated my role as faery-queen, wife, and mother. I know he truly felt the words he spoke on that day, and I know that he cherished each and every one of you as dearly, my dear bride-sisters. Each of you bearing your own special fruit made his garden one of light, pleasure, and happiness."

At the conclusion of the prayer circle, the pallbearers stepped forward. Chosen by Sur Sceaf, they represented special friendships and alliances. Mendaka and Son, Going Snake, represented the Sharaka. Walter Shanks represented the Quailor and Ruhm, the Hickoryans. Herewose stood in his father Pyrsyrus' stead, and El Yid, representing his father, the revered Rabbi Amschel.

Alph Hegele, representing his father, Hartmut Hegele, Sur Sceaf's dearest friend and Quailor brother, had the great honor of bearing the golden reliquary containing the king's heart.

With Alph in the lead, and the family and closest of friends following, the pallbearers carried the open sarcophagus out of the hall, circling around the golden obelisk three times, then carried on through the narrow eastern door of the temple into the Urth Chamber and out the western door to the Ever-Living Tree where he was to lie in state on a hazel wicker platform surrounded by yew fronds and magnolia wreaths. With great reverence Yellow Horse slowly unfurled Sur Sceaf's personal White Horse standard with its scarlet ground and golden runes. He laid it over Sur Sceaf's body leaving his face visible. "Yellow Horse then took up his position next to the high king, Lord Arundel, and Redelfis.

Long serpentine lines of mourners threaded slowly through the hedgerows around the mound, waiting patiently for the opportunity to view the king for the last time, and to bid him safe journey to Valhalla. Long Swan as prothonatory scribe gave the benediction.

At the conclusion of the prayer, Sur Sceaf's personal twelver led his fyrd in a rousing Syr Haka, while Paloma stepped forward to lay a magnolia blossom atop the flail, crook, and misseltwig. One-by-one his wives followed suit with asters of purple hues. Taneshewa, as the last bride chosen, carried both a bundle of sage she had collected nigh thirty winters ago at Di-Ahman after their first encounter. With tears streaming down her face, she tucked the sage next to him along with her placental talisman, offering up her own spiritual protection to him as the ultimate token of her supreme devotion. She suddenly let out a keening wail of anguish and threw herself across his chest and showered his face with kisses.

"Oh, Surrey, the sun has left my sky. How could you leave me to drown in the darkness of this world?" Her sobs filled the air, inciting a crescendo of grief from the crowd.

Paloma's heart was breaking for her Sister as she stepped forward to stroke Ahy's hair. Bending forward, she whispered, "Dearest Sister, do not despair. Our beloved husband is not lost, only absent from us for a brief span of mortal time. His love was great unto you, and cannot be severed by the cruel blade of death."

Taneshewa slowly rose, and turning to Paloma, choked out, "Would that this was just a nightmare, and that on the morrow I may wake to find my dearest lying next to me."

Sur Sceaf was held in a dream-like limbo by the outpouring of love and grief over his exit from the Realm of Mould. Watching from his ethereal perch like a hawk from a crag, he agonized over Taneshewa's raw suffering. He knew full well that his spirit should be able to swoop down within the blink of an eye to comfort her, but try as he might, some force restrained him.

"Please release me! Let me go to my beloved wives and give them relief from their pain."

Woon took him gently by the arm and said, "Taneshewa's heart will break its vessel and spill into the well of life. When it is her time, she shall join you in the kingdom of our ancient tribe. See, we must go and prepare a place for you, your bride-covey, and all your posterity as all your worthy fathers have heretofore done, and as the thread of destiny has been woven on the looms of the Norns."

In a twinkling of an eye, Sur Sceaf was as naked as a newborn babe, but strangely felt no accompanying shame. Father Woon handed him a shimmering garment with the luminescence of mother-of-pearl tinged with radiant silver. "This raiment has been waiting for you and will shield you and grant you protection upon your readmission into the Higher Realms.

The robe hung loosely from his neck to his ankles and had the smooth feel of the finest of silk. On his feet appeared winged slippers with a quicksilver shimmer and curious turned-up toes. Both the garment and slippers bestowed the gift of elevation above all earthly powers.

The light intensified as they stepped upon what at first appeared to be a solid bridge of glass in the colors of a rainbow but soon began flowing like a mighty river into the heavens. Stars turned in cyclonic activity, as wave after wave of thunder rolled over them until they landed before the Great Blond God, Heimdal, standing as a sentinel at the end of the bridge. Acting under his command a double flaming sword swirled in front of the portal to Os-Gard, thus effectively blocking the entrance.

The Fairest of Gods rumbled in his deep voice, "Who comes here?"

The All Father answered, "A traveler from the Realms of the Mould and Flesh, having been found worthy of all acceptation into the Society of Gods, Elves, and Holy Men, like unto all the proven fathers before him."

"You shall pass," the Guardian God declared. He raised his hands, and the flaming swords moved to the side, allowing free passage, after which they resumed their former position.

Together, they passed along a flourishing path, through an enormous outer garden to the gates of a magnificent city where a welcoming host of kith and kin similarly attired were gathered. The place seemed strangely familiar, as if long-forgotten memories were returning.

As he approached the crowd he discerned the face of his beloved mother, Mahallah; to her side stood Redith, and Sagawis. He fell upon their necks and hugged them. As he looked around he saw Elfbeard, Crooked Jack, Onamingo, and Thunder Horse, and his heart swelled with overwhelming joy.

Onamingo made his way over to him. "I welcome you as a brother, Sur Sceaf. I have looked through the veil and seen my daughter, whose heart is at the point of breaking asunder with the unbearable weight of grief that no mortal should ever have to bear. I pray for the day when we shall return together for Taneshewa. At the appointed time, we shall close her eyes to suffering and spirit her away from the realm of mortals."

Her absence caused a tug at Sur Sceaf's heart strings, and his heart was drawn out for his beloved, as it was for all of his wives and loved ones thus left behind. The comforting thought came to him that a thousand years on Ea-Urth was like a single day in Os-Gard. He rejoiced that his wives would soon join him.

Onamingo stepped aside, allowing Redith to take his place. Her countenance aglow, she took his arm. "There are many, many friends waiting to see you, my dear grandson. Some, you never knew in mortal life. Some from eons before you, and others from your Seed who shall take up residence on the Ea-Urth eons after you are laid to rest. Many who will make a pilgrimage to your dolman, and others who would employ your casketed heart as protection in battles that yet lay in the future, for it is the design of the gods that there will never be an end to war on the Ea-Urth; for only thus can the spirits be proven for the battles that await us in the heavens."

Sur Sceaf covered her hand with his, and, as they strode through the exquisite pathways of vegetative exuberance, he was overtaken by the singular beauty of landscape and architecture that flourished all about them. Soon they came upon a large party of old comrades gathered beneath an enormous agathus tree.

It seemed that Redith had some design for their excursion. He felt overwhelming feelings of love for everyone there and a great sense of utter well-being as he reacquainted himself with friend after fallen friend. There was the noble Aethelstan, the ever-stalwart Crooked Jack, who was no longer broken across the back but in the prime of his life and, to his surprise, even his brother, Melyngoch, whose smile beamed as warm as sunlight.

A memory of deepest affection filled his heart. It was suddenly made clear to him that his friendship with this troubled brother was far more ancient and had gone far deeper than either had realized during their brief mortal span of life together. Memories flooded in, of pleasant times and shared adventures. His heart was filled with instant forgiveness.

"Dearest Brother, our mortal existence in this life blotted out the friendship of our previous life. But now we are once again friends at last, and once again joined in the eternal spiral journey upwards."

Melyngoch was moved by his words. "Dear Brother, we shall indeed be friends and make full amends for past slights and transgressions incurred under the dark veil of flesh that blinded us of our holy bonds to one another."

A group of tall fair men approached Sur Sceaf, led by Wilona and a powerfully charismatic man whom he instantly sensed had to be the Grand Patriarch, Hrus-Syr-Os; father of their nation.

The longfather embraced him and said, "We have sorely missed your company, Surrey. Your mission to Ea-Urth has been well done, and we look forward to your wisdom as you join once again in our heavenly council fires."

Wilona smiled warmly. "You are newly arrived here, Lord Sur Sceaf. It takes the passing of many days before you regain your former memories of your life here before the Ea-Urth life." Pointing to one of the tall youths with raven black hair, Wilona explained, "This is Ri, who will soon be the son of Il-Alim, to be born of Yffe's hearth. He was chosen and elected by you and the others of your extensive clan to be king over the many lands after the long reign of my son, Anghrus, is fulfilled."

Turning to a tall tawny haired man with sharp green eyes and ten maids clustered about him, Wilona said, "This is Suryggyrus, who will be born to Anghrus of Pyrsyrus' granddaughter, Siff's hearth, and will become a great military commander. It is woven by the Norns that his feet shall be on the bows of all our enemies during his generation, that our enemies shall come against him as one, but will depart from him in a hundred directions, and he shall hunt them down to the ends of the Ea-Urth.

Faint memories of his days spent in these gardens started breaking through to his consciousness like the outline of a distant skyscape on a foggy morning. Images of a time when he had been introduced to Hrus-Syr-Os after the death of the Great King came to him in crystal clarity, as did the memory of the Longfather Hereward telling him that he would one day take up residence on the Ea-Urth and become a King of Three Bloods to unite three tribes to defeat tyranny and break the bonds of oppression over his people and prepare the soil for the return of the sovereignty of Tribes.

Wilona turned to a towering red-haired man of manly proportions and superior physical strength. "This man will be born Tyranus-Sur-Hrus. He is to be the son of Forsetti, of Ka-Luna's hearth. He it is to be fated to be Suryggyrus' right arm in the coming Age of Wars. This will be a time when the evil forces of the Old World will pour over the walls like a typhoon, beating in wave after wave against the gates of Panygyrus, the freest of nations under the heavens."

Finally, Redith led him to a rose-covered bower where two of the most beautiful women he'd ever seen stood smiling an eager welcome. Like unfolding blossoms, he recalled that one was Syr-Ah and the other was Fae-Rah. Both had been fated and sealed to him before they had left for mortal experience. Memories cascaded over him, of saying a heart-wrenching good-bye to each of them before they descended to the Ea-Urth. Both had passed through very trying and unhappy marriages before returning to Os-Gard with the hope of this day's reunion with their eternal husband and king.

Redith's smile was gentle. "It has been decreed by Odhin that Freya shall put it in the mind of Brekka to officiate in the sealing of these promised wives to join your bride-covey with the authorization of Paloma, so that what is above may be below, and what is below may be above in the order the elves have decreed and the gods have set in firmness and beauty."

Deep feelings resonated in his heart, and he found himself speechless with delight at how much love he had instantly felt for these lovely women. He was overwhelmed with the gratitude that the gods were good, and that the gods were great.

At high noon, stallion fights commenced on the promontory and continued throughout the day, as was custom after the death of a king. The spectators and handlers were shocked when Arundel led Sur Sceaf's last mount, Altar Fire, into the paddock by the Elf Waters where the contests were being held.

Ruhm, who was acting as horse master in charge of the stallion hrink, rushed up to Ary. "My lord, surely you are not proposing to put forth the king's mount as a contestant. Such a magnificent steed does not deserve to be marred by the teeth or hooves of these wild mustangs, Dzungarians, and cobs."

Ary ran his hand over Altar Fire's teeming mane. Ruhm had the right of it. Altar Fire was indeed a magnificent product of his brother Aelfheah's brilliant breeding programs at Powers. He stifled a sigh. "This horse was beloved by my father and is my gift to the gods in token of remembrance of all my father has given me, just as my longfather, King Sur, offered up his father Leofric's Stallion, Woon Fyr, to the gods in memory of Leofric's steadfast love of his people. The gods love those who give sacrifices and gifts, and the windows of Heaven are opened to their posterity."

"My Hanoverians are fine steeds indeed, but I'd trade half of my stable just to have this steed." Ruhm bit off his covetness, shook his head and sighed. "The ways of the Herewardi are rich indeed. Who am I to question their values?"

Altar Fire handily defeated every opponent put against him, suffering no injury unto himself. His swift hooves readily dispatched his less skillful opponents, and, in fact, he showed such great heart that several of the stallions bolted after the first encounter. After the ninth and final counts of the victory rings, the stallion was declared the ultimate victor. Ruhm signaled to the lur blowers to announce the placing of the traditional and highly prized magnolia wreath over the triumphant horse's head.

Standing next to Altar Fire and Ruhm, Ary declared in a booming voice, "I decree this magnificent stallion that was greatly prized by the mighty Warrior King Sur Sceaf is now marked as property of the gods. Let it be found in no man's possession under penalty of swift death no less than by drawing and quartering."

At Ruhm's direction, a handler opened the paddock gate whereupon Altar Fire bolted free and galloped away at great speed, his shimmering white mane flowing past the wreath in the afternoon sun. At the top of the promontory, Altar Fire paused, turned around, reared, pawed the air with his great hooves and shouted his farewell. Seconds later, he shot off at lightning speed through the trees into the savannah lands of the Shenandoah, where he would forever run free. Never to be ridden by a mortal man again.

# CHAPTER 18 :
## THERE WAS A QUEEN

THE PROCESSION OF MOURNERS SEEMED endless. As day turned to night, they kept coming in droves, now bearing torches and lanterns to light their way. Children and women wept. Men, many in uniform with ashes of mourning for a fallen comrade on their faces, passed by and saluted.

Paloma and the bride-sisters had agreed to remain by the body until midnight, at which time one after another would take an hour's shift for their watch. Lana took the first shift, sitting on Sur Sceaf's favored bench and graciously accepting the condolences of those passing by.

As the bride-sisters took their leave, Paloma noticed Brekka and Verushka approaching the byre. Brekka carried a decanter of Cacapon crystal containing Liza's green liqueur, while Veru carried three matching crystal glasses.

"My ladies," Paloma said, "this is so thoughtful of you. I was thinking of taking a measure of peach brandy myself to ease the bite of grief."

Brekka was hollow-eyed but resolute. "Dr. Shanks has recently begun using Liza's liqueur instead of poppy milk because he says it eases the pain, but the patient remains aware. He bade me to administer it in small doses. Never more than three glasses in a twelve-hour period. Shall I pour a measure for you, Mother Superior?"

Paloma thought for a moment before answering. "Yes, please, my dear. That would be most gracious."

Verushka held out a glass, and Brekka poured a full measure. At first a bit hesitant, Paloma merely wetted her lips, but found the taste so delicious, she swallowed several sips. A pleasurable sensation of warmth and well-being gradually enveloped her from head to toe. "I must compliment Liza. This is indeed restorative to the spirits." She drained the glass before handing it back to Veru. "Have you sent a sample of this marvelous concoction to Xelph for study?"

Veru nodded. "Oh yes, to both Xelph and Siwel. Face-of-Stars wrote back to say that Xelph is working to perfect its salubratory properties along with several other mixtures garnered over the past few years from the mountain witches which he has taken a particular liking to."

As Paloma hurried along the path, following the glow of shining moon's lantern, she noticed one of the sisters veered off toward the procession and disappeared behind the hedges enclosing the elf waters. Realizing it was Ahy, she hurried to intercept her, but Ahy was too swift. She did manage to keep her in sight and followed her path to the elf waters where she found her sister sitting on a rectangular block of limestone so common to the crystal springs.

The clear water bubbled up from the dark depths, creating ripples in its black mirrored surface. In the distance she heard the haunting cry of a loon, a counterpoint to the soft shuffle of feet on the path worn down by the multitude of the passing mourners.

Paloma slowed her pace in order not to startle Ahy. As she approached, she saw tears streaming from her sister's swollen eyes and realized they shone golden in the reflected torch light.

"Ahy, it is I, Paloma," she whispered softly. "May I join you?"

"If you wish." Ahy moved over to give Paloma ample room.

As Paloma stretched a compassionate arm around her sister-wife's shoulders, a surge of unbearable grief ran through her, releasing the sobs she had kept so rigidly at bay during the day's trying proceedings.

The two wept together for several minutes before Ahy gasped out, "Oh, Paloma, my heart pounds like eagle's wings so furiously against my ribs, I fear they shall break asunder and it shall soon take flight."

"My dear Ahy, I do so understand." As they fell to weeping once again, the air began swirling around them. From above came the rhythmic sound of powerful wings. In a blur of white a flight of nine swans swooped down to land without a splash on the surface of the rippling water. Immediately following a shower of light appeared, out of which two figures of celestial hue levitated several feet above the water, and approached them like a cloud.

Paloma had been visited many times by the elven lords, rulers of the heavenly realms and faithful allies of Odhin, but Ahy was clearly stunned, her mouth agape, and her tear-filled eyes now wide open in wonder. Paloma put her hand over Ahy's to reassure her. "Fear not, these are they who are for us."

One of the elven lords spoke in a melodious tone that was musical to the ear, "Ye daughters of Os, why sit ye weeping on the banks of the elf waters? Know ye not, fair Paloma, that you shall be known as a grand lady and live to see the fifth generation of your offspring. Your name shall be found praiseworthy from one end of the heavens to the other. Your devotion to Sur Sceaf and support for his difficult commission as well as your steadfast commitment to your folk and the causes of goodwill toward all mankind shall be held high as the model for all rising generations."

The second exalted lord, an elf of splendid red hued skin spoke, "Fair Ahyyyokah Taneshewa, weep no more, for this night, ere the sun rises on the morrow, you shall join with your beloved. The Herewardi minstrels shall sing of the love between Sur Sceaf and Taneshewa until the last generations of time." The lord stepped forward and gently touched her with a fingertip between her eyes. "Peace unto you, my daughter," he commanded. "Leave behind your mortal cares and enter into the rest on the arm of your lord."

Without warning, the light gathered again around the elven lords and became a ball of lightning that shot skyward, sending the swans into a spiraling flight once again to trail the lords and soon to disappear into the star-lit darkness above.

When Paloma gathered her senses, she realized that Ahy had gone limp in her arms. Gently, she placed her hand over Ahy's tormented heart and felt not even the slightest flutter. Nor did any discernible breath escape her nostrils. The breath of life had departed her and her spirit had taken flight with the swans.

Even though her own heart grieved for the loss of a dear sister, she couldn't hold back a sigh of envy. Perhaps the elven lords had deliberately cut short the silver thread of her life out of pity for her intolerable suffering, which, no doubt would have continued without surcease. Or perhaps Ahy had consciously willed herself through the veil. No matter the reason for her spirit's departure, in all likelihood, her beloved Surrey waited on the other side to receive her.

Paloma whispered through her tears, "Take your rest now, my dear sister, in the bosom of Hereward, Odhin, and his friends the Thunder Beings, though I will greatly miss your company and your counsel. Daily, I shall feel the loss of your endearing smile and laughter, but you shall enjoy far better company among the exalted in the halls of Valhalla on high."

Paloma sat holding Ahy to her heart for she knew not how long. The procession continued without cease long into the morning hours. At the first sound of lark song, she gently laid Ahy on the smooth stone and rose. Though she was exhausted, sleep had to wait, as there was much to do. That day, at Sunset, the gods willing, and the Roufytrof yielding to her pleas, the two lovers would be laid to rest together atop the Mound of Heredom.

Cocooned in warmth and surrounded by her favorite scents of lavender and sage, Taneshewa floated above the Big Springs. Directly overhead, the Elven Lords appeared as trailing streaks of light. Below her, the flight of swans took to the skies and passed into the west. Looking down, she watched as Paloma cradled her body in her arms, rocking her gently to and fro whilst weeping.

Though she grieved for causing her sister this added pain, she realized that her own grief that had wracked her to the bone was now gone. In its place, a feeling of well-being and joy filled her bosom. Slowly, she was engulfed in otherworldly ether like the soft mist of a summer morning in Di-Ahman. As though from a distance came the musical tinkling of chimes.

The mist slowly took form until it resembled the gossamer veil in the Daleth Tent when she was wed to her most beloved. Now, as then, a hand reached out to her through the veil. Slowly, she was pulled through the gentle squeeze of the mist until she came face-to-face with her darling Surrey. Happiness exploded inside her as the flames of their love joined into a blaze of celestial ecstasy.

"My dearest love," he whispered before drawing her close in a royal embrace and kissing her tenderly. When he released her and she opened her eyes, she found herself surrounded by those she loved best. Her father, Onamingo, her mother, Dancing Rabbit, her Aunt Sagwi, and the beloved Thunder Horse clad in brilliant robes of light and winged slippers. And their faces were wreathed in smiles of welcome.

Surrey whispered, "By the grace of the elven lords, the all-father has acknowledged my desperate desire to comfort you and has granted a special dispensation to us that the cries of his daughter may no longer come up before the ears of Heimdal. It was he who pronounced an end to your suffering and a shortening of your mortality." Smiling his beautiful smile, Surrey took her hand and together they passed over the Rainbow Bridge of Bifrost.

Brekka had wept well into the morning hours and slept badly, rising well before the larks took wing for their morning song. Not wishing to disturb Ruhm lying beside her, she left the warmth of her bed and went out onto the balcony. Though it was not yet dawn, the sky had an orange hue from the myriad of signal fires in the surrounding hills. On the green, the procession of mourners continued its serpentine path, flickering torches lit great expanses of hedgerow like a luminescent green dragon. In the distant Sharaka encampment, the steady throb of funeral drums and continuous chanting in honor of a fallen chief accompanied the sounds of grief from below.

The morning air held the crispness of autumn with a slight breeze carrying the distinctive scent of burning torches. As she looked out over the sad scene, she heard the door open. Ruhm came up behind her and mantled her with a blanket still warm from the heat of his body.

He brushed a kiss against her temple before wrapping his arms around her. "Dearest Brekka, I wish I could lift this pain from your shoulders."

She turned into his arm and nestled into his warm chest. "Oh Ruhm, my heart is grieved indeed for the loss of my father, but my grief is tempered with knowledge that the time of his passing was fated by the Norn Sisters. I am comforted knowing that he is resting in the company of the ancient elven kings in the bosom of Hereward, and that someday I shall see him again in the plains of the Summer Lands. Yet I feel a certain heaviness in my soul, as though a weight of some kind has been added upon my heart that extends beyond the grief for Fa."

A sigh escaped Ruhm's lips. "I have learned to put my trust in such feelings from you. In the past, such intuition has saved lives, and often bodes an approaching doom. The last time you felt this way we soon heard that Lorna had parted mortality in childbirth."

"Poor Ily, he suffered so, and then to hear that Fa has died so soon after losing Lorna and his newborn as well. But I'm very glad he's coming for the internment. Mother Taneshewa's bride-sisters are so worried about her, and say she cannot be comforted no matter what they do or say. I'm hoping that Ily can relieve some of her grief sickness when he arrives. Ahy has spoken often of her eagerness to meet his new bride, Siff. I pray that will at least lift her heart in some small measure."

"I've done much thinking during these past three days about loss and grief and the bane of our mortal existence. I have observed how Paloma and her bride-sisters have come together to comfort one another, and then I thought of my own mother and her suffering over the loss of my sister. I don't think she really ever got over it." Ruhm stroked her back. "I found myself wondering if she'd had bride-sisters to help her through the pain, if her suffering perhaps might have been greatly lessened. Father and I did our best, but we'd often find her keening on the front porch and holding Sissy's doll against her breast with empty eyes and that haunting hollow expression of an irreversible loss."

Brekka sighed. "With Lorna's death, tragic that it was, Ily has been released from his vow of monogamy. I take it as a very good sign that he has taken a royal daughter of the land. I can think of no better faery-queen to assist in his search for a covey than Fa-Bro's black-haired granddaughter, Siff. Ilkchild has sung her praises even before Ily took a liking to her. Apparently, she was one of his best students at the Academy at Moon Door." She chuckled. "As I recall, he referred to her as a wizard wrestler, and said she often confounded many of the Wizards at the Academy with her profound knowledge of the sciences, often excelling their own."

"Little wonder Ily chose her. She does indeed sound remarkable and praiseworthy, but she will never surpass my many-talented wife."

"I thank you, my love, but it is not a contest."

They passed a few silent moments before Ruhm admitted, "It troubles me that Il-Alim has not yet arrived. The harrier he sent was very clear that he intended to arrive yestereve at the latest. I heard from a traveler of flash floods and tree-ripping winds near Front Royal on the way to the Winchester Pike. Perhaps he's been forced to take the longer road through Leesburg, which could very well add a good half day to his journey."

"I imagine Mother Ahy and her sisters have sent up her prayers for his safe arrival. And Bithia mentioned yesterday that Going Snake has posted sentries on Winchester Pike to alert us as soon as Ily's banner is sighted."

"What happens if he is delayed?" Ruhm asked. "Will the unveiling of the burial site and the internment of the king be postponed?"

She shook her head. "The law governing the burial of a king demands internment on the third day and cannot be unwritten."

For a time they stood in silence, wrapped in their own thoughts and somber reflection while the sky turned to purple and lavender and the Morning Star, Earindil, heralded the arrival of a new day.

Ruhm said suddenly, "Look, Brekka, isn't that the Lady Paloma walking up from the big springs by herself?"

Following his gaze, she spied her nigh-mother moving slowly through the hedges, her head bowed and hooded in her silver cape like a ghost passing over the green sward. "Something's amiss. This does not bode well. The ur-fyr tells me that Paloma bears sad news. I pray no harm has come to Ily. See! Let us go to her at once."

When Paloma reached the great hall, she found Brekka and Ruhm waiting in the foyer. "Our dear Ahy has followed Surrey into the summer lands," she told them before haltingly recounting the events by the elf waters. Even if her voice cracked several times, she managed to maintain a semblance of composure.

Although clearly stricken by the news, neither Brekka nor Ruhm seemed unduly shocked. Prompting Paloma to ask, "Brekka, did you scry this?"

"No, Mother Superior, but I did have a heavy sense of dread in my being."

"As did I," Paloma was finally able to admit. "Though I hoped I was mistaken."

Brekka took a deep breath. "Forgive my impertinence, but you look utterly exhausted. If you will allow me, I will summon stewards to convey Mother Ahy to the House of the Dead."

Paloma offered her a look of gratitude. "It would be wrong of me to refuse such an act of kindness. Thank you."

The House of the Dead was located in a consecrated underground chamber with passageways beneath and beyond the temple. The royal embalmers were also trained priests who would minister to Ahy with great care and respect, just as they had served Surrey only three days before.

Brekka rang the bell near the door to summon a green beetle. When he arrived, Paloma recognized the lad as Raedwulf, the son of one of Brekka's field commanders, Il-Hammer the Splitter, and Pata's younger brother.

Brekka quickly explained why he had been summoned, then ordered him to call forth four stewards she listed by name. "Inform them that it is my command that Lady Taneshewa's body must be treated with the utmost reverence due a queen. Use the canopied and veiled litter reserved for ceremony of internment to transport her to the House of the Dead. Please tell no one, so that I may make the announcement at the appropriate time."

After Raedwulf departed, she summoned another beetle with similar instructions to the Master Embalmer in charge of preparing the body.

"Make sure the Master Embalmer understands that his task must be completed in all due haste before eventide."

In the meantime, Ruhm had poured Paloma a glass of Liza's green liqueur. "My lady, let this take the edge off the anguish you must be feeling."

More than anything Paloma wished for sleep. But that must wait. "That is most thoughtful of you, dear Ruhm. I have to admit the glass Brekka proffered earlier did ease my soul. But only a half measure this time. I must be of clear mind. I have much to do this day. I have not yet broken this sad news to my sister-brides, and they will need time to ready themselves for the ritual of preparation as soon as the embalmers are finished."

"Do not worry, my lady. One drink will not cloud your mind. In fact, it will lubricate your words and give you the energy you so desperately need."

Paloma was grateful for his concern and support. As she accepted the glass, she asked, "Has Ily arrived yet? I must go to him first before I break the sad news to my sisters."

"Not yet, my lady. We have heard that thunderstorms in Front Royal have delayed travel. Not even the post can get through."

Paloma took a sip of the sweet sage-scented liqueur. Somehow, she had to summon the strength to carry out the duties required of her as faery-queen and head of the council of women. She took another sip, and then another until the glass was empty. Her blood gradually warmed, and as Ruhm had predicted, her mind seemed to sharpen into unusual clarity while easing some of the cut of her emotional pain.

"Brekka, with your permission, I would like to convene the Council of Women here in the hall as soon as possible. Somehow, we must address this unforeseen dilemma."

Two hours later Paloma convened the Council of Women in the council chamber of the great hall. Her and Brekka's bride-sisters were still shaken by the news of Taneshewa's sudden passing. They took their seats in silence and somber reflection. Little Doe, as the wife of Sur Sceaf's blood brother, was an honorary member of the council, and often attended the meetings. As soon as she'd received word of Ahy's passing, she'd hurried to the springs from the Sharaka Camp to offer her condolences and to comfort Shining Moon who was particularly close to Taneshewa.

Arundel, as the high king represented the executive branch, and as king, always had a seat in the Council of Women as had his father before him. With him, he brought the three wives who'd accompanied him to the springs: Zschamillah, Ilklilith, and Ilkfae.

When all who were summoned had arrived, Paloma instructed the door tiler to seal the meeting to non-members, no matter how prominent or insistent. She cleared her throat, and then began, "I've called this meeting on behalf of our dear sister, Ahyyyokah Taneshewa, who has taken an unexpected flight to the Summer Lands. I am here to attest to the fact that she was granted an early admission by the elven lords and the Nunehi, whose visitation came in on the wings of a wedge of swans from on high during the wee hours of morn.

"The purpose of this meeting is to petition the Roufytrof for permission to inter our dear sister with her beloved husband at sundown today. To this end I've invited the high king, Lord Arundel, the prothonatory scribe, Lord Long Swan, son of Sur Spear, his first counselor, Lord llkchild, son of Ilker, and second counselor, Lord Forsetti, son of Melyngoch the Unready, thus constituting a quorum of the Roufytrof in accordance with the Forty Four Laws as established by our Great Patriarch, Howrus."

Verushka raised her hand. "Mother Superior, may I have the floor?"

"Of course, Verushka."

Verushka stood. "May I ask the prothonatory scribe to relate what the law concerning royal burial specifically states?"

Long Swan stood. "The law, as it stands written, states that the body of a royal personage must be prepared in the prescribed manner and interred in a suitable and consecrated crypt, grave, or dolman on the third day after death. And as you know, that is today."

Verushka frowned. "To be clear, Lore Master, to follow the law, we must wait three days before interring Ahy. Is that correct?"

"That is correct, according to the law."

Ilkchild claimed the floor. "If I may, Madam Superior, I should like to call to memory the words of our longfather, Elrus, in which he stated that in matters of love and the Forty-Four Laws, love should always take precedence."

"Also, remember that it is written in the scriptures of Leofric," Godgifu added urgently, "that when the Kingdom of Baldur is restored to the Ea-Urth, that love will be the prevailing law that governs all."

Sensing the passion of the women mounting, Paloma decided to intervene. "These are excellent points for consideration. The fact that dispensations have been granted for other paradoxical situations would appear to argue in favor of our petition to have our sister interred with our husband. Let me ask for the voice of the sisters of the council in this matter. I ask those members who agree to tender a petition to the quorum of the Roufytrof here present to stand in favor."

Verushka was the only dissenting vote. All others stood to be counted.

As her sisters resumed their seats, Paloma addressed the quorum. "My lords, you have witnessed the manifestation of the will of the Council of Women herewith. Now I ask what will be the binding decree of the quorum? Shall you grant a dispensation, or no?"

Long Swan rose again. "Mother Superior and women of the council, since time immemorial, the Council of Women has been greatly valued by the Roufytrof. It has ever been our shield of protection in troubling times, so we needs must give your petition the greatest of weight. In accordance to the laws, each member of the quorum shall have the opportunity to speak his vote openly. Remember that the vote must be unanimous in favor for the dispensation to be granted. I turn first to Lord Forsetti."

Just as Forsetti got to his feet, a knock at the door forestalled his reply. The lady tiler opened the door and exited. Moments later, she returned. "Mother Superior, I have been informed by a harrier just arrived from Lord Il-Alim with the news that he and his party had camped yestereve at Wizard's Clip on the Opequon and will be arriving here at the great hall within the hour."

Paloma took a deep breath. *Praise the Gods of Os-Gard. One problem solved.* But, she hated the task before her of telling a son already so acquainted with grief that his mother had just departed the mould.

"Thank you, Lady Eaydth. Lords and ladies, this news adds to the urgency of a decision on our petition."

Forsetti nodded. "Here is my view. I believe it is in the highest and best interest of Herewardom to grant a special dispensation as a tribute to our most revered king, Sur Sceaf, and his most beloved wife, Lady Taneshewa." He smiled at Paloma as he resumed his seat.

"Your opinion, Lord Ilkchild," Long Swan requested, pointing his caduceus in his direction.

Ilkchild stood up with the aid of his ivory-winged hazel rod. "Lords and ladies, I have had the great honor of witnessing the timeless love shared by our great warrior king and his ever adoring Taneshewa. It was a love one had to envy, and I for one must grant my voice of approval for this special dispensation. I do this to honor what I believe would be the wish of my beloved nigh-father."

Long Swan rose slowly to his full height. "Lords and ladies, as you know, Sur Sceaf and I considered ourselves twins of separate mothers, but always of one heart and one mind. If my heart tells me correctly, and I believe it does, he would grant this dispensation without any hesitation or qualms. Therefore, acting in the official capacity of prothonatory scribe of the Roufytrof, and cognizant of the unanimous vote of the quorum here convened, I hereby issue to the Council of Women the requested dispensation. This evening at sunset, the Lady Taneshewa shall take her place beside the king." He smiled. "So mote it be."

Il-Alim, his bride of one moonth, Siff, and their escort of bushmaster knights arrived within minutes of the adjournment of the Council of Women. Brekka and Ruhm were there in front of the hall to offer a hearty welcome. The two old friends and comrades embraced warmly with much back thumping and laughter, while Brekka hugged her cousin, Siff.

Brekka had not seen her young cousin in seven years. At that time Siff was just budding into womanhood. The promise of beauty that she had shown then had blossomed into full-blown flower. With the exception of her porcelain-fair peaches and cream complexion, she was the very image of her raven-haired mother, Dona, a most renowned Mexus beauty of great elegance.

"My father sends his love to you and Ruhm, and wishes me to express his deep sadness. I, too, wish to offer you my heartfelt condolences. I remember how close you were to your father. But I have to say, it is so good to see you again, dearest cousin, so I come with a mixed bag of joy and sorrow."

"And I must say it is good to see you again. I had only hoped you'd bring Lorna's children, especially the new babe."

"We did consider it, but Ily decided that the speed at which we had to travel was too rigorous for such young children. And, of course, we would have had to bring baby Ur-Tyr's wet nurse as well, and since she has her own baby to nurse, it would have been ill-advised. I don't have to tell you that Lorna's father is blaming Ily for the death of his daughter down in Charleston. He says it was a heathen spiritual arrow that smote her to death this summer by breaching the child."

"Sadly, Merriman Wallanwood manages to be the author of all his own unhappiness. If he could only learn to accept differences and not try to bend everyone into his mold."

"Oh, before it flies out of my mind, I must tell you I received a message by pigeon relay from my brother, King Thror, who bids me tell you that he and the people of the Sand Wand Island and also his see of Haida Gwai Island are holding a memorial service today in remembrance of Sur Sceaf."

"I know Fa would appreciate that."

"Copper Locks, do you not have a hug for your baby brother?" Ily asked with a grin.

"Oh Ily, I'm so glad to see you." She started to cry. Ily pulled her into his arms for a long hug. "There! There now! It'll be alright."

When he released her, he glanced around. "I know mother must be in the depths of grief. If you would excuse me, I should go to her now. Siff and I hope she'll consider living with us for a time."

Brekka exchanged an anguished look with Ruhm, who encouraged her with an understanding nod. She knew Paloma should be the one to tell him of his mother's death, but her nigh-mother was already burdened beyond bearing. Though it would be painful, she would gladly shoulder this most grievous burden for Paloma's sake.

"Oh Ily, by the gods who love us, I wish I didn't have to be the one to tell you this. Your dear mother was so stricken with grief that her heart simply broke in two. She left us this morning. I must declare to you that she was touched by the elves and took early departure from this vale of sorrows. She could not bear to live without Fa at her side, and so has joined him in the Halls of Valhalla."

Ily let out a gutteral moan and could not speak for several minutes. Siff wrapped her arms around him and he wept on her shoulder. "The fates have not been merciful to me," he choked out. "How have I offended them? First my wife dies, then my father, and now my beloved mother."

"My dear husband, you have done nothing that the Norns would find worthy of punishment. Their ways are not ours to know. They see into the unseen and into the far future. Weeping shall endure for a season, but hope must spring anew. Though your mother and I have crossed paths but rarely, my mother always spoke of her kindness and wisdom, and most of all, her deepest love for you and your siblings. I beg you suspend judgment of the weaving of the Norns, for I believe that to deny her wish to join your father would have been a far greater curse."

Taneshewa lay on the same cold marble table where Sur Sceaf had lain only three days prior. By the time the royal embalmers had finished their work and returned Ahy to the great hall, it was wearing into mid-day. Since time was short, her bride-sisters had foregone the mid-day meal in order to prepare her properly for the ceremony at sunset.

It had been an emotionally rending afternoon, with grief added to grief. Perhaps even harder to bear than their dear sister's passing had been the expression of utter bereavement on Il-Alim's face when he had arrived in the chamber to pay his respects to his mother.

Paloma's heart had gone out to her nigh-son who was as dear to her as the children of her own hearth. Many were the times she bounced the little one on her knees. As Ahy's firstborn, Ily was particularly close to his mother, who, though not an active participant in the affairs of government, did not like to be parted from Sur Sceaf for more than a few hours, and so she always had Ily with her. Now he was mourning three great losses in his life, and Paloma was struggling to know how to address such a titanic chain of suffering. So for the time being, before he took his leave, she simply held him as his mother would have done.

Her reverie was interrupted by Lana. "Sisters, it wondereth me how to get this beautiful dress on our dear Ahy without rending the back."

"Don't even think that, Lana," Swan Hilde exclaimed. "Ahy made this dress with the hands of love and hope. It must have taken endless and tedious hours to sew on these beads one-by-one."

Faechild ran her hand over the intricately beaded design. "I agree with Hildy. This was her wedding dress and it would be tantamount to robbing a tomb to mar it in any way."

"We can manage," Paloma said. And they did.

"She looks so happy and peaceful," Milkchild whispered when they finished. "Just as I remember her when first I saw her. I'm as jealous of her beauty now as I was on that day."

Paloma nodded. "And she's even more beautiful," she murmured. "I must confess that I burned with jealously too when Surrey informed me that he was actively courting the Sharaka maiden. She was so young, so fresh and so lovely, I was sure my husband would find me so much less desirable. It grieves me now that I even considered rejecting her at the vetting, for I can now say, as I know you all agree, that she enriched our lives much, much more than if she had not been with us."

"Yes, our husband wisely chose her as our bride-sister. I will miss her terribly." Faechild dabbed at the tears on her cheeks.

"As will I," Shining Moon whispered in a choked voice. "But I take comfort that she can now accompany our husband on his journey."

Paloma's eyes filled once again. "And I take comfort in the Baldurean Resurrection, when we shall all be together again and have lifespans as long as the yew trees, when we shall drink freely from Kvasir's blood and eat the fair apples of Idun so that all will find the cause of their sorrows, and that they may sing the song of their own healing. Comes the day then, that all will be whole, and every man, woman, and child shall see eye-to-eye with the gods, the elves and the faeries. The doors of heaven shall open and we shall commune with the other worlds. Death shall then be but a twinkling of an eye when we pass from one life to the next in an eternal upward spiral." She sighed. "But now, sisters, we call in the pallbearers that Il-Alim has selected from his bushmasters. And then, we must ready ourselves to say our final good-byes to our beloved husband and sister."

By Brekka's decree in her capacity as haeligawicca, the procession was to begin under the large rowan tree marking the entrance to the courtyard of the great hall. Those participating in the dirge march had been told to assemble at the fifth point on the medicine wheel. Ary had arrived even earlier along with his three wives, who'd accompanied him to the Big Springs.

Brekka had assigned members of the godija to assist the mourners in finding their places and positions in the procession. In addition, the maidens of the godija passed out yew fronds as well as a warning that it was unlawful and illegal to cut yew branches within the confines of the mound.

The night before, Ary had gone with Chief Forester Ido to the forest of D'If to assist the Men of the Mark and woodcutters in the gathering of the fronds. It had been his private tribute to his fa, who had taken him at the age of six to cut the Yule Log. He still could hear his father's deep voice in his head, admonishing him that the Yule Log was a sacred symbol and reminder of the ur-fyr that should ever burn in a king's heart. '*Remember, Ary, when you become king, all of your comings and goings must be open for all to see and executed with only the purest of intent.*'

It had been near dawn by the time they had trimmed off a sufficient number of fronds from the coppiced yews and piled them into thirty-three long-bed wagons pulled by teams of the finest sorrel mules, superb products of Quailor jackstock studs.

Ary had dozed off sitting next to the muleskinner driving the lead wagon, but had slept only a few hours before he'd been jarred awake by the stony roads through the orchards of the Arden leading to the Stream of Avon.

When Ary arrived at his station under the rowan tree, he encountered Brekka and Anghrus deep in conversation. The young prince was clothed in fallow buckskins tied with the royal red sash, a perfect mix of Apache and White Mountain Herewardi cultural attire befitting one reared under the tuteledge of the acclaimed shamanic priest, Red Knife. The boy's shoulders were slumped, and in his hand he held a cluster of rowan berries, which he was throwing one-by-one at the tree's trunk.

Ary sympathized with the young blood's situation, as he too had had great responsibility thrust upon when he had been but a stripling.

Both broke off their conversation when he joined them. Anghrus turned to him with pleading eyes. "My lord, I beg you remove me from this task Brekka has assigned me."

"What task is that, Lad?"

"To bear our late king's crown, I am unworthy of this great honor. I have accomplished nothing of import or praiseworthy such as you and my father, and both Brekka and Ruhm have. I have no experience to commend me to the seven nations. I will most certainly earn the mockery of the other young bloods, who will hate me for my pretense to accomplishment."

Ary directed a questioning glance at his sister, who appeared distinctly frustrated. "I have explained over and over that no Herewardi, young, old, or in the middle, may refuse the order of a haeligawicca. Even though I have no responsibility to do so, I have explained my reasoning." She looked directly at Anghrus, who was looking down at the berries he was dropping on the velvet ants crossing his path. "Anghrus, once again, I repeat, you have been called and anointed by the Roufytrof as the future king of the seven nations, and the lost tribes of Ur-Ope, and this is no small thing. Under your feet flows the blood of the noblest of generations. Your calling is to redeem all of the seed of Odhin under the four corners of Heofonum. The gods do not err in their appointments. And believe me, in the days to come, they will require you to earn every inch of that crown."

"But--"

"Enough," Ary declared sternly. "The haeligawicca has spoken, and even I would be bound to obey. Never would she ask amiss. So, Young Prince, I command you to straighten your shoulders, take a deep breath and remember that you represent the name of your noble father and your holy mother. That is the only assurance you need. Gird up your loins, take up the mantel of your royal seed code, and do as you've been asked by the haeligawicca."

Anghrus flushed bright red. He dropped the berries, straightened his shoulders and took a deep breath. "It shall be done as you will, my king." The young blood turned to Brekka and added in contrite tone, "My lady, I beg your forgiveness for causing you distress on such a sad day. That was never my intent. I only sought to avoid causing reproof or embarrassment, but I now understand that I must put aside the selfishness and inconsiderateness of my childhood and become worthy of both my mother and my father."

Ary grinned. "You have just embarked on the first step toward kingship, owning your own behavior. So mote it be."

Anghrus took another deep breath, shook his long golden mane, and excused himself. When he was out of earshot, Brekka said, "Thank you, my dear brother. My patience was worn to a dagger's edge. I know he means well, but we don't have the time to indulge him, for his commission is becoming ever more pressing with each day that passes. It is as if the wheel of time is turning ever faster."

Ary drew her close. "My sweet sister, remember when we were striplings how we resented being reminded of our obligations as bearers of the holy blood? I remember how stern Starkwulf could be when we chose frivolity and lightheartedness over duty."

"And I remember mother warning me that Starkwulf was not a man to provoke to anger." Brekka sighed. "And she was right."

Though she was trying hard to present a stoic facade, Ary saw the pain and weariness of grief in her eyes. "You know, Brekka, everyone would understand if you turned over your priestly duties today to Ka-Luna. You have taught her well, and she would do you proud."

"I know she would, Ary, but I owe it to Fa and Ahy to do my duty to the best of my ability. I cannot give in to my selfish feelings lest I shirk my responsibility just as Anghrus was wont to do."

He leaned down to brush a kiss across her forehead. "Dearest Brekka, once again you have evoked my deepest love and respect for your commitment to the right and true. And I know Fa is looking down from the heavens with approval and love."

Brekka straightened her shoulders and took a deep breath. "And I may say the same about you, dearest Ary. So let us make it so!"

Watching the shadows climb the golden shaft Long Swan stood at the base of the towering obelisk with his winged staff in hand. On his right hand stood First Counselor Lord Ilkchild the Wizard of Moon Door. On his left stood Second Counselor Lord Forsetti, newly awarded his wizardry over the Shenandoah. Custom dictated that Long Swan, as prothonatory scribe and high weardean of the Roufytrof, preside over the interment of a king, but he found himself worried that his emotional connection to Sur Sceaf and Ahy would render him unsuited to offering the proper eulogy.

He would miss his brother more than most. After all, they were of like mind and spirit. Family legend had it that when his mother and Surrey's were in proximity, the babes they carried would leap in their wombs, a phenomenon noted by all the bride-sisters. Their father, too, had recognized the connection of his two offspring, and thus had treated them almost as one. Both had been given identical educations at the academy, and both had trained under Fork Beard and Crooked Jack.

His memories were heavier than any yoke, weighing down on him and threatening to release a flood of tears. In an effort to preserve the dignity and solemnity of the day, he'd asked Ilkchild and Forsetti to assist him.

Behind him, royal musicians in full red and gold regalia were arrayed in precise rows, trumpets, lurs, and drums at the ready, waiting for Long Swan's signal to herald the beginning of the funeral dirge.

As the sky gradually took on an amber hue, a shimmering silver cloud resembling Brekka's round iridium shield slowly moved downward until it was hovering directly above the obelisk. The White Wizard Long Swan clarified, "Behold, the celestial barge of the gods. Many are the times I have witnessed it. It is given unto me to know that this is a vessel of the gods, one among their many, but to the uninitiated, this is but an unusual cloud."

Forsetti shaded his eyes for a better look. "I recall, Lore Master, a conversation I once had with Lady Mahallah when I was but a strapping youth. She said that a sign was given in the heavens when a silver cloud appeared over Witan Jewell and DiAhman on the fourth day of the dark moonth when both you and Sur Sceaf were born in the wilderness of Di-Ahman."

Long Swan smiled. "My mother, the Lady Soma-Frey, reported the same sign in the heavens which endured throughout the night."

Ilkchild spoke up. "Recall that our lord and king, Sur Sceaf, had often recounted visitations of a vessel of this self-same appearance. It seems. I believe it is no mere coincidence that this vessel should arrive to consecrate these proceedings of his death."

Long Swan nodded. "In the days of Elrus and Arundel the Great, such visitations were much more commonplace. It is written in the most ancient of Herewardi boks that the gods and the elves communed with those great kings and exchanged information as freely and warmly as one friend to another."

Forsetti looked eager. "Lore Master, do you think they have come to impart information to us this day?"

Long Swan shook his head. "No. Our people are not yet prepared for such communion. Even I trembled during the first time I met with them at the Haliggryft in the Umpqua. The gods are both too terrible and too beautiful to look upon without being consumed by dread and terror. It will require another generation of gradual conditioning before we are prepared to commune openly with the heavens as in the days of Elrus, when the skies were cloven. In the meantime, Ilkchild and I will school you in the signs and tokens you will need to approach the gods, so that you may then go forth to prepare the rising generations to endure the glory of the gods."

No sooner had Long Swan finished making his pronouncement than a beam of white lightning shot upward from the tip of the obelisk. The silver shield of the vessel took on a vapor-like appearance, transforming it into what now appeared to be an everyday cloud.

According to the rite laid down by the Roufytrof in the time of Arundel the Great, when the shadows reached the ur rune at the midpoint of the shaft, nine potent songs nine were to be sung and precious honey mead passed around to the immediate family. The mead was a sacred brew called 'the Saliva of the Elves' and purportedly stirred inspiration—and, at times, even the visitation of the departed.

Most of the temple mound was now deep in the shadow of day's end. He looked toward the yew tree to the west of the temple behind which stood the dolman. Though the canvas walls behind the hedges had been dismantled by Sur Child's multitude of grown sons and grandsons, the dolman itself was still shrouded in the traditional three ritual veils.

As he had instructed, as the sun reached the horizon, Uffa and Ugga began lighting the many torches surrounding the crypt as the sun reached the horizon. Though the ceremony would begin at twilight, it would end in darkness.

Next to each torch stood a fallow-clad temple guard, either a godhi or a godija, each possessing a sword and a staff to ensure that no profane person could pass up to the mound.

As soon as the shadows touched the ur runes, Long Swan gestured to He-Man, the master singer to begin the nine songs of praise and exultation. The elite chorus of five soprano women and four oktavist men began with the 'Ode to the King and His Lady', newly composed by Ka-Luna. At the same time, maids in dirndls passed around leather krugs filled with the sacred mead to the family members.

The shadows climbed higher, striking the sun runes at the top of the shaft. Turning to the ramrod-straight lur master, Eyvind, he signed, 'Make ready.'

Immediately, the lur-men readied their lurs. Long Swan gazed upward, his scepter raised. At the precise moment when the sun's rays struck the base of the pyramid so that only it remained in golden brightness, he lowered his staff.

The funeral procession began at the precise moment when the sun's shadow reached the base of the pyramid atop the obelisk. From his position, Long Swan was able to view the caravan of official mourners lined up from the great hall along the elf waters and up to the promontory. Brekka as haeligawicca, and Arundel as the king-in-chief of the Seven Kingdoms of the Herewardi, led the procession. A lump came to Long Swan's throat at the sight of his favorite nephew and dear friend. Attired in his robes of royal red trimmed in ermine, and wearing the Crown of Howrus, Ary looked so like his father that Long Swan had to fight back tears. Yet, even as he grieved for the loss of his brother, he took heart that the spirit and mantel of Sur Sceaf now rested on his firstborn son. All who had spiritual eyes could clearly see it.

Following Ary came Sur Sceaf's bride-covey wearing the hooded aubergine robes of the priesthood. Anghrus, designated the heir presumptive by the Roufytrof, bore atop a woolen cushion in the shape of a ewe's foot the last crown worn by Sur Sceaf as high king of the Seven Herewardi Nations. The young prince was both proud and nervous.

"Ilky, your nephew reminds me very much of you at seventeen winters—all arms and legs, and a sun-filled lion's mane. But fortunately, he lacks the cockiness that got you into such constant trouble. And so far, I have not seen in him that inclination you had to woo every woman you encountered."

Ilkchild looked both amused and shame faced. "That's to his advantage, my friend, for he shall not have to suffer the lost friendships and burning shame that I did before I came to my proper senses."

Next came the king's sarcophagus, born by his chosen compatriots. Then came Ahy's sarcophagus to be proudly borne by six of Ily's elite bushmasters in their striking saxon green uniforms. It pleased Long Swan that Il- Alim was once again clothed in a white robe and the royal red sash of the Herewardi bloodline. The great cryptic warrior nobly waited with a stoic composure in front of his mother's sarcophagus.

It grieved Long Swan that Surrey had not been able to personally restore the royal sash to his son, a duty that had thence fallen to him as executor and sealer of the king, and which he had carried out earlier in the day.

The swollen ranks of the family came next, followed by honored friends and guests. Silent mourners waited alongside the path of the procession to wave yew fronds in tribute and farewell as the sarcophaguses passed in a somber parade. The lurs droned. The deep-throated sound reverberated over the elf waters, rippling the surface and shaking the ground. The last good-bye to a great king as his spirit passed like a falcon into the west.

# CHAPTER 19 :

## THERE WAS A KING

AT THE SOUND OF THE LURS, Arundel exchanged looks with Brekka. She nodded. With her at his side, he began the procession, measuring his stride to the slow and steady beat of the Sharaka drums. The route led across the courtyard of the great hall and onto the path lined with a box-hedgerow marking the serpentine passage way to the mound.

Alcoves had been pruned into the thick branches every one-hundred and forty-four paces, and in each alcove, stood a temple guard from the ranks of the godhi or godija. Dressed in their traditional fallow garb, each guard was armed with a spear tipped in a steel point in the ancient design of an elm leaf. Since the reign of King Sur, these elite temple guards had been known as spear-shakers, and were universally venerated as protectors of that which is most holy. It was even said that a guard is so well-trained that he or she can recognize a spy, an impostor or an intruder on sight, even in heavy crowds and at great distances. As he and Brekka passed, each guard gave a fist to chest salute.

Following the gentle contours of the mound, the path passed under the Hoar apple tree, now heavily laden with its winesap fruit. It was fitting, as the apples were his father's favorite fruit. His fa had been especially partial to the hardened wine from those apples, called Dumpsie-Dearie. Arundel thought it a pity he had not lived to enjoy Nigh-Mother Lana's apple medlar pie one last time. He stared up at Wilona's gleaming white marble dolman a few steps below the crown of the mound.

At the top, he and Brekka were met by Long Swan, Ilkchild and Forsetti waiting at the base of the obelisk. As haeligawicca and queen of the east, Brekka represented the Morning Star, Earendil, as well as Mother Urth, the spinner of the fate of all mankind from birth to death. It was Brekka and Brekka alone who had the authority to conduct those not initiated into the Herewardi rites from the eastern womb to the western womb, from birth to death. As prescribed, the three weardeans, who formed the First Quorum of the Roufytrof, were to follow as her train.

Careful to keep four measured paces behind, Ary followed the quorum into the east door of the temple, a deliberately narrow passageway representing the portal of birth, then through the Urth Room representing the lands of toil and strife where mankind and womankind serve their mortal probation, and then out the western door, representing the shedding of the mould, the flight of the spirit, and the beginning of the journey into the celestial realms. As he emerged from the temple, directly ahead, the dark form of the ever-living tree was now silhouetted against the lavender twilight sky.

The canvas walls that had hidden his father's crypt for so long had disappeared overnight, revealing a towering pillar draped in the traditional three veils, red, blue, and purple. Greatly widening at the base where the veils pooled, its massive form indistinct in the dusky twilight, the dolman aroused both Arundel's curiosity and awe. In the flickering light of the hundred and forty-four torches, the dark red veil seemed to flutter and flow, reminding him of a fountain of king's blood.

Long Swan directed him to halt beneath the canopy of the ever-living tree. "Behold my brethren, when an ancient yew falls in the forest, the oak, magnolia, and hawthorn howl as vassals for their lord. Behold your king is fallen; his wood was close grained and sound to the core. He was pleasant of fragrance, and a pleasing color. He is now indestructible to the dry rot and borers of death and shall ascend into the heavens, worlds without end."

Above Arundel, the torch-lit branches appeared to turn like the Wheel of Heaven. Behind him, the rest of the procession fanned out beyond the low-growing box hedge encircling the dolman.

The sarchophagi were lowered to two sturdy, but temporary hazel wicker byres. While the pallbearers stood guard, Alph Hegele reverently settled the reliquary containing the king's heart onto the white horse ensign draping the sarcophagus. Anghrus followed to place the cushion containing the king's crown on top of the polished yew-wood reliquary.

Brekka then stepped forward. Beneath the golden runes adorning the hood of her pure white priestly robe, her face was drawn and pale. From inside the bosom of her robe she brought forth a holy talisman of wholeness composed of a single snowy-white swan feather and a single gleaming black raven's feather bound together with golden rope of silk, tied in a Herewardi knot. The talisman symbolized the integration of good and evil, light and darkness in profound and perfect balance.

For a long moment Brekka stood perfectly still, her gaze fixed on the carved replica of her father's face. She began biting her lip, a familiar sign that she was attempting to hold in her emotions. Finally, she leaned down and kissed her father's forehead before joining Ary under the tree. Tears ran down her cheeks.

In the distance, whistling ducks lent their melancholy songs to the gentle breeze stirring the branches overhead, followed by a cry from a loon. Once all of the mourners had found their proper places, Long Swan raised both his arm and staff to the heavens.

"O ye. O ye. O ye. Dear royal family, friends, citizens, and mourners, we are gathered here to bid a last farewell to our beloved king, father, husband, friend, and brother and to commit his spirit into the hands of the Os Syr and elves, who have loved us from the beginning of times."

At a nod from Long Swan, Ilkchild stepped forward, handed his walking staff to Forsetti, and using his good hand, unfurled a parchment scroll bearing the royal red border. In a strong and clear voice, he began to read:

"Hear the words of your king.

*'Do not mourn for me, my beloved family and friends, as I go to prepare a place amongst the gods for you. To the seven nations of the Herewardi, I say, take comfort in the leadership of the new king-in-chief, Arundel. And when it comes time for Arundel to hand over the scepter of the high-kingship to the Young Prince Anghrus--whose commission is yet to be fulfilled--I shall rest in peace knowing that you will fare well under these kings anointed by the hands of the gods and confirmed by the hands of the Roufytrof and the haeligawicca. Know ye all and sundry, this is the king's will. Whosoever departs from this decree shall suffer the curses of former days to be added upon them, including the loss of the new liberty so dearly purchased. When you arise, you will*

*say, 'Would that it be night.' And when you lie down in your bed at night, you will say, 'Would that it be morning,' so great will be your misery. May the gods ever watch over you from this holy mound'."*

Ilkchild lowered the scroll and gazed upward. "You have heard the words of the king. So mote it be."

A rumble of thunder came from the cloud above. All eyes cast upward along the length of the obelisk to the unmoving cloud that momentarily shone silver against the darkening sky. As a murmur of disbelief raced through the observers, many of the mourners cringed in fear, afraid that a bolt of lightning was sure to follow. Ary heard someone call out, "It must be that our hearts are so impure, we are about to incur the wrath of the gods!"

Long Swan raised his wand. "There is no need to fear what is above," he declared in a commanding tone. "We all stand here as friends together. This is but the rumbling approval of the gods you hear." The spectators gradually calmed, and silence was restored.

"As is ordained by Arundel the Second, and required by the custom of the Roufytrof, a dolman must be thrice veiled in order to protect it from the prying eyes of the profane. Here you see the red outer veil. Symbolic of the royal blood, this first veil or hood serves to remind us that we are a nation of kings and queens, priests, and priestesses, warriors and warrioresses. Red is also the fervent color of zeal and reminds us that we must always be willing to spill our blood for a righteous cause. As the red veil is removed by the temple guards, I charge you to remember that the blood of our ancestors has purchased all the liberties and freedoms we Herewardi enjoy today. No redemption ever comes without the shedding of blood."

At his sign, thirteen godhi and thirteen godija encircled the dolman and carefully unhooded the underlying veil of a rich royal blue. They then rolled the red velvet shroud into a tight bundle which they bore to the side to lay it upon the knees of the ancient yew.

Beneath the blue veil, the dolman was beginning to take form but still left much to the imagination. Sur Sceaf's wives stood leaning on one another a few paces from the sarcophagi. Their faces were partially obscured by their hoods, and several pressed handkerchiefs to their lips to muffle their sobs. Arundel's own bride-covey stood with Brekka's sister-brides, grieving openly.

He, himself, felt much the same way, but as the high king, he must present a composed facade throughout the proceedings. However, his composure wavered when Long Swan choked out a call for Little Doe to offer Ahy's eulogy.

Some of his earliest memories were of the summers he spent in the camp of Little Doe and Mendaka in Di-Ahman. Their eldest son, Redelfis, was blood-brother to him, and had served as his first lieutenant throughout the many campaigns of the war. Though he greatly respected Mendaka, he loved Little Doe as much as a nigh-mother.

In her sixties now, she was still vibrant and lovely, as slender as a reed, with only a hint of silver in her long raven black hair. She wore a white buckskin dress with the beaded totem of an owl on the back, and two coiled serpents adorning her breasts. Hanging at her side was the peace pipe Onamingo had once given to Sur Sceaf.

Taking up her position next to Taneshewa's sarcophagus, she addressed the multitude in her musical singsong voice. "Most of you know me as Little Doe, the daughter of Blood Smoke and Curling Snake. Ahy was but a child of three winters when I came out of the Cherokee Lands of Tahlequah. I was a young bride to a hungry and handsome Sharaka brave named Mendaka, son of the Thunder Horse, who had found a new home in Di-Ahman under the wing of the Herewardi. Twelve winters later I saw Ahy again when her father, Onamingo, brought his family to live at Di-Ahman with us.

"As a maiden of fifteen winters, Ahyyyokah Taneshewa was so full of the spirit of life, like a dainty freckled fawn kicking up her heels. Soon she was beloved by all in the village.

"Her beauty was like honey to a bear, and tales of her ripeness spread through the tribes like fire in dry grass. Braves came as suitors from as far away as the White Mountains. Others came from the Buffalo Nations. Many of those suitors were sons of chiefs. But in her carefree youthfulness, she set her eye on a handsome brave named Standing Bull. It was a mistake, one which other maidens had made before her.

"Though charming, this conniving brave thought more of his horseflesh than the long chain of throw-away maidens he had violated while living with his own Klamath Tribe. But that love went sour fast, for, as she discovered, it was filled with worms and maggots."

Little Doe straightened her spine and fought back tears before proceeding. "Soon, Standing Bull shattered her soul when she discovered his cheating heart. Sweet Ahy fell hard into a hard pit of grief, so much so that few of us thought she would ever return. And even if she did return, her heart would most likely be as a stone in the hands of any man who dared hold it.

"But that was before the Thunder Beings arranged a chance and magical encounter with the Young Prince Surrey; an encounter that would sorely try the reins of both their hearts. We all knew Sur Sceaf had set her heart aflame again, but starting a fire and being able to approach it are two different things. Surrey, too, was to be tried by those flames, as Ahy did not know the ways of the Herewardi, and was much put off by the prospect of sharing her man with his six other wives. I have never seen before or since such agony as afflicted those two souls in their turbulent courtship dance. They were like two lovers always reaching for each other while the currents of their separate cultures kept pulling them farther and farther apart. After the constant sawing motion of their attempts to unite but being pulled apart repeatedly, the two finally joined in a bond that ultimately grew stronger than death.

"In life, they were one. In death, they could not be parted. She became Herewardi and made Surrey's people, her people, Surrey's wives, her sisters, and their children, her children. She loved them and they loved her, and all of us had cause to marvel at how rich their love was from the beginning. It is a testimony that their love had roots elsewhere in some distant fore-life or world the veil of flesh conceals from us."

She paused to untie the leather thongs attaching the peace pipe to her belt. "Now I have one more duty to perform before saying a final good-bye to my dear friend." Holding up the pipe with three fingers on each hand for all to see, she continued, "In the days of the courtship of Surrey and Ahy, her father, Chief Onamingo, gifted Surrey with this peace pipe that had come down through the line of Sharaka Chiefs from the Great Longfather, Tah-Man-Ea. It was given as token of his approval and full-confidence in Surrey's leadership.

"Surrey took great stock in this pipe, and ofttimes used it in an occasional lodge. Recently, he gave it into my care with the request that I keep it safe. It was Surrey's wish that after his departure for the summer lands, I pass this pipe to Ahy's firstborn son, Il-Alim, so that it remains in the hands of a descendant of Onamingo's blood-line."

Little Doe walked over to Il-Alim standing with his young bride, Siff, at his side. Ary felt a knot come into his throat. He couldn't help remembering the proud day when his father had passed down to him the Sacred Signet Ring. How like Fa to find a way to reach beyond the grave and offer his son a token of his great love and encouragement as he goes forward to fulfill his destiny.

Little Doe passed the pipe to Il-Alim, and then took several deep breaths before she could speak again. "Dear Ily, my people and your people believe that our spirits leave part of ourselves in our most treasured possessions. The breath of many chiefs runs through this pipe, as well as the breath of your father and grandfather. Should you ever need to employ it, the breath of your ancestors will reach the ears of the Thunder Beings on your behalf where the smokes of all great beings will be bound to do your every righteous bidding."

Beneath the look of surprise and pride, Ily was too emotional to speak. Instead, he genuflected, took Little Doe's hand and brought it to his forehead in the traditional sign of respect.

After he rose, Little Doe leaned closer and whispered something in his ear. When she was finished, tears were streaming down his cheeks—and hers.

Taking a step backward, she turned to face the mourners once again. Raising her hands to the sky, she uttered, "I wish you god-speed, our beloved Ahyyyokah Taneshawa and our adored Sur Sceaf. Go in peace into the bosom of the Thunder Beings."

Mendaka stepped forward, put a strong arm around Little Doe's bowed shoulders and gently led her from the circle of torchlight. Most of the women were now openly weeping as well. Even the usually composed Paloma had tears streaming down her cheeks.

Long Swan was particularly moved by Little Doe's tribute. He had been at Sur Sceaf's side during much of his time in Di-Ahman and had done his best to support his brother during those times of despair. Once again, he stepped forward, cleared his throat and began, "Cast your eyes toward the king's dolman once again. The royal blue veil is to remind us that zeal without knowledge and blood without a moral science will only serve to destroy us as a people. We must ever be focused on taking a higher road that leads to life, liberty, and the pursuit of happiness for all folk, great and small, red, black, or white. Blue serves to lead us to the certain knowledge that no society can survive without chastity and virtue. We are Os-Syr-Tru. We are true to the gods, to those we have married, and to our posterity down to the last generation." He signed to the temple guards, who once again drew the veil free, revealing a final veil of rich purple hue. The blue veil was rolled into a tight bundle and carried to the ever-living tree where it was placed next to the red veil.

"Behold the marriage of the red and blue. Behold the purple veil. It represents the marriage of zeal and knowledge and betokens the mastery and fulfillment of a life well lived. There never lived a nobler soul than Sur Sceaf. And, as the Grand Lady Queen Paloma has said, 'Never was there a more devoted, doting, and loving wife than Ahyyyokah Taneshewa.' They lived among us as mortals, enriching our lives immeasurably. Yes, we will grieve their absence, but we rejoice that they have marked the path and shown the way toward entering the society of the gods and elves in the heavens above."

Long Swan turned toward the dolman and gave the sign for the final unhooding of the raven. As the guards approached the dolman, Ary sensed a heightened anticipation running through the mourners surrounding the crypt. Many crept forward for a better view, while others appeared almost entranced. Every eye was turned upward.

Ary was reminded of the time Woon came to Elrus who was tending his flocks in the fields of the Taxus Hilly Country. The All-Father ordered his ravens to guard the flocks by day and his wolves, by night so that he might impart the teachings of Os-Gard to the Herewardi king. Woon then personally supervised Elrus as he wrote the Book of Elrus.

Ary's chest burned when he silently recited the final passage in the book. *In a day when men's hearts shall fail them, I will send a King of Three Bloods, who shall bind the nations together and wield them like Thor's hammer to lay low the Pitter Empire into the dust, never to rise again. He shall establish a foundation of a kingdom which shall never be removed from his people again, and shall establish the peace of all nations, races, kindred, tongues and peoples.*

Inch-by-inch and with great solemnity and reverence, godhi and godija drew down the veil, gradually unhooding the noble head of the Raven Guardian Protector with its fierce and gleaming emerald eyes and formidable beak as sharp as a spear, forever on guard and eternally vigilant. The powerful chest and mantling wings, each feather cleverly etched into the gleaming onyx surface, evoked the ferocious majesty of a traditional Herewardi sentinel ever keeping the sleeping king and his seven consorts from earthly violation.

Gasps of awe and wonder ran through the mourners. Ary, too, was awe struck by the sheer beauty of the gleaming grave guardian that seemed to be gazing directly at him, as though filled with an unexplainable living essence.

The veil finally fell away, revealing a stunningly beautiful clam shell of white marble so translucent and flawless that it appeared to be crafted of the finest porcelain. Exquisitely carved, the shell seemed alive, lovingly opening to receive eight sepulchers within its protective embrace.

Long Swan read aloud to the gathered friends,

"'*Be it known, that I, Sur Sceaf, commissioned Master Builder Sur Child to fashion me a tomb in which I may sleep with all my bride-covey until the time and season when our eternal spirits may all reunite with our mortal coils once again and come forth in glory on the morning of the first resurrection along with Baldur, the Fair.*

"'*The tomb and its crypts are now complete, and my hour appointed to me by the norn sisters has come. The tomb is fashioned like unto a large white clam shell out of the finest Parian marble in the manner of the Tlingit Haida-Gwai, an art form introduced to the Herewardi by Raven's Tongue. Fitted out as a mausoleum, it has been especially crafted to accommodate our eight yew sarcophagi. I have also commissioned Horst Gimmelhausen to carve our personal images into the lids in a way that it appears we are climbing out of the mouth of the clam.*

"'*Atop the dolman stands the ever-attentive Raven as guide to our emerging resurrection, carved out of purest black onyx stone fetched from the heart of Mexus, which came to me as a gift from my friend and ally, Admiral Juan Carlos de Bevar y Sajones.*

*Blessed be this tomb, and all those who reside beneath its protecting wings.*'"

At a nod from Long Swan, Paloma led her five bride-sisters into the soft golden glow of the torchlight where Brekka waited in front of the dolman. As they formed an outward facing prayer circle, they were the epitome of Valkyries gently lifting the slain from the battlefield of Ea-Urth into the heavens.

Following Paloma's lead, the bride-sisters and Brekka intoned in unison, "Oh Holy Father and Mother of the Heavens, we your daughters commend into your hands the spirits of our beloved husband, father and sister, and beseech you to allow them to prepare a place for us in the Halls of the Gods and the Elves. In your tender mercies, we ever trust. As above, so below. So mote it be."

Ary joined the other mourners in echoing, "So mote it be."

Long Swan waved his staff. Anghrus stepped forward to remove the cushion bearing the king's crown, and then stepped aside. Alph Hegele, his cheeks wet with tears, stepped forward to claim the reliquary before joining Anghrus to one side. At twelve high, both items would be carried into the holy of holies in the temple, where the crown would reside until Anghrus would claim it through his deeds and actions. The king's heart would be carried into battle as a measure of protection against all Dark Elves and enemies. Until such a time, it would remain veiled in the Holy of Holies.

Through the blur of tears he could not suppress, Ary watched the pallbearers step forward to take a firm grip on the two poles supporting his father's sarcophagus. Both Mendaka and Walter Shanks were openly weeping as they lifted the heavy burden. Yellow Horse, in his jesters' harlequin costume was weeping beneath his mask as he stepped behind the sarcophagus.

At the first note of the lurs, the drummers began a slow and steady beat while the lurs continued to drone a somber dirge. Step-by-step Sur Sceaf's dearest friends carried him to his final rest. When they reached the crypt, they turned around, and gently slid the sarcophagus into the snugly fitting crypt, withdrawing the poles at the same time. The pallbearers then joined Brekka and the bride-covey standing to one side of the dolman.

Despite the solemnity, Ary found himself amused to see Yellow Horse, as contrary as always, stride to the opposite side where, with a jester's dispensation, he broke protocol by placing one hand on the clam shell and wept openly aloud.

Then, accompanied by the musical sound of a Sharaka chant and ceremonial rattles, Il-Alim's bushmasters bore Taneshewa to her final rest.

The lurs and drums ceased. Muted sounds of weeping mingled with the soughing of the wind through the yew branches and the whipping of the torches. With tears streaming down his cheeks, Long Swan nodded to Forsetti, who stepped forward.

In a voice choked with emotion, he began, "Since the dawn of Herewardom, no man has done more for the salvation of the Herewardi than Sur Sceaf of the Three Bloods. But in addition to that, he broke the yoke of the Pitter oppressors over the Land of Panygyrus, gave the red man the manifest destiny of repossessing the lands of their inheritance as the gods had ordained, and gave the quailor unmolested peace in the land under the Rule of Law. He revealed to us that every race, kindred, tongue, and people has one of the weapons whereby the death blows may be administered to the enemy of all mankind—the dark elves.

"For twenty years he toiled without surcease to give the Herewardi the final prize of their ancestral home at Mount Heredom. Many were the nations that profited from his benevolence and guidance. He was unexcelled as a father and a husband.

"There was a king."

# THE END

# AUTHOR BIOGRAPHY

Russ Howard was born in the North end of the Shenandoah Valley. He grew to manhood in rural West Virginia, where the mountaineer culture conveyed to Russ a sense of fierce independence, which is a running theme in his books. In his youth his first passion was for the animals he kept, an assortment of creatures from owls and pigeons to chipmunks and foxes. As he entered adolescence he developed an obsession for running and became an accomplished cross-country and track athlete.

His education spanned across international borders. He attended four major Universities in three states and for a number of years he lived abroad as a student in various German cities as well as Kitzbuhl, Austria. During his stint there he learned to love and appreciate the German tongue and culture.

He is greatly influenced by English Literature, Germanic, Keltic, and Slavic Mythology. He is an admirer of the operatic genius Richard Wagner, the political innovator and democratic theorist Thomas Jefferson, and reveres J.R.R. Tolkien as the greatest modern story-teller. Russ's spiritual philosophies have been condensed from sources of mysticism and Kabballah. He especially praises the works of Rudolph Steiner, Bruno Bettelheim, and Martin Buber.

Most of his life he worked as a Mental Health Investigator, and a Marriage, Family and Child Therapist. Now Russ lives with his wife Kathryn, a dancer, in Roseburg, Oregon. He spends his time as an avid gardener, small-scale farmer, and shepherd.

I wish to take this moment to thank all of you who have read these books and have been fellow travelers with me on this odyssey of the Syr Folk. May the Ur Fyr light your path on future journeys to discovering the gods anew. May the names of the elves, faeries, and ancestors be as alive in your homes as they were in times past.

Until we meet again, Adeiu.

***The Rebirth of the Elven Gods*** is the eleventh and final book in the eleven book series, ***The King of Three Bloods***, which follows the many trials and tribulations faced by the freedom-loving Syr Folk.

If you liked the book, please leave a review for this book on whatever platform you purchased it. Every review gives me renewed vigor to carry on with the stories of Panygyrus, and leads other readers to enjoy the fantastic world you have come to love.
Thanks again, Russ L. Howard

Be sure to check out

**TheKingofThreeBloods.com**

for future book releases, articles by and about the author

and other news concerning the series.

CPSIA information can be obtained
at www.ICGtesting.com
Printed in the USA
LVHW090416291120
672397LV00011BA/131/J

9 781945 130250